ARCHER

ON THE RIVER OF TIME | BOOK THREE

ESSENTIAL POETS SERIES 292

Canada Council **Conseil des Arts**
for the Arts **du Canada**

ONTARIO ARTS COUNCIL
CONSEIL DES ARTS DE L'ONTARIO
an Ontario government agency
un organisme du gouvernement de l'Ontario

Canadä

Guernica Editions Inc. acknowledges the support of the
Canada Council for the Arts and the Ontario Arts Council.
The Ontario Arts Council is an agency of
the Government of Ontario.

We acknowledge the financial support of
the Government of Canada.

ARCHER

ON THE RIVER OF TIME | BOOK THREE

CARL HARE

**GUERNICA
EDITIONS**

TORONTO – CHICAGO – BUFFALO – LANCASTER (U.K.)

2022

Guernica Founder: Antonio D'Alfonso

Carolyn Zapf, editor
Cover Design and Artwork: Kyle L. Poirier
Interior Design and Artwork: Jared Shapiro
Guernica Editions Inc.
287 Templemead Drive, Hamilton (ON), Canada L8W 2W4
2250 Military Road, Tonawanda, N.Y. 14150-6000 U.S.A.
www.guernicaeditions.com

Distributors:
Independent Publishers Group (IPG)
600 North Pulaski Road, Chicago IL 60624
University of Toronto Press Distribution (UTP)
5201 Dufferin Street, Toronto (ON), Canada M3H 5T8
Gazelle Book Services
White Cross Mills, High Town, Lancaster LA1 4XS U.K.

First edition.
Printed in Canada.

Legal Deposit – First Quarter
Library of Congress Catalog Card Number: 2021947751
Library and Archives Canada Cataloguing in Publication
Title: Archer / Carl Hare.
Names: Hare, Carl, 1932- author.
Series: Essential poets ; 292.
Description: Series statement: On the river of time ; book three | Essential
poets series ; 292
Identifiers: Canadiana 20210327995 | ISBN 9781771837071 (softcover)
Classification: LCC PS8615.A7243 A73 2022 | DDC C811/.6—dc23

A wanderer is man from his birth.
He was born on a ship
On the breast of the river of Time.

— Matthew Arnold, "The Future"

To all those

who were part of Company One

and whose work inspired

many of these pages

TABLE OF CONTENTS

ACT THREE: 2007

ABOUT THE TRILOGY

This huge project—an epic trilogy, *On the River of Time*, that spans the ages from the ancient Greeks to the present day—was instigated on a Fringe Festival tour by the chance purchase of the collected poems of Edmund Spenser. In Spenser's biography lay the shock that sparked my need to respond. I discovered that Spenser, one of the great poets of the English language, while writing his epic poem *The Fairie Queene*, had written a treatise advocating the starvation of the Irish to quash their rebellions in order to fully conquer their country, in essence proposing genocide. How could one of the great poets of the English language, who could speak with the tongue of angels, hold simultaneously in his mind such contradictory attitudes with such conviction?

As time went on, the implications of that question spawned the themes that pervade this work: the nature of our most basic perceptions and drives; our encounters with the Other; our use of the Mask as an integral part of our lives; our acceptance or denial of the consequences of our actions; and the continuity over the millennia of these universal human attributes.

To explore these themes, I have related three stories in the three books of the trilogy, each one depicting the journey of an extraordinary individual. All three protagonists endure journeys both external and internal; all three must face critical moments that in different ways change them significantly. And each story's form of expression reveals in its utterance the time in which its protagonist lives—a suggestion of the Greek epic poem; the Spenserian stanza for the Elizabethan period; and free verse for today—with further variations that link the separate tales to form a mosaic of word and action and character.

In the first two volumes of the epic, we saw the thorny journeys and struggles that Odysseus endured to propitiate the wrath of the god Poseidon; and the wracked four months at the end of Edmond Spenser's life, haunted by his memories of earlier journeys. In this final volume, we follow the fictional actor/director Ray Archer as he takes his theatre company across Canada performing a masked production of *King Lear*, while he fills his notebooks with what he learns about this vast land, research for his new event on the history of the country; we see the creation of the event and its tour across Canada and later through Ireland.

And so, after twenty-eight years of thought and composition, I come to the end of my three-thousand-year epic adventure—from the initial shock to my quest to gain more awareness of us as humans caught between love and hate, ambition and beneficence, power and submission, with always the sense of death just beyond our vision, its fear whispering to us; to my search to find the vehicle of expression that led to the vision of an epic poem; to my insight to reveal in this vision our intimate linkage with those who have lived and died over the past three thousand years, from the ancient Greeks to ourselves, as we have plunged from one century to another; to my endeavour to reveal those people from then to now in their struggles; to my labour over the long years, away from the tasks of each day, so as to plunge deeply into the times of these men and women, and to find a way to express in a contemporary way verse of the past and verse for the present.

Why did I ultimately choose to write in the form of an epic poem? Because a shock, a sudden realization, forces the need for a response, and if that insight is important enough and large enough, it requires a form expansive enough to express its implications. And throughout these many centuries, the epic form has fulfilled this need with its great scope and the power of its poetry.

And so, what you are about to read is the final volume of an epic journey that reaches back three thousand years and finds its end in our new century.

ACKNOWLEDGMENTS

Over the now almost thirty years since this project was sparked, I must acknowledge still its instigation through the tour of Christopher Logue's brilliant interpretation of the first two cantos of *The Iliad* performed so admirably by my son Kevin and the old Winnipeg bookstore where I purchased Spenser's poems and biography, and discovered the terrible paradox of his holding simultaneously in his mind the great virtues and genocide.

Because of the length of time, I also acknowledge the huge help of the books and resources I found in the libraries of the Universities of Victoria and Alberta, and then later the scholarly sites found on the internet. I am indebted to the late Jim Munro of Munro's Books in Victoria for tactfully suggesting a change from the original title "Journeys," and to Matthew Arnold for his poem "The Wanderer," which has provided the line that is now the title for the whole epic. My various trips, tours, and adventures over this vast land have also deepened my understanding and appreciation, adding experience to study.

My major gratitude goes again to my late wife Clara, both for her patience over the hours I have spent on this work and as the first to read it and to have faith in it. Also, thanks must go to Sharon Thesen, the next to read the epic and to continue to follow it over the years.

For this final book, however, I must also acknowledge, as I have in the dedication, Company One Theatre, my troupe who worked tirelessly with me as we explored new territories, continually working eight hours a day in physical, vocal, and imaginative routines and explorations on events written by our playwright and dramaturge, Carolyn Zapf, and for several events, on their own materials; and to which I brought the experiences I have had in training with Jacques Lecoq, Rudolph von Laban's Art of Movement Studio, Keith Johnstone, Clifford Turner and James Roose Evans at the RADA; and also the experience of seeing many of the major theatre companies of the world, such as The Moscow Art Theatre, Grotowski's Theatre Laboratory, Théâtre du Soleil; and Joan Littlewood's company, as well as various productions in England, France, Norway, the United States, and Canada, including, of course, the Stratford and Shaw festivals.

I must again thank Douglas Campbell for his meticulous editing of my words in the mid-stage of the creation. But even more I must acknowledge Carolyn

Zapf as the principal editor. And I give my praise to Kyle Poirier for his fine cover designs and maps for the trilogy in the digital versions.

A good editor is a godsend to a writer, whether it be in correcting errors in word or sentence, asking questions about aspects in the work, finding a way to allow writers to find their own words, thoughts, style, querying rather than dominating, but always honest, not afraid to question something if it requires it. Throughout these many years Carolyn has worked with me in this fashion, sometimes with arguments (not quarrels) that can last months, but always keeping the work in mind. I acknowledge with deep gratitude and admiration what she has done for this trilogy.

PROLOGUE

Dust
and the odour of old books
linger on the packed sway-backed shelves,
drift among the heaps
of journals, magazines and maps
scattered on the worn, uneven floorboards
of this prairie bookstore
on this prairie summer day.

The shaded incandescent lights,
suspended with their caps
like the green eyeshades of old bookkeepers,
lose the battle with the brilliant sunlight
projected through the casements
of another era
to make the bindings and the covers
glow with the life that they contain.

Within this gleaming maze,
sidestepping piles of books to navigate the aisles,
distracted both by literature and store,
I spy in a far corner,
just before the light angles into darkness
The Poems (the prose, I later learned,
tactfully left out) *of Spenser*
and my student days rush hurly-burly back.

The whiles the woods shal answer—
an alien word and world
Upon a bed of roses she was layd
heard as an erotic patchwork
As faint through heat, or dight to pleasant sin
encrusted in words archaic
even for that rhetoric time—
And your eccho ring.

And now—for who knows
what reason ... a prairie guilt
over something left unfinished?
a twinge to read the whole
of a vast quirky epic,
to join the few crumbs of it
half-digested so long ago?—
I buy the poems of Edmund Spenser.

To say the least,
this had not been my intent.
The faded store stood close
to where the Fringe Festival
displayed its variegated wares
and where my son's one-man *Kings*,
touching in a modern poet's words
The Iliad's great opening strife,
played in the transfigured room
of an aging downtown hotel.

Bookstores are for browsing—
a nibble of a novel here
a taste of fancy there
and the hoped-for discovery
of some succulent curious volume
of ancient and forgotten lore—
and with this intention
I had sauntered in.

Well, that's how I remember it—
the store can be checked out
if it still exists—
but the luminous image of the place
still glows in the recesses of my memory;
I can still feel the wry twinge,
the impulse to acquire,
and the book now rests in my hand.

How our butterfly events
shape our future acts
when seen through the twisting prism
of our mazing past.
Who can really read our fractal patterns
except as a convenient history
in which one slight event
can change our lives?

The reading of his poems,
the reading of his life,
leads to this moment,
leads to this need
to sing of journeys,
his and two others,
all from different times and places,
of a poet who can hold together in his mind
Magnificence and Genocide,
of an ancient Greek hero,
"he who inflicts or receives pain,"
and an aging artist
pursuing his own unfolding quest,
all enmeshed in our chaotic life,
to trace the filaments of this web
like the subtle strands of the spider
hovering in the quiet dusk.

ARCHER

Preface

ARCHER

At the beginning of this epic trilogy, we followed the second forced journey of the mythical Odysseus three thousand years ago; then we witnessed the struggles and journeys of the Elizabethan poet Edmund Spenser. Now we come to the twenty-first century to follow the fictional Ray Archer on his journeys, both external and internal, through Canada and Ireland. And with Archer's story, we complete our exploration of how we human beings relate to each other and to ourselves.

But this fictional character Archer is, of all things, an actor, a director, a creator of events that move strongly and strangely among the more conventional performances of others. Why an actor, an artist? Because an actor, director, creator must gain insight into the nature of the characters performed, the actions they attempt, the journeys they must take. And even as artists struggle to accomplish these tasks, they reveal themselves and the meaning of their own struggles. Also, of course, actors, including myself, have toured in productions across this country.

For this volume, I wish to describe its particular interest to us now. In his journeys and in his subsequent production, Archer becomes aware of the extraordinary size and history of this northern country—from the Indigenous peoples who inhabited this land for thousands of years before our trilogy began; to the explorations, battles, conquests, and subjugations of the European colonizers here for the last six hundred years; and to the remarkable nation that now exists, still with unsettled problems like lava beneath the surface. Of the three journeys, this one must touch our hearts, whatever our backgrounds and cultures.

So Archer's journeys across the breadth and depth of Canada let him discover the history of this segment of a continent at the same time as he explores the ruptures of family and country in Shakespeare's deepest, if not darkest, play, as well as his own unsuspected, disturbing revelations and relationships.

The poetry of this book follows the principle that guided the forms of the other books, which had for *Odysseus* a sense in modern verse form translations echoing the Greek poetry found in *The Odyssey* and for *Spenser* a modification of the Spenserian stanza. *Archer* employs a variety of styles that reflect the historical periods to which they refer—the literary ballad for Batoche, rhyming couplets for the eighteenth century, free verse and other forms for the present. In this way, I have striven to create a sense of the period in the historical episode portrayed.

We see our protagonist in Canada and Ireland as his story winds out. And in the end, the epic reaches back to its ancient beginnings.

ACT ONE
2005

Canto 1

SASKATCHEWAN

Light
pressing warming on closed eyelids black starred brightening speckled
Open
shaft through slit in curtain adjust slightly let streak of warmth on cheek
See
enamelled curve above in streaks painted by factory sun
Eyes flicker left for curtain window wall small desk litter curtain wall
Feel
body naked next to naked body close soft warm snug
Hear
quiet breathing close to ear gentle slight gentle slight
Adjust
head to see her next
fair hair nimbus pillowed clear delicate lines of face eyes lashed shut
Look
down the soft curves neck vulnerable shoulders lightly placed
smooth arms relaxed askew breasts buoyed by breath up down easily
young stomach fine silk after sweep of slim waist isthmus between hips
casual toss of legs so richly shaped their journey long
Aware
of own body aged silvering beside hers stirring
Sigh
Reach for her ripe breast

Still the chill outside the bus
Early sun foretells later heat
but the asphalt space clear for now
No people   no squadrons of mosquitoes
just rhythm of trucks' roar on highway near

In sweats and ponytail
she focuses on him before her
Warm-up done

Archer starts the Tai Chi set
tall   taller shadow cast
GRASP BIRD'S TAIL
   male body she knows intimately
   still lean   firm
WHITE STORK SPREADS WINGS
   movements graceful   exact
STRUM THE PEI PA
   hair a silver mane
BRUSH KNEE AND TWIST STEP
   glimpse of craggy face
CHOP WITH FIST
   Others beside her
APPEAR TO CLOSE ENTRANCE
   Yumiko to her right
   tiny   delicate-featured   adept
CARRY TIGER TO THE MOUNTAIN
   Michael to her left
   handsome Chinese face   absorbed
FIST UNDER ELBOW
   effortless in the flow
GO BACK TO WARD OFF MONKEY
   James much older
FLYING AT A SLANT
   stocky   powerfully built
PUSH NEEDLE TO SEA BOTTOM
   at ease
FAN PENETRATES THROUGH THE BACK
   Ann   wiry   slim
MOVE HANDS LIKE CLOUDS
   her face angular   Haida
REACH UP TO PAT HORSE
   Behind her others more tentative
   Gary   athletic   black
STEP UP   DEFLECT   PARRY   PUNCH
   starting to master the sequence
PARTING WILD HORSE'S MANE
   Luke   sensitive-faced   young
   not yet connected

CREEPING LOW LIKE A SNAKE
   struggling to keep up
   Lance   tall   blond
GOLDEN COCK STANDS ON ONE LEG
   excessive effort
   Behind them Ursula
WHITE STORK SPREADS WINGS
   dark   statuesque   new discoveries
WHITE SNAKE TURNS AND PUTS OUT TONGUE
   Gillian   company manager
STEP UP TO SEVEN STARS
   older but comfortable in the sequence
TURN AROUND TO SWEEP LOTUS
   Behind all   watching attentively
   Jack   heavy-set   balding
CLOSING OF TAI CHI

When all ready
breakfast in the café
beside the motel   old   shabby
Baseball-capped farmers
in for coffee   gossip
faces tanned   lined
look up to see them
look them over
purse lips   resume their daily ritual

At tables made one
the company sits
Ray Archer at one end
Deirdre   Gillian on either side
Jack the far anchor
Ripples of desultory early morning chatter
punctuated chuckles   laughter
Jack's wit already on tap
Archer quiet   attentive
watching nuances   relationships
Deirdre sensing his presence
Gillian focusing on the company
but aware of what he captures

As breakfast ends with coffee   tea
Archer brings them to silence
his voice quiet but surrounding them
"Gillian will give us our orders for the day."

She smiles at him, turns to the others briskly
"Twenty minutes before we leave..."

Comic groan

"...including you, Jack."

Relaxed chuckles from all

"No long stops as yesterday at Batoche..."

Everyone alert

"...but we will have a good lunch break."

Theatrical sighs of relief

"This morning, an intimate rehearsal on the bus,
but you're free in the afternoon.
We expect to reach Regina before dinner.
Any questions?"

Jack clears his throat
glared at by the others
looks at the waitress   the ceiling
says nothing   grins

Gillian looks at Archer
Their eyes meet
He smiles   nods
looks back at the group
Her eyes stay with him
for a brief moment

"See you at the bus."

They clatter off as Gillian clears the bill
The farmers retract their antennae

The old long bus speeds
down the quiet highway

Gillian at the wheel
company in front
equipment   possessions   at rear   below
office   bed   between

Rehearsal starts
Avoid heat with closed windows
Actors shift in small clusters
sitting close   leaning over seat backs
lines murmured intensely into straining ears
against the roar of the bus
faces   bodies   absorbed in the scattered huddled drama
When not caught in a scene
Archer moves among the clusters
listening   watching
his own concentration contagious
The play moves inexorably
toward its dark conclusion
actors submerged in the fatal working out
unaware of the rising heat   closeness
Then the final dread ending
in clustered quietness
all exhausted   sweating
open windows to relax
in the rushing   cooling breeze
itself warming as the sun moves on

Lunch in another small town
spaced every few miles
In another café like the others
farmers joined by their wives
again look them over
judge them alien
leave them alone
Little conversation
tables separate
company drained

Quiet discussion
professional

intimate
from long experience
together
between Gillian and Archer
over plans on arrival
Deirdre always sensitive
to his presence   voice
but carefully quiet   watchful
ready for the dregs of a glance

As the sun scorches its path above
the bus snarls down Highway 2
to connect to Highway 11
Gillian wheeling it along
as if it were a bug
Inside the noise of rushing wind
little else
everyone quiet to themselves
looking   reading   napping
Archer in his cubicle
leafs through
his notebooks on BC and Alberta
his mind already drifting
away from *Lear*
toward an as-yet-unformed creation

This palimpsest of a land
written over more than once
by turbulence and ice
after a tropical existence
Tri-oceaned
West stroked by the Pacific
East buffeted by the Atlantic
North frozen stiff
reluctantly thawed

He flips through the pages
of a BC notebook

British Columbia
by the Pacific ocean

coast jigsawed with islands
tips of gigantic tectonic plates
interior erupting in mountains
rich in valleys   lakes   rivers
most of the province unceded land
from the almost two hundred First Nations

How I glanced at the side of mountains
saw the broken conduits
that brought water for irrigation to the fields
built by young men
before the First World War
to which they marched
and never came back

He looks out the window
focusing on nothing
then reaches for another notebook

And Alberta
Traders   farmers   ranchers
Bible-thumping premiers
and theorists
Oil
I see at sunset the radiant yellow of canola fields
I see at noon the dark haze over Edmonton

He closes the notebooks
looks out the window
for a time
watches the prairie passing
Then he opens a new notebook
pen ready in his hand

Batoche
museumed neatly
like letters of passion
ink bitten deep in paper
now tied in lavender ribbons
But the fields   hills
if more domesticated

still alive with grasses   grains
woods   clumps of bush
The wind-swept ridge
still looks down on the curving river
fur-edged with poplars

The Ballad of Batoche

The village sits beyond the ridge,
The river bending wide;
The valley small, not much at all
To show for those who died.

The graveyard simple, simple too
Memorial chiselled there:
Village remains don't show the stains
That former days must bear.

Nor does this quiet nestled place
Reveal the shift so wrenched
Through battle in our country's dawn
That territories were redrawn
Colonial world entrenched.

Archer looks up
crisp angles of his face
catching highlights
from the prairie sun
beating through the window
broods over the plains
flowing beside him

The Métis
This people of commingled blood
in this vast land

Brilliant in their nomadic hunts
over these buffaloed plains
distinct from the two bloods
hissing in their veins
knowing themselves

in their own drifting nationality
triumphant in the birth of their own government
at Red River in a new province
then losing what they had
selling their land to speculators
because they lacked the means to farm
or the desire to do so
locked in against their need to roam
then travelling farther west
farther on to the plains
to hunt again the now shrinking herds
until some come to terms
with the farming life

The Métis, driven farther west,
Had found a place at last—
A valley, fertile, wooded well,
Through which a river passed.

The South Saskatchewan could give
To them the settlement
They needed now, with land to plough
And villages content.

And where the Carlton Trail did meet
The river on its route,
Letendre made his ferry trade,
A move both shrewd, astute.

Métis, by river and by cart
Did business on that trail,
And at this landing built a stop
That with its ferry and with shop
Flourished and could prevail

So that the village grew to house
Five hundred in its bounds,
And Batoche, by its founder named,
Served the men on their rounds.

And ten miles south had Dumont forged
His farm, and roundabout

His father and his brothers lived
And so farmed thereabout.

Gabriel Dumont had earned fame
—In most things he succeeds—
A leader who had won respect
From Métis for his deeds

And from the Blackfoot and the Cree
For his audacious skill,
His knowledge of the buffalo,
His swiftness in the kill.

And so he laboured with the rest,
Their farms, shaped as before
In long strips that were river lots,
As they had done of yore.

But now the vast North-West awoke
To troubles on it carved:
Buffalo annihilated,
The Cree and Blackfoot starved,

And from the far more distant East
Word broken, aid delayed,
Treaties not kept, parleys not heard,
So that all felt betrayed.

Archer pauses
glances at the notes before him

The Métis
1,400 strong
fifteen years on
from the last crisis
again caught by pressure
East and West
their land precarious
from surveys oblivious
to their traditional siting
the tribal rights
to the land unextinguished

as a fire
ravages a forest
then lurks
submerged beneath a smouldering turf

Commercial factors at work
for all in the region
The Canadian Pacific Railroad
more to the south
to devastate their land value
settlers' titles to their land ignored

White settlers met to call for rights,
Their resentments simmered;
Surveys and scrip began to nip
At Métis, who felt their life slip
With their requests unheard.

Cree with Blackfoot disagreed
Cree Council decided then:
Demands unmet, revolt was set,
The only question, when?

The Métis turned to Gabriel
To lead them, find the way,
But since no English he could speak
No government could he sway.

Instead, he went to see Riel,
In exile in the States,
To now return and then to earn
Their rights in these dark straits.

Riel, whom the Métis revered,
Had been the major force
To fight for their place in the land
In Manitoba their resource.

Shaggy head rises again
penetrating eyes gaze out
unseeing

Like a huge sculpture
that shifts its shape
from the many sides
it can be viewed
evoking awe in some
angry rejection in others
but cannot be ignored
so Louis Riel
in this country
then   now
His greatest act
the painful gestation
birth of Manitoba
his greatest blunder
the execution of the racist bully
Thomas Scott
the convenient excuse
the simple catalyst
to inflame
Protestant   Orange East
against those French   Catholic
Métis in the West
Manifest Destiny
not the sole property
of Americans
also looking with the eyes
of any predator
on the enticing plains
of the North-West
For Riel
the aftermath of Manitoba
voluntary exile with cash
then legal exile
amnesty

Riel considered, then agreed
To lead them, lead them all,
The whites, Métis, Blackfoot, and Cree—
Make others hear their call.

To the East he then called out…

Lifting his pen
Archer smiles grimly

Intrigues again
But the East did not reply
Riel
feeling betrayed
claimed to be God's envoy
with nightly revelations
claimed saints
the Holy Spirit
talked to him
at the same time
wrote eloquently of the situation
participated fully in political acts
whatever he could do
to persuade the East
by any means he had

Archer shook his head
then saw more

With rumours
on both sides
rebellion feared
a force appeared
at nearby Fort Carlton
Riel reacted defiantly
took prisoners
seized arms
cut telegraph lines
set up a Métis government

> The blue skies and broad prairie plains
> Now saw the fatal act
> That changed their state, the Métis' fate,
> And on the West impact.

Crozier
Major in charge
to hold Fort Carlton

sent police to deliver munitions
near Duck Lake
Dumont turned them back
A second attempt
through accident at the parley
left Dumont's brother Isidore
and with him a Cree elder
dead
A battle began
with the police in their sleighs

The rebels, who before each shot
Had started to outflank each sleigh,
Quickly fired back, and in
This bullet storm, back to his men
In haste Crozier spurred away,

Left the Cree and Isidore dead.
Dumont his carbine used
With deadly aim; fierce fire poured down
On the sleighs, now confused,

And to their left now appeared, swirling
Forward as the snow, with
Huge crucifix in hand, Riel
And his Métis, a myth

Now brought to life, and roared
As bullets raged at him,
"In the name of God, the Father
Who us created, now with power
Reply with vengeance grim!"

Redcoats retreated, had to flee.
Dumont went on ahead,
Ambushed them, but stood up, exposed,
And a bullet gashed his head.

Tied to a horse to Duck Lake
The Métis led him, where
His deep wound was dressed; meanwhile back
The redcoats fled from there,

A quarter of the forces wounded
Or killed, to five Métis,
And the rebellion had begun,
A taste of what would be.

Archer looks up again

So it started
by panic   accident

He shakes his head
returns to the narrative

And now the slumbering East awoke:
The volunteers poured in;
For the campaign they came by train.
The great trek did begin.

Macdonald's railway now stretched west,
But four gaps were not filled;
And through the snow they had to go,
And ice and frost storm-laid.

They suffered from the wind and cold.
With flatcars, sleighs, and march,
Four dreadful weeks they struggled thus,
The land to overarch.

Middleton, their General, was
From British forces come;
At fifty-nine he thought to shine,
Rebels to overcome.

But when he finally saw his troops
Back in the East his heart
Began to sink; for they could not
Shoot straight to do their part.

Without experience and untrained,
They trained but little there;
And now in war they would learn more
Than they might ever bear.

At Fish Creek crossed the major trail;
In the coulee Métis hide;
Exposed at the top the soldiers
Are shot—pure suicide.

But to the thick willow bushes
The Métis withdraw then,
Below in the coulee, and rain
Falls lightly on the men.

Some Métis and Cree now decide
To leave; forty-seven
Are left to face four hundred men,
And they pray to heaven.

Riel in his diary writes,
"O how hard, hard it is,
A war to wage! O my God! Guide,
Guide me from this abyss,

That with good fortune I may wrest
Peace, honourable peace,
Before God and Men." And he waits.
For two weeks both sides cease.

And in this time his government
A true prophet names him;
Days' names are changed, and a miracle
To win the Métis hymn.

Defence is now in Dumas's mind,
Digs pits around the town,
Asks all the Cree and Blackfoot to join;
But most now turn him down.

They have their own battles to fight;
And Dumont counts his men:
Two hundred seventy-five face
Eight hundred fifty then.

Archer
lips compressed
checks
what happened next

An attack
is planned on two sides
The first
a steamer made a gunboat
is ambushed
when the Métis
slyly decapitate it
with a cable
across the river
The second
starts with army
exposed on top of the hill
Cut down

Archer grunts
then exclaims
at what he finds

Middleton uses cannon fire
At Batoche; in terror
The women with their children flee,
And a tragic error

His Gatling gun commits against
The hapless village group,
For a girl of fourteen years dies
In the shots from the troop.

But the tchou, tchou, tchou, tchou from the
Rattling gun does not harm
The nesting warriors there, and whom
Its vague spray does not alarm.

Senseless
vicious

Archer snarls

The first day done
with stupid loss
Now change of tactics
no attack

just bombardment
Métis low on bullets
those who stay
mostly old
stones in their guns
Middleton lunches
His men mount their own attack
Métis slip from the site

Archer shakes his head

Dumont   Riel
escape to the bushes
Dumont finds his family
helps others
evades troops for two days
sees his father
takes his advice
escapes to "the free U.S.A."
but Riel is caught

For Riel a trial is:
He's found guilty, sentenced, and hung.
And the upheaval he had sprung
Birthed a genesis:

For the railway had won the West,
Métis independence gone,
Conservatives lost in Quebec,
And all tribes were withdrawn

From freedom of mountain and plain.
And Dumont from crass shows
Returned home to farm and to hunt,
Find what he could in repose.

And Batoche and its Métis stayed
And for a while prospered;
But a new railway chose a route
For white settlers doctored,

And by 1915 one store
Only the village had;
And many then moved farther north,
And their fortunes turned bad.

And now only a monument
And a graveyard are seen
To show where the earthquake began,
And where their stand had been.

But how to show
the politics of Riel's trial
the ancient statute
under which he was sentenced
the stacked jury
prejudiced judge
all to salve the atavistic hunger
of an aroused central Canada
against which
soared his spirited defence
his words still cherished by his people
his legacy to them

The power of his character
in his ecstatic mysticism
like Lear
raging against the elements

Then suddenly
a revelation strikes him

Of course
Riel is in real life
what mask and contra-mask reveal
His mask that of the patriot
strong in character
eloquent in speech   thought
risking all to bring his people justice
His contra-mask
the deep disturbance in his soul
in his religious journey

his mania that he is
an instrument of God
expressed both in word
and physical symbol of himself
Mask   contra-mask
were made for him

Archer feels the bus slowing to a stop
looks up
sees the outskirts of Regina
leaves his cubicle   down the aisle
stands by Gillian at the wheel

"It's still early,"
Gillian mutters
as she swings the bus
to another street

"Yes.
Drive to the Exhibition Grounds first."

"We're already on our way there."
Gillian grins

It was not far away
Gillian turns at the wheel to the others
"Time to stretch your legs.
We'll be here for half an hour."

All stumble out
to scatter in small groups
gazing at the grounds   the city
Archer   Gillian   Deirdre
stroll together
Archer looking intently at all

"This is where it happened,
the space different now
but still a large space."
He stops speaking
still in concentration
while the women wait

Deirdre unsure of why they are here
Gillian watching him
as he lets the sense of the space
permeate his memory

For a time he stands there
Then he turns
looks about
starts to stroll
the others on each side

"Take a short tour through the city,
then find the motel and dinner."

Afterward the company is released
for the evening
with admonitions to be back early
a warning that the next day
would start early again

Deirdre wishes to stay close
But Archer smiles
"I have to work tonight.
Go join the others."
He returns to his cubicle
as she stands motionless

He sits down
the image of the grounds
etched in his memory
Then he reaches in among his papers
brings out a copy
of an old photograph
Music sounds in his mind

"We meet today in freedom's cause
And raise our voices high."

An old tune adopted
by workers in the dirty thirties
first in Vancouver
brought with them

to Regina
The Great Depression
all afraid
Men fear lack of jobs
humiliation of needing help
to feed their families
Governments fear
communist agitation
the shock
of the Russian Revolution
still spreading hope   anger

Archer's head bends over his notebook
as he begins to write

On to Ottawa Trek

In '32 the plan is hatched
That McNaughton has laid,
Set up camps for us unemployed
To make sure no one strayed.
Relief camps they now will be called,
Remote from cities found,
Where we must work with simple tools
On roads to nowhere bound.

Camps run with army discipline,
Pay twenty cents a day,
With food we find not enough,
No future yet in play.
Over the dreary years we men
Grow restless, angry, mad,
And the Workers' Unity League
Our confidence now had.

We'll join our hands in union strong
To battle or to die!

April, 1935
1,500 from the relief camps
strike

move by train   truck
to Vancouver
organized by Slim Evans

> We're angry at the poor conditions,
> Tired of bad benefits,
> Sick of feds' kind of silly work,
> Our wages shrunk to tiny chits—
>
> Scorn to take the crumbs they drop us,
> All is ours by right!

The strikers organize
make divisions
make alliances
demonstrate
interviews with government officers
Premier Pattullo
Mayor McGeer

> Two months we stay here in Vancouver,
> Occupy the HBC;
> Do the same with the museum
> And with the library.
> Then we parade on that May Day
> To Stanley Park for all to see
> That we are now twenty thousand
> Workers, others, with esprit.
>
> Scorn to take the crumbs they drop us,
> All is ours by right!

Local governments
refuse to be involved with
the workers' welfare
They grow restless

> Our movement hasn't worked for us,
> We've had no real success.
> Now Slim and his associates
> Think up a new redress:
> We'll take the strike to Ottawa,

Tell the nation of our cause,
And lay down our just complaints
Before Bennett without pause
And at the feet of parliament.

Over ten thousand strikers
the On to Ottawa Trek
commandeer freight trains
stop in Calgary
in growing militance
meet with the mayor
with government officials
demand three days
of relief assistance
pin them in City Hall

Mr. Mayor, we won't let you out;
We are prepared to wait
If you don't mind being hungry.
And we don't mind to state
That we can really outlast you
Without a real debate,
Since we've been hungry more often
Than you could even appreciate.

They receive three days
of meal vouchers
are joined
by hundreds of Alberta men
as they travel to
Medicine Hat
Swift Current
Moose Jaw
arrive in Regina

Onward, men, all hell can't stop us;
Crush the parasites!

Bennett sends an edict
The railways
refuse further access to their trains

Evans sees no way to have us
All to travel farther on.
Instead eight Trekkers we choose
For real consultation
With Bennett off in Ottawa.

And now off they are dispatched
While two thousand of us remain
In Regina Exhibition Grounds.
Food and shelter we gain
From townspeople and Sask Government,
And there we hope maintain.

But in Ottawa the talks are short:
Shouting between both sides;
Bennett attacks them as radicals,
Slim an "embezzler" besides.
Slim then calls Bennett a "liar";
They chuck them on the street outside.

The delegates return
decide to disband
the Trek
call for a rally
for July the first,
to secure last-minute assistance
from townspeople
Although the Trek is dispersing
Bennett decides to arrest its leaders

Three hundred of us at the rally.
Then while Evans talking,
Constables and RCMP
Hidden round the square
Move into the crowd, stalking
To arrest him and other speakers,
With a whistle signalling.

Just four minutes in Market Square
A battlefield is made,
People beaten and arrested.

We with cars barricades made,
Throw stones, make clubs—riot grows,
Mounties' guns in the raid.

Three hours the pitched battle rages;
Several set upon and beat
To death a plain-clothes policeman;
A small troupe make a retreat
Are cornered by three hundred rioters;
Shots are fired in the street.

Archer shakes his head
his face grim

Seventeen wounded
five of them citizens
By morning
more than a hundred in hospital
forty are police
Premier Gardner wires the P.M.
accusing the police
of instigating the riot
while he had been negotiating
with the Trekkers
"Men should be fed where they are
and sent back to camp
or home
as they request."
He promises to "undertake
this work of disbanding the men."

We are now fed and kept,
And four days later Gardner helps,
Which most of us accept,
Returning on passenger trains
To Vancouver, except
Not back to the camps again—
A choice we make unwept.

And the next year at last
Bennett loses the election.

King shrewdly has forecast
The public's hatred of the camps
And kicks them into the past.

But he puts nothing in their place,
So things are not so well.
What people wanted was a way
To solve unemployment hell.

Archer sits
still
Then he glances at the photo
looks at it more closely

A picture of strange contrasts
An ample space
to the extreme right the corner of a building
in the background a street
with fifteen people standing around
in front of them a bank
with a single policeman standing below it
on a road
buildings just seen on the street
In the centre of the picture
a squatting policeman
holding a half-upright man
three men in front of them
moving toward them
to their right a man crouched   running
a small crowd to the left   in the foreground
observing some moving forward
one in the process of throwing a rock
one with his hands in his pockets
In the foreground right
a man in a white shirt walking swiftly toward us
passing a woman in a coat standing quietly watching
along with six male bystanders
hands also in their pockets
the strange violent action

with still observation
chaotic   unfixed
just like the Depression itself

He shakes his head
puts down his pen
finished
except for the thoughts
that will run through
his head while he sleeps

Canto 2

WINNIPEG

Ruler-straight roads   past the wide fields   punctuated by winding down
over slight rivers   larger   small lakes nearby   larger waters   level fields
all caught in the bright   bright   omnipresent sun

Light flashes through the window
from a sun shifted in the sky
yanking Archer from his reverie
Landscape skips by the window
Another body near
He turns   sees Deirdre
quiet   sitting on the bed
absorbed in him

Empty of thought
he looks at her   impassive
lets his watch inscribe the time for him
"How long have you been here?"

"A while."

Hunger to know
to understand him
all   all of him
infect herself with his art
He's been through it before
Nothing to say
"Let's see the others."

Out of the office into the aisle
two seats
She does not know what to say
A comforting smile to her

He looks out the window
to the flat plains
deer crumpled

at the side of the four-lane highway
Map out   hand touches
hers
"Have you noticed the names
of the places around here?"

"No."
tentatively

Finger traces a crooked path
on the workbook page
where names are scribbled
as he says them metrically
regardless of location
"Tuffnell   Springside   Rocanville   Guernsey
Wynyard   Meacham   Bredenbury   Saltcoats
Kirkella   Sheho   Virden   Elfros
Elkhorn   Insinger   Viscount   Wakaw
Leslie   Theodore   Foam Lake   Griswold"

Hypnotized as his voice rolls on
each place shining in his sound
each unique   living
map shrunk in folds

"Each place baptized for identity
by native here or across the sea
or by the land itself."
Spoken to the drifting landscape

Deirdre looks up at him

Why does he tell me this?
What is he doing?

"The land is pockmarked by us,
infected with our lives and history.
How to show this…"

Sinks into reverie

"Are you working on something?"

"What?… Yes…"

A roaring silence
against the bus's drone

Nonplussed
Then
"Can you tell me about it?"

"Not yet."

Crushed   withdraws
Blinks
No tears

Feels her emotion
sees her profile vulnerable
"I can't talk about it yet
until it gels more in my mind.
But how did the rehearsal
go for you?"

Brightening
telling him what she learned
without the mask
in the strange intimacy
of the noisy bus
lips to ear

Sun retreats behind them
sky with tarnished light
as the bus lumbers through
the outskirts of Winnipeg
to find the marked motel

Disengagement
Gillian disentangles rooms
bookings bus business
Dinner at a cheap restaurant
then she and Archer
leave the rest to find the playing space

As the bus wends through the streets
"How long do you think she'll last?"

"Until she's learned all she can."

"Let's hope it takes the tour."
She glances at him
shrugs
eyebrow raised

He grins
"It will."

Bus noses into a church space
Dark figure at the door
They peer into a hall
seats in three segments
embracing a space
simple   open   uncluttered
large
He paces about

Gillian in conference with the one in charge
"We can come in tomorrow morning."

"Good. We'll warm up here."

"Can I have time first to unload and set up?"

"Yes."

Return to motel
Gillian to her room
to phone key people
publicity
in all the scattered ways
she knows so well
He stays in the office
playing the scenes in the space
in his mind

Knock at the flimsy door
then Deirdre enters warily
"Can I come in?"

A nod

"May I stay?"
A look embraces her

"What are you doing?

"Living the play through the space."

"Oh. Should I leave?"

"No. I'm done."

Body   face   relax
slightly
He studies her face
good cheekbones
eyes large   dark   attractive
watching his study
mouth full   sensitive
vulnerable at the moment
clean jawline   nice chin
desire to know
desire
tumbled together
He takes her hand
She shivers
slight blush
slender fingers
long   strong
feeling his fingers
feeling them
Four eyes on the two hands

"Deirdre..."

Her hand tenses slightly
stays willing in his grasp

"...I like you here,
and you can come any night."

Her hand responds more to his touch

"In the next few days
we both will be deeply involved
in the play..."

Her hand passive in his

"...and I will need
to continue to work
with each of you
toward each performance."

Eyes up to meet hers

"I will not neglect you
but must be with the others as well.
You understand?"

Dark eyes uncertain
apprehensive
a little lost

A deep stare into them
"You understand?"

Tentative "Yes..."

"Do you really understand?"

Keeps the stare
Long moment
each probing
then a desperate leap to acceptance
"Yes."

He pulls her to him
lets her receive
assurance from their bodies
Light out
From garish streaks
of motel street lights
through the curtain
they begin their nightly ritual

Breakfast next morning
Archer with Yumiko
"You will need to practise
during set-up?"

She smiles   nods
Discussion between bites
cues   shadings   tempi
She listens carefully
says little   nods at times
absorbed in nuance
unfolding of the petals
of the play

While they travel to the site
he sits behind Gillian
who wheels the hulk
through morning traffic
tells him what she negotiated
that last evening
brief but sharp
witty
Archer chuckles
She smiles
eyes fixed on the road

At destination
drums unloaded first
set up by Yumiko
the others trudge in
the properties   lights   board   mask cases
set up
to her deep reverberations
pounding rhythms

Again the rituals of exploration
set by Archer
from rehearsal to performance
enacted from the birth in the West
Vancouver Victoria Kamloops Calgary Edmonton

Slow warm up   Tai Chi
Then the half masks revealed
the work begins

Archer lets his mask live first
the others watching closely
His mask a craggy face
heavy-browed
with deep-set eyes
prominent nose
ambiguous mouth
by its absence
no beard
A moment of stillness
body quiet
in neutral stance
He takes a quick glance
at the face in his hands
absorbing the whole without judgment
slips it on
For a brief moment
stillness again
then his body
seems to expand
grow taller
yet with an aggressive stoop
his hands age perceptibly
yet reflect great strength
like the gnarled branches
of a dead redwood
still towering high into the sky
The head rises
immense authority
emanates from the commanding figure
It looks around shrewdly
if erratically
speaks the first lines
the voice ravaged   magnificent
holding them transfixed

the power of the figure
overwhelming
The speech finishes
the figure relaxes
diminishes
Archer takes off the mask
All release breath held unconsciously
He looks at them
All nod
The mask has lived

Then in groups each explores
a first mask   then the next
Archer observes keenly
quietly works with them
Michael's Chinese classical training
he softens   makes the actor more receptive
as he has continued to do
Luke still inexperienced
but sensitive
Archer nudges to go deeper
Lance must be handled carefully
helped to find the boundaries of definition
Ursula he treats gently   carefully
helping her not to push
to embrace the mask
channel the energy   the strength
without personal tension or catalytic outburst
Ann he softly praises
her mask terrible alive
James has worked with him before
they communicate in quiet shorthand
Gary is a natural
but needs to find the constraints
paths of the play   character
Jack he helps to settle in
Deirdre he pushes calmly
to find the exact energies
for the masks of her two characters

Lunch break
then a cue-to-cue
adjustments
the first moments
of the birth of each mask

They finish early
to rest for the opening
that night
except for the Gillian-scheduled interviews
Archer gives
using his charm to good effect
Gillian's work done well
his name   company
are known here in Winnipeg

A solid audience
full of critics   actors   directors
followers from previous shows
They see
standards with banners
ranged in a curve behind
dim stations at the sides
for masks   mirrors   costumes   props
farther back and to the side
the great Japanese drums
Yumiko's other instruments
A grid surrounds the playing space
spans   girders
like an uncompleted building
or cage
lights mounted
bright   unforgiving

Blackout
Distant rumble of drums
Light stabs the darkness
Banners at the back
held by black figures
angled for a multicoloured wall

penetrated by three figures
Gloucester in rich tunic cape
his mask beefy sensual
Kent in worn brown leather jacket
with darker leather jerkin
great leather boots
worn brown gloves
mask weathered strong
Edmund in black leather bomber jacket
thin black leather gloves
mask sharp like a fox
Their presence charges the space
Behind them the banners straighten again
With each thought they speak
each mask acutely shows its character
relationship
A clear trumpet ushers in
through the ranged banners
Lear's court in all its pageantry
Lear
huge towering over all
in rich scarlet robes
hands gloved in wrinkled leather
ringed with jewels
his mask lined strong-featured
crown of barbaric richness
Goneril with harsh high features
richly bound black hair
tall angular
opulent black dress set off with great jewelled necklace
Looming beside her Cornwall
equally harsh-featured
black leather studded jacket gloves
vicious boots
Regan taller full-bodied statuesque
scarlet dress to show her figure
voluptuous hungry face
bound dark brown hair glittering with jewels
Albany tallest with her

long English face
severe green tunic   cloak   gloves
holding the great map
Then Cordelia
tiny among the rest
face fair   delicate
blond hair cascading to her hips
simple slim cream gown

So the tragic game plays out
against the huge stooped figure
king   father   dupe to himself
Family breakdown before the map
No contest between France   Burgundy
Cordelia   France leave
as does their banner
All played with primal energy
through the archetypal masks
against the dense nuances of the verse

Scenes of loyalty   betrayal follow
Lear's curse at Goneril   electric horror
as behind the dark figures
ninja-like
remove   add   use the banners
Always the drum pulses
Clothing shifts   is discarded
The fool follows
small   slim
wry face
Deirdre   her blond hair up beneath a twisted cap
always a song poised on the lips

Stage now bare for two dark moments
In the centre spotlight Lear now staggers
clothes in shreds
hair a wilderness
drums moving from the distant rumble
to the beat of thunder overhead

Fool huddled at his feet
keening
Lear orders the thunder
It obeys
punctuating his dark cries
with ear-deafening strokes
Harsh terrible moment
Then found   led away

Dim scene of intrigue
Gloucester   his betrayer son
the pitiless spectacle
with the hut of banners held over
mad   loyal indiscriminately
Then Gloucester busied with kindness
thrust into the centre light
eyes torn out leaving strands of red wool
where they weep blood

Then the plummet
to the final catastrophe
Lear found with flowers
Cordelia with him
In the battle
whirlwind of banners
drums   brassy sound
Their capture
the final conflicts   deaths
Lear with Cordelia in his arms
dying as the play sinks to its end

Silence in the blackout
Lights up on cast
masks in hand
who now look small
so small
They bow
The stunned audience
bursts forth

They bow again
leave the stage together
no separate bow for Archer's Lear

There is no reception
All quietly pack away costumes   props
exhausted
file into the bus
leave the space
now dark   void
to shrink back to their own lives
somehow

But Gillian and Archer meet
in his cubicle

"Well?"

She grins
"Good show—just a few notes."
Sharp   precise
Moments where timing of the changes
could be better
Adjustments to the sound of drums
Adjustments to the lighting
Sense that the characters are still
developing

He grins back
No thank you from him
Both have done this so many times
A mutual recognition
A mutual understanding
She leaves

Next day
quiet morning
all with personal preoccupations
Then after lunch
off in the bus to the space
Discussion of the previous night
warm-up rituals

work on precarious moments
with the mask
technical moments
then an early break
Yumiko left
the great drums startling
the birds and dogs outside
That night
the cataclysm enacted again

So the habits set for the week
For Archer
Deirdre in the night
the city in the morning
wandering the streets alone
or with another member of the company

He sees monuments to Riel
one statue heroic in a leader's stance
another twisted   enfolded
in the curves of sheltering walls

His battle still goes on

He takes in the city's feel
central towers   concrete
broad avenues   traffic
parks   waterways
the older neighbourhoods
some neat   some not
houses with faded dusty stucco
forlorn trim with defeated paint
vestiges of thirties bungalows
the cheap small houses of the forties
greyed fences   caragana hedges
old tired stubborn trees
shading the streets   narrow backyards
He imagines
like an archaeological dig
the old muddy town
of shacks   horseshit

the Red River carts
wood   leather tied together
their two great wheels
with shattering squeals
lurching west along the pitted roads
with loads bumping along
as far as Edmonton

Archer spends time
walking through neighbourhoods
not fully noticing where he is
until after a time
he finds himself
at the Old Market Square

Here
Winnipeg's Bloody Saturday
took place
sixteen years before Regina's riot

Winnipeg General Strike

1919

A year after the war
one dreadful year after the other
Men coming home
from the horrors of the front
still dealing with the Spanish flu
which killed thousands of Canadians
those two years
now facing massive unemployment
inflation that took away
what money they had
see the success of the Russian Revolution
feel they have to act
Across the country a wave of strikes
and rising up
revolutionary industrial unionism

Early Spring
March in Calgary
Western labour unions meet
discuss creation of One Big Union

May
In Winnipeg
negotiations break down
between management and labour
The Winnipeg Trades and Labour Council
call a General Strike for
collective bargaining
better wages
improvement of frightful working conditions
Within hours thirty thousand workers leave their jobs
almost unanimous response
closing factories
crippling retail trade
stopping the trains
leaving the public sector
policemen   firemen   postal workers   telephone operators   utility workers
The Central Strike Committee
delegates elected from each union with the WTLC
bargain with employers
coordinate the provision of essential services

The Citizen's Committee of 1,000
created by influential manufacturers   bankers   politicians
supported by the leading Winnipeg papers
oppose the strike
never seriously consider strikers' demands
without evidence
declare the strike
a revolutionary conspiracy
led by a small group
"alien scum"

In the next four weeks
the feds get involved
Two ministers go to Winnipeg
to see the Citizens' Committee
but refuse a meeting with the other side
and support the employers
Fed employees ordered back to work
or be dismissed
Immigration Act amended
so that British-born immigrants
can be deported
Definition of sedation broadened

June 17

Government arrests
ten leaders of the Central Strike Committee
two One Big Union "propagandists"

June 21

Bloody Saturday outside City Hall
Royal North-West Mounted Police
charge crowd of strikers
Thirty casualties
one death
Federal troops in the streets
Six labour leaders released
Dixon and Woodsworth arrested

June 25

Strikers decide to return to work

Aftermath

Bitterness and controversy
the legacy
wave across Canada of increased unionism
militancy
sympathetic strikes across the country

Seven arrested leaders unfairly convicted
"conspiracy to overthrow the government"
Charges against Woodsworth dropped

Almost three more decades
before Canadian workers obtain
union recognition
collective bargaining

Western Canada
These turbulences
and the Great Depression
and two World Wars
A hard beginning

Archer stands for a minute
taking in the Old Market Square
for a last time
his mind filled
with the dark struggles
of the prairies' past

Red River Rebellion
Batoche
The riots in Winnipeg   Regina
First Nations suffering   physically
politically

Then
he trudges back
to his other world

One morning he walks with Ann
They stop for coffee
in an older shabby café
sit at a battered table
with its scarred chrome legs
beside the window
where they can watch
whoever straggles by
In cloudy morning light
the counter is greyly visible

Several Cree sit there
at a table
all male   all with worn clothes
quietly punctuating long silences
as they drink coffee
in the old thick white mugs
All glimpse Ann
when she comes in
The silences grow longer
as they make occasional
covert glances at the couple

"Your first time here?"

"Yes. It's so different from the coast.
The air is heavy here as well
but sticky with dust,
not like the sea-washed air there
with its seaweed and ocean smells."

He chuckles
"Dust defines the prairies
whether the air is dry or sticky.
I'll hear what you think
when we go over the Shield
and beside the Great Lakes."

She smiles back
They sip their muddy coffee

"Do you feel more comfortable with your mask?"

"I'll never feel comfortable with it."
Looks out the window   haunted

The power of her Goneril
taken by the mask
a force unleashed
so fierce a merger of flesh and leather

Turns back   slight smile
"But I won't give it up."

"Have you done much work with mask before?"

"Some. None when I was young."

Her face angular   sensitive   intelligent

"How did you become an actress?"
Question open to allow an answer

She works hard but keeps to herself
First time we have really talked

Silence thought-filled
Decision
"No theatre where I come from,
far west, Haida Gwaii.
Pretty isolated.
But my mother was a knowledge keeper
and taught me and my sisters
all her lore and our traditions."

A torrent of memory bursts forth
Child absorbed in a wonder
of herbs   ferns   cedar
scents   emanations
senses attuned to air   life
more than linked
more than part of
a child's identity
immersed
in this totality
In the totemed lodge
against the flames   smoke
flickered the stark rich masks
of animal   bird   water creature
possessing their transformed humans
spirits alive with power
alien   natural

But later years bring darker times
struggle with the local schools
with whites

with her Haida friends sometimes
but she had some sense of the whites'
language
from her mother
who had escaped going to
the residential schools
but learned the language
seeping around her

She looks toward the men
at the counter table
cool appraised understanding
They avoid her inspection
busy for the moment with their coffees
forced subdued talk   laughter
with each other
but ears still alert

Trouble with friends
too drunk to avoid pregnancy
males too drunk to care
Once in her teens
out in a boat with her brother
sees her best friend
married at fifteen
pushed out of another boat
her drunken husband
pushing her head under
even as she couldn't swim
Ann and her brother
rescue their sodden friend
The marriage staggers on

Bright
recognized as bright
by an observant teacher
who persuades her to get away
go to university
finds grants   funds
pulls strings

She leaves
tries to subdue the thoughts
of problems back home
By chance she takes a course
involved in theatre
By chance she meets a mask teacher
Not by chance
she works on dance   movement
mime   gymnastics   martial arts
Small success as actress
Then sees his work
Meets him

So much lived by one so young

Now silence at the counter table
each in a reverie
Archer reaches across table   gulf
takes her hand
looks eye to eye
Silent acknowledgment
They pay   exit
changed

Many from the theatres come to see his *Lear*
some more than once
After a performance
he speaks cordially with them
With some known from years past
he has a drink   listens to their gossip
the currents of the intrigues   failures   triumphs
dissatisfactions
all of which he has heard before
only the names changed
circumstances
Sometimes Deirdre   others
from the company would also come
to listen to the circumscription of their world
But he never meets the theatre folk
in the day

nor goes to see their theatres   their shows
Instead he continues to prowl
streets   cafés   small stores   parks
of Winnipeg   St. Boniface
absorbing the thick textures of the places
Native people   some working   or in the gutter
some mothers with young children
walking with tidy elders
others in ganged small groups
leather-jacketed   showing wealth
from sources undisclosed or unmentioned
still others sitting in the doorways of shabby buildings
rich in time   nothing else
Michif   dialects of French
heard in some neighbourhoods
with their own patina
of custom   history   style
Some Yiddish   Ukrainian   German
more Eastern tongues
The jumble   swirl of districts   signs   clothing
the concrete   steel   aluminum
core of the city
all windows   cars   fumes
oppressive in the reflective heat

When the Red River carts rolled through
the Natives   the Métis   saw
the new European mixtures
as they clattered in   out
saw the settlement
become a town
become a city
become what it is today
while they have tried to make their own settlements
still on the edges   the fringe
still outsiders

Even as he again walks the streets
the memories reverberate of his own city
Edmonton

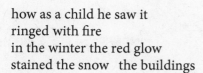

how as a child he saw it
ringed with fire
in the winter the red glow
stained the snow   the buildings

The great valley rent the city
the North Saskatchewan meandering
between the wide deep-slanting sides
the scars of new roads   bridges
against the steep old wooden steps
from valley floor to northern top
the long-girdered two-decked
High Level Bridge
used by many to go "over town"
between the banked segments
of the north   south sides
On the top deck still ran the rails
on which trains   streetcars
now had ceased to rattle
but cars below still sped through
the long caged thoroughfare
others walked or cycled
on the precarious sidewalks
extended past the iron structure
where the river could be seen
directly below from the elbowed railing
not yet secured
from prospective   desperate suicides

Happier for him in those child-full days
was the ravine
Mill Creek beside Bonnie Doon
just before it too was ransacked
for pleasure   for traffic
down whose gashed sides
he could sleigh or ski
or trudge beside the frozen creek
with its few patches
of reeking sewage
beside which the world was silenced

by the white-blanketed trees   shrubs
the snow-treed sides
of the ravine's steep banks

Elsewhere construction's blare   hum
growled always in the ear's underground
but even with the snaking roads
the huge valley still hid quiet groves
from which spectacular sunsets
glinted in the slow currents of the river
He could still paddle a canoe
up dense tree- and bush-lined creeks
away from the frenetic adolescence
of the burgeoning city

The sudden blare
of a car's horn
startles him

Enough of then
keep your mind
on this present journey
What was it like before
where here the Red River carts
groaned through the sucking mud
as they lurched toward
their distant destinations?

He lets himself dwell
on the image in his mind
then opens his notebook
to add a reminder to work on this idea

Each night the production deepens
as Yumiko's drums find
the heartbeat   the pulse
of each inevitable scene
each mask possesses its wearer
in each nook   cranny
of the mind   imagination   being
grips the audience

spellbound in the power
of the play   the creatures
striding across the space
with such clarity   passion

What saves the company
from being swallowed
in the maelstrom of their acting
is the discipline
stringent   concentrated
of the warm-up
with its work on bodies
voices   imagination
Gillian each night
enriching the possibilities
with her notes on each performance
discussed with Archer
Archer among them
a touch here
a murmur there
for that actor only
to which each responds
some tentatively at first
Ursula   Lance   Jack   Luke
then with a growing trust
wonder at their work
the ensemble birthed

The run finally comes to an end
the bus is packed
they can relax
with a last night party
which is hosted
by a theatre friend of Archer's
Some bring friends
Lance has picked up another handsome man
Ursula an old actor friend
appearing in a play
Jack several young actresses
also in shows

whom he charms   entertains
as only he is able
Yumiko has also met a friend
who plays the drums
they chat happily
Gary   Michael
focus of a group
of women in
multicolourèd dress
Ann converses with a Cree woman
both chuckling through their conversation
James   Luke sit quietly
watching the others peacefully
Deirdre tries to mix with the others
but still gravitates back
to Archer   Gillian   his friend
on their outskirts
listens quietly
absorbing the atmosphere around her
the sounds   laughter   from different rooms
but mostly what the three are saying

"Ray, you know the impact of this show—
why don't you settle down
at one of the big festivals
or in a major city?
You know that you can write your ticket
with this work."

Intimate smile between
Gillian and Archer

"No, I'm happy this way.
I like the road,
and the only strings I have
are those that Gillian pulls."

They both laugh comfortably
A pang of jealousy
as Deirdre feels immediately
the close connection

the years between them
more a marriage
than a business
The man persists
but he sees that Archer
will not budge
so the conversation turns
to the usual theatre gossip
that seeps across the country
Gillian with a scalpel wit
dissects the theatres   companies   plays
with devastating accuracy

The party winds its usual way
preliminary chat   acknowledgments
noisy climax of happy babble
relaxing to contented murmurings   laughter
The host toasts the company
applause enthusiastic
The company thanks the host
applause again
All take their leave

Deirdre   some of the company
go in the bus
Others such as Jack   Lance
go off with their conquests
Little conversation in the bus
all now tired and relaxed
but when they have retired to their rooms
Deirdre confronts Archer in his cubicle
"What is it between you and Gillian?"

Raised eyebrow

"Have you slept with her?"

Chuckles
"None of your business,
but, yes, I have."

Eyes fill with angry tears

"Deirdre, Gillian and I
have worked together for many years.
We have been intimate.
Now we are friends, and happy
with our relationship.
I could not do what we do
without her. She is my true support,
and I appreciate and admire her work."

A wide-eyed look
Such a relationship
she has never thought of   imagined

A look   gentle smile
"Just relax. That is all there is
and all there should be."

He holds her quietly
as she sobs
with relief
but still vulnerable

The next day
all are free
On the following day
the bus starts out
to traverse the Canadian Shield
the Great Lakes

Canto 3

NORTH BY THE GREAT LAKES

The country shifts roughly
Plains   fields   stutter out
encroached by dark forests
an outpour of lakes   swamps
the omniscient granite
Rocks grow to hills
small mountains
through which the bus labours
on the wide track
cleaving the scarred faces
or skirting or engulfing
muskeg   rivers   creeks

Archer sits behind Gillian behind the wheel
to watch the Shield's rim appear
the exit   entry to the provinces
marked by substantial icons
a discreet distance from each other
Brief smile

A polite demarcation
But before?
Wrestling for territory
Rat Portage the wrestling mat
bureaucratic spats for fourteen years

A glance at the swift panorama
the ancient bedrock slumbering for eons
below the immense gouge of the patient glacier
whose souvenir is the present Lake   lakes
festooned with its fourteen and a half
thousand islands   of the Woods
A brief 8,000 years
of Indigenous habitation

who two hundred fifty–odd
years ago were found by incipient traders
to live on hunting   gathering   fishing
to name the northern end
Wauzhushk Onigum in honour
of the muskrat

Business   power always fought here
Territories wracked
by tribal raids for generations
a never-ending ritual of violence
this small hiccup on the main water route
east to west for fur trade caught
between the
Hudson's Bay Company
the North West Company
until they meld in 1821
Time now moves in decades
a post on the old Fort Island
in the Winnipeg River from 1836
then the Portage des Rats on the mainland 1861
as the community of Rat Portage
then the provinces move in
claim the town
both build jails   what better way
to show your territory
both issue titles   yes a better way
for mining   timber
Then heavier punches
a Manitoba municipality in 1882
members elected to both legislatures in 1883
Finally the referee the next year
the pinnacle of Victoria's legal empire
the omnipotent Privy Council
decides for Ontario
Better the devil you know
particularly if he frequents your club
Then it took five years more
for the official stamp

Goneril   Regan   without Cordelia
the King a Council

Archer had done his homework
For several years he trawled the net
his laptop   always with him
omniscient   as he worked on his growing idea

One last pressure on the little town
its name   corrupted to begin with
now an embarrassment   especially for business
A climax when the Maple Leaf Flour
(O! Canada!) Co.
refused to build a mill
because "rat" would emblazon
each flour bag
So in 1905
three close relatives contribute to a name
Keewatin   sister town
Norman   brother village
Rat Portage   a necessary amputation
Ke-no-ra

In Kenora the bus now arrives
Gillian in her own ingenious way
wending through the thickets of grants
she had procured by fair means
or by better
had insinuated the company's *King Lear*
into Kenora's Harbour Festival
which in the patriotic way
of many Canuck communities
included at least one summer play
by the patron saint of Canadian theatre
William Shak(e)spe(a)r(e)

Wry grin

What do we bring them?

After the inevitable motel
where the company moves in

Gillian and Archer walk to the location
a tent in a park by the shore
in the midst of Kenora

"Good location."

"Mmmmm."

An eyebrow raised slightly
A glance at him

In the tent they check
where to put their lighting trees
how to use the stage
where to place Yumiko's drums
where the actors change
how the town sounds interfere
Satisfied   they return

Their first performance in a tent

Evening   still light
audience   two hundred or so
townspeople   the local Shakespeare crowd
tourists who had seen enough scenery
wanting to be entertained
a First Nation scattering
who had heard a Native had a big role in the play
Chattering   noise peculiar
to chairs on grass in a tent
flaps left open for air until the play begins
but still in the air the unique smell of tent and grass
a slight breeze outside cooling a warm evening
even as the flaps are shut

The stage lights up   the play begins
The tent walls   roof   still faintly shine
from the sun not yet ready to set
The drums begin   dimly glowing at the side
The actors   their masks
softened in the tent's dun light
now seem to act within a sheen

that lends a strange unworldly sense
to what unfolds

In the hour in which this gleam holds sway
all actors   audience   all
are caught up in the magic of the scenes
Even the breeze-fluttered tent
breathes in spellbound unison
Few notice as the glow fails imperceptibly
the stage lights harshen
At the intermission the audience
stumble into the cool dark outside
the actors stumble
away from the others
Few speak but look instead
at the dark lake with its darker shapes
away from the town's
halogenic   neoned light

The second half
changes the world again
Harsh light in company with harsh drum
giant grotesque shadows
creep   leap along the tent's sides and ceiling
The sighing of the wind grows louder
the terrible power
of verse   scene   form
engulfs performer   participant alike
The play ends
the last drumbeat lingers
the actors   naked of their masks
move forward to bow
But catching the glazed dazed moist eyes
before them
a stricken confused congregation
they look in bewilderment at Archer
who gently nods to the audience
They nod as well
then quietly leave the hushed space
Gillian discreetly opens the tent flaps
The audience slowly dissipates

The Shakespeareans
who had hoped to meet their fellow thespians
walk slowly away
unable to speak coherently
The organizer of the festival
remains for business   for courtesy
but to Archer   the cast
can barely choke out a corporate thanks
is saved from more by Gillian
herself in wonder
from the experience

No one can talk with others
this strange powerful night
All quietly return to their rooms
including Deirdre still lost in that other world
Archer lies in his bus bunk
to fathom the profound experience

The tent's gleam
the shadows
the breakdown from the usual space
a naïve audience

All these he felt were the main ingredients
of a potent potion
but still
all performances had surged forward
in power   in depth   in definition of an action   a scene
He felt the mask force him
to new nuances   new meanings

The challenge to the daughters
on the knife edge of willfulness   anger
Each daughter forced to state a love
pricked with disturbed bitter memories
His stern control of their younger actions lost
in their marriages   subtle rejection
Later that vicious moment with Goneril
the scream of curses venting all that sooty past

But as he works through the stark trajectory
of his character's declensions of his fate
he does not yet see
how these revelations shape his own journey

Sleep does not seduce
the company that night
For each the huge images
shadow-tormented
of the characters
loom without restraint
in the amphitheatre of their dreams
the emotions   unhindered
that rage unabated through them

In her bed
Gillian stares
unseeing
through the dark
thought disrupted
Never
never before
not in exploration
not before the stage lights
have the stark heavy masks
wrenched her emotions
disrupted her mind
Now
her body
lies there
rigid
the graven images invading
emotions so long dormant
swaddled by her clamouring tasks
awakening her intimacy
sense of dislocation
loss
overwhelming need for
something

densely trapped
not yet understood
She lies there
vulnerable
lost
in this new
undefined
awareness
until
a faint whisper of reason
begins to penetrate her panic
Finally
exhausted
she sinks into sleep

In the morning a subdued company
gathers for the long drive
to Thunder Bay
No impulse to speak is born
as the bus trundles off
snuffling for the far-off destination
They seat two by two
or alone
staring out ahead
but seeing nothing
Archer sits behind them all
Deirdre at his side
both firmly silent
A moody rain-driven day
the drone of the indefatigable bus
punctuated by the rhythm
of the long wipers
as they snick-snick over the rain-whipped glass

Archer finds himself vulnerable
nerve-ending raw
his emotions   feelings
exposed with no defence or barrier
to his surprised   shaken consciousness
As a great wave can agitate

the depths below
to scour   disturb the sleeping sand
the force unleashed last night
bursts through the actors' sensibilities
to touch the deepest chords
of their imagination   feelings   body   all
In this new   disconcerting state
Archer is acutely aware
of the same turmoil in the others
studies them with sharp   painful sensitivity

Ursula behind Gillian
Jack at her side
She's chosen to sit there
because he's chosen to sit with her
Look at her
shocked into lassitude
Regan hard on her last night
bitter hate   unendurable lust
brewed with insatiable ambition   envy
Today the scars ripped open
of her breakup   her breakdown
the solace of her work
turned inside out against her
Only Jack's presence prevents
her giving way   totally
New experience for Jack too
Gloucester took him down the dreadful path
as if his eyelids had been sliced off
to leave him no choice but to stare
without abatement
New emotions for him
jokes wiped from his lips
his easy sensual familiarity with women
scattered by his intimate proximity
to Ursula's agony

He remembers
Ursula's wary enjoyment
of Jack's comfortable wit

pleasant badinage
during the early rehearsals
his lack of affectation
in his experience of the mask
his unobtrusive support
for Ursula   those others
who entered into new territory
On the aisle's other side
sits Yumiko   Ann at the window
Japanese looking through the sprayed windshield
Haida through her own now private window
both faces inscrutable

How far both have come
Ann's Goneril
that frightful look when my mask's hand
gripped her shoulder before the curse
All released in this performance
deep   harsh   barbaric feelings
like a wolf on its prey
Yumiko's drums awakening
to the power   the act
her own surrender
to the different masks
as she underscored the greater figures
with her servants   soldiers
Order in surrender
a potent force
Both will need time to refocus

Behind Ursula   James
the oldest but for Archer

That strong   sturdy body
his shortness gone with Kent's mask

Memory slips in moments
from fifteen years before
and later

He has never lived through this
There he sits   alone
as usual
brooding at the window
How will this new full life of Kent
anger   loyalty   compassion   grief
all spent by the end
only the thinnest hope of better change
affect his own life so intruded on?

Michael at the window opposite
so strong   agile
so used to focus through the ordered
wildness of the Chinese classical mask
now penetrated by his own emotions
magnified tenfold
by Edgar's struggles
betrayal   despair   grief   deadly anger
mask on mask
madness   warrior   brother   son
his whole range   way of expression
shattered in this struggle
of rehearsal   performance
last night
How will he rebuild himself?

Behind him   Lance
He is the one concerns me most
His Cornwall burst through last night
tall himself   he became huge
went to the heart
of the mask's blunt viciousness
heavy sexuality
The dying was hard to watch
The mask kept him in thrall
but I must work with him
given his own personal disturbances
He must not twist the mask
to give vent to his own explosive turmoil

Luke attracts him
but there's nothing for him there
A tricky situation
It's no coincidence
that Luke sits at the window opposite

Luke
for all his inexperience
or perhaps because of it
he has also broken through
his Albany not weak
but caught between his love for Goneril
his growing horror
of the catastrophe he sees unfolding
Fascinating the Oswald
found by Lance   him
each finding a common character
but with different   subtle nuances
appropriate to someone who shifts with the tides
I must help him to consolidate what he has learned

Gary behind Lance
His Edmund   his Edmund
fascinating appalling   contra-masks
Deep bitterness
deeper ambition
a true sociopath
always a devastating sincerity   charm
irresistibly attractive to both sisters
That final dying contra-mask
or was it the true mask
Gary has much to ruminate today

My Lear
my mask
what their masks
released in mine
In that first scene
his initial sense of power over family
over all

his feeling of no loss
in dividing his kingdom
that he will still hold
the power in his divided kingdom
forcing his daughters to declare their love
as a competition
his shock at Cordelia's response
his fury
the mask so strong
emotions titanic
all through buffeting me
as the mask pushed
farther than I have ever gone
What nuances
What massive   tangled states
Yet even as I remember it
I can sense it will drive me farther

For a moment
a chill grips him

How powerful imagination is
but what it can reveal
That's what the actor must find
but it can come at cost

Then
Deirdre shifts beside him
letting her shoulder
rest on his

He senses her there
quietly vulnerable
Slowly he lets her
help him to relax

She is lost today
Her Cordelia a fascination
her father's child
honest but proud   proud
her royal passion grounded in loving

courage
Her Fool on the verge of madness
seeing too simply   too sharply
wit the only anchor
song the only outlet
All this she found
today too raw   vulnerable
frightened of her need for me
but helpless in it

He sighs
Deirdre looks at him   startled
He gives a reassuring smile

Thank God for Gillian
Goddess of Management
I owe her more   much more
than can be repaid

Thoughts of their past shows
their long association
their comfortable animation

We must talk

In the early afternoon
the road permits their first sight
of Thunder Bay
Beyond
the Great Lake
the dark   turbulent clouds
scud across the rain-swept water
Lunch   the ritual of the motel
Then the company wheels to the site
the civic auditorium
Within a space in contradiction
to the tent the night before
fifteen hundred people can see them

In the large space
Archer at the platform
that will be their stage

"We all know what happened last night:
a rare and wonderful performance;
and we will talk about it later.
But now we must adjust to the size of this place
and so—to work."

He first lets them find their voices in the space
uses exercises to let them fill the auditorium
without strain or shouting
whispers heard
dynamics explored
Then they adapt to the space itself
their groupings changing subtly
Finally the masks are brought out
exercises lead them back in control
to find the mask   the space   themselves
Short segments of scenes are explored
In the work the actors lose themselves
let the memories of the night before
slip quietly into the shaded crannies of their minds

That night the auditorium is full
This time many Natives can be seen
Their compatriots have swiftly passed on the word
of Ann's performance
the masks
The masks now work fully   powerfully
but in the larger space they easily fill
new meanings now emerge
not only the intimate responses of the characters
but their whole social   political existence
The family becomes a royal family
whose actions reverberate through the kingdom
Cordelia is engaged for kingdoms
the kingdom itself roughly divided up
Lear   his dwindling retinue
betrayals not only personal but shaking a country
war
an accounting that leaves no one
in the country   at rest

In the audience the Ojibwe   Cree
are disturbed by the dividing of the country
for they do not think of land
as owned or divided
but they are sensitive to each nuance
of the characters' relationships
When the play ends
a great roar fills the auditorium
like the lake's fierce storms
sweeping uncontrollably
over the wind-lashed waves
beating at the swaying evergreens

After the play as the audience is leaving
some remain
A group of Natives waits quietly
until Ann goes to them
They smile
a quiet conversation   intimate
heard only by themselves
Archer is intercepted by a man
once handsome
now going slightly to seed
his hair dyed
betraying the birth of a paunch
Archer knows him

"Gerald."

A wide painted smile
"Ray, a wonderful production, wonderful!
You always amaze me."
Tiny crease at the brow
"But why didn't you tell me
you were coming here?
My theatre could have sponsored you."

"A problem of grants—Gillian can tell you."

"Yes, I'll ask her, of course.
But can I take you and the cast for a drink?"

A patient smile
"If you like. But our sponsor should come too.
And we have to pack first."

The smile flakes slightly
"Naturally—I'll invite them now.
Just wait and I'll lead you over."

He goes off to see the sponsors
ricocheting from actor to actor as he goes
shaking their hands
exclaiming over them

Gillian raises her eyebrow
looks at Archer

"Tell everyone we're going for drinks
with the Artistic Director
after we pack."

Gillian raises both eyebrows
but says nothing

Ann comes to him quietly
"I'm going with my new friends."

A nod   a smile

At a noisy bar
the A.D. holds court
Archer makes sure
Gillian is on guard on one side
he on the other
The cast sit quietly at bunched tables
insulating themselves against the raucous barrage
surrounding them

"Well, you were all splendid, just splendid!
A brilliant show."

All nod slightly in acknowledgment

"But Gillian..."
immediately getting to his sticking point
"...why didn't you contact me?
We could have worked out something."

"The conditions of our grants
wouldn't allow it, I'm afraid."

"Oh come, we all know how to
get around the grants, don't we?"

Gillian watches him
without expression
says nothing

Archer intervenes
"You know I don't like connections
with the commercial theatre."

"Do you still have that bee in your bonnet?
There's nothing wrong with a professional company
and what we have today."

Archer smiles
"You go ahead with what you're doing,
and I'll go ahead with what I'm doing."

"But it's such a shame!
You could be..."

For an instant he betrays
the tiniest hint of envy

"...Artistic Director of Stratford,
for God's sake!"

Archer's smile remains
but thinner
"You know I'm not interested
in any of that."

"Well, I think it's such a waste.
And have you a place yet?
Still living in the bus?"

Archer's smile relaxes   broadens
"As usual."

The A.D. rolls his eyes
sighs in mock exasperation
"You're incorrigible!"

He changes the conversation
to how successful
his last season was
the glories of the next
gossips with the cast
who receive him politely
try to maintain some form
of conversation
By now they begin
to talk among themselves again
more relaxed after the release
of this night's performance
After a half hour in the maelstrom
Archer excuses the company   himself
using the reason of moving on tomorrow
They return to their motel
with easy banter about the A.D.
the bar
A little later Archer
in his bunk hears outside his window
the almost imperceptible sound
of Ann as she returns

The next day they leave for Nipigon
a short drive
Archer remains in his cubicle
to consider what he needs
to glean from Thunder Bay

As he pulls out a notebook
nestled with others
their box on the floor
he pauses
fingering its surface
looking at the stuffed space
before him
with an affectionate grimace

Living here in the bus
parked always beside
Gillian's house
when not on tour
She is a good cook

Grins
Then aware again
of his workbook

But her books
every room with shelves of books
even in her kitchen
for her cookbooks

Chuckles

Those meals
how we ate   talked
or how she talked
about any subject at all
Then afterwards
in the quiet of the evening
she'd curl up in that large chair
her eyes tearing through
yet another book

He opens the notebook

Thunder Bay
inhabited even longer than Kenora
11,000 years
Because of its position
a pivot in the middle of the continent
at the head of the Great Lakes
a natural meeting   trading site
or so it is considered
definitely for Europeans   the fur trade
who build a fur trading outpost at Baie de Tonnerre
Then in 1728 another company   nation
North West Company's Fort William
near the Kaministiquia River

a wild medley   Scottish traders   French voyageurs   Native trappers
Then the new metallic transition
copper   silver   gold   amethyst
Then the railroad
grain   manufacturing   shipbuilding   pulp and paper
The Finns migrate here with their traditional pleasures
for the tourists   Ojibwe Keeshigun
the marriage of Fort William and Port Arthur

Archer is now acutely sensitive
not only to the swirling currents of relationships
the deep undertow of feeling   emotion
but now the full spectrum of the social world
peoples   tribe   community   nation
the shifting structures of business   politics
shoved forward by the brutal clarity of *King Lear*
In this light his pen turns to the legends
of Thunder Bay

Ode to Ojibwe Legend

In the fractured light of our inconstant world
How legend can pierce with unobstructed brilliance
To the lodestone of our existence.
The territories of land and water and sky infuse
The life in and around our flesh and blood and nerve
And we in turn use the mirror of ourselves
To make them part of, make them unite with,
Our perceptions of ourselves.

In the uneven shores of the Great Lake,
The ruffled, illimitable waters,
The bays, islands, mountains, forests,
The rivers, falls, uncountable lakes, and muskeg,
Our personal dramas play out in a vast panorama
Described by a people, ancient in the way of years
By the thousands, striking to the heart
With their complex and sometimes violent world.

Their Gods play out their stories
Much like the half-wild divinities and creatures
So lovingly and chillingly delineated
By hard-headed, subtle Ovid.
In this northern country the hierarchy starts
With the Great Manitou, a divine chieftain
Both beneficent and vindictive—
Not one to meet when he is angry.

Subservient to him, but to no other force,
Nanabijou, Great Spirit of the Deep Sea Water,
Who controls two elemental creatures:
The Thunder Bird, from whose terrible eyes
Lightning streaks forth, and whose thunderous screech
Births the huge storms that scud across the reaches of the lake;
And Nagochee, his constant companion,
A great lion of the sea, with the wings of an eagle,
The feet of a duck, the speed of the wind,
Who not only can fly but can swim like a fish.

Like monstrous actors in dramas violent
They play out our turbulent passions and repercussive acts.
Take the triangle described before:
Nanabijou has only to fly off hastily
On the great wings of his pet Nagochee
And his beloved Thunder Bird forget to take,
And she, hurt and jealous in assumed rejection,
Will as they return screech up a furious storm,
Forcing the wing-torn Nagochee with his master
To plummet to the hungry waves and confused separation.
The Great Spirit feels betrayed that his pet
Did not rescue him from the waves
And turns him to stone.
And Nagochee lies still petrified on Silver Islet,
Solemn in immovable granite,
Still loyal to his master.
Jealousy and betrayal win the day;
Honour is suspended, all by mistake.

Or consider how humans become entangled with them,
As in the case of a renowned, kind Ojibwe chieftain's
Youngest daughter, deeply sensitive to plants and animals,
Whom Nanabijou selects for his son North Star,
And appoints for her the time and place of assignation.
The human tragedy then unfurls—
Jealous sisters deriding her.
("Drink herb tea for your disordered mind!")
They lash her with deer hide as a result,
Envy distilled to hate;
The ambush at the appointed time, arrows through her heart,
But borne up to the skies by her Spirit lover;
The three sisters, fleeing in terror,
Nanabijou, who has seen all,
Catches them up in a wild storm,
Turns them to stone,
And drops them as islands in the Lake.
And for the final irony,
Sailors have rejoiced since then when they see
The Welcome Islands that lead them to the safe harbour
Of the Bay of Thunder.

Or the Spirits see unblinking humans' own heroic acts:
As when young Princess Green Mantle,
Daughter of revered old Chief White Bear,
Saves her tribe from the ravaging Sioux warriors
By tricking them to be carried over the Great White Falls
To their deaths and to hers.
The Great Manitou respects what she has done,
And he places her as the Maiden of the Mists
At Kakabeka Falls.

Legend turns in the end to another end:
The coming of the white man
And the inexorable retreat of the Great Spirits.
Nanabijou, fighting the invasion of his territory,
With his Thunder Bird raging at the camps along the shores,
In a tempestuous fight with his angry wife
Over his continual absence, strikes her down,
But cannot in his later grief find her again,

For Manitou, to keep her from harm,
Turns her to stone and places her on Pie Island,
Where still she can be seen
Peeping from behind the large plateau,
Hoping that he who approaches will be her beloved husband.
But now the legend continues:
If Nanabijou returns,
If Manitou forgives him,
Then the stone will disappear
And she will never leave his side again.

And legend finally tells the passing of the Spirits
In this multicultured world;
Tells of the Ojibwe people,
Peaceful, industrious, and loyal,
To whom Nanabijou from his mountain temple
Awards the gift of a silver mine
With admonition to keep it secret or he will die.
They do so, but their wealth attracts the interest of the Sioux,
Who, when torture fails, resort to treachery,
Sending a scout as a spy
Who unveils the secret.
But through two white men's alcohol and treachery,
He leads them near the hidden place,
Ends crazed in his canoe,
The white men drowned in a vicious storm.
But in the wide entrance to the bay,
Which before was clear,
There now is found a large new island—
Nanabijou, Sleeping Giant, arms folded across mighty chest,
In the sleep of death as he had forewarned.
And since then no one has gained access to the silver mine.

So legend permeates the land, the Lake,
Giving significance to object and location;
Its lessons of our digressive lives
Lost and relived painfully
As long as breath and blood animate our confused acts.

Archer looks up
Caught in the labyrinth

How these myths
echo in the ruptures
found in Lear
family riven
country riven
how they echo
in the country I explore
profit
love of power
leading to acquisition
conquest
across the vast expanses
trickery   bigotry
against the hard struggle
to find the means
for a life valued
for a family sustained
for a hope
to break past
the maze of different views
of seeing how we exist
together in this immense space
Yet we enact
watch Lear
live through the horrors
end with the corpses
the scarred
but still upright
Edgar and Kent
who yet try
to make the kingdom sound
So this country stumbles
through drives mistaken
wealth   conquest   power
still streaked with dreams
of its communities

He stops
gazes out unseeing
lets his mind revert
to his bus-ridden place
alone

Canto 4
THE CANADIAN SHIELD

By noon the bus arrives at Nipigon
where they have lunch
Then Archer leads them on
to the mouth of the Nipigon River
to see the rock paintings

Another ancient habitation
at least 9,000 years
these paintings in the last thousand
dark stickmen
occasionally with dark stick spears
ochre stripes that curve
sketched animals
all creeping through the ribbed sheen
of the forbidding cliffs
The oldest trading post here
Claude Greysolon Dulhut in 1679
on the north shore of the Great Lake

As they scatter to explore the shore
Archer gazes over the waters

Edward Umfreville started his exploration
near here
A good exploit for our exploration too
his journal of his canoe voyage
from Nipigon to Winnipeg
this voyage
brings in the conflicts
of commerce politics

He pulls from his pocket
the notebook
glances at it for a moment
then pauses
looking out at the river

In 1783
the boundary with the U.S.A.
lost for traders their Grand Portage
at the Great Lake
They had to establish a new base
to link the Lake with the vast interior
with a route on this side of the boundary
In 1784
the North West Company directed a new exploration
for a route from Pays Plat on the Lake
to Portage de l'Isle
to make a link to the River Ouinipeque   the interior
Edward Umfreville was commissioned
from his long experience as a writer
with the Hudson's Bay Company
Said to be sober   diligent   durable
but did have a temper

A Canoe Exploration

Archer smiles

A fascinating journal
written with both fact   comment
on their ordeal
from the sixteenth of June
until the twenty-third of July
1784

The first day involved packing
But the second day is typical
of what he and the five Canadiens
in their canoe
"with provisions only"
had to deal with throughout
the exploration

Thursday, 17 June 1784

Along a shallow river we canoe
With gentle current until we pass through
A half-mile rapid that we must subdue.
Then, past a small lake with sturgeon filled,
The Portage de Roche Capitaine fulfilled.
We leave the river for a creek, then make
Our first Grand Portage, for the which we take
Seven hours to pass things over to make
The four long miles with cargo and canoe.
And the experience? Myself and crew
Packed in with cargo paddling each long mile,
Fighting rapids, then packing—a great trial—
Canoe and contents over portages short
And then for seven weary hours to resort
To the trek of four miles each arduous way,
While about us we cannot keep at bay
The swarms of mosquitoes and biting flies
On our necks and arms, in our faces, eyes,
And always overhead the sun's harsh heat,
And always branches that our bodies beat,
And at this slog's final weary end
To still make camp as night starts to descend
And finally eat and finally sleep
With the hard rough ground our reward to reap.

Archer is rooted at the shore
absorbed in the journal's narrative
as one of Antony Gormley's sculptures of a man
planted along beaches
evoking power   mystery
so Deirdre
returning down the shore
sees him from a distance
standing tall   motionless
She stops to gaze
stilled by the sight

Throughout the trip
they meet "Indians"
though it is their hunting season
With discretion they use
constant diplomacy
Their first guide unreliable
several dangerous incidents
Their next guide
Edward learns to trust

Tuesday, 13 July 1784

Our first guide the most villainous,
and this the best
Indian that ever I met with. Thus blessed
Are we, for without him found,
then, tempest-tossed,
The fruits of the voyage must have been lost,
And we probably perished for want.
But still, with such struggle we are now gaunt.
At Lac de Monteggé we are now found.

More adventures
many caused by drink
a trading staple

Friday, 16 July 1784

And so it befell,
As traders had advised, that trouble came
With drink, for an Indian lamb-meek became
When drunk a mere devil when given
This infernal stimulator. When driven
By exploration, an expedition
Should at all costs try such spirits to shun;
But on a trading voyage, I own
The necessity of it.

How his journal reveals
the chasm between
these two cultures

one alien to the harsh land
through which they
hack   paddle   struggle
the other alien to the group
to which exchange is paramount
who provide them
with the fiery means of madness

Friday, 23 July 1784

And so we searched for five long weeks and more
To find a route. We struggled to explore
The way while gambling on a guide to show
What portages were best, and we didn't know
When we encountered Indians whether they
Were friend or foe—we had to display
Fortitude and courage, and honesty
Throughout. I got them there at last
And sent in my report the route had passed.

Archer pauses
is about to close the notebook
but discovers an unfinished stanza
which he had not completed writing

But the company did not agree,
And though for a new treaty we did plea,
Were unsuccessful. Yet...

Yet the British still
kept Grand Portage for many years until
the U.S.A. taxed their goods   and even then
they did not move to his new route again
but to Fort William and the old route
of the Kaministiquia   the fruit
of a rediscovery in 1798
An ironic end at such a late date

Archer
images scuttling
in his head

looks at the shore
sees Deirdre
now the others
watching him
He smiles
leads them back
to his own civilization

The bus returns to Nipigon
They search for   find the motel
Then off to the playing space
this time the recreation centre
to use the skating rink
chairs set on the flat floor
a high platform
Their task is to defeat
the echoing cavern
to let the words be heard
Archer finds ways to let their voices
insinuate their meaning through the space
to let the masked figures
share expression with the audience

That night four hundred come
many are First Nations
many have seen the production before
driving to Nipigon

Because of the acoustics
the performance must slow
to let the words be heard
against the reverberation
A strange tapestry of form   sound
the figures high above   huge   iconic
the slight echo fills the space
to give a new dimension
to the stately progress of the tragedy
Despite the time
the audience is still

Even at intermission little is said
When the end comes
masks are doffed
the actors move quietly forward
to take their bows
the audience is subdued   exhausted
files out silently

As they are striking to pack
Ann approaches Archer
"Can you bring the cast?
We've all been invited
to a gathering."

Archer gives her a sharp intent look
nods
When the bus is packed
a guide comes with them
to a place outside Nipigon
where in a space enclosed by woods
a bonfire blazes at the centre
Surrounding it are many people
sitting on the ground
or on logs or portable chairs
Three greet them
two men   a woman
Elders
Ann introduces them
as from the nations of the region

The woman Elder
"We wish to thank you
for your play
and for showing that our sister…"

She nods to Ann who acknowledges her salute

"…can show such strength
on your stage.
We could not understand all the language…"

Appreciative chuckles from the flickering ring

"...but we understood what they did
and what they meant,
and we understood also your masks
and felt their power and their spirits.
Ann has told us of the ceremonies of her nation
and the masks of their Great Spirits,
and here you have let us have a glimpse
of what they must be like.
Thank you for this."

Then the company are led
to be dispersed among those at the fire's edge
There they talk   laugh
as the fire blazes to show the faces
more open than they had ever seen before
Archer sits with the Elders
asking them about their legends
explaining things in the play
about which they question him
Ann sits nearby among another group
who talk happily with her
ask about the differences
between the shows that they had seen
In this wood-shrouded space
the fire sending sparks
into the clear night air above
the stars shifting in the coiling smoke
time burns away
Only when the fire abates
collapses into embers
the chill air invades the smoke-riven place
do the actors feel in their bones
their deep fatigue
need for sleep
Partings are made
the fire extinguished   the ashes raked
The company climbs wearily
into the bus back to the motel
dreamless sleep

The next day brings the long journey
to Sault Ste. Marie
Archer no longer feels
the need to watch his actors closely
The three different performances
have given the ingredients
to cook a much looser   more relaxed
comradeship
or the right to be each alone
if the need arises
Again he sits behind Gillian
as she steers the ungainly vehicle
down the continually curving highway
Beside him still sits Deirdre
now no longer afraid
to let him remain silent
as he gazes in thought
but she makes sure that her arm
touches his as it rests on the
seat's arm between them

To see where Umfreville began
imagine what it took
for him to navigate those long weeks
of trek   portage   negotiation
that we traverse in hours
on our convenient highway

The bus drones down the twisting highway
Many of the actors doze
dazed by the continual rush
of red and grey rock folded into hills
dark trees invading them
the glint   sheen of sun
on endless water
Deirdre sleeps
her head on Archer's shoulder

All that struggle for a route
to aid a corporation

All the gambles with life
the unknown
the "Indians"
for whom the journey   their life
were one   the same
with their families   their canoes
their life in hunting
trapping for trade
The careful rituals with the Europeans
who change every few years
leave their old rotting settlements
The desire for the white man's liquor
that unhooks the hard-won disciplines
for all the members of the family
The need to keep the invaders
in quiet surveillance
to see where next they go
what encroachments
on traditional territory
will sidle through
a strategy now long lost

The show last night
a new facet
The rituals of our strife
fixed in inevitable forms
what we call evil
destroying others   itself
in the mad pursuit of power
revenge
hatred
Yet the good could only destroy evil
in having more power
in the courage of the individual
when all is stripped away
in helping through illusion
Edgar as Tom
the field as cliff
to cauterize the wounded mind

The campfire after
the friendly talk
Faces opened
by the penetration
of the masks' rituals
the need to recognize
what is deep below the surface
where the monsters   the angels swim

He watches the grey hills roll by
as the miles unreel

The continuous rippling
of this primordial rock
oldest visible in the world
beside these vast waters
vast land
through which we rip
our threads of roads
rails
ships
Did our masks
show last night
the undulating ageless rock
of our frail selves?

He falls asleep
For a lunch stop
they picnic
After the quiet time
in the breezes of the near lake
Archer takes the wheel
lets Gillian rest
while they snake down
the long winding highway
to Sault Ste. Marie

The last stop
for this north shore
ancient in its rock
ancient in its peoples
Two thousand years

lived beside the rapids
at Bawating
The French defined them from the rapids
the Saulteaux
at the hurl of waters
between two Great Lakes
St. Mary's River

Commerce stamped the place
North West Company
with trading post   tiny lock
destroyed by the Americans in 1814
in our one continental war
Fur money changed to mineral money
which the U.S.A. won in locks
that we rented for the next four decades
until 1870 with passage refused
to the Chicora blockade runner
at the time of the Red River expedition
Humiliation with negotiation
Then wheat money with the mineral
the Canadian lock
cut through the bedrock
with Southern Ontario   Quebec
profiting from their industry

Decades of ships passing through
then full circle again
locks broken in 1987
the four American locks used again
a pleasure lock shrunk
into the old laboured lock
Like the drifting clouds
the economic shift again
with the great steel complex
in danger of creating its own rust
as we drive into town

Mid-afternoon when they arrive
settle in road weary

Gillian contacts their sponsors
for a morning expedition
She and Archer confer
but not for long
Then Archer   Deirdre
walk along the locks
Silence as dusk begins its overlay
He lets her take his hand
as they stare at the stone passageway
then move on to see
the sidetracked rapids
as the sodium-vapour lamps
begin to eradicate last glimmers
He tells her of the Soo's past
of the thoughts he has
of that past   of this present
She listens
but always she strains to sense
what he means behind his words
each glance
each pressure of the hand
each brush of the body
still his is a foreign language
to her   her feelings
He is sensitive to her
responds with mature intimacy
but the path to him
seems to twist   turn
with abrupt endings
sudden quicksands
or lead off into infinite distances
with no signposts to help her on her way
Yet she is still engulfed
in her desire for him

That night
when they lie together
after a tumultuous union
when her hunger could be barely slaked

a quiet moment
when both breath   heart
slowed to their normal dance
he speaks to her
his voice barely a breath in her ear

"You must accept us as we are,
not as you want.
I don't know,
can't know,
all of you,
even with what you use for your masks.
You don't know,
will never know,
all that I am.
I don't know,
barely know parts of myself.
We must accept what we can have,
for now,
not for some other time.
Don't make plans for a future
that we cannot know.
This is our relationship.
This must be how we know each other.
There is no other way,
not with what we do."

She hears
her eyes wide in the glooming
a moment after he finishes
then her body convulses
racked with sobs
He holds her
until she subsides
lies limp
unresisting in his arms
Then both sleep

Light glimmers through
the window of the bus
a ray lighting quietly

on Archer's face   naked shoulders
as he lies asleep
Deirdre nestled still
within his arms
but now awake
She gazes at the tranquil face
so near to her
softened in the subdued light
his features moulded   shadowed
Without thought
she lets her fingers lightly trace
the firm contours
As she does so
the image of his face   body
as it would have been
when he was young
floods her mind
She sees how beautiful
his face
still handsome
must have been
in those bright years
how firm   smooth his body
a young Apollo
his hair dark   abundant
without restraint
She lets lust move deep within her
coaxes the sleeping man
into erotic life
lets the image
take her
in complete abandonment

The next day
the routine continues
inspection   warm-up   rehearsal
This time a regular theatre
this night an audience of seven hundred
in a space that could hold more

but few First Nations people
The show rages on
against the comfortable surroundings
Afterward a scattering
all in small groups

In the morning
they leave the lakes
drive to Sudbury

The change in the basin
from my last time years ago
then a trash land of slag
ravaged country
as industry ate at its heart
its raw skin
ripped from its face
Now plastic surgeons
have been at work
green taking over from blood rust
for the healing
but the smelters still belch
their reminders to the sky

That night
a church again their venue
the audience small   bemused
Again they return to their motel
in small groups or alone
Again Deirdre writhes in Archer's bed
Again the next day they drive on
not far
to perform in North Bay
Again a community centre
the ritual repeats
the audience repeats
if larger than in Sudbury
With their routine set
they finish the north of Ontario
prepare to invade the south

Archer takes the wheel
from North Bay
leaves Deirdre with Gillian
as he drives   thinks
skirting Lake Nipissing
plunging into Algonquin Park

Stone   water   trees
an eternity of Shield
wilderness
where spruce   pine
birch   hemlock
maple   fir
start to jostle for territory
Not like Lear's moors   cliffs
softened by foxglove piercing the blood
Here old battles were intimate
ambushes   skirmishes
within the forest
by a lake
but much scarcer
than farther south
It's the numbing scale
difficult to enumerate
The size from a thin ribbon
that still takes days to drive
would take at least
as many days north as east

Rearward sit Ursula   Jack
tender still
from the masked nights
their nervy insights
the past furrows newly ploughed
Rock   trees
sweep past their window endlessly

"It's like the old panorama."

"What?"

"You know, it's like—
we're just sitting here
on a stage
in a prop bus
while the scenery rolls by us."

Ursula smiles
It's an old stereotype
but a theatrical one
she can be comfortable with
She likes the way
he can ease the situation
his humour tailored to her tastes
But she is still
still wary with a man
grateful
that he accepts the situation
They remain silent
but not alone

The bus rides the curves
blasted from the rock for convenience

This wilderness picturesque
but harsh
harsh as the play
Lakes give relief
but their enclosure
provokes the heavy feeling
of the overwhelming rock   forest
How can I portray
the vastness   the emptiness
the huge wild gaps of this country
with its human millions
spread in a thin band in the south
or scattered in brief pockets
elsewhere

Gillian   Deirdre
sit some seats behind
to the side

of Archer
Deirdre trapped
at the window
her gaze tugged to him
They sit silent for a time
letting the roar of the bus
the scenery shifting by
fill the moments

Gillian breaks the routine
"So what work did you have
before the tour?"

Deirdre
startled
glances at her
She knows Gillian
has studied her résumé
knows all she has done
fully
that she had done well
at the National Theatre School
"I did a few things
after the school,
but then I felt restless,
lacking something,
and took some workshops
in physical theatre
and mask."

"That's why you auditioned for us?"

Deirdre notes the plural
"Yes."

"How have you found the experience?"

"The work has been wonderful.
I've learned more than I thought I could."

"What particularly have you liked?"

"The mask work, the discipline,
the ensemble,
discovery in character and playing."

Gillian sees the enthusiasm birthed
She smiles
looks directly into Deirdre's eyes

"Anything else?"

Deirdre stares back
the moment long
"And Ray."

"You have learned from Archer?"

Deirdre notes the use of his last name
"Oh yes. I've learned from him."

Gillian's smile is warm   sympathetic
"Want to talk about him?"

Deirdre knows this is the destination
She wants to arrive there
on her own terms
"I will if you will."

Startled
No one before had asked her this
Then
laughter   warm   amused
"Of course!
What would you like to know?"

"How long have you known him?"

"Over twenty years."

"How did you meet him?"

A chuckle
"At a Fringe Festival.
I was very young,
just starting to learn the business.
Fringes were kindergartens for many of us,

and I was busy with a student group—awful!"
She shudders affectionately at the memory
"He had a small group—perhaps two others,
I don't remember—
but what they did,
the force and discipline of their playing,
shocked me,
forced me to see the power of the stage
and its experience.
Ray was brilliant,
and, of course, twenty years ago
he was gorgeous."
An affectionate sensual glance
at him as he drives
"Naturally, I had to meet him,
and I did.
And I had to have him,
and I did."

Deirdre   despite herself   blushes

A mischievous grin
"In those days,
at nineteen,
I never looked better—
and I looked good!
I gave up everything to follow him,
and for a year,
despite the work and the touring,
it was bliss.
And then..."

Breathlessly
"And then?"

"Then one night
after a particularly vigorous session..."
She looks his way
the memory igniting a spark of desire

Deirdre turns red
can hardly breathe

"...as we lay together
he told me that he had no more to teach me
for now
and that I needed to leave him
for a while
and learn as much as possible
about the business,
about the stagecraft,
and then return.
I was astonished, stricken.
'What about us?' I whispered.
And he said,
'You have got all you need of me
for now.
You must learn to distinguish
what your desires are,
both for your body and your work.'
I did not understand then.
The next day he sent me away,
and I hated him for it,
and I worked hard to show him
I could do the business
as well as, and better than, anyone else.
I went back and finished my commerce degree;
I worked on connections with the right people—
my father knew a lot of them, and I made sure I saw them.
And I plunged into theatre.
I worked at everything:
stage management,
building sets and props,
lighting,
the business of theatre,
promotion, management...
And in a few years
I had done it all,
and I went back to show him,
and I saw he was right.
We have been close friends
and colleagues ever since."

Deirdre can say nothing
for a long moment
Then   hesitatingly
"Have you been lovers
since that time?"

A chuckle
"Oh, there have been occasions.
He's still a sexy man, for God's sake,
and I'm not unattractive yet!"

She pauses
memory flooding back
how she had helped create companies
how her background
parents with influence
money
gave her contacts and means

"I've had my share of lovers…"
She suddenly is struck
by an insight that shakes her
All her lovers
resembled
him

She forces herself
back to Deirdre
"Sorry,
I just thought of something
I need to do—
but it can wait.

"Both Ray and I know
our friendship
and our work
are more important.
Now, what about you?"

Sensitive face
drawn   vulnerable

As one stone
kicked   dislodged
begins its journey down a slope
gathering other stones   debris
as it begins a steeper plunge
until the single stone
provokes an avalanche
that sweeps all away before it
so Deirdre
disarmed by the older woman's frankness
in a trickle
then surge
of feelings   words
describes how she is lost
in him
famished for what he knows
for the new horizons   experiences
explored
hungry for his body
eager to devour him in all ways
shaken by her desire
unslakeable need
never   never ever
felt by her before
her surprise   confusion
over her desperate attraction
for a man old enough to be her father
grandfather
So the young actress
blurts out her revelations
ends   exhausted
her head on Gillian's shoulder
whose arm shelters her
A long silence
as wilderness flashes by
Then
head still on the safe shoulder
"But why did he send you away?
Why has he stayed with no one?"

Gillian
while hearing the girl's wracked thoughts
could not help returning to
her own turbulent time
sighs
"You must remember this:
There is one thing,
and one thing only,
to his life—
that is his work.
Everything—
relationships, women, men,
where he lives,
what he does—
are fuel for that fire.
He does not hurt anyone willingly.
But unless you can live
within his obsession,
be part of it,
you have no chance
to continue with him."

She gently raises Deirdre's head
turns it to look into the wide eyes
stained with fear
"Learn all you can from him,
stay in the company
for its discipline and ensemble,
and when you feel you have learned
all you can,
or he feels you have,
and you have exhausted your desire,
then leave
with good memories,
not failed dreams."

Deirdre cannot answer
Gillian lets the head return to her shoulder
For the rest of the ride
they both let their intimacy
sustain them

But thoughts
memories
rush through Gillian's mind

Her head resting on my shoulder
so intimate
so open
so honest
The first one to be so with me
about him
Those before excited
eager
passionate about him
wanting everything he could teach them
wanting everything with him
as I had
but unquestioning

Her eyes widen

As I still am
Over these years
the glances of the other actresses
how I had to work with them
some jealous
some disturbed
but I helped them all to sense
that it was the actress
who made the first move
always

This cast less involved with him
personally
surprised when Deirdre
started the relationship
was so open about him
but they sensed
her openness
her honesty
his care of her
Only Ursula disturbed to begin with

then her concern lessened
as she saw what has happened
although she probably still has reservations
But what she has brought back to me

She closes her eyes
lets the drone   rhythm of the bus
be a ground note for her memories

was I actually so young as she is   o yes   younger   even at school   skipped a
grade even at a posh Vancouver girls' school   father   proud of his only child
but quizzical   distracted by his work   important positions   distinguished in
an eagle kind of way   whom my mother tended as a gardener her plot   such
parties growing up in her foliage   house perpetually in flower   plenty of
friends   acquaintances

Deirdre shifts slightly
For a brief moment
Gillian is aware of her
Then

loved clubs   running them   my own garden to plant   hoe enticing them to
flourish   theatre the best   even over reading   ravenous to learn things
reading the great books at an early age   Euripides   Chekov   Shakespeare
my friends   prickly as they could be   fast learner   got me through   like a
cheetah in full flight   graduation a rush   a release

A shadow past the window startles her
but the bus's drone lulls her back

then   the university whirligig   the boyfriend I first gave myself to   so young
devoured courses   devoured clubs   theatre devoured me

The bus whines up a hill

two years   then Archer   smashing into a whole new world   so hungry to
learn   to learn him   body and soul as they say   and the hurt when he sent
me away   the rupturing hurt   then fury   then determination   finished
degree   commerce   for what I needed   for him   my parents relieved
ruptures healed   though they worried about time wasted in theatre
no problem   high marks   recognized at graduation   a social life with my
father's influential friends   collecting connections as a collector stamps
theatre odd jobs   any backstage work   learning lighting   tough shows

tougher shows   stage management   company management   anything I
could find   I was good   my parents aghast   then resigned   then   then
then I confronted him   he grinned   took me on   we meshed as a team
our bodies meshed   occasionally   the years go on   I still want him

Canto 5

THE GOLDEN HORSESHOE AND THE SOUTHWEST

Now past Algonquin Park
the bus wheels around
the many lakes
until they open up
to the greater water
of Lake Simcoe
As a sea
laps toward the mouth
of a great river
its salt water
mingling with
then diluted by the flood of fresh water
issuing from the shore
so the country begins to change
the evergreens now living
in close habitation
with the birch   the maple
then both retreating
before the clearings
of farms
nestling in the slightly rolling landscape
opposite the shining bulk of the lake
The bus comes to Barrie
where Archer attends to his notebook

Barrie
our portal to the teeming south
reverse of where we've been
all these southwestern cities
reflecting the later century
in their names
with Indigenous names

territories
shoved out
Barrie after Sir Robert in 1832
commander of the naval forces
portaging from Lake Simcoe to the Georgian Bay

For the next week or more
they tour around
southwestern Ontario
Nottawasaga Bay brooding on the right
to a hazy horizon
country to the left
like moulting skin of a mule deer
lush fields and old barns
shoved among woods   forests
themselves undecided as to their composition
Archer keeps a notebook handy

Owen Sound
water   city
across the patchwork land

Owen Sound
Ojibwe elbowed out by 1841
after William Fitzwilliam Owen
surveyed in 1815   gave the inlet
his older brother's last name of many
Admiral Sir Edward William Campbell
Rich Owen

Glimpses of more horizon-stretching water
Lake Huron
down Bruce County
past Empire towns
Kincardine   Goderich

Goderich
named in 1827 for Frederick John Robinson
First Viscount of Goderich
then prime minister in the old country
Goderich

*connected to the Irish
now by its Celtic Roots Festival
then to the country
by its response in 1866
to the Fenian Invasion*

The Fenian Invasion

"We are the Fenian Brotherhood
skilled in the arts of war,
And we're going to fight for Ireland,
the land that we adore.
Many battles we have won,
along with the boys in blue,
And we'll go and capture Canada,
for we've nothing else to do."

Men from the Union side, men from the South,
All of them Irish, and all of them broke.
They were tough veterans, and all with one thought—
Revenge on the British, with one savage stroke.
Two places they planned to attack with surprise,
To win at Fort Erie, then the Welland Canal,
While there in the west, their strategy lies
In winning Goderich for its harbour and all,
For Lake Huron, the railway lines, and farther on
Both Stratford and London were in their sight.
For they thought once they were winning then thereupon
Canadian Irish would rise up and join in the fight,
And England would then have to agree
To let Ireland rule itself, independent and free.

"Tramp, tramp, tramp, our boys are marching.
Cheer up, let the Fenians come!
For beneath the Union Jack, we'll drive the rabble back,
And we'll fight for our beloved Canadian home."

And in Upper Canada, there was much fear;
Formidable they found them, ten thousand suspected
Without truly knowing where they would appear.

121

Troops were frequently mobilized, drilled, and inspected,
Then left in barracks until something occurred.
But in Fort Erie, the attack a surprise,
And villages mobilized, young men undeterred,
And were joined by the troops to increase their size.
Then they all met at the Battle of Ridgeway,
Where defenders, outnumbered and poorly led,
Were brave but defeated, and retreated instead.

Meanwhile in Goderich worry had mounted,
In Chicago was rumoured five thousand would board
Ships to invade them, and so all the town hustled
To find arms and find youths, others, a horde
To fight and resist, all determined to save
Their town and their country with all that they gave.

But truth was, though Fenians promised,
And had dreams much too large and plans colourful,
They delivered but little and much that was missed,
With conflicting orders, and with ships really not full,
So that in Chicago ships stayed in port, and in the east,
Reinforcements were held up by Grant at the least.

The invasion thus failed, but out of it came
With deep conviction something far more important.
For both town and country found they were the same—
They wanted their country and kept their opinion,
And one year later, they got their Dominion.

Archer smiles wryly
watches as other places
whizz by
Chatham   Sarnia

Sarnia
another Ojibwe hunting ground taken over
surveyed in 1829
called The Rapids in 1835
Stubborn deadlock over the next name
by the English who wanted Buenos Aires
by the Scots who wanted New Glasgow

broken by Sir John Colborne
Lieutenant Governor of the Channel Isle of Guernsey
who offered Port Sarnia
the Roman name for Guernsey

Southampton
colonial recognition
Tecumseh
the land now settled comfortably
with the occasional protest of woods

But the cost
First Nations dispossessed   decimated by disease
clearing of the land
painful   slow
from trees   stumps   rocks
generations of struggle
always a gamble

The creeping suburbs of Windsor
haze now a fixture

The oldest
Windsor
the oldest European inhabited city
west of the Quebec border
a French agricultural settlement mid-eighteenth century
a place of many names
Petite Côte   La Côte de Misère
Sandwich after the American Revolution
Windsor after the town in Berkshire

For the company
the only constants are
the bus   the discipline
Each performance on a different stage
a different space
some intimate
others   large auditorium   arena   festival tent
Each time the need to set up   warm up
slip into the skin of the playing space

Each audience different
some resistant to the style
but always the shock of involvement
whatever the initial preconception

During this section of the tour
Archer lets Gillian drive
as he slouches brooding on the landscape
Deirdre now sits with him intermittently
getting to know the others more intimately
Yumiko attracts her
the drums   her still   strong   presence
They sit together in silence
for long stretches
Then Deirdre asks
Yumiko responds
about her drumming   her past
her joining the company
She speaks quietly
but every word is needed
for what she has to say

"I was raised in a family
that turned against its past.
My father was the second generation,
his father raised in Vancouver;
the family caught in the war,
torn from their home,
shunted to the interior.
They returned after the war
but the scars cut deep
for both generations.
My father became an artist,
a good one.
He married my mother,
also Japanese.
I was born,
then a son.
Neither of us knew what had happened
during the war,

all things Japanese were discarded,
denied, or hidden.
We were Canadians,
lived as Canadians,
but still
my brother was the hope of the family,
the one who would take over,
the one on whom all dreams rested.
No one,
especially me,
questioned this—
it was part of our life,
like breathing,
understood without words.
But with the responsibility on him
I had more freedom,
when I realized I had freedom.

"Only when I was in my teens
did my East Asian look,
my Japanese side,
release its current.
In school I learned about the war
and knew I must find out
what had happened to my father
and his father then.
It took patience
and nerve,
but finally,
even as he was painting late one night,
he told me the story,
the violation and the shame.
In his telling his own dam burst
and it took time before he could reconcile
the two sides of himself.
As for me,
I plunged into a search
for all things Japanese,
disturbing my family

in my rush to learn.
I took lessons in Japanese
and broke the taboo
of using the language
with my grandparents,
who hesitantly,
then with more enthusiasm,
would talk with me,
and tell me stories
and things that only Japanese
would understand.
And so my skill in the language increased
even as it still was basic.

"One day I heard of
a concert of Taiko
to be given by a group
from Japan.
I had never heard of Taiko before,
but that it was Japanese
and done by Japanese
immediately persuaded me to go.
I had never experienced
what that concert gave me:
the beating of the drums
entered into my heart, my blood, my soul.
At the end I could hardly breathe,
but I knew that this
was my calling,
that I could do nothing else.
After the performance I stayed
and spoke to the performers.
They looked at me warily,
with some condescension
and some amusement at my halting Japanese,
but I persisted,
and finally the leader of the company
spoke with me.
He remained expressionless

as I told him of my desire
to train with him;
then, looking at me closely,
he told me what I must do.
First, I must perfect my Japanese;
next, I must audition;
finally, I must endure the training,
which few—and few women at that time—truly complete.
He told me to come to Japan
in a year and try then.

"I returned home in ecstasy
and told my family of my plan.
They were thunderstruck,
and opposed to what they felt was
a foolish cause.
For them I should get an education,
find the appropriate husband,
and settle down.
Finally, after a furious quarrel
I turned to my father
and asked him what he did now.

"'I am an artist,' he replied.

"'And did your father want you to be an artist?'

"'No, but it was what I had to do.'

"'And this is what I have to do.'

"'Yes, but I had talent for what I did.'

"'How do you know that I don't have talent
for what I want to do?'

"He looked at me, his face dark,
then strode from the room.
All were silent;
I heard only the rapid beating of my heart.
An eternity went by in this silence;
then he returned, calmer,
but his face determined.

"'You have made your choice:
you must be tested.
For the next year learn fully
your language' (*MY language!*)
'and find someone with whom to practise;
then go to Japan and audition.
If you succeed, we will support you
in your training;
if you fail, you must return,
go to university,
and finally marry.
You agree?'

"'Yes!' I said,
'Yes!'

"For the next year I plunged into the work,
learning Japanese and using it and nothing else.
I found a teacher in a company in the city
who auditioned me,
shook his head,
but let me stay.
I also began to study Tai Chi.
And then I flew to Japan
and I auditioned.
And he accepted me.
For five years I studied and practised,
learning the mysteries of the drums
and the importance of *Ma*."

Deirdre looks at her

"The space, the silence between each hit.
I also became proficient in Aikido
as well as Tai Chi,
and came to understand how all these
became part of a whole.

"I played with the company for a time
and then returned to Vancouver,
where I continued my work.

I was in a local company
but was restless and dissatisfied.
Then I saw Ray and his work.
I talked to him afterwards;
he told me his ideas for this *Lear* production
and I offered myself and my drums.
He accepted.
And here we are."

Deirdre looks at her intently
"Are you happy doing this?"

A smile
"Oh, yes.
Taiko has always been involved with theatre,
as well as temples and festivals.
Working with Ray has been fruitful for me."

A lapse into silence
Yumiko glances at her
smiles when Deirdre
does not offer to continue
turns to watch the speeding scenery

Deirdre wants to learn more
but is not ready yet to reveal
her own desires
still swirling like a mist
in her mind
against the shadows of her desire
for Archer
But now she watches more closely
at each set-up
realizes that when Yumiko arranges her drums
other instruments
there comes a moment when Archer joins her
Together with precision
concentrated strength
they tighten the drum heads
with the cords around the great bodies

How do they find such strength?

Now up to London they drive
the humid air muggy
enveloping as it has since their descent
to the toe of the province
A full week in this city of trees   rivers
gives them time to renew
after the travels before
Their venue now is a proper theatre
the old Grand
with its comfort of dressing rooms
green room
but its audience as well
The Artistic Director
a woman quiet   attractive   unaffected
greets them cordially
Archer warmly
"I never thought we would get you
to play here."

Archer and Gillian smile at each other
"I never thought so either,
but Gillian can be very persuasive."

All three laugh genuinely
They have the company unload
set up
for the opening next day

The next morning
Gillian and Archer
have brunch with the A.D.
at a small pleasant café
Reminiscences
past associations
fragments of blossoms in the wind
drift through their conversation
Then
they turn to the business of the week
Archer sits back

as Gillian takes over about
audiences publicity interviews technicians rehearsal
Then
business food done with
new mugs of coffee

"What about next fall, Ray?
Have you anything I can put in the season?"

A wry smile
Interjection from Gillian
"Ray will tell you his plan,
and you can decide if you want it.
But it would have to be in a different space."

She looks at Archer

"Yes. I want to create an event
about the history of this country—
a grand sweep
with multiple shadings."

Gillian
eyes shining
"Not the country
in the political sense,
though that is part of it.
But the whole gigantic,
whole ancient land
since animals,
then humans,
began their treks
and established
their networks
over it."

Archer
enmeshed
in the same vision
"What we humans have done
as we spread throughout the vastness,
adapting,

changing its face,
ourselves,
like the ever-swirling eddies
of an inevitable current."

Gillian nods agreement
Their eyes meet
in their bright
excitement
their companion
caught up
in their mutual spell

A pause
Then their friend
forcing herself
back to reality
raised eyebrows
"A pretty tall order.
How many weeks will it take to show?"

All chuckle

"It will definitely not be short—
but around three hours.
After all, if Shakespeare can play that long,
why can't we?"

"Mmmm."

"The work is still fizzing in my mind,
but I see it with moments where the audience
sees it together
and other moments when they are broken up
and hear intimate vignettes, anecdotes.
All this in a large space
like a circus tent.
The audience stands,
action swirling around them,
and they may move into small groups,
find themselves surrounded,
or they surrounding."

Breath exhaled
"That's big—and expensive.
Couldn't you use a gym or arena?"

Archer grimaces
Memory of a past event
when he had tried simultaneous staging
in a gym
Chaos
much rewriting and staging
before the event
truncated
could play before an audience
"No. Not for what I have in mind.
I can give you details why later,
but this is the only way I see."

"What size of cast?"

"Large. Over fifteen..."

She looks at him in surprise

"...as well as the technicians and tent people."

Silence for a moment.

"But the cost!"

Gillian intervenes
"Actually, the production is underwritten."

"Where could you find such money?"

A grin
"We have our sources.
I can't tell you for now
but the costs have been taken care of
so that tickets will be affordable.
But we do need your help
to find a suitable location here
for the tent.
And if you want to incorporate it
as an extra for your theatre,
we would be delighted."

A wry smile
She has known him for a long time
knows what he can do
knows that always it is an act of faith
"When do you intend to play it here?"

Gillian responds
"This next tour will take in
the country.
The whole east we can handle
in August and September,
perhaps October."

The A.D. leans forward
face open   serious
"Let's say for now that I am definitely interested.
Keep me informed about the dates
and anything else you can send me."

Archer grins
"I'll drink to that!"
Laughing   the three
clink their mugs
drain the dregs

Opening night
conglomerate audience
season subscribers   formal dress
tourists   any dress
actors   directors   others
from Stratford not playing that night
some critics from out of town
Words of welcome before the performance
from the A.D. on the stage
incongruous against the banners   drums   the rest
The beginning
audience watching   to examine   to analyze   to judge
Shock of the Taiko drums
shock of the masks
shock of the lines   articulate
against the visceral   primal emotion

Some discomfited
some fighting for protection
all lost in the power pulsing
through the theatre
Intermission
little conversation
even among those whose defensive shields
shattered by what they had experienced
now painfully   ineffectually   reassembled
Second act
in its avalanche
of horror   tragedy
irresistible
At the desolate end
stunned silence
then actors in the audience jump up
crying out
applauding
The whole audience
like the speeded film
of grass sprouting
lift from their seats
a roar resounds
through the old space
The company realizes now
that fellow actors are here
move forward   moved
to acknowledge the acclaim
with a simple bow
Archer keeps them standing there
for a long minute
then they quietly leave the tumult and the stage

The first backstage is the A.D.
weeping
embraces the sweat-streaked Archer
then the actresses
the actors
Yumiko

Gillian
Then others
filling the corridor
some who know Archer
some who want to see their fellow actors
close up
others   directors
who need to see them all
Praise breathlessly given
invitations to see them in Stratford
the wave sweeps out
The A.D. invites the company to her place
not far away
When clean-up is finished
the company   the technicians who assisted them
walk quietly together to her flat
the technicians normally removed from what they see
in awe of what they too experienced
The party is calm
not comfortable
but given the A.D.'s subtle hostessing
a time to release the aftershocks
of the production
She gradually makes her way
among them
sometimes talking of the play
sometimes finding out about them
sometimes answering their questions
Deirdre notices her familiarity with Archer
"Do you know Ray?"

"Oh yes. We've known each other for some time.
I've seen his work; he's seen mine.
We did work together once
and then went off in different directions,
but I've always respected
and admired
what he does.
He walks another road from most of us,

and it is a road that few can travel,
but he is one of them."

Deirdre wants to find out more
but the A.D. excuses herself
for hostess reasons
goes off to the kitchen
For an hour and a half
they remain in quiet chat
then Gillian rounds them up
they walk back to the bus
back to their motel
That night Deirdre asks Archer
if she may sleep with him
but not to make love
just to be there

During the days
except for the late afternoon disciplines
the actors are left on their own
Deirdre notices
Archer and Yumiko
disappear early each morning
She wonders what they do
but does not ask Archer

One morning her curiosity
pushes her to follow them
stopping when she sees them
facing each other
in a slow beautiful dance
of the Tai Chi routine
They spar
one counteracting the other
Then they move quicker
and quicker until
their movements become a blur
but still counter each other's actions
Deirdre watches
in wonder at what they do
then quietly slips away

In the later morning   the early afternoon
she walks with Archer about the city
He points out the history of the place

"A place for centuries,
for Algonquin, Iroquois villages—
Kotequogong, an Algonquin village
at the fork of Askunessippi."

Deirdre looks out at the city
fascinated by the sounds of the names
as he pronounces them
shows her in what direction
each of them had their territory

Archer's tone changes
"Then the Europeans came.
This site was selected by him of the great title
Lieutenant Governor John Graves Simcoe
as the site of the future capital of Upper Canada
with England's names attached:
London, the Thames."

Deirdre looks at him
an inquisitive eyebrow raised

Archer grins
"But Guy Carleton rejected it.
Access to London would be limited
to hot air balloons."

She grins with him
He looks out again
continues
more thoughtfully

"London abandoned sectarianism
in 1877, forming the Irish Benevolent Society
open to both Catholic and Protestant Irish,
forbidding the discussion of Irish politics.
The Orange Order and Catholic organizations
quickly lost their influence in the city,

and the Society survives yet.
All this when other Protestant cities in Ontario,
particularly Toronto,
remained under the sway of the Orange Order
until sometime into the twentieth century."

Deirdre looks up at him
puzzled

Archer looks at her
pauses for a moment to reflect

"The Orange Order
is a strongly Protestant organization
founded near the end of the eighteenth century
to commemorate William of Orange's victory
over the Irish rebels at the Battle of the Boyne
in 1690.
And when Orangemen immigrated here,
a lodge was established
and became influential on the Conservative side,
although not so fiercely anti-Catholic
as other more extreme associations.
And that's why London acted as it did.
But the Orangemen remained a force in Canada
until the 1950's
and still can be found in rural areas."

"Thank you."

They walk on.

Deirdre and Archer take more long walks
not through the city centre
with its usual high-rises
peppered among old churches   buildings
but along the river's cool edge
within the tree-saturated park
through the university
where he told her
that many years before
he had seen a golf course
spread out in the middle of the campus

"What were you doing there?"

"I was at a religious conference."

A startled look
A responding smile
"I once wanted to be an Anglican monk
but my minister gently persuaded me
that this was probably not my calling.
I think he knew that my young urges
for theatricality and sex
I had confused with religious ecstasy."

Deirdre now looks at him in a new light
She finds herself listening
not so absorbed in being with him
as in learning from him
Her desire is not slaked
but deepened
without the former desperation

So the week wears on
unobtrusively as busy weeks do
Archer with Yumiko in the early morning
walks   reflection on the area's history
Gillian constant
phoning ahead
to later destinations
publicity
appointments
the continual detritus
of a theatre tour
the others on their own
warm-up   performance
brief meetings afterwards with actors   others
who attend the performance
Saturday the last night of the run
then three days off
Through Gillian's ingenuity each of those days
the bus trundles off to Stratford
returns late at night

Some of the company had been there before
Ann Yumiko Deirdre Michael Luke Gary
had not
All are caught up
in informal meetings with actors
an occasional director
the sensuous beauty of the river
with its walks   trees   swans
in contrast to the hordes
visitors   tourists   buses   streams of cars
shops with tourist bait
jostling old stoned buildings
all permeated with the humid air
then
the Festival Theatre
projecting dramatically from its hill
its encircled events
the Avon
still with the scent of productions
distant by a hundred years
lingering in new seats
on its picture-window stage
the Tom Patterson
adapted each year from
the quarters of the badminton club
for less popular work
the small Studio Theatre
for experimental works

They are given tickets
choosing *The Tempest*
in the Festival Theatre
Measure for Measure
in the Patterson
After each production
casts take them for drinks
in their lounge
where they are surrounded
by the panoply of the Festival company

older actors who have made their home
in Stratford   the company
young actors from the schools
in the school there
actors in the middle of their careers
some now stars in the Festival firmament
others partway through their climb
to the better parts

Deirdre finds herself surrounded
by some of the younger actors
the occasional more mature actor
in conversation that
after a brief congratulation
on her performance
turns to gossip
about where the Festival is going
what will happen
in Toronto
the media
She finds herself taken aback
when the head of the school
suggests that she might try out
for the company   become
a member of one of his classes
She looks for Archer
sees him in conversation
with one of the directors of the Festival
whose torrent of words
is greeted with a casual shrug
an enigmatic expression
Ann   Yumiko sit at one side
quietly watching
with few if any talking to them
Lance has found some kindred spirits
is drinking heavily with them
Michael has found an actress
of Chinese origin
with whom he is having an intense conversation

Luke is among a mixed group of younger actors
listening intently to their conversation
Jack James Ursula
discover actors that they have known before
catch up on each other's lives
Gary finds himself talking seriously
to several other black actors
Gillian has several people that she knows
around her in an animated discussion

After this evening
Archer is invited by an old actor
whom he has known for years
for a chat
At his friend's bidding
they meet at the counter
in one of the cheaper department stores
The actor ruddy-faced
greets him warmly
if quietly
"I like coming here
if I want to have a cup of tea
with someone
without being interrupted
or gossiped about."

Archer smiles sympathetically
He remembers roles the actor played
a superb comedian
who brought humanity depth
to the smallest part
who had developed
into a clever if eccentric
director and teacher

"So what do you think of us now?"

A chuckle
"Really, I've seen only one production..."

143

A wry smile
They sip their tea

"I saw your *Lear.*"

Eyebrow raised

"Splendid work.
The first time I have seen
the full power of the play.
Devastating."

More tea
"Why don't you come here to direct and teach?"

Archer laughs
"You always try, don't you?
But, as usual, no thank you.
The whole structure and ambience of the place
does not attract me,
as you well know.
I prefer my way,
each project different,
sparked by something
that affected me
to the point that
I have to do something about it,
sometimes with those
with whom I have worked before,
sometimes with new,
those who can accept
my way of working.
And we need to travel,
to keep the work alive
for many performances,
for months to let it mature,
let it grow,
even as I may in these journeys
find the spark to light
a new possibility."

Archer puts his hand
on his friend's arm
"Why don't you join my company?
You know I respect your work."

A twisted smile
"Ah, it would be wonderful
to work with you again.
But…
I'm too old to be a vagabond once more.
I like living
in this little Eden
where I can play my roles,
direct occasionally,
work with the younger actors,
have tea with friends like you.
The cost is too great for me.
But I do appreciate and respect
your work, you know."

Archer gives his friend's arm
a small affectionate squeeze
After another sip of tea
they indulge
in the usual gossip   comment
on the theatre world

The next day
after a late breakfast
during which small groups
began scattered fragments
of conversation
the company buses
to Brantford

Michael   Gary
find themselves
seated together
Neither speaks for a while
Gary looking out the window
Michael lost in thought

Gary turns to Michael
"Where are you from?"

"I'm a native Vancouverite."

"Any problems there?"

"There is a large Chinese community.
Little problem."

"I'm from Toronto.
Third generation."

"And problems?"

"My father is a lawyer
so things are pretty good
on the whole.
Although I think not much better
than before.
My grandfather was a
CN porter."

"Ah.
How is it for parts?"

"The usual.
Not yet a great place
if you're a person of colour."

A nod from Michael.
"Similar to Vancouver."

A pause
Each thinks of
what the other has said
against the drone   vibration of the bus

Then Gary sits up
"Have you seen Chinese classical actors?"

Michael smiles
with slight embarrassment
"Yes."

"When?"

Michael lowers his head
for a moment
Then
"I spent five years in Hong Kong,
from the time I was eight.
My parents had emigrated from China
to Canada in the 80s.
But their hearts were still back there,
and they loved the Peking Opera.
So much so
that when I was born
they worked with friends
in Hong Kong
to get me into the Peking Opera School.
They were successful,
and I went there
with my dad
who left me at the school.
The school owned you.
Eighteen hours a day you worked
at martial arts—Aikido, Kung Fu—
and all the acrobatic and vocal skills
needed for that art.
It was hell.
If someone made a mistake,
the whole class was beaten with bamboo.
For five years I endured it,
but finally the school decided
I would not be appropriate,
and I was sent back here
in shame."

"What did you do then?"

"My parents put me in
a Canadian school,
and I had to change again.
But I did hold on to

many of the old skills,
and no one in the school
dared bully me.
When I graduated
I went to a drama school
in Vancouver
and since then
have done stunt work
and a few parts.
But it was only
when working with Ray
that I could find my voice.
I have learned much here."

He turns away
looking out the window

Gary
astonished   moved
by what he has heard
"I appreciate your telling me this.
Thank you.
We both have something in common.
We do occasionally get parts of colour
but most roles are those
of white people.
That's what we're playing now.
And even though we've grown up
surrounded always by whites,
to move into their bodies,
their thoughts and emotions,
is still, frankly, like speaking
a foreign language that you sort of understand
but not altogether."

Michael nods
Their eyes meet
then they return
to themselves
in silence

stare at the landscape
speeding past them

Archer glances at his sheaf of notes

Here's a brief intersection
between first   later nations
Let me think of it again
Thayendanegea
leader of the Six Nations
Joseph Brant to the British
led his people for them
against the American rebels
He and his followers
forced out of New York
to Canada in 1784
Rewarded with much land
on the Grand River
for their loyalty to the Crown
his Mohawks settled
where they could land their canoes
where he crossed the river
Brant's Ford
Then the settlers from Europe
by 1847 began to settle farther up the river
from the Mohawks
the new village Brantford
More settlers
The Mohawks abandon their settlement
only the old Mohawk chapel left
Ontario's oldest church
the last souvenir

What story lies behind this shift?
What can I use of this
for my work?

Warm-up
rehearsal
performance
strike

Mohawks   Ann
As a river can be streaked
with different waters
from a tributary stained
with wastes or glacial debris
so the Mohawks appear to Ann
Some are young   restless   with hawks' eyes
others   Elders and the rest
quiet   wary-eyed
A young man   heavy-set   speaks before the Elders   angry toned
"Why do you waste your time in a white man's play
with masks that mock your own
and which you could never have worn?
Why don't you tell your own stories?"

Before Ann can reply   an Elder
"Masks do not belong only to us.
What you did in this play you can be proud of.
And the play speaks to us as well.
We too know about land title disputes,
so we understand the way
they saw each other
and the calamities that could occur."

Angry muttering among the young warriors
One of them   leaner   sharp-featured   energy-riven
"The play did not tell the truth!
Both old men got what they deserved.
The only reason that the others lost
was that they were invaded by another country's army!"

"And we know what that's like!"
mutters another

Ann   now alert
"You think that Lear and Cordelia
deserved what happened to them?"

"Of course!
If he had that right
to own his territory
and was stupid enough to break it up
and try to get his daughters to praise him for it,

then he bought everything they did to him.
And that daughter was also stupid not to have seen
what was going on.
When she came back,
she got what was coming to her too."

The others noisily agree with him
Elders look at each other   frown
at the memory of that fatal confrontation
with the Canadian army
over land they knew
was theirs

Ann suddenly rises up
eyes blazing
aware they do not want discussion
only a release   confirmation of their feelings
their rebellion
"I know how you feel.
This question of
ownership of land
you know only too well.
Oka was not long ago,
and you still struggle
with laws and treaties that bind you in.
On Haida Gwaii
we also suffer,
our forests decimated,
our fishery barren.
We have ourselves begun to fight,
blocking the loggers' highways
and searching for our own means
to live in peace, survive!"

All are stunned
by her presence
the power of her words

Disturbed   Ann takes her leave
Later she tells Archer what happened
He points out the uneasy situation
among the Mohawks

Not only territory
but who controls the territory
a struggle not yet finished

She understands
but is not consoled
Each leaves the other
isolated in thought

I should have remembered
how little the First Nations
have regained in territory
their own sovereignty
Still the federal   provincial governments
reluctant to move on
unwilling to acknowledge rights
afraid of territories
no longer under their control
the effect on business   corporations
over rights to strip the forests
ravage the resources
for more profit
In the cases that disturb Ann
vast areas of Haida Gwaii clear-cut
fish stocks vanishing
no wonder the barricades at Oka
to protect land stolen from the Mohawks
no wonder the logging roads
blocked successfully on Haida Gwaii
So much deceit   intrigue
manipulation   deception

Hamilton next
for a three-day run

Like modern Rome
a city built over an ancient past
smothering the settlements
of the Haudenosaunee Confederacy
The French explorers passed through it
but it took a war to bring the Europeans

to settle there
as usual   United Empire Loyalists
the War of 1812 when here
British defeated American invaders
at the Battle of Stony Creek
Then the official business
George Hamilton's townsite laid out in 1812
Confederacy shoved from the area
Canals cut through
sandbar
create major port
Steel town
centre for manufacture
spreading out in all directions
then partial shift
to service sector
Hum always there

Audiences now a bouillabaisse
of regular theatregoers   working-class families   Natives   young
Archer's productions had played here before
Gillian had worked carefully on the cultivation
of those who had seen them   on others
The houses build through the brief run
Like clouds layered in the sweeping sky
some gliding swiftly below others
drawn out   trailing wisps
some rising majestically above the swifter current
so these audiences respond
with   confusion to the older language   shock at the power of the masks
rapt wonder   fascination   horror   deep tragic feeling
helplessness to keep apart from the event
With these new fluctuations
the actors first are startled into slight shifts
in their own response
but Archer
by the fierceness of his own concentration   power
then by more rigorous warm-ups
brings them back into focus

When the run at Hamilton finishes
two days break
off together to see
the Shaw Festival
Again tourists amble through the village
with its honey-trap shops
They split up to see
matinees   evening performances
visit the dive bar
where the actors congregate
A different atmosphere
more relaxed   apparently convivial
No one has seen their production
so more of a social time
They also sense the evocation of different eras
that span the long life of the old articulate trickster
They enjoy performances
some without strain
return to their motel
with the sense of a brief holiday
Then off to Kitchener-Waterloo

Old farms   lush fields   sheen of silos   stolid cattle grazing
solid houses for generations   slightly rolling hills   then suburbs again
thick factories   streets   river   parks   motel

Archer has gazed out
at the passing landscape
occasionally
away from the notes
he has been working on
Now he looks up
thinking

A different invasion here
Six Nations property
part of the land along the Grand River
deeded to them by Haldimand in 1784
They sell part of the land to a United Empire Loyalist
Colonel Beasley
Dutch Mennonites from Pennsylvania
persuaded by concern over the American Revolution

move to the area
Colonel Beasley
sells 60,000 acres   90 sections
from what he bought from the Six Nations
as a German company tract
A large colony grows
Lutheran immigrants attracted
Waterloo named for the 1815 battle
Berlin   county seat   village   city   prospers
First World War
Name changed against violence   the News Record against change
118th Battalion breaks down its door   smashes equipment
Lord Horatio Herbert Kitchener of the Boer War   First World War
dies in 1916
Other names lost in the election of his name
The two cities grow side by side

Again a stew of an audience
As at London a smattering of university students
faculty
now growing in number
at the start sitting in critical detachment
then lost in the power of the unfolding
the characters
Still a tincture of First Nations
One performance
the short drive to Guelph

A different importation here
a developer's dream
planned from the beginning
one of the first in the country
very British

The pattern of the tour continues
alternative space
more students   faculty   theatregoers
fewer First Nations
similar response
They finally take off for Toronto

Canto 6

TORONTO

Place where trees stand in the water
the lake   Toronto   Simcoe to the British
tree saplings installed by Hurons to corral fish
but the name   ominously   Iroquois
Toronto portage to Lake Ontario
its history a narrative of the East's settlement itself
the French at Fort Rouillé by 1750
the United Empire Loyalists by the 1780s
a British naval base
the capitol of Upper Canada as York in the 1790s
captured   burned by the Americans in 1813
a main destination for immigrants from the 1820s
Toronto again in the 1830s
Here we are
perhaps the unifying force for the country
having been hated equally by the West   the East
Toronto the Big
Toronto the Good
Toronto the Superior
Toronto the necessary
Haze-ridden
neighbourhoods of every nationality
towers of every business
financial centre of the country
but in the 1830s also
one of the settings
for a major change

Archer gazes out at the Ontario landscape
then reaches for his notebook

Rebellion in Upper Canada 1837–38

How this country stumbled to existence.
The First Nations spread across its span,
Then explorers struggled with persistence,
And traders eager for the furs began,
And wars sprang up without consistence,
And treaties made, and settlers overran
The East, until the nineteenth century
Found towns, farms, British rule pre-emptory.

The East (forgetting its Atlantic fringes)
Now finds itself so large it splits in two:
Upper Canada on the western fringes,
Lower Canada the eastward accrue.
But in both commerce quickly impinges
On any common voice that might ensue;
Landowners, businessmen, contrive to rule
By just themselves—a convenient tool.

People are unhappy, which sparks unrest,
Brought into focus when such sly intrigue
Stops legislation despite strong protest.
Now the economy slumps in great fatigue;
Farmers with two crop failures are distressed
When sued by merchants after debts in greed,
While thrown in prison until debts paid off.
No sign of mercy with pigs at the trough.

William Lyon Mackenzie

Here in my sixty-sixth year, my old age,
I make no apology for what I've done
In this hard life on a corrupted world.
In Scotland was I born, and my mother
Poor, our living harsh, same our religion,
But she upheld all that was good and right,
And I am proud to be descended
From a rebel race who held all borrowed

Chieftains fully in abomination.
And when I came across to this new land,
Later my mother, we pursued the same.

For I have seen this country in the hands
Of a few shrewd, crafty, covetous men
Under whose management one of the most
Lovely and desirable sections
Here, in America, remained for long
A comparative desert, exploited.

Against this Family Compact I fought,
Elected member of the Assembly,
Whose bills were sneered at, haughtily ignored.
But I would leave the House, and with my cart
In the woods see the farmers so downtrodden,
Give my speeches that quickened their anger
And give them hope that tyranny be overturned.

Then came the time when all British troops went
To suppress, in Lower Canada, rebellion,
And our best chance to gain democracy.
I quickly proposed a plan
To attack at once Toronto—dismissed.
But at a secret meeting was embraced
A December date for winter revolt,
Published quickly a draft constitution.

My plan was clear—secretly assemble
At Montgomery's Tavern, three miles back
Of Toronto, in the evening, proceed
To the city, friends joining with us there,
Seize the large stand of arms stored in City Hall,
Take Head, the Lieutenant Governor, and
His advisors into custody, place
The garrison in our hands, then declare
The province free, call a convention then
To frame a suitable constitution.
And do this without any bloodshed.

I expected thousands to join us.
But the dates and orders were confused,
Only several hundred farmers marched along
Not told that battles might occur.
Some misadventures stumbled now and then.
In a confrontation the riflemen
In the first line fired, and dropped down to let
The second line fire. But the farmers, by now
Nervous from dire tales of what to expect,
Eight hundred men, ran where not one pursued
And, unfortunately, in the wrong way.

And so this bold, delightful, dangerous course
With other mishaps failed, and I escaped
To America, where I invited men
To join me; on Navy Island, created
The Republic of Canada. But it
Was lost, I imprisoned briefly, and stayed
In America for eleven years,
Pardoned and returned to Canada,
In both countries despairing at such loss
Of morals, discordance in democracy.

But still I remember my good farmers.
Had they possessed my feelings in favour
Of freedom, they would have then stood by us,
Even if armed but with pitch forks and broom handles.

I know I am a diminutive little
Creature who wears a red wig and rants much.
But I have always condemned any vice,
And despite our poverty have loved, cared
For my wife and family in all these times,
And do not regret whatever I have done
In my persistent expecting that human
Affairs should reach the condition found
In the great kingdom of Heaven itself.

A slight smile
The rebellion of 1837
An extraordinary man
A tragi-comic revolt
And yet
He turns the page

Aftermath

And from all these revolts and suppressions,
What consequences in these colonies
Now took place? For the British, that it had begun
With strong U.S. support, and strong unease,
In Lower Canada. What then began
Were punishments—hangings, shootings—but these
Provoked more war. And some were transported,
But more were pardoned, rebellion thwarted.

Mackenzie, eleven years later,
Pardoned, returned, political again,
Preferred reluctantly U.S. annexation.
More important was Lord Durham's report
For responsible government. A stir.
The British North America Act truly
Brought the country together in THAT year,
And still later, the whole country cohere.

Archer gazes out the window again
as he thinks of how these events will work
in his gradually forming event

Gillian has prepared carefully
for this run   two weeks
the venue an old church downtown
haunted by former productions of varying quality
played upon the platform built where the altar was
extended to where the pews used to begin
She has made sure there has been much publicity
word from where they have played
stories about Archer himself   his companies
She had stayed for some time earlier

in contact with theatres   actors   universities
people who had seen his work before   the media

Opening night was like many opening nights   critics
comps to friends and actors
those who might be influential
Natives that she knew   her friends suggested
The old church with its high arches   stained-glass windows
enveloping the platform   the stark setting
A buzz echoes through the cavernous space
of different conversations in anticipation
Then the change of light
Yumiko's drums reverberating
overwhelming flood of pulsed sound
the masks
their dialogue rolling sonorously through the nave
with clarity and power
their figures somehow filling the huge space
Intermission
Audience in fragments   hushed conversations
as they move outside for a reprieve
Then the remorseless second half
like a Bach fugue moving with relentless   beautiful logic
to the ultimate conclusion
Silence
Then a roar erupts   rolls through the gigantic space
people on their feet   eyes running   glowing
the bows from the now shrunken actors
Afterwards when the audience has stumbled out
there still remain knots of people
some who know Archer
some who want to see the actors
some who importune Gillian for interviews
The company returns exhausted
to the usual motel
Deirdre to Archer's bed

Gillian confers with Archer
the next morning
over breakfast

She has read the reviews
but knows that he does not look at them
ever
"Some criticisms,
but the response is good.
The usual raised eyebrows
about the use of masks."

He grunts
"I think too good."

Sharp glance
"You may want to talk to the company
at the session this afternoon.
You know they will have read the reviews."

Grimace

"The usual speech when this happens?"

A nod

"I know you don't like to have interviews
after the first night of a run
so I have booked you with the CBC tomorrow.
They want to do an interview for the local station
and one for the Sunday morning radio show."

Groan

She smiles
"We do need them."

Grunt and reluctant nod

"And please..."
Hand placed on his arm
"...try and cooperate with them?"

Sly look grin

"Ray!"

He takes her hand in his
"I'll do what I can."

She is not reassured
but continues to talk of the other interviews
with papers   magazines   stations
as he sips his coffee
without comment

That afternoon he faces a company
the younger ones of whom
cannot conceal their excitement
Before he can speak
Luke bursts out
"Ray, what do you think of the reviews?
Aren't they great?"
Some murmur their agreement

Archer smiles
"I don't read reviews."

Surprise and disbelief on younger faces

Luke again
"Why not?"

"Because I have had to learn
to trust my own vision
and also listen to the response of the audience,
which is always truthful."

Lance   frowning
"Can't reviewers be truthful too?
And can't they talk about a show in terms
of how it relates to what else is happening?"

"Of course.
But as an actor and director
I don't want that distraction.
I know how my work relates to other work
because I see the other work.
A reviewer sees a particular show,
usually on a preview or opening night,
the worst possible time to see it,
and they have to write their review

quickly for the next morning
or even that night, fighting a deadline,
unless they are writing for a magazine,
and even then their comments are based on one performance."

Lance persists   disturbed
"Then you don't feel that reviewers are needed?"

"Not at all. They hopefully have an informed opinion,
And can be useful to those who want to see shows.
But they sometimes doubt their own value—
I remember a reviewer of a major newspaper
telling me in a weak moment,
and not when he had been drinking,
that he considered himself a pimp for the theatre."

A brief silence
"But don't you think getting such feedback
is useful for us?
And keeps our names in front of the public and directors?"

A quiet smile
"It can be, but it can also be dangerous.
Suppose that a critic disagrees
with your interpretation of a role
and attacks you for it?
It is difficult to distinguish a criticism of interpretation
from a criticism of the acting itself,
and you can be left with a reputation
of not being a good actor.
Worse in some ways, I think, is praise,
particularly if it is unqualified praise.
It creates a reputation
that you are always trying to live up to."

Dubious look from Lance

"The hard part, and the aim,
is to learn to know ourselves,
to sense when the performance is worthwhile,
whatever the play."
A wry grin

"And that takes a long time."
He sees that some in the company are deflated
"In this case I'm sure that the reviews
reflect what you're doing on the stage.
But you have to keep doing it well,
and so, back to work!"

He takes them through a careful rigorous workout
further exploration of the space
the habit of the mask
That night there is a full house
they retain the power of the production
for a curious shaken audience

The next morning
Gillian takes Archer to the CBC
They walk through the tall rotunda
to reception
where they are met by the producer for the local program
Archer is made up, then sits quietly on the TV set
listens politely to the interviewer
answering questions about the production   the company
but saying little about himself
The female interviewer is nonplussed
by his reticence
but is won over by his charm
much to Gillian's relief
The interview is over within a few minutes
then they are led to the radio studio
where they are met by the interviewer
a man of the same age as Archer
slightly heavy-set
with a trim beard   genial manner
The interview flows as before
with expressions of enthusiasm
for the production   the actors
but this time
the interviewer
with a quizzical expression
"But why the masks?"

"Did you find the performance powerful?"

"Oh yes, I did. But couldn't the actors
have played even better
without their faces covered up?
Why did they hide behind their masks?"

"How do you see me?"

"I beg your pardon?"

"If you had to describe me,
what would you say?"

The interviewer
uncomfortable
gamely tries
"Well, I'd say you are tall,
shaggy headed,
strong aquiline nose and jaw line—
powerful eyes…"

"What kind of feeling
do you get from me?"

"Hmm. A sense of authority,
a very strong presence…"

"How did you come to that conclusion?"

"Well, by the way you look,
by the way you hold yourself…"

"Precisely. I am defined by the way
I look and act,
as are we all.
The mask does the same thing—
it defines the character
rather than hiding it;
and the actor,
responding to this powerful definition,
explores the full dimension
of the character."

A dubious look.
"I'm not sure how that takes place."

"I'll demonstrate."
Archer lets his features contort
then keeps fixed the face he made
One side of his mouth twisted
with a pendulous lip
one eye seems larger than the other
the chin sags into the throat
Immediately his body changes
even sitting there
the chest concave
the shoulders hunched
the hands splayed   aimless
Then a voice emerges
as contorted as the figure
rasps slowly
"Now d'ye see?"

"My God, yes!"
exclaims the startled man

Immediately
Archer returns to his normal self
"That is the power of the mask."

"I wish our listeners
could have seen you,
but at least they heard that voice."
For a few moments he describes
what he has seen
Then in relief turns to a different topic
"I believe that you tour a lot, is that right?"

"Yes."

"And you don't usually play in theatres."

"At times we do, but on the whole, no."

"Why not?"

"Many times it is difficult to book them,
or they may be irrelevant to the audience we attract."

"Do you have an audience that you do attract?"

A chuckle
"Yes. Over the years we have built up a following
in different centres."

"And that's why you're in a church here?"

"Yes."

Slight desperation
A new tack
"I also hear that you actually live in your bus?"

"Yes."

"You have no other place you live?"

"No."

"Don't you feel that you miss something,
living in a bus?"

"No. What would I miss?"

Almost incredulous
"Well, family for one."

"I've no one left to visit,
and I'm not married."

"But don't you find yourself rootless,
living in that way
either in a city or on the road?"

"Not at all. I'm focused on what I do
and on working on possibilities for the future."

"Are you working on one now?"

"Oh yes."

"Can you tell us about it?"

"No."

"Well, I must admit you live an unusual life…"
The interviewer quickly congratulates Archer again
closes off the interview

With a wry grin
as they leave the studio
"Well, I have to admit that
you're one of the most difficult subjects
I've had the fortune to interview."

Archer grins   shakes his hand
Gillian   who had listened from the booth
meets him shaking her head
"Oh, Ray!"
They both leave the building
shaking with laughter

There are full houses
for the rest of the run
frustrated interviewers
for the week

When not occupied
Archer tours areas
that interest him

Cabbagetown
even more gentrified
then I remember it
a long history
now sterilized

Cabbagetown

The forties of the nineteenth century past
Starts the way this place began:
Desperation from a famine vast
Caused by many an Englishman,
Absent landlords who did not care
About their lands except for profit
And did not let their peasants share

In the produce grown, but forfeit
All they grew, except the potato.
And when a plague destroyed the lot
The Irish peasant suffered a death blow.
Millions died, and many sought
To sail to a new country.
And to Toronto thousands came
To find work in a factory
Or distillery, all in the same
Location, which was this place.
But times were still bad, wages poor,
And so in the small front space
Of the workers' cottages dure
Cabbages grew to ensure some food.
Thus the name started, still found today.
And for decades the neighbourhood
Remained working-class all the way,
And in the Depression it was hard hit—
"An Anglo-Saxon slum the worst
In North America," and it
Appeared to be cursed.
But twenty years later real change began:
First the worst slums were razed and replaced
By Regent Park's housing and plan;
Then later decades it came to life
With Victorian homes bought and saved
And now it is gentrified, with inflation rife.

Down below it
Corktown
about as Irish as can be

Corktown

In early nineteenth century
From County Cork immigrants came
And found work in a brewery
Or brickyard and their home claim
Close to the place of their employment.

Cottages gave way in later years
To late-Victorian row housing, remnant
Of which in side streets still appears.
But in the nineteen sixties days
Much of Corktown was demolished
For elevated roadways.
But the rest still old and polished.

He strides through the streets
absorbing everything
thinking of their pasts

After one performance
Archer invites Deirdre   Yumiko to walk with him

"Where are we going?"

"To Leslieville."

They look at him
not understanding   but willing
He takes them down Eastern Avenue
along a gritty stretch
where faded storefronts line
the scruffy   ramshackle street
Archer says nothing until he stops
in front of a shoddy cinderblock building
like a Legion Hall of bygone days
"This is the headquarters of Hell's Angels.
Take a quick look and we'll pass on."

They start walking again
as he explains the significance
of what they have seen
But as they walk a distance away
Archer senses
a car has been following them
but makes no indication to the others
It suddenly moves
stops ahead of them
Five younger men
with shaven heads

dressed in jeans   boots
battle jackets
open to show their wide braces
block the sidewalk
One of them
slightly older   larger
with twisted smile
steps before the others in their way

"Well, what have we here?
Two nice looking girls with an old man?
And one girl a Jap?
That doesn't look right to me.
Not here in Toronto.
What do you think?"

The others grin   murmur their assent
Deirdre   frightened   looks at Archer
sees Yumiko and him with strange impassive faces

"I should let us by if I were you."

Twisted grin widens
A snarl

"Really? And what will you do if we don't?"

Knives appear   glinting through the group
He moves forward   knife extended

The next few moments Deirdre later can't remember fully
A look between Archer and Yumiko
a sudden blur of speed
crack of bone   grunt of pain
bodies flying in all directions
but inevitably down
She sees   amazed
the two with swift precise movements
show the real menace of a martial art
Within a minute all the youths lie
unconscious or writhing in pain
In disciplined calmness

the two move among the bodies
collecting knives
Then Archer takes Deirdre's arm
"Please don't tell anyone of this."

They continue down the street
without further incident to the motel
dispose of the weapons
in a trash can on the way
She is chilled by the calm deadly skill
shown by the two
That night sleeps in the motel

Midway through the run
when they have finished for the night
Jack quietly speaks to Archer
"Come for a drink with me."

Archer looks at him surprised
sees Jack's face   unusually serious
nods

They walk for several blocks
to a bar Jack knows
among many in Toronto
They sit in a secluded booth
away from the blare of the music
the over-animated gabble
of the other   crowded   booths   tables
"We have a problem."

Archer gives him a quick searching glance

"I know Ursula wouldn't say anything
but it affects me too."

Archer listens carefully

"Lance's Cornwall is becoming much more violent.
Ursula has bruises on her arm from where he grasps her
and I am becoming really afraid as Gloucester

the way he manhandles me—
and the eye scene..."
he shudders

A grave nod
"I'll work on him tomorrow in the warm-up.
Any idea why he's doing this?"

Jack shrugs
"I'm not sure.
I do know that he's keeping apart from the rest of us.
For a while he showed an interest in Luke,
but when that didn't pan out,
although he seems to get his kicks
outside the company,
he has gradually withdrawn.
He's a good actor,
and he doesn't have to be chummy with us,
but he does have to work with us on stage."

Nod of agreement
"Thanks, Jack.
I'll see what I can do."

Business done
conversation turns to gossip
Jack has picked up in Toronto
the comments he has heard
about the show
Archer listens
gently turns to another topic
Drinks   talk exhausted
they return to motel   bus

Archer   alone in bed
lies for a long time
working through the problem
reflecting on the other members of the company

That same night
still shaken from the attack
Deirdre dreams

Harsh white street light
everything so clear   so   delineated
pack of five fanned across the sidewalk   the street
The leader   black leather jacket
of the Lear battles
face also a mask
grin turned rapacious   snarl
slim   taller than Yumiko   me
but not so tall as Ray
steps forward   knife ready for Ray's stomach
Sweep of Ray's left arm
crack of broken wrist   drop of knife
face   astonished before pain
then grunt as Ray's right pointed hand
slams into solar plexus
the body drops to the ground
Surprise on every face
then rage   all attack
A hulking figure   heavy face distorted   pig eyes glaring
lurches toward Yumiko
She stops him with a high kick to his thick neck
Gagging   unable to breathe
he topples to the ground
Ray kicks another   pasty face wrinkled in fury
breaking his leg
a scream on the way to the pavement
stilled by a cut to his head on the way down
Yumiko breaks the arm of a smaller man
trying to raise his knife to stab her
slashes the wrist of another   fat   slower
then wheels about
to kick each unconscious
As trees mowed down by giant machines
so these five bodies spread across the pavement
But the faces of Ray and Yumiko
devoid of expression   impassive masks
of total concentration
their movements graceful   balanced   exact
in a deadly beautiful dance

Deirdre awakes   shivering   adrenalin shocked
lies looking out at the night sky
until exhaustion seals her eyelids

Next afternoon
warm-up   then mask exercises
Archer brings new masks
"For a change we'll explore these full masks
first for what we see."

They explore the masks
each with a definite physiognomy   expression
Archer watches closely
but especially Lance
who chooses a mask   sharp-featured   skeptical smile
Each actor works alone within a specified space
Their masks in this first exploration
ignore the others   lost in their own world
but Lance's mask paces within the confines
looks out at the others with an attitude
of skeptical contempt
For the next exercise two masks meet each other unexpectedly
Lance's mask meets the mask of a sweet old lady
At the sight his mask brushes by her brusquely
almost knocking her down
She moves on cowering
As usual   Archer gives the signal to take off the mask
ingrained in his actors for safety
"Now let's try a meeting with contra-mask."

This time the masks show new dimensions
The old lady meets a fat man with a scowling face
As he stands before her   blocking her way
she suddenly becomes a wild cat
confronting him aggressively
he sidles around her   timid and submissive
Similar encounters take place with the others
Lance comes at the end
This time his mask meets a tall mask with a placid face
As this mask ambles toward his

Lance's mask   with its contemptuous walk
sees it   goes into a rage
The other mask   seeing this
seems to grow even taller   bigger
also signals anger
Just as they are about to strike each other
Archer gives the signal
The one actor removes his mask
but Lance   still in the fury of the mask
attacks him
knocks him to the ground with no apparent effort
Archer quickly moves forward
yanks off Lance's mask
Lance stumbles forward   confused   still raging
Archer   a comforting   firm   hand on Lance's shoulder
speaks quietly in his ear with such authority
that the distraught actor's shoulders slump
he subsides
Archer still with his arm around him
Other actors have gone to the aid of Michael
whose mask it was in the encounter
He is not hurt but he   all
are disturbed by what has happened
Archer brings them together
In the discussion he lets them talk
asking what happened
Was it the nature of the mask?
Why had Lance not heard the command?
Lance himself cannot answer
shaken   confused by what he did

Finally Archer intervenes
"We all know the power of the mask…"

Murmurs of agreement

"…and we've seen the mysteries of the contra-mask,
which shows us the mask in a new light
with what appears to be a new personality
even if it may be the true submerged character
of that mask or something released in the mask's psyche."

177

Nods

"But we have worked on and used
our masks so much
that we have forgotten our own relationship
to the mask.
For when our imaginations are released
in the playing out of the mask,
our emotions are also released and expanded;
and if we have not come to the mask
in a receptive condition,
if we are at all upset, disturbed, or unsettled,
the mask will provoke that emotion or feeling
to our own detriment,
as we have seen."

A smile   comforting hand on Lance's shoulder

"Now, let's get back to work and see what we can do."

A half hour of exercises   physical   mental
to set up the right condition
The *Lear* masks brought out
quiet   isolated   exploration
encounters between them
brief   carefully shepherded by Archer
Then exploration of the contra-mask
for each character
looking for new   unexpected   insights   actions
Archer particularly watches over Lance
encourages him when he hesitates
persuades him to move more deeply into his masks
All show new facets of the characters
pleasing shocks to the actors
The afternoon finishes in excitement   anticipation
of the night's performance

That night the production moves to a new phase
the characters richer   more complex
none simply good or evil
but with nuances   shades

that make the characters more ambiguous   disturbing
but also plunge deeply   profoundly   into the human psyche
The words   lines
acquire new dimensions   clarity   musicality
the play now a great cathedral of sound   character   meaning
The audience becomes enmeshed fully
at the end respond
not with wild enthusiasm
but with deep respect
to acknowledge the depths to which they have been taken
Backstage the actors acknowledge one another
for what each has done
Michael makes sure that Lance knows
how much he has grown in the role

Archer takes Lance out for a drink
They sit quietly for a time   sipping
then
"I'm sorry for what happened today."

A smile
slight shake of the head
"It could happen to any of us—
and everybody understands."
A pause
"Can you tell me what caused it?"

Another pause
Archer waits patiently
Lance looks at his drink
cupped in his hands
twice he tries to speak
cannot
finally
"I… don't belong here."
Archer waits
"I'm not really connecting with anyone."

"What do you mean?"

"I feel isolated.
Not able to talk to anyone."

"Why not?"

"I don't know. I… don't know."
Another pause
"They don't go out after the show.
I suppose I don't mind that so much."
A wry smile
"I can find my own company almost anywhere."
The smile sags
"They don't sit with me in the bus.
I don't seem to be able to join in conversations at meals."

"Have you tried to talk with them?"

Pause again
"For some reason...
for some reason I can't seem to make the effort."

"Any idea what that reason is?"

"No… no."

"Do you like acting in the production?"

More animation
"Oh yes. I've learned an incredible amount.
But I do find it exhausting…
And I'm almost shaking at the end of the show."

Only the bright gabble of the bar is heard around them
"Sit with me the next few days—
at meals, in the bus.
Let's see what happens."

Lance looks at him   face clouded
"If you want."

"I want."

With that they finish
leave the bar

Back at the bus
Archer finds Deirdre in his cubicle
Timidly
"May I be with you tonight?"

A reassuring smile
"Of course."

He looks carefully at her
sees her trembling slightly
A gentle kiss
Then he guides her hand to undo his shirt
they slowly strip each other
he lays her in the bed
She is now trembling strongly
With care he kisses her
without urgency
begins to stroke her hair
slowly   rhythmically
As she begins to relax
he lets his hands explore her body
slowly   slowly
until she begins to respond
then his stroking becomes more urgent
Finally there is a willing union
she lies exhausted in his arms

"Archer, I…"

"Sleep now. Sleep."

She looks at his eyes
then her long lashes flutter
she falls asleep
He looks at her in his arms
her face child-innocent
For some time he looks
falls asleep

The next day Archer keeps his promise
Lance joins him for lunch   dinner
but he has others sit with them as well
Deirdre   Gillian to begin with
then James joins them
Yumiko
Luke   Jack   Gary

Ursula   Ann
Michael
so that over time
all the cast has sat   eaten with him
Lance is silent at first
but Archer and Gillian are adept at this game
they draw him out   make him forget himself
the others do the same
But as the several days go by
Archer notices that Lance both enjoys and detests
the attention
As he loosens up
Archer also sees that he begins to manipulate
the others   makes little comments
On both men   women   he now uses great charm
as if seduction is his aim
Archer sees that there are deeper problems
He says nothing   keeps Lance occupied at the meals
Every warm-up he keeps working on
the centring of the actor
the rich dimensions of each mask
The performances continue to grow
in depth and power

By the second week
the reputation of the production has grown
full   enthusiastic houses
The media
tired of being frustrated by Archer himself
turns its attention to the performers
The more experienced actors
Ursula   James   Jack
know how to deal with their interviewers
making sure that the questions are directed
to the production
referring to Archer only as a director
revealing nothing about his personal life
Yumiko   Ann also are tactful
But the younger actors

Gary Michael Luke Deirdre
cannot suppress their enthusiasm   respect
for what they have learned from him
Deirdre moves dangerously close to
revealing her feelings about him
but manages to keep her admiration centred on his work
Only Lance is different
Without saying anything directly
he intimates that the cast does not fully get along
that he is ignored
that Archer is an overstrict disciplinarian
that he favours some actors over others
that he is having an affair with one of them
The media loves it
the company is besieged with reporters

Archer has not read or listened to any of the interviews
Gillian has to tell him what has happened

"You will have to do something—
the company is outraged by Lance's comments
and Deirdre is shattered."
She tells him what Lance has suggested

"Bring them together.
And find me an actor we have worked with before
who can play Lance's roles.
Cancel the last two performances…"

She winces but nods

"…and delay the remainder of the tour for a week."

A grimace
"That will be difficult to do.
We will probably lose some bookings,
but the publicity and reputation may help us."

That afternoon the company meets
mutters   glares at Lance
who sits smugly   arrogant

With Gillian   Archer strides in
face impassive
Deirdre sees it   shivers
the face she saw when he fought the gang

Gillian   calm   precise
"You have all seen and heard the interviews,
and you have been bombarded by the press."

Angry mutterings of assent

"As a result, we have to do three things.
The first, to refuse more interviews;
the second, to write a statement from the company
in support of what we are doing.
Please signify if you are willing to sign such a statement."

All hands rise but Lance's

"Thank you. I have one with me for you to look at
and revise if you feel it needs it.
The third, Ray will tell you."

All look at him expectantly as he steps forward

"We are here because we want to perform
and to perform good work as well as we can.
I have taken the route I have
because it is the only way I know
to do what I truly want,
and you have joined with me for this reason.
We see the results in this production.
You have every reason to be proud
of what you have done.
And you have worked as a company to do it.
Do you agree?"

A shout from all except Lance
"You don't think we have worked as a company, Lance?"

Lance shrugs
Archer's voice changes slightly
still quiet but with something
something   underneath

Deirdre again shivers slightly
the company as a whole becomes very still
"Yes or no, Lance."

Lance spits out
"No."

"Why, Lance?"

Lance
in a torrent of words
finally expresses what he feels
that they have been doing bizarre
exercises as if they were a cult
that they don't really play together
that he is ignored by them
happy to be ignored
that he thinks the production is weird
not what a real Shakespearean production should be
that Archer plays favourites
Deirdre is only in the company because she sleeps with him
A gasp from the company
Deirdre turns white
Archer remains impassive
Finally Lance subsides into silence
his poison fully released
The company is frozen   breathless
waiting to see what Archer will do

"Lance has made some serious accusations
about our work and about us personally.
Is there anyone who agrees with any of them?
Any of them at all?"

Silence

Lance sneers
"Oh sure, none of them would speak up.
They're too frightened of you."

Archer turns to the others again
"Is that true?"

James rises
"I've worked with Ray before,
and I've never known him to do the things
Lance says.
And no, Lance, I'm not afraid of Ray
because I know the work he does
and how he does it,
and I know how good it is.
And I know the work you do—
at least I thought I did,
until what you've done recently.
I've only one thing to say to you:
you are a disgrace to this profession."

He sits.
Lance colours   looks at the company
sees the terrible look on their faces
falters for a moment
then   contemptuously
"Well, you're not much yourselves.
And I quit.
I don't want any more of this."
He looks at Archer
who looks deeply into his eyes
He face whitens
then he turns   swaggers from the space
Silence

Then Gillian smiles reassuringly
"Well, he's done what I thought he would do,
and a good thing too.
No problems with Equity on this one!"

Archer now smiles
"It is better to let someone like that
speak without answering him.
We knew that he would quit—
what else could he do, after what he's said?
And so Gillian has been looking for another actor,
someone who has worked with me before

and who is the right size to play Lance's roles.
He will be with us tomorrow morning.
The production is cancelled
for the two nights we have left here,
and we are delaying the tour for a week
while we rehearse him into the show."

The performers shift in their seats
still trying to assimilate what has happened

"One more thing.
I take full responsibility for having cast Lance.
He showed talent and an aptitude for the work,
and he has given us good performances,
even if there were problems in the last week."

Jack   Ursula nod agreement

"But I had no idea that his problems
were so deep-seated
or that he would turn on all of us
as he has.
And so I apologize to you all
for the problems that have resulted."

Murmurs of denial
but the situation still is too new   raw
for full understanding

"Now, take the rest of the day off
and say as little as you can to the media,
who will be making hay with this."

Actors rise   do not leave
but talk among themselves
Archer goes to James
thanks him for his support
They shake hands warmly
Others also come up to him
to give their acknowledgment
of his work   leadership
Gradually they leave

Then Deirdre moves to Archer
deeply troubled
"You didn't cast me just to sleep with me?"

Archer laughs heartily

"Of course not!"
Seriously
"I cast you because I could see your potential
and how well you could play in this company.
Did I come on to you during casting?"

"No…"

"And did anything happen between us
for the first few weeks?"

"No."

"And did I seduce you?"

"No!"
She giggles at the thought

He takes her by her shoulders
looks deeply into her eyes
"You have turned out to be better
than I could have hoped,
and I respect you for it."

A vulnerable look
eyes brimming
He hugs her

Then
"Now, Gillian and I have work to do.
I'll see you at dinner."

He and Gillian sweep out
leaving her standing nonplussed
Luke
who has watched the encounter
comes to her
"Let's go for coffee, Deirdre."

He takes the dazed girl's hand
leads her quietly from the room

The next day
Archer leads in an actor
tall   slim   angular face   thick-haired
"This is Patrick."
The company   curious   murmurs greetings
"We have worked together before..."

They grin at each other

"...and enjoyed it—right, Pat?"

A voice   angular as the face
"Right."

Without further comment
Archer starts
the warm-up
the Tai Chi
the mask work
Patrick immediately slips into the work
proving the previous connection
His exploration of Cornwall's mask
brings out qualities unseen before
making the character like a leopard
relaxed when at rest
but ready to pounce instantly
His contra-mask
plumbs the depths of a vicious sexuality
a ravening hunger for power
concealed away from the mask proper
Oswald's mask brings out a smooth bureaucrat
invisible when necessary
adept at adjusting his status
to those above
below
his rank
His contra-mask
fear   hate of those above him

an intense rapacious sexual desire
for his mistress
deep   subterranean
a longing twisting pricking
to kill
In the break after the warm-up
Patrick moves to James   Jack
They greet each other affectionately
happy to see him
They start to reminisce
about their previous shows together
broken off
only when rehearsal begins
The read-through
becomes for everyone
a new exploration
as across the table
the speaking of the lines
probes the relationships
actions
As rehearsals progress
Patrick shows the ability
to retain lines quickly
both in words   understanding
After the initial rehearsals
he is off book
The masks
each day explored in the warm-up
are again in use in the play
His voice shows remarkable range
rich or harsh for Cornwall
higher mellifluous insinuating
or like a snake
as Oswald
The cast catches fire
from his work
their masks adjust
to the new traits   nuances
The play glows
with the refurbishment

Gillian has been busy too
She arranges for the two cancelled performances
to be performed again in the church
honouring the tickets sold previously
She manages to reschedule
the tour along Lake Ontario
by a judicious cancelling
juggling
so that they will be on track
when they get to Ottawa
During the week of rehearsal
the media is busy
trying to research the backgrounds
of the performers
especially Archer   Deirdre
Photographers try to get their picture
take pictures of the bus
The change in cast brings new stories
that suggest Lance is a victim
Finally
Gillian has a journalist friend
with whom she has a quiet talk
who digs more deeply
into Lance's past
A story is published
the affair dies out

The new performances
show that the production
has improved on the last
The company
now feels much closer
after the onslaughts
Patrick reveals
a sharp   ready wit
though he shows his independence
mingles easily with the others
They leave Toronto
with anticipation
of the rest of the tour

As the bus negotiates
the north shore of Lake Ontario
the past again haunts Archer
as he opens a notebook

Oshawa   a practical name for the Seneca
crossing of a stream
we leave our canoes   walk
the eastern anchor
Greater Toronto
the Golden Horseshoe
transfer point for the fur trade
from 1760 with the French

Belleville
Asukhknosk

Kingston
Katarokwai
Cataraqui to the French
traditional Mississaugas First Nation site

Brockville
Ontario's first incorporated town   1832
Industria   Intelligentia   Prosperitas

Cornwall
home of the Akwesasne on their Mohawk reserve

For the company
it seems the beginning of a new tour
the production fresh
the interest in new relationships
Patrick sits with different members
each time on the bus
They enjoy his wit
Jack and he convulse the others
at the table
the whole atmosphere
charged with brightness
The trips are short this time
the mornings again free

One morning Patrick
after breakfast with Archer   Deirdre
"Would you like to go for a walk?"

Deirdre glances at Archer

"Go on—I've got to do some work."

They are in Kingston
where the company has two performances
The two walk to the old canal
"You and Ray are an item, eh?"

Deirdre blushes   nods

"But it happened after the play opened?"

Relieved
"Yes."

"Well, I don't blame you.
He's an interesting man."

She glances at him
then stares out at the canal
"How long have you known him?"

A laugh
"A donkey's age.
I've done two shows before with him."

Still staring at the canal
"Did he rehearse as he does for this one?"

"No. Each show is completely different.
His approach changes depending on
the needs of the production.
Many of the exercises in the warm-up
are the same, including the Tai Chi,
but then he will use other exercises
for each rehearsal
and for the performances."

For a while they chat
about the plays he had been in
the techniques that Archer used

Then
"Was he alone when you worked with him?"

"Alone?
Oh, you mean, did he have a woman."

A blush
"Yes."

"Yes, he did. But not necessarily from the cast.
There were always women after him."

Patrick glances at Deirdre's somber face
quickly adds
"And he always treated them well."

Silence

"Are you afraid of losing him?"

A slight nod

"Deirdre, me love, let me give you a word of advice.
Be with him, take what you can from him.
And when you separate
—and you *will* separate,
sometime—
keep what he has given you,
which will be worth far more
than the hurt of his loss."

A defiant look
"But I want to stay with him!"

A gentle smile
"Of course you do.
And stay with him as long as you can.
Just don't forget what I've told you."

He changes the topic
as they trudge off
tells stories of previous shows
that finally make her smile
then giggle

finally laugh helplessly
until they return to the motel

Gradually they traverse
the northern shore of Lake Ontario
playing in the old towns
with their stone   wooden houses
dusty against the trees   lawns
travelling past the lush fields
ripe for harvest
They play again in different venues
the audience returns
to its mixture of different peoples
classes
The production continues to mature
with its new provocations
interpretations
In a mood of deep confidence
they enter Ottawa

Canto 7

OTTAWA

Algonquin country
beside the Kichi Sibi
Kichissippi
Great River
for a long long time
but the river also named
Outaouais
for the Odawa
Odaawa
relatives of the Ojibwe
The same drama played out
on the crease between
Upper   Lower Canada
Europeans settle in 1800
Philemon Wright   American   on the Quebec side
flood after the War of 1812
through military   immigration schemes
Irish Catholics   Protestants
labour for carving out
the Rideau Canal in 1832
when it is named Bytown
for the colonel who built the canal

Archer
looks out for a moment
sees where they are
returns to his notebook

The Rideau Canal
two hundred kilometres long
one of the great engineering feats
in North America
fifty dams

forty-seven locks
But what a terrible cost
in human life
Built in virgin forest
all done by hand
great hardships
for the almost two thousand
Irish labourers
Many died of malaria
five terrible summers
insect ridden
working continually
with axe
or shovel
But the river   its people
recognized in 1855 with its new name
Ottawa
Finally Victoria chooses it
as the compromise capital
for the Province of Canada in 1857
its final shift for the Dominion
in 1867

Gillian
politic as always
has accepted the invitation
for the run to be
in the National Arts Centre
The notoriety from Toronto
has followed them
but in a less sensational fashion
as has the reputation of the production

After the company is settled into their motel
Archer and Gillian go off to see
the powers that be
The Artistic Director
of the English program
whom they both know
as affable   an astute politician

greets them   takes them
to see the theatre
"I hear that the show is wonderful—
I'm looking forward to seeing it."

Archer smiles politely in acknowledgment

"But I'm concerned about your set-up.
You didn't send a lighting plot with your stage plan.
Do you have a designer to work with our crew?
We can't do much in the time we have
more than add some specials to the house plot."

Politely
"We will set up our own lights as part of the setting.
We won't need your lighting men."

A dubious look
then a slight frown with the realization
that Archer means what he says
"That may be difficult—union rules being what they are."

Gillian intervenes
"It's all right—I'll direct them in the set-up,
And I'll be running the show."

Still hesitant
not fully comfortable
but still affable

"Well, I'll put them at your disposal
and we'll see how it goes."

They discuss the technical aspects of the set-up
finally leave the building

Archer looks at her
"This will not be an easy run.
We will look like part of a museum
in there."

Gillian shrugs
"I know.
But the performances will take care of that."

"They'd better."

Archer works the company hard
during warm-ups   rehearsal
in the space
particularly on the voices
to fill the space without effort
Opening night
brings a crowd in which
tuxedos   evening dresses
mingle   overcome
the mixed dress
of the rest of the audience
The atmosphere pre-show
is one of comfortable anticipation
helped in some cases
by visits to the bar
for others
by the theatre's décor
Even when the house lights lower
Yumiko's drum bursts through the space
the pleasant anticipation does not change
This is an audience accustomed to effect
But when the company's lights rise
the masks accumulate
the first scene ricochets
to its disastrous end
the rustles of the dress   the program
cease
The audience is still
shocked
cannot wrench their eyes away
as the play moves arduously forward
For a moment
when intermission comes
the audience does not realize the act is finished
Only when the house lights
slowly make their ascendance
do they come back to themselves

The centre's bars are very busy that night
When the audience returns
the atmosphere is less strained
but the anticipation is no longer comfortable
The second half is even stronger than the first
with the implacable drum
beating at the back of each head
As the disaster reveals its dreadful folds
the masked figures seem to grow
to fill the whole space
not only the bright square on the stage
The audience is transfixed
through the last desolate moments
The usual stunned pause at the end
then the audience as one arise
in a clamorous acclamation
as the company takes its usual quiet bow
the theatre dims to normalcy

Following the performance
the company attends the first-night reception
a tradition at the Centre
They mingle with the animated crowd
unrecognized for the most part
except for their casual clothes
Archer is introduced by the A.D.
in fulsome terms
The crowd gives him
an enthusiastic reception
He then introduces Gillian
the company
who are immediately surrounded
by audience members
with city actors
vying with the tuxedos   dresses
for their attention

One richly dressed lady
of indeterminate years
with a strong face   voice

confronts Archer
"Well, you have a very accomplished company."

A nod in acknowledgment

"But I'm not sure you do Shakespeare a service."

An eyebrow slightly raised

"The performance is very powerful,
there's no denying that.
But the use of masks and drums is so eccentric,
so far from what is appropriate
for the play."

A smile   slightly sardonic
"What do you think is appropriate
for the play?"

With definitive conviction
"Something more realistic,
more like what is done at Stratford."

The smile   fully sardonic
"Ah, I see."

At this point the A.D. hurries up
to apologize to the authoritative lady
lead Archer away
to meet a tall man
aging but still with full powers
an aquiline face with piercing eyes
under shaggy brows
The A.D. introduces him to Archer
indicates to Archer that
he is the Director General of the NAC

"Congratulations. A fine performance.
You should have a good run here."

Archer nods acknowledgment

"Your work is unique, a little like Lepage's."

Eyes meet
"I know his work and he knows mine,
but we come from very different starting points
and work very differently."

"Really? Yes, I suppose you must.
But please keep us informed about what you are doing.
I would be happy to see you here again."

"If the space proves appropriate,
I should be happy to."

A look of surprise
A shrewd glance
Then a hearty unaffected laugh
"Well, I hope it will be.
It's been good to meet you.
Have a successful run."

He leaves
the A.D. following him
uncertain as to what has just happened
As Archer watches them go
amused
the Artistic Director of the French section
greets him
They have known each other for some time
a happy conversation
in rapid-fire French races between them
Gillian is in animated conversation
with several people
from the Canada Council
other funding agencies
collecting cards
arranging appointments
Deirdre is off to the side
with Yumiko Ann
nursing her drink
watching Archer and Gillian
when she is not distracted
by audience members actors

who praise her   the others
for their work
The men of the company
are with Ursula at the bar
enjoying the audience
each other
Deirdre glances at Ursula
realizes suddenly
how relaxed   open she has become
how engaged
there at the bar
with the men
how she herself
is less turbulent
less fearful of her relationship
as an actress
In the middle of the swirl   chatter
she begins to look at herself afresh
to see where this new condition
will lead her

The week proves pleasant for all
Archer takes Deirdre along the canal
into the parks
soft-footed on the grasses
shadowed by the green leaves
of the lush clothed trees
They walk among the banks of flowers
in a comfortable silence
They row a boat on the small lake
become tourists on the canal boats
wander through
the vast clever spaces of
the National Art Gallery
the Canadian War Museum
the other museums
of the city engulfed
in national significances

After performances
the company meets
many of the French actors
The whole week
goes by as if they were
encased in a picture postcard
Gillian has ensnared
those she needs
in the bureaucratic jungle
with Archer's help
has set up the economic prospects
for his next event
When they are finished
the sets   lights   costumes struck
the motel vacated
the bus shifts its gears
they all look with interest
to playing soon in Montreal

Canto 8

MONTREAL

The bus growls along the Number One
through clusters of woods   fields
glimpses of the Ottawa River
broad sullen waters
outraced by the bus

Montreal
my sainted city
second home
if there is any home
island of confluence
Saint-Laurent   des Mille Iles   des Prairies
Seaway   port
races
French New York
ancient home of Huron   Algonquin   Haudenosaunee   8,000 years
their battleground
First European steps with Cartier
into Hochelaga in the scarlet time of year   1535
Another three score and ten
Champlain finds the scarlet soaked into the earth
Hochelaga gone
Algonquins   Mohawks hunting in the valley
too dangerous for permanent locations
But in the second decade of that bloody century
La Place Royale   furs
yet encroachment fended off by Haudenosaunee
Another two decades
French tax collector   Jérôme Le Royer
makes foreign settlement permanent
then religion   Ville Marie   1642
Paul Chomedey de Maisonneuve   Jeanne Mance

expansion of New France
New century   new peace treaty with the rattlesnakes
Three more score
Battle of the Plains of Abraham
Generals Montcalm and Wolfe both killed
Surrendered
by Pierre François de Rigaud   Marquis de Vaudreuil-Cavagnial
to Jeffrey Amherst   his British army
officially British with Treaty of Paris
end of the Seven Years War
Battered by fire 1765
Now Montreal
occupied by American Revolutionaries   1775
briefly
British immigration   local North West Company
A quarter into another century
Lachine Canal
A city
five-year capital of the United Province of Canada
anglophones   francophones same size of population
largest city in British North America
CPR   CNR   St. James Street
Then three score and ten
into the last century
loses   as financial centre
to Toronto
Québécois   Bill 101
anglophone exodus
a new millennium
new immigration
refurbished city

The bus soars over the Pont de l'Île-aux-Tourtes
rushes along the Autoroute Métropolitaine
into Montreal
finds the motel
then the Saidye Bronfman Centre
Climbing the steps to the gleaming glass front
a flood of memories

Walking into the building in the 70s
energy so different   volatile
space rarely quiet
different pulses
walking by a room bulging with Yiddish clamour
its ethnic theatre director small   vital   shrewd

Archer and Gillian meet the Centre's representative
After warm mutual greetings
they are taken to the empty theatre

Like any theatre
but for its tall walls of windows
At matinees
the curtains still let in a strange light
that diffuses through the space
leaving the audience in a twilight
watching the brightly lit stage
where   with no front curtain
blackouts   the ends of acts
become small dramas in themselves

Technical details resolved
unloading   set-up accomplished
break for lunch in the cafeteria

No changes here
Still the same booths
same counter
all with discreet dividers
but the waitress different
from the Moroccan Jew
so tactful thirty years ago
with kosher preserved
by my leaving the space
between one course   the next

Workout   rehearsal on the stage
The first performance
a different audience again
the space filled with chatter

English flavoured by many countries' tongues
a field of heads like the seeded tops of dandelions
The dimming of the lights
provokes a hushed mutter
beaten down by Yumiko's drum
but through the act
small emotional exclamations
At intermission
a tumult of excited exchanges
Attentive silence to begin the second half
greater silence as the tragic machine
grinds on
but now involuntary gasps   groans
some weeping
when Lear howls   hopes   dies
the body of his daughter in his lap
Silence when the light dims out
some bewildered shock
when the actors stand shorn of their masks
then applause like steady breakers on a long beach
After the company descends to the dressing rooms
the Centre's Artistic Director
others from the Board
come backstage to congratulate them
Archer politely acknowledges them
but he is distant with memory

That night when Deirdre comes to him
they make love
she feels that he is not there
Afterwards
head on his shoulder
"What is it, Ray?"

A moment
then he holds her more closely
stares   sightless in the dark
"Too many memories here."

She waits a moment
"Can you tell me?"

A long pause
"I happened to be here
in the 70s
and was in a show
that profoundly affected me
gave me a look
into real evil,
huge loss,
resilience under horrific conditions."

He stops
remains   silent

Deirdre   her head on his chest
can hear the quicker beating of his heart
his uneven breath
She does not know what to say

"Let's go to sleep."

She lies there   listening
while gradually his heartbeat slows
his breath becomes regular
They both drift into sleep

The 70s
in Montreal
seeing French theatre here
everyone was exploring
I was part of that world
audition-workshops
for a project at the Centre
Director in his early forties
with him the Playwright
watched throughout the process
the creation of a work
about the Holocaust
based on the stories of survivors
living in Montreal
Eight of us selected
six men, two women

we began to work on one of the stories
to perform
for the Committee of Jewish Survivors of the Holocaust
who would make the decision
whether it was appropriate

The evening when we did the scene
performed in a classroom in the Centre
we filed into the room
found twenty survivors   their families
quietly sitting to watch us
The Director had chosen
the toughest scene in the work
the story told by the Chairman of the Committee
who had been at Janowska
a concentration camp in Poland
had been taken out
to the piaski
sandhills   dunes
ditches
where the prisoners were executed

We told his story
sitting on stools
Readers' Theatre style
then lining up
As each actor came to the front of the line
waited to be killed
their character was telling stories
or was crying   or was praying
For a moment
each face showed naked
in the moment before death
then the actor quietly returned
to a stool
My turn
my character   the Chairman's story
how he stepped   terrified
onto the plank
slipped on the blood

pieces of brain   skin
fell into the ditch
lost consciousness
That night he crawled out from the bodies
found another   shot through the leg
crawling out as well
They found clothes
from the piles on the sand
walked past the dunes
to a farmhouse
where the farmer gave them a meal
then turned them in
for two kilos of sugar
At the camp the SS officer
joked with them on their survival
slapped them on the back
gave them a bowl of soup
as if nothing had happened
That was the concentration camp
on the highway that went to Janow

When the scene finished
a dead silence
We rose
left the room in silence
Then   in a moment
the man whose story we had told
came out
He embraced me
for a long long time
the man who had portrayed him
I knew then
that we could do the play

The run for the week
lets Archer re-explore the city
brings back fragments
from that past
thirty years ago

St. Catherine's
a bus moving into it
where I sat behind
a Hassidic Jew
black-tasselled   black-clothed
sitting beside a nun
black-habited
both in their own other world
of prayer   reading
The heady days just finished
of the Olympics
the great energy   openness
of the city
barraged with French   English
street cafés
vibrant French theatre
the excitement
of the new election
the ascendance
of the Parti Québécois

The darker side
how a Belgian friend
spoke in Parisian French
to a parking attendant
was told to go back
to where he came from
an Acadian girl
refused admittance
to the French section
of the National Theatre School
because she was not from Quebec
the first stirrings
of the new language law

During the run
audiences fill the tall space
for the production
French   English actors
begin to come in increasing numbers

animated conversations
over coffee or wine or beer
at night or in the mornings
But after each show
when Deirdre lies on his chest
he does not tell her stories
and when he falls asleep
the hauntings begin again

Those voices from the Holocaust
shaped the script

The Director of the Library
handsome   distinguished   courteous   witty
but still removed from us
in the war disguised as a priest
caught while working for the underground
tortured
had to scream in Polish   not Yiddish

Rehearsals in the basement of a synagogue
An old man
came to rehearsal
brought a small old suitcase
As he took out objects
told us the story
how in Warsaw his family had been taken
while he was at work as a factory slave
In the suitcase
all he had left   memories of them
a framed photograph
his daughter Lilka in an opera costume

Quietly he sang her last song

We sat stunned   breathless
He almost crumbled at the end
but then he straightened   smiled at us
carefully repacked the suitcase

A man whose wife had carried her sewing machine
all the way to Treblinka

where she was separated from him
immediately gassed
He wanted to die
But instead he and a small group
of prisoners conspired
to blow up Treblinka
Under those impossible conditions
the camp was destroyed
two hundred escaped
he one of sixty who survived
After seeing his story on the stage
he embraced the Playwright
for five long minutes
overcome

After the war
survivors went essentially
to three places
Israel   New York
Montreal
twenty thousand in the city
Many come to see what we performed
rapt   spellbound
each night
the power of the play
on the Centre's audience

The images refuse to fade away
the echoes of the two plays
Holocaust   Lear
reverberate in his mind
as he lies dreaming
or awake
the glare of streetlights
bleeding along the edges
of his blinds

How can anyone survive?
What does it do to them?

Despite his nightmares
during the day
Archer keeps working hard
The nights begin to settle
even as something new
begins its birth in his mind

After so many years
the impact of these stories
so deep in personalities
in tragedy
to me as an actor
to those who relive them
to those in an audience
Now as Lear I feel
that same power
the dramatist reaching so deep
the audience immersed

Is this why
I was impelled so strongly
after that production   over twenty years ago
to search for my own way
to find the meaning   the experience
of how we live   what we live for
life in all its complexities   its paradoxes
that could be shared   with others
an audience?

Now I search
for the life   the character   the history
of an entire land   country
as it lurched to where it is today
I must do it
I cannot help but do it
All this history

But the journey must be
the stories of the people
their lives   their experiences

I sift through all that I have found
searching for the plots of my new event
We must show people

He keeps digging deep
into the history of the area
its Indigenous past
Ann also wants to know
its history   so different
from her own people's past
They sit together
in his cubicle
as Archer tells the Eastern story
that he has just written

The Beaver Wars

Sometimes on a map
changes in territory
are tinted like a watercolour
though all the tinctures
may blur to pink blood

But other times such changes
are like a volcanic torrent
with lava searing paths
like red twisting rivers
over the scarred
and outraged land

Such is the effect
of the Beaver Wars

Long before pale faces
gaze at this supposed
New World
arise those tribes
Ongwi Honwi
superior people to themselves

Ann looks up
"We had our nobles
and our sacred craftsmen,
and the rest were slaves
that we captured from the Coast Salish."

Archer looks at her searchingly
before returning to the piece

              Iroquois
        rattlesnakes to the Algonquin
          and to other enemies
          bad snakes to the Ottawa
           adders to the Ojibwe
          and other tribes

      At home they are named Haudenosaunee
          people of the longhouse
          and the Five Nations
          then the Six Nations
    but the French from the Algonquin
      keep still the indelible label
           Iroquois

          Long ago
  they begin to live in their clan longhouses
       long dark smoke filled
        Turtle Bear Wolf
    the Seneca with five more clans
     Crane Snipe Hawk Beaver
           Deer
     and their clan mothers
         owning all
      keeping kinship clear

"We Haida were different.
Two moieties we had,
Raven and Eagle,
both descended from the mother,
many families and chiefs
under each,

but one from Raven
could only marry one from Eagle."

Archer nods
then continues

And long ago
they say
four of the tribes are a single tribe
in the valley of the St. Lawrence
under the sway of the Adirondack
Algonquin speakers
and they grow in number
but they chafe under the Algonquin
and leave the valley to move south
to New York
where they grow in number
and split into opposing tribes
Cayuga Oneida Mohawk Seneca
But the Onondaga begin
with merger of two villages
in New York
and their villages increase in number
as other tribes war with them

The Algonquin still threaten them
and they threaten each other
as their tribes fight in constant war
in blood feuds
in revenge killings
and they would have bled into the earth
but for the coming of a Huron holy man
the Peacemaker Deganawida
Two River Currents Flowing Together
to whom the Great Manitou
sends a vision
All the tribes of Haudenosaunee
smoking the peace pipe together
helping each other in peace and war

Deganawida struggles long
to make himself understood
and over time he wins support
from Ayawentha
He Makes Rivers
an Onondaga who is now
because of his famed prowess
a Mohawk war chief
and with great effort
they convince the other Haudenosaunee tribes
to end their fighting and to join together
in a League

They say
to convince those who are reluctant
Deganawida blotted out the sun
And so the League begins
founded on its primary law
Kainerekowa
The Great Law of Peace
Haudenosaunee shall not kill each other
And it is cemented with a written constitution
based on one hundred fourteen wampum
reinforced by the Condolence
shared mourning at the passing of a sachem
from a member tribe

Each tribe obeys the Great Law of Peace
but all are free to find their own way
and that way lets them come together
to fight the Great War against any people
who act against them
and there are few tribes who could avoid
the terrors of the Great War
They make confederacies
the Neutrals
Susquehannock
Huron
There is peace in the League
and great prosperity
from its subjugations

"We had no such treaties.
On our islands we were secure.
No tribe could match our seamanship,
could stand against our war canoes,
so large, so beautiful,
holding sixty men and women."
Her eyes flashed
"Yes, and women!
We fought as fiercely as our men,
fought beside them in the canoes
and on the shores,
were feared by our enemies."

Archer continues
a new tone in his voice
as he reads the next line

And then the white man comes

1535–1610
Down the St. Lawrence
Cartier travels in that year 1535
and as his canoes pass
he sees the villages
in their elm-barked walls
eleven in their number
from Stadacona
to Hochelaga
with its strong fortifications
its tribe three thousand strong
its expansive corn fields

When he passes by six years later
it still stands as before
but as the next century begins
no villages stand beside the shores
no fields are tended
but new tribes
drift through the surrounding woods

Near the end of the first decade
of this fresh century
the French have dug in at Quebec
now search west to where
Hochelaga once stood
find as they move up the river
for days no other person
Mohawk war parties have harassed
the Montagnais and Algonquin
and they remain away
from the now deadly river

The French are in the New World
to trade for furs wanted by the aristocrats
for their fashions
Champlain gets them involved in this war

Ann sees Archer gazing out the window
lost in thought
For a moment
she studies his face
profiled   lit by the sun
sees his eyes
haunted
the lines
that begin to groove
the lean face

More to explore
Champlain
in his voyages
finding his canoes
slip into the wood-fringed expanse
of a vast lake
shimmering in its beauty

For France he thinks
for me
with my name

Then his confrontation
with the League
where they discover
the deadliness of guns

His establishment
of official New France
"Father of New France"
Governor of Quebec
now enemy of the Haudenosaunee
developer of the whole trading area

Archer's attention returns
he continues

The League learns about guns
when Champlain shoots three chiefs in a battle
and they soon adjust
They learn quickly about the white man's
armament
and they learn soon to turn the captured guns
on those who lost them
They are feared by them as well

But still the League is driven
from the St. Lawrence Valley
and the triumphant Algonquin and Montagnais
take control of the area and the fur trade there
for the next twenty years
Now wars and skirmishes light up the unhappy wilderness
Truce made
truce broken
another peace made

1620

Great Britain's colony
Three European powers
play the Great Game
Allegiances and treaties shift the powers
the stakes throughout this lengthy time
the beaver furs

222

1633

Total war erupts
arms race started by Swedes
European plagues
indifferently decimate the villages and tribes
complex alliances
massive assaults on all sides

1650

The League a great empire
but now the second phase of this long war
murders and decimations
a failed siege by the League

More alliances against them
Thirteen tribes attack
huge canoe fleets
each homeland devastated
slaughter

He stops
She sees him again
lost in thought

So six generations have seen nothing but war
massive battles   sieges
sudden ambushes   attacks
warriors swift   brutal
men   women   children massacred
scalped
women   children taken as slaves
or forcibly adopted into alien tribes
all against a swirl of politics   intrigue
between tribes
between Europeans
between tribes   Europeans
the winds in the forests   on the lakes   rivers
shifting   uneasy

1701

Smallpox, battles, weaken the League
Peace is signed with the French
but the Haudenosaunee shrewd
use the balance of power
between English and French
to keep independence and power

1763

Until the French 1763 defeat at Quebec
Then neutralities fail
alliances fail
Settlers and militia
swarm across the land
and the end comes

The American Revolution
The Onondaga put out the council fire
each tribe finds its own path
the Great Peace ends its long life
and the League is gone
Betrayals and reserves
become the Natives' life
in North America

As he finishes
Ann exclaims
"Like the Haudenosaunee here in the East,
the Haida ruled the West Coast.
No one could resist us
when we raided their villages
in our massive dugout canoes.
Those we captured became our slaves.
Our villages had great longhouses,
and our art and fine possessions,
our carved poles,
were the world's wonder.
We were many chiefs and families
and large in number..."

Ann's eyes grow dark
"But then the white man came to us
and could not defeat us in battle
but unleashed his diseases,
and we shrank in death to a few hundred
from the thousands who had gone before.
We were deceived
and rotted with liquor
and infected with greed
so that we helped the traders
and helped the companies
to rape our ancient forests
and became destitute."
Her head lifts
eyes lock with Archer's
"But we are now truly ourselves
retuning to our former ways
despite my people's losses from disease,
despite the residential schools,
despite what happened to our forests,
and the decimation of our fishing grounds.
And you can see the renewal of our culture
in our new carvings and our art."

Archer returns   holds her gaze
"You know your own history
only too well,
and you know personally
how much it takes to find the way.
I don't need to condone
your violence and theirs or your invaders.
In the Europe of that time,
the time of the Great Law of Peace and the League,
men were still ripped apart by horses,
disembowelled while still alive,
then hung slowly;
men and women were burned alive,
tortured in a thousand, thousand
ingenious ways,

all in the name of justice,
or religion, or the nation, or the colour.
In *Lear* the same.
But still there glows
the need to be together,
the possibility of connection
even in the flicker of the fire."

Each still holds the gaze
for a long   lingering moment

That night
Archer sleeps alone
but his mind is disturbed
by violent images of war
mixing the older with the newer

Canto 9
MONTREAL: TOUR'S END

Change now
change in the audience
a loaf leavened with many peoples
many Québécois actors scattered through
all involved
all intent
After each performance actors
Archer
invited out to talk   vigorous debate
in the lively cafés

No longer do they talk about their need
to have their language paramount
Now it's about the form   the way
the insight
Little talk of a new country
they have their country
Now they can trek beyond their woods
All these companies here now
so many different approaches
the Québécois as usual vibrant
so many small anglophone companies
fighting to find new ways
from old models
They all sniff about each other
these two theatre planets
sometimes the solitudes collide
sometimes they stay in their separate orbits

Montreal itself
downtown towering with new buildings
the world intruding
with those from the mid-east   far east   Africa   Caribbean
many comfortable in two languages

others comfortable in more
a city of more villages
But the old streets still persist
the outside walk-ups
women on the balconies
always watching the life in the street
each area oozing out
from its former ghettos
polyglot
despite politicians' tribal gestures
Still downtown the same old flavours
smelled   tasted
the comfortable animation
in the sidewalk cafés

The last night
the last time on this tour
no death like the death of a show
At the equator the sun plunges into the sea
night sweeps in like a closing curtain
for a play
The actors   their support
emerge from the stage's spell
blinking in their curtain calls
so final   irrevocable
still uncertain of this final moment
the stage lights still dazzling their eyes
Only when undressing
does the final truth sink in
Then the mortuary preparation
the striking of the sets
packing of costumes   props
embraces   chatter with the last visitors
the final twitches of the production
the dream
So the troupe goes through these motions
touching for the last time
the surface of their masks
now devoid of their life
like a lover touching a beloved's face

soon to disappear on the train
to some war
from which he may never return
All find a way to touch Yumiko's drums
The bus is packed with special care
takes them to a final party
in a hotel
in the centre of the night life of this night city

For the first time since they came together
the performers find each other strangers
seeing faces so familiar but now reframed
as at some special time   a funeral   a wake
A separate room
with a buffet   bar
awaits them

For a while they stand about
Then the ice of the situation begins to melt
drip
trickles
of conversation begin with initial drinks
Ursula smiles at the drolleries
of Jack and Patrick
who attract for the moment as well
Luke and Deirdre

"You remember that tour long ago
when Ray was driving us
in a minibus in BC's interior?"

Patrick's eyes roll upward
"How can I forget?
We had to make a ferry,
and he thought he was in
a Formula One race,
skidding around those curves…"

"…and we were going down that
godawful hill and he was trying to pass
a car and another car was coming up…"

"…and it was only two lanes wide…"

"…and he made it by a whisper—
that's the only time I ever heard
you silent for the rest of a trip!"

Patrick grins
"Well, at least he made the ferry.
But what about you?
Those apple cheeks were white.
But I seem to remember on that tour
that you had a habit of leaving things
in every place we played—
a razor here, laundry there.
It was a miracle you had anything
left on your back by the time we finished!"

Jack gives a mock sigh
"Well, what else could I do?
You kept me distracted the whole way,
what with your gabble and your jokes."
He stakes an appetizer from Patrick's plate
as the others chuckle at their antics

In other clusters they talk
about the show that night
the nature of the audience
the hotel
the life of Montreal
any matinees they might have seen
as they pick at the buffet
sit in small groups
Archer   Deirdre
with Gillian   Michael
Ursula with Jack
Patrick   James
Yumiko with Gary   Ann   Luke
more animation chatter

At Ursula's table
"So how often have you three
worked with Ray?"

A glance among them
a nod to James

"I suppose I've worked with him
the longest.
We go back over twenty years."

Jack exclaims
"I thought you were old,
but not that old!"

James smiles
"Ah, appearances are deceiving."

"Do you find him working the same way now?"

The three men laugh
Patrick picks up from James
"Working the same way now?
We have never known him to work
the same way for any show.
Everything he does is in a different style,
and his choice is always different."

The other men nod

James
"It's hard to place him in a box.
He's like the surface of a lake,
sometimes smooth, a huge mirror,
sometimes rough, white-capped,
sometimes with the shadows of currents
curving through it."

Jack
for once serious
"You're right.
Everything he does is different from before,
and every rehearsal is designed
for that show only."

Patrick
"We all learn together from him,
and he from us.
Always new territory,
always hacking new paths."

James
"The work is not easy—
it can be bloody hard.
If there is anything common in what he does,
it's that he pushes both your body and your voice
and your probing of the character.
And his experiments don't always come off.
It's like skydiving
without a spare parachute."

The other men nod
For a moment none speak
Then Ursula
thoughtful
"Would you work with him again?"

Patrick
"In a shot."

The others nod gravely
all for a time
concentrate on their food

At Yumiko's table
the talk turns to what now
concerns them most
Yumiko turns to Ann
"Are you going back to Vancouver?"

"Yes. After I visit home.
Do you know what you want to do?"

"Oh, back to drumming,
at least for the moment.
Yourself?"

"There's an Indigenous company
I might be interested in.
And you, Gary?"

A shrug
"Probably Vancouver too.
Then—who knows?
What about you, Luke?"

Luke
His decision made
"I think I'll go to Toronto
and see what happens.
The people at Stratford
were nice to me.
Perhaps I'll try out for them."

The others smile at him
They eat quietly for a time

At Archer's table
after talk of Montreal
what they have seen
of the city
of its theatre
Michael turns to Archer
"While I have the chance
I want to thank you for this experience.
I had no idea of what we would do,
and what we have done
goes beyond words to say.
I will never forget what we have learned—
nor will I forget my mask!"

They all chuckle

"But now I want to learn more,
grow more in this kind of work.
What can I do?"

Archer smiles
"There is always training in different ways—
for the body, not only the discipline
of Tai Chi
but more work in mask, in voice,
in movement of various kinds,
either here or in Europe.
You have seen companies here
that explore this kind of work,
and there are others too."

Gillian interrupts
"I have a list I will give you.
Check with me tomorrow."

"May I have that list too?"

"Of course, Deirdre."

Archer thanks Michael for his gratitude
the conversation veers off
onto the differences between
the French   English theatre

Soon   with stomachs satisfied
the groups begin to drift to the bar
to reform with others
either at tables or standing around
As a river's waters
become rapids
the previous quiet flow
now loud with the rush of current against rock
so does the chatter rise in the convivial room
Archer and Gillian work their way
through the scattered groups
Then after some time
Archer calls for quiet
"Well, as is our lot as actors,
we come to the end of another run.
Every production each of us performs
is unique
but, as Keats would say,
it is 'writ on water' and stays only
in our memories and
in a few words and photographs.
These are my few words:
I thank you for what you have explored
and probed and created;
for your courage and patience in doing so;
and for your fortitude in moving always forward.
What you have done is fine;
you should be proud, as I am, of it.

Now we all move on to new projects.
As you may have suspected,
I have been working on something new
while we have toured."

They all laugh in their full knowledge
of the research he has been doing
in each place

"Now, what I am about to tell you
is a secret between us,
and I ask you not to bruit it about
because it still is early stages."
He describes for the first time
what he now has in mind
which will involve the sweep of the country
the span of its ages
the turbulence of its peoples
All this in a huge tent
with the audience sometimes enclosed
by the performance
sometimes moving among individual scenes
"And the performers will be stretched
to their utmost,
even more than in *Lear*.
Again it will tour,
and there will be a bigger company involved
than we have had this time.
It will not be in the shape of
the usual play;
it will have its own shape
and experience.
If you are interested in working on this project,
see me tomorrow in the bus."

They all look at him
stunned by this revelation
But before they can respond further
he nods to Gillian
who slips out

Then the door bursts open
some happy Québécois actors
who bring with them a jazz trio
Tables quickly shunted to the sides
the trio begins to play
The arrivals mingle with the troupe
whom they have met before
Chatter increases
dancing begins
The actresses of the company
all find themselves out on the floor
both with their colleagues
the Québécois men
as do some of the men
with the Québécois women
As he talks to one of the visitors
Archer watches while Deirdre
as a petal on a small stream
is whirled gracefully along the current
dances with one   then another
Ursula finds that at last
she can dance with happy abandon
stays on the floor with innumerable partners
Ann   Yumiko are more reticent
but warm to the infectious enthusiasm
of their gyrating partners
as do the men
Like all end-of-run parties
the noise   dancing   gaiety
lasts   time lounging
until clusters sit at the sides
while the dancing slows in tempo
numbers
As the trio moves quietly to other pieces
the atmosphere becomes quieter
Like a sky with its ribbons of clouds
so do the conversations drift
some of the troupe
begin to talk more intimately

"What do you think of Archer's project?"
Jack asks Ursula

"I'm not sure.
I've never heard anything like it."

"Are you interested in being part of it?"

"I don't know... I'll have to sleep on it."

He grimaces
"Oh, I'm a sucker for anything he does.
I'll give it a try,
if he doesn't break down my body
any more than he has."
A slight breath
"But it would be nice to work with you again."

Ursula looks at him   smiles
"It would be nice to work with you too."
Then, a softer tone
"I want to thank you, Jack,
for having been so considerate
over these weeks.
You kept me going,
and I feel I can talk again
to men—if they are like you."

For once Jack cannot joke
He sits quietly for a moment
"I wasn't being your nurse,
you know.
I enjoyed you as an actress—
and as a person.
I would like to get to know you
better."

Ursula reaches across the table
to take his hand
"I like you, Jack,
and would like to see more of you
as well.

But things will still take time
to work themselves out."

He nods slowly
"I know.
Being a friend is fine for now.
But think about his project—
I hope you have nice dreams about it
and not nightmares!"

She grins
"I hope so too!"

For a while they sit
with their hands still enclosed
listening together to the trio

In another corner
face flushed
eyes shining
Deirdre finally has stopped dancing
sits with some of her partners
some of the troupe
Across the room Archer catches her eye
She smiles
then turns back to the others
Archer suddenly realizes
that for the last two weeks
except for their nights
of lovemaking   nightmare
he has rarely seen her
as he has been lost
in his research for the project

Now each member of the company
begins to realize how final
this time is
They move about to meet
to say last things to each other
The dregs of the party are drained
all bid goodbye

to their visitors
trek quietly out to the bus
Gillian takes them home

In Archer's cubicle
Deirdre and he make love
without a word
She has him slowly
take in her face   her hair   her body
with his eyes
with his hands
while with open eyes
she memorizes him as well
his body
how he looks at her
Gradually they become more intense
but he suddenly realizes
that her hunger is not so desperate
as before
that she accepts him fully
responds with all her being
but seems to savour
to linger on
each moment
He reciprocates
as if it were again the first time
After their lovers' eternity
exhausted they fall asleep
with no word spoken

The next morning
Archer awakes
to find Deirdre lying beside him
taking him in with her eyes
He turns toward her
She moves against him
in the quiet light
of the blinded sun
They make love again
as if what they had done the night before

was now compressed into
one ecstatic moment
When again they lie quietly together
she looks into his eyes
as her hands gently caress his hair

"I didn't talk to you last night."

"No... I could see you were having a good time."

"Yes. I was."

For a moment she continues stroking
his hair   face tenderly
Archer lies quietly
watching her
but somewhere deep inside
he is puzzled

She has never been like this before
Always before she would nestle in my arms
her head on my chest
as if she needed my protection   my strength

She smiles
"So now we can have our talk."

"All right."

"Thank you for all you have done for me.
Thank you for what you have taught me
as an actress..."

She chuckles

"...and as a lover.
I had no idea how deep I could go
in either case."

He waits to hear what else she will say
She softens
her face vulnerable   open
but direct
"I have truly loved you, Ray—

still love you.
And you have made me understand
myself and, in some ways,
you."

Surprise at this last

"Last night you asked us
to tell you today
if we wished to join you
on this new project.
It sounds enormous, crazy,
just as anything you do seems to be,
and if anyone can do it,
you can.
But I can't do it now,
not now.
During the last two weeks
while you have been doing your research
or were lost in your past,
I began to go out on my own
with no one from the company
and explore
with the new eyes you have given me,
and I have found that doing that
alone
has let me be freer than
I have ever been before.
And I realized that I cannot be
dependent on anyone else
but must find out more about myself."

A short pause
He waits in silence again

"And so…
I must leave you
before you leave me,
and I must search more
and live a little more

before we can meet again.
I am grateful for last night
and this morning
and all those other nights together,
and it will hurt
not to be with you
and hear your voice
and touch you
and smell you,
but you will still be with me.
Thank you."

She stretches across
gives him a soft loving kiss
puts her finger to his lips
to keep him silent
then gets up
without hurry
dresses before him
leaves

Archer lies there still
musing
No woman before now
has done this
left him before he left her
in such a way
He now realizes
how much Deirdre has matured
grown
He admires her for it
But still he is haunted
by her loving look
presence
even as her scent
still lingers in his bed

That morning
all the members of the troupe
visit him

both to say goodbye
to tell him whether
they will join him

Some
all the men save Luke
accept his offer
Yumiko and he have talked before
but now he makes clearer
what he has in mind for her
She agrees
Ann he spends some time with
finally persuades her
how important she will be
in the planned production
Ursula is the last
"I must admit it has taken a long time
for me to consider it.
Before I make any commitment
what do you have in mind for me?"

He explains

"Do you think I can do all that?"

"Of course. You have come a very long way
in *Lear*,
and I know you can go farther.
It will be hard work but satisfying,
I think."

She thinks a long moment
takes a deep breath
"All right. I'm in."

He smiles   gives her a hug

"Are the others in as well?"

"All except Luke and Deirdre."

Her eyebrow rises
"I can understand Luke—
but Deirdre?"

"She feels she must be on her own
for a while."

"I see.
Well, she has to make up her own mind."
She turns to go
then turns back
"And thank you for everything.
You not only made me a better actress
but also helped me personally."
She gives him a big embrace   kiss
then rushes out

By the end of the day
all have left
leaving Gillian and Archer
at the bus
with all the play's paraphernalia
stored away again
They go off to dinner
at a small restaurant
favoured by Archer
She knows that the tour
is not what he wants to discuss
His mind already winds toward the future

"You're off tomorrow?"

"Yes. I'll get a car,
drive through
the Eastern Townships,
then along to the Maritimes
and Newfoundland,
fly over to Labrador,
across northern Quebec,
and stay in the north,
then back down
to meet you in Toronto,
and we'll drive back together
to Vancouver.
I expect it will take
several months."

Gillian
brow furrowed
"That will give me some
time to get the tour
and funding organized
in Ottawa.
But we'll be driving back
in December,
not the best time of the year."

A grin
"Well, weather will be involved
in the project.
We might as well explore it."

A sigh   shrug
"I'll get the chains."

The evening spent quietly
at the restaurant
on the plans
some talk of the project
That night
Archer sleeps alone
for his last night in the bus
before his long journey

Canto 10

QUEBEC

The morning spent with Gillian
renting the car for part of the voyage
Lunch   farewell with quick embrace
which Gillian found she desired longer
Then off he drives from Montreal

For three months Archer journeys
to absorb colossal territories
that he had not explored before
Through the tangled veins
of the Eastern Townships
he drives in the patchwork
of fields rich and yellow for harvest
Trees in their greenery spread
the hills in their fecund undulations
Into the steeple-towered villages
he goes   meets in the quiet streets
the old cafés of brick or stone
or clapboard occasionally verandaed
the anglophones   francophones
sometimes the anglophiles   francophiles
He chats a while with them
about their world of weather
economy   politics
gossip   senses the acceptance
of their shoulder-rubbing cultures
By the wood-wrapped lakes
by the curving streams   rivers
he hears First Nation myths   legends
to nestle with the newcomers' tales
scents the winds of the abrupt mountains
or the continuous hills
or the valleys with their dappled fields

ancient barns   houses
At night he writes down his thoughts

So much at peace now
these fields woven among the hills
these villages   towns
content to host their visitors
the cities to promote their wares
but every foot holds grains of history
of the ancient struggles
both between First Nations

then the seep   onrush
of the Europeans in their quest
to capture the land
here particularly
where the towns reveal
their early births

St. Hyacinth   village in 1670
town in 1679   city in 1857
Granby arising after 1792
when Loyalists permitted
to colonize the Eastern Townships
incorporated in 1816   made a city in 1971
Sherbrooke birthed between
French   Abenaki
in the conflict with the Mohawks
in the seventeenth century
a place the Abenaki called
"Shacewanteku"   "where one smokes"
in 1802 Hyatt's Mills
in 1818 renamed for Governor General
Sir John Sherbrooke
but now truly French
Drummondville in 1815 founded
to provide a home for British soldiers
guard against American attacks
Victoriaville   the Abenaki Arthabasca
"place of bulrushes and reeds"

in 1802 named by a fur trader
in 1861 named after the queen
in 1890 a town   in 1993 a city

He shakes his head
as he forages north up to
the southern shore
of the defining St. Lawrence
to cross to Trois-Rivières

Trois-Rivières   the halfway point
between Montreal   Quebec City
1634 the second permanent settlement
in New France
but seen in 1535 by Jacques Cartier
its name used since 1599
captured by the British in 1760
site of a great battle
with Boston invaders in 1776

Now on this north shore
driving toward the distant capitol
he finds the flavour French
more Québécois
steeples no longer towered
or battlemented but more Catholic
the towns   villages
saturated in their culture
with their own unfrenzied pulse
announcing their descent
Champlain   Batiscan
Ste-Anne-de-la-Pérade
Déschambault-Grondines
Portneuf   Cap-Santé
Neuville   St-Augustine
then into Quebec

Quebec City
always a site
"where the river narrows"

old to the Algonquins
who named it
old among cities on this continent
continually changing
Cartier with his fort   settlement
abandoned because of tribes   winter
Champlain started the city 1608
Stadacona abandoned long ago
by the Haudenosaunee
captured by English privateers
returned in exchange for Louis XIII
paying the dowry for King Charles's wife
then the Battle of the Plains of Abraham
ceded by France along with New France
the Battle of Quebec
when American revolutionaries
tried to liberate it   lost
British North America split
into what we have today
in 1820
its Citadel construction
still in military use
the other big historic changes
Conference on Canadian Confederation in 1864
following the Charlottetown Conference
that same year
capitol of the new province 1867
but National Capitol to the inhabitants
two crucial allied conferences
in the Second World War
Its picturesque   ancient stones
reek with our history

All this
coming to a boil
only a half century
after the fall of Montreal
the fall of New France
British occupation

immigrants
French habitants

He pauses before
beginning to write
in his notebook

Rebellion in Lower Canada 1837–38

Now revolt
suppression
British concern
over strong U.S.A. support
for the rebels
Parliament sent Lord Durham
to become Commander-in-Chief
of the British North American colonies
report on the grievances
find a way to appease the population

First   punishment
Hanged
Shot
Strongest reason for continuing
the Patriot War
Much later
many pardoned

Durham's report
Lower Canada
"Two nations warring
within the bosom of a single state"
Unite the two provinces
Encourage British immigrants
to overwhelm the French population
hoping they would assimilate
into the British culture
Rescind the freedoms
granted to the French
but little change
in the structure of the government
The French response

Louis-Joseph Papineau

I was for twenty years elected, always
with a large majority, President
of the Assembly, perfectly aware
of all that did occur until the point,
the moment when, disorder started here.
In 1827 the majority
of the people complained in petitions
signed by 87,000 persons
of serious and numerous abuses,
and in 1832, in
a province of 600,000, of whom
525,000 of French origin,
75,000 of British,
the French appointed to inferior
offices, some British with several
at once, forbidden by law, but still done.
An insurrection we had not resolved
to start. They seized our papers, slandered us,
to justify their presentation. For
historians cannot say all there is
to describe this time of military,
occupation of these provinces
that were plundered, set on fire, decimated.

On May 1, 1837, all
over Canada were frequent meetings
to denounce oppressive measures by the
British ministry. We wrote a plan for
legal resistance, an elective body
separate from their vicious institutions
viciously administered, and
recommended people choose in every
parish conciliators to receive
their complaints. All the people welcomed this.
And then they raised up for me a column,
papers called a "tree of liberty."
But the Crown's lawyers called it "overt
act of treason," a call to emancipate.

Their judicial power was mercenary,
servile, either corrupted or partisan.
And the storm arose. We, the Patriotes,
defeated the British at Saint-Denis
but lost twice in turn, with those stricken towns
pillaged, ransacked, their women raped, their men
slaughtered. And in Durham's report the British guilt
was proven: their systematic corruption,
antipathies against the peoples,
examples of irresponsibility
among the shameless agents of power,
monopolization of the public
domain. And yet, not shown in the report,
that the British people, few though they be,
in a majority hold their wishes
and interests in common with fellow French,
that the one class love the country of their
birth, the other that of their adoption.
And these British resist the schemes tempted
to them of monopoly and abuse,
and all without distinction anxiously
wish for an impartial and protected
government.

Sir Louis-Hippolyte La Fontaine

I speak in English as a courtesy to you.
I am Louis-Hippolyte La Fontaine.
In the Assembly I knew well, I worked with
Papineau to reform it, to achieve
responsible government instead
of what we had; to no avail despite
all we did. But when my friend called us to arms
I could not agree but sailed then to England
to plead our case in a responsible way.
But I was arrested, thrown in jail,
then released without trial—a warning?
But that did not stop me, for I became
a leader of the French Canadian

moderate reformers, and after that,
with the union of Upper and Lower
Canada, I founded a united party
of all our reformers. In the Assembly
I persistently spoke French, then forbidden,
until the prohibition was repealed.
There were many struggles, but in 1848
Lord Elgin, who truly, fully, recognized
responsible government, then called me
to form a ministry, and I did so.
I was, in effect, in Canada
before it became a nation, a real
Prime Minister. Then I showed truly what
a responsible government could do:
bills to recompense reformers' losses,
to forgive them for the old rebellion,
to create universities—Toronto,
Laval. These are the things that please me
the most. Other things were given me,
of course—a chief justice, a baronet,
a papal knight. But that I helped create
a proper governance allows me now
a fulfilled life and a contented death.

For a moment
Archer looks up
then again
muses

Durham's report rejected
in 1839
No responsible government
for a decade
but it opened years of debate
Then
British North America Act of 1840
British North America Act of 1867
Canada is born

but the French riddle
still simmered

Archer leaves Quebec City behind him
as he crosses to the south shore
drives to Berthier-sur-Mer where he can ferry
to Grosse Isle
the island that was
the quarantine station
for ships coming to the port of Quebec

So many died
in the horrors of ship fever
in that third tormented decade
Yet still thousands of Irish
managed to survive
to make in that time
with the French Canadians
the largest ethnic groups
in the country

Grosse Isle

Above the cliff and rocks
against which the waves
break restlessly
stands the great Celtic cross
to signify
the charnel house
of this country's troubled past.
Neat federal signs
also indicate this heritage
and the areas so disturbed
are now mown trim,
dressed by trees and shrubs,
with the whole island
standing rugged against the current incessant
of the mighty St. Lawrence.

1832

On Grosse Isle
Lower Canada sets up a depot
with sheds built hastily
to contain an epidemic
believed to be caused
by European immigrants.
Cholera
rages like a vicious conflagration
runs swiftly through Quebec, Montreal,
races into Upper Canada.
On arrival ships not permitted
to sail on until they have assured
authorities
they are free of disease.

1845

Across the ocean
in Ireland
the atrocity begins.
Small land renters
forced to give their harvests
to the absent landowners
have to exist
on what potatoes they can grow.
Disaster strikes:
blight,
potatoes rotting
over the whole island.
A million ultimately die.

People desperate
struggle to emigrate,
jammed in ships,
tricked into believing
food will be on board.
Little or no food.

Typhus creeps through.
At least five thousand die,
bodies thrown into the sea.
At the island
corpses kept in the stinking hold
until land burial possible.
Dead dragged out of holds,
stacked like cordwood
on the shore.

1847

Island quickly overwhelmed.
Ships lined for two miles
up the river.
Quarantine regulations
physically impossible to carry out.
Immigrants cooped up
onboard their ships
for days.

Tents set up to house the influx,
but with no bedding.
Many arrivals left lying
on the ground without shelter.
Hundreds literally flung on the beach,
left among the mud and stones
to crawl onto the dry land
as best they can.

People lying opposite a church
screaming for water.
People left in reeking pestilence
up to their ankles in filth,
crowded together like cattle,
corpses long unburied.

Children:
one seen covered in vermin,
another who has been

walking with some others
sits down for a moment,
dies.
Many orphaned.

Sheds filthy, crowded.
Patients lie in double-tiered bunks,
allowing dirt from top bunks
to fall onto the lower,
two or three invalids
placed together in one bed
irrespective of age and sex.
No ventilation,
new sheds built
with no privies.
Hospitals have little equipment,
little bedding
spread out on the ground
becomes soaked.

Water
never enough for fever patients.
A priest gives water to invalids
who have not been able to drink
for eighteen hours.

Very few medical personnel.
Attempts to recruit nurses
from healthy female passengers
fail from fear of disease.
Nurses expected to sleep alongside the sick,
share their food,
tea, gruel, or broth three times a day.
Prisoners released from local jails
to carry out nursing.
Many steal from the dead and dying.
Only two doctors arrive as passengers.
Dr. Benson from Dublin
volunteers to help the sick,

contracts typhus,
dead within six days.

More than forty Irish and French Canadian
priests and Anglican clergy
try to help,
many becoming ill themselves.
Bishop Power contracts fever,
dies after delivering last rites
to a dying woman.
Mayor of Montreal dies
in the course of caring for the sick.

As for those who pass
quarantine "check,"
many die soon afterwards.

June 8, 1847

Warning to Montreal and Quebec:
epidemic about to strike.
Previous Sunday,
four to five thousand "healthy"
had left the island,
estimated that two thousand
will develop fever
within three weeks.

Thousands discharged into Montreal
weak, helpless,
some crawling because they cannot walk,
others lying on the wharves, dying.
In Quebec,
immigrants described as emaciated objects
huddling in the doors of churches, on wharves and streets,
in last stages of disease and famine.
Three to six thousand die from ship fever
in fever shacks set up at Windmill Point.

Other cities,
including Kingston and Toronto,

anxious to push immigrants on,
and it is recorded
that one family is seen
sheltering under boards
by the side of the road.
Winter comes,
and no one knows how many survive.

And later:

1859

Remains of six thousand discovered by workers
building the Victoria Bridge,
and the first recognition happens.
The Black Rock memorial erected
for their remembrance.

1909

In August is erected
a national memorial,
the Celtic Cross,
largest of its kind in North America.

1974

The government of Canada
declares the island
a National Historic Site.

1997

A memorial again erected on the island.

Along the south shore upwards he travels
the huge river stretching its shores
beyond the naked eye
the settlements sparser
or clustered near the fruitful shore
while the dark-forested mountains
brood over the rippled land

around cliffs   bays that
stand against the gulf's waves

The difference in naming
of these many settlements
between First Nations
Europeans
The latter name their villages
towns   cities
for leaders of any stripe
or for a saint or sacred one
But the names given by First Nations
"where one smokes"
"place of bulrushes and reeds"
describe what distinguishes
the place   a signpost of nature
"Trois-Rivières," "Three Rivers"
a rare union
between them

On he goes
through Trois-Saumons   Saint-Jean-Port-Joli
La Pocatière   Rivière-Ouelle
Kamouraska   Saint-Alexandre   Notre-Dame-du-Portage
to find himself
at Rivière du Loup
the traditional stop between
Quebec City   Gaspé Peninsula
and the Maritimes
After a brief pause   coffee
he plunges south

Canto 11

THE MARITIMES
AND NEWFOUNDLAND

He descends into New Brunswick
the vast spaces of the interior
shrouded in their mountainous heaps
rolling   thick with evergreens
down to Edmundston
where the old   ancient
mix again in language
in culture
the two languages
official not officious
As with the Quebec terrain
he finds the sense of roots strong
Though he can talk
comfortably with those he meets
on the street   at the table
he knows he is the stranger

As he roams through these Atlantic provinces
observing   taking notes
always scribbling
he sees the small cities moulting
with their high-rises bursting through
the bricked and clapboard streets
the lumber towns
refining towns
fishing towns
rivers   trees
lakes   trees
bays   trees
the furious Fundy tidal bore

Again in these Maritimes
the ancient conflicts
lie buried in these fertile fields
in winding rivers
in powerful bays
in placid lakes
Here clearly seen
the waves of different cultures
as each is dispossessed

First Nation   Acadian
both fanning the embers
of their shattered pasts
One First Nation
shows in its history
the conquest of the country

The Mi'kmaq

Mi'kmaq
Maritime peoples
of the Atlantic Provinces
the Gaspé Peninsula
North-Western Maine
first area exploited
by Europeans
"resource extraction"

From prehistoric times
small semi-nomadic bands
related by families
centred on fishing   hunting
according to the season
Relationships revealed in words
mi'knaq   the family
lnu   human beings or
the people
and as a greeting
mi'kmaq   my kin
Their name rich

in possible sources
migumaach my brother my friend
my dearest for a wife
Words for their land
led to their being called
for some at least
the Red Earth People

As time passed
they became a national territory
Mi'kma'ki
their government
of their seven districts
Santé Mawiómi
the Grand Council
Each district had its own
independent government and boundaries
a district chief
a council
enacting laws and justice
apportioning fishing and hunting grounds
making war and suing for peace

Then the Europeans came
early in the sixteenth century
fishing ships
caught fish and salted them on board
then set up camps for dry-curing cod
In these camps
traded with Mi'kmaq fishermen
expanded to include furs
by 1528
350 ships
around St. Lawrence estuary

The increasing trade
changed the way the Mi'kmaq
began to think
For more trading goods they moved
longer from the coast for fishing

to the interior for trapping
As they trapped more beaver
and other animals who did not migrate
they became more aware
of the importance to them
of territories

As traders preferred good harbours
more Mi'kmaq gathered
in fewer summer locations
which led to larger bands
who were led by
the shrewdest trade negotiators

Then expansion of European settlers
and they needed to join
the Wabanaki Confederacy
with other Algonquin-related nations
allied to the French colonists
in Acadia

The wars began
seventy-five years
six wars in Acadia and Nova Scotia
against British conquest
When the French lost
the Mi'kmaq were entangled
in treaties that betrayed them

In 1713
the Treaty of Utrecht
did not include them
Mi'kmaq
never conceded any land to Britain
In 1715
they discovered Britain claimed
their ancestral territory
protested to the French commander at Louisburg
that the King could not transfer land
he did not possess
then were informed

the French had claimed legal possession
because of a law that decreed
no land could be owned
by any non-Christian
conveniently forgetting
that Chief Membertou and his family
had converted to Christianity in 1610

Over the years
four other treaties
In 1763
with the Treaty of Paris
Great Britain formalized its colonial possession
of all of Mi'kmaki

The peace agreements
on the one hand
did not establish
limits on British settlement expansions
but the Mi'kmaq assured access to their
hereditary territories
along the coastline
in the woods
But
the Mi'kmaq thought they could
share the land with the British growing crops
hunt as usual
get to the coast to fish
But
more settlers
more pressure on land use
treaties

So
the Mi'kmaq tried war
to enforce the treaties
supported the American Revolution
were part of the Maugerville Rebellion
attacked in Miramichi Valley
but unsuccessful

In the early nineteenth century
they appealed to the British
to honour the treaties
reminding them of their duty
to give "presents"
to occupy Mi'kma'ki
But the British offered "relief"
told them they must
give up their way of life
begin to settle on farms

The treaties did not become legal
until placed in Section 35
of the Constitution Act
of 1982

In the whole Maritimes
New Brunswick
Nova Scotia
Prince Edward Island
the first wave of settlers
French   Acadian
swept aside
by the victorious British

The Acadians

In New France
two cultures distinct and separate
Quebec and Acadia
In Acadia
descendants of French colonists
of the seventeenth and eighteenth centuries
and of the Wabanaki Confederacy
with whom
they had friendly relations

Then the wars
final French defeat
the Great Expulsion

1755–1764
11,500 Acadians ripped
from their homes and lands
deported from the Maritime region
One-third die from disease and drowning
ethnic cleansing
deportation similar to others of these times
sent to American colonies
forced into servitude
desperate lifestyles
sent to England
then the Caribbean
or to France
lured by Spain
to now-modern Louisiana
where they developed
the Cajun culture

Some finally returned
most to New Brunswick
barred from Nova Scotia
where their lands and villages
had been settled
by English colonists

English colonists
who were themselves dispossessed
after the American Revolution
by the dispossessed Loyalists

The United Empire Loyalists

The American Revolution
changed much here as well
Many fought
or were on the British side
both white and black
Huge numbers migrated
fled here
during and after the war

In the main waves
of 1783 and 1784
swamping the population here
forcing to be created the colonies
of New Brunswick   Cape Breton
Thirty thousand in the Maritimes
and many thousands more
In Quebec
along the St. Lawrence
In Ontario
the Niagara Peninsula
later the Thames River
Long Point

As the first great influx
they caused the creation
of a separate province
Upper Canada   1791
In 1789 Lord Dorchester proclaimed
"EU" to be added to their names
to represent the Unity of Empire
although this not recognized officially
in the Maritimes
until the twentieth century
They have had strong
lasting influences
a certain kind of conservatism
evolution rather than revolution

Off across the long bridge
a millipede to link the mainland
with Prince Edward Island
forever remembered where the debates
the quarrels in private rooms
the rough gestation
gave birth to a new country
in a place of settled beauty
There the red sands   soil
the quiet farms   towns
infused with tourist shops

the spread of large potato farms
the unwholesome tincture
of various chemical fertilizers
staining the waters of the quiet streams   rivers
He feels the sense of a people
rooted in the isolation of the island
the vague distrust of their
new umbilical cord to elsewhere
Always among the gentle hills
the farms   comfortable settlements
there is a sense of the ocean
restlessly prowling nearby
even as it wards off from the mainland
the extremities of a frigid winter
As before when he has been there
he feels a sensation giddy slight
of living off the edge of the world
known at the other end of the endless bridge
but when he leaves he senses
that he gives up the feeling
of a deeply settled land

Back to cross the isthmus
that holds Nova Scotia
to New Brunswick   the continent
to traverse a province
parts of which he has lived in briefly
Around he goes to places
embellished with names carved
by Scots   Irish   English
French   First Nations
to bays   beaches of white grey beauty
to the formidable hills   cliffs
of Cape Breton Island
clothed in their greenery   scarlet colours
through the innumerable fishing villages
across the lush fields   woods
the fecund Annapolis Valley
He remembers how long ago

each night for the run of a play
he had driven black Canadian actors
back from Wolfville to their home in Middleton
along a narrow winding road
crossed many times by a railway track
how they were plagued by a train
that always found a way to cross their path
throughout the tiresome journey
on those dark star-infested nights

Halifax
the Great Harbour
"Jiputug"   the Mi'kmaq call it   "Chebucto"
From the time the British settled it in 1749
it has struggled with conflicts   wars
British against Mi'kmaq   French   Acadians
until the end of the Seven Years War
refuge for Loyalist refugees in the American Revolution
major bastion of British strength in North America's East Coast
important financial centre for Britain   then Canada
until the twentieth century
involved in the Riel Rebellion   Crimean War
American Civil War   Second Boer War
First and Second World Wars
inner turmoil
the press gang riots in 1805
Africville
the Halifax Riot on VE Day
catastrophes
the 1917 ship collision
largest man-made explosion before the atomic bomb
another explosion in the Second World War

He remembers the story about a man
who stood on Citadel Hill   saw sail into the harbour
three of his sailing vessels from
the east   the west   the south
how that man told his friend John Cunard
that he was not interested in the new steam vessels

would stick to sail
He did

The Maritimers that he talks to
regal him with stories   legends
so do the First Nations people
the Acadians still there
Like the rest of the Maritimes
the houses are old   clapboard
with verandahs   Victorian towers
old trees sweep the streets on either side
The older people are like their houses
especially by the sea   weathered
like plants stretched up
from the ground   the sea they inhabit
But he also walks down darker streets
houses shabby   wearing badly
He senses elsewhere the deep currents
of estrangement between French   English
white   black   red   new tinges of brown   yellow
in scattered segments of a changing population

Newfoundland he finds wrapped in its seasonal mantle
of fogs   mists   wind   rain
as he moves through the cliff-laden St. John's

The history of the place in terms of Europe
goes further back than any western place else
touched by Vikings then by others
vying for the honour of first contact
A history stained dark with the
eradication of the Beothuk
hunted for sport
infected by chance

The Beothuk

In their full centuries' span
is seen the splintered crystal
of this country's long past
imbedded in a single people
the Beothuk

It's thought their ancestors migrated
to this rocky and sea-wracked island
from the mountain-riven Labrador
around the time of Christ
spread gradually throughout
a millennium and a half later
had settled in their culture

Hunter-gatherers
living in their extended family groups
independent   led by band leaders
dwelling in their conical mamateeks
fortified for the winter's frigid attack
sleeping in the hollows dug in the dirt floor
their fire in the centre

In spring all things red ochred
in the great spring celebrations
the newborns decorated
in welcome to the tribe
For food the caribou   salmon   seal
other animals   plants
following migrations

In the fall deer fences set up
miles in length to drive caribou
to the hunters with their bows   arrows
For clothing the skins of trapped animals
fur side worn next the skin
When they died
elaborate burials with birch-wrapped bodies
carefully buried with objects offered
to accompany the dead

Strangers first saw them
a thousand years after they had come
Norse Vikings in the north of the island
saw   named them skraelings
barbarians

Almost another five hundred years pass
when John Cabot arrives for the British Crown
Then starts the waves of Europeans
explorers
traders
settlers

Other groups had interacted with these strangers
sometimes in war
sometimes in trade
sometimes in alliances
but the Beothuks were different
They tried to avoid contact

As European settlements grew
they moved inland
Only when former camps were empty
would they pick up metal objects   tools   materials
left by European fishermen

But the contacts between them were hostile
except for a meeting with John Guy in 1612
Settlers disrupted the caribou hunts
pillaged their camps   supplies
Beothuks stole traps for the metal
took supplies from European homes   shelters
ambushed the Europeans
But the settlers had guns
Beothuks wanted none

They tried to move to coastal areas
where the Europeans had fishing camps
but were soon overrun
Inland they lost two main food sources
fish   seals
had to overhunt the caribou
which began to dwindle
no longer had land to support them
became undernourished
starved

As well there were new migrants
Mi'kmaq from Cape Breton
Inuit from Labrador
A new cycle of violence

Loss of Beothuk food sources
violent encounters
finally infectious diseases
no immunity
smallpox
tuberculosis

There may have been no official genocide
with proclamations prohibiting mistreatment
No person ever was punished
for killing a Beothuk
But they were hunted by Europeans
Hunt's Harbour in Trinity Bay
a group arrived for hunting
trapped four hundred Beothuks
driving them out on a peninsula
then massacred everyone
men   women   children

1829

Shanawdithit   the last Beothuk   died
The Beothuk officially declared
extinct

Leaving St. John's, he travels
around the outports
Most he finds consist of their
sturdy wooden houses   sheds
perched on the slabs of rocks around them
most with no trees in sight
alien outposts against the rock   sand   sea

*Here   now in the oldest settlement
in Canada
apart from the First Nations*

communities
Over a thousand years ago
Vikings in L'Anse aux Meadows
for a while at least
Then John Cabot in 1497
sailing into the harbour here
on the feast day of St. John the Baptist
This place is seen on a 1519 map
one of the oldest European settlements
in North America
By 1540 the French   Spanish   Portuguese
fished near here
but in 1583 Sir Humphrey Gilbert grabbed it
as Britain's first overseas colony
Forty years later England's West Country fishermen
controlled most of the east coast
By the 1630s there is a permanent community here
Then fracas with the Dutch   the French
ending in the Battle of Signal Hill
permanent English control
Now a new danger in 1800
with the United Irish Uprising here
British army took care of it
But the British feared it would not be the last such
a new reputation as a "Transatlantic Tipperary"
a semi-Irish colony   all that suggested

It has lived through all the travails of its province
poverty   immigration trudging hand in hand
conflict between Protestant   Catholic Irish
rejecting Canada
born as a Dominion
collapsed to colony again
marriage to Canada in 1949
revived through ownership of oil in 1985
A vivid 550 years

He ploughs along the slick snake of the road
against the driving rain
senses through the unfocused sheets

the harsh beauty of the bays
the sea snarling just beyond them
the rugged barrenness
with only a modest garment of spent green
clothing it
the ancient Long Range Mountains
anchored along the west coast
north end of the Appalachian chain
parts of which are vast in age
605 to 1,500 million years old
When there is no rain
there is the wind
in the tablelands the first drifting dusts
of snow

All along he meets the people
rugged   weathered as their place
hears more stories   more legends
all in their words   dialect
that they own wholly
A country different from the mainland
still with its own identity
coming to the others
as a woman from another land
comes to her arranged betrothed
The sea   fish shape their life
now the fish thin   disappear
outports sag to ruin
or become tourist curiosities
He remembers men he met in the West
who came from Newfoundland for work
So here the women keep their kin
work much of the time alone
only slightly more than when their men
sailed out to fish on the Grand Banks
or joined the sealing expeditions

But these Newfoundlanders now
here rooted by their generations
from those who looked hard

for a way to live away from poverty
in Ireland or Scotland or the rest
of another island
This people shows
a pride that comes from struggle
with a constant barrenness

Canto 12

OVER THE NORTH
AND HOMEWARD

Now he takes a plane in Newfoundland
Over the unnumbered ancientness
of the Canadian Shield he soars
looking down on the towering cliffs
fjords of Gros Morne
the trees   soon snow-shrouded
lands of Labrador
to villages with reassuring French or English names
but where Inuit have spread
most huddled in the bays and fjords
among the great cliffs   heights
of the Torngat Mountains
its neighbouring ranges
all shrouded in heavy clouds   fresh snow

The hours spent passing over
unending mounds   levels of tundra
great dark reaches of the boreal forest
now dusted in their virginal white
as he speeds from the busy south
drum in his mind how immense the territory spreads
through this ribbed kingdom of the north
With the renewed shock of its size
comes the deepened insight of its growth   age
over the near four billion years since its birth
how the fiery mantle broke through the newborn plate
to generate its molten pustules
rich in their pressured ores
how these huge mountains weathered
how mighty glaciers ground   crushed them
leaving in their annihilating wake

the thin soil in which the evergreens
scrabble to find sustenance for their roots
how in a mere twitch of time
ten thousand years from us
tribes made sacred deadly instruments
from precious translucent stone
in which were embedded souvenirs
of life from still more ancient times

In these fjorded villages
he meets the Inuit
who listen carefully when he speaks
then measure their response
or when their sense of humour
finely tuned
he provokes they laugh or chuckle unaffectedly
But he also sees the encroachment from the south

As the glaciers with the mountains
will they also be ground down
their culture levelled   made dust?

Now he wings northward   westward
the forest giving way to barren tundra
perforated with its thousand freezing lakes
iced with the new thickening snow
Then the wide expanse of Hudson Strait
littered with its growing ice
to Iqaluit presiding over Nunavut
filled with new buildings
laid out in the streets beloved of the south
with an accumulating people
searching for a new means
to find themselves
Then he crosses over to
the great land mass of Nunavut
the Northwest Territories
riven with huge   smaller lakes
to visit other communities
that he finds growing

as families leave their nomadic treks
to settle in these villages
sometimes laid out neatly
sometimes with haphazard roads   houses
always finds Inuit
still grappling with their new ambiguous ways
or succumbing to the old scourges
gifted to them by the whites
alcohol   drugs   despair
suicide

Always he finds it hard to grasp
the enormous land
over which he flies for unceasing hours
in which so few traces
of humans can be found
except in the great gashes
to root out the ores from the ancient shield
Again throughout this long journey
as he has continually done
he collects the stories   legends   histories
sense of the people
Finally returns to Toronto
after these variegated months
during which he feels
he has explored a huge mine
with tunnels leading every which way
to reveal after much labour
their secret   surprising lodes

At the airport Gillian is waiting for him
with the inevitable bus
They spend the few hours left of the day
in their plans for the journey back
That night Archer sleeps again
in his lair in the bus

At the start of the next day   December
they begin the drive across Canada
Sometimes the weather is bright   clear

the roads clean of ice   snow
At other times they fight through
blizzards with snow lashed against the windshield
drifting across the road
to blend it with the ditches on each side
Gillian would sleep in a motel at night
Archer in his usual cubicle
but one night they find themselves
stuck in drifts where the bus is imprisoned
for the night
In the bus   even with its heaters
the cold creeps in
They share his bed once more
first to keep warm
then to renew an intimacy
they had known from previous times
Gillian does not need further motel rooms

Then Gillian
finds as she drives
that Archer starts to tell her
of what he has seen   heard
Never had he done this before
when he would talk about business
the tour
the production
but never the creation of an event
although they did talk
did argue animatedly
about many things
across her dinner table
she remembers affectionately
But after
when she always curled up
with the inevitable book
she had barely noticed
him browsing her shelves
that sometime later
he would take a number of her books

back to the bus
until he announced to her
the new project
gave her a rough idea
of what would be involved
read to her
the poems he was writing
Now there flooded from him
the immensity
of what he had seen   heard
from innumerable people
in the towns   cities   villages
on the farms   tundra
As the rush of what he felt
from this vast panoply
both from what he lived through
what he had read   studied before
she realized how open he had become

As he takes his turns driving
she is shocked that he now asks her advice
They enter into discussions freely
where he listens closely to what she says
She discovers that she can respond
with depth from her own observations
extensive readings of her own
her mind alive with ideas
as they explore
the waves of subjugation
of the First Nations
near the present
residential schools
treaties
for the French   relationship
changing life of Quebec
pockets of this life
throughout the country
for the European

the shifts in immigration
She finds the interplay between them
open   deeply satisfying

At night
close together
she finds herself talking intimately with him
until both are aroused
speech becomes unnecessary
Now she realizes
that the physical desire for him
which always simmered in her
has not changed
but the new intimacy   frankness
has awakened her to a deeper feeling
for him
that she is falling
falling in all its senses
deeply in love with him
Such intimacy
vulnerability
she now lets overwhelm her

So they work their way
across the perimeter of the Great Lakes
along the perpetual highway of the prairies
wending up to Edmonton
to take advantage of the more gradual grades
of the Yellowhead
Next a heart-stopping drive
over the Coquihalla as snow rages
batters at the bus
Then into Hope   the rain-sodden delta
finally their home in Vancouver

Now the odyssey of the creation
of the new work begins

ACT TWO
2006

Canto 13

VANCOUVER: CREATION

In the lush gloom of green   mist
he stands
the tall columns soaring out of sight
In the shining wet shade
emerald underfoot
the mosses settle in
or quietly creep along the gnarly trunks
Ferns arc delicately upward
fronds open to the small droplets
clustered on their greening surfaces
Congregations of huge trees root everywhere
to circumscribe the place with no boundaries
except their own innumerable presences
Above
the branches of the Douglas firs
straggle up in close abandon
with their neighbours' needled limbs
or the western red cedar
spreads its multitudes of particoloured boughs
so that the lowering sky overhead
the treetops themselves
are obscured by such traffic interlaced
All sound is muffled in this vast cocoon
Only the tapping rustle on boughs high above
the steady drip from needle   twig   bough

Archer stands rooted as the trees
water dripping from his fisherman's hat   slicker
letting himself be taken in
by the rain forest
sensing the quiet inexorable life
of the ancient trees standing there
through wind   rain   snow   heat
for hundreds of years

Even dead hulks occasionally lying
like long low hills in which small life seethes
can take eight hundred years to rot

Time slows here to drip   breath

How long he stands there he neither knows nor cares
Then above he hears the muted roar of a jet

We do not live with this
we use it for our own needs
leaving the rest as trash   desolation
This forest can endure most of what nature unleashes
but it cannot endure us

Then he slips quietly away
to cross the slick suspension bridge
return to the City of Vancouver

Another time in this tail end of January
on a rare sunny day
he travels to a promontory in West Vancouver
where he can view the strait
with its dark gleaming waters
punctuated with near   distant islands
dotted with freighters waiting to unload
their alien cargos
Then he turns back to see the arching bridge
the gateway to the vast inner harbour
He can see the shining high-rises
multitudinous as the rainforest trees
He remembers a couple who lived here
long ago
who told him when they heard
the wail of the sirens
signalling the end of the world
they would sit with cocktails on their deck
facing toward the harbour
so that they might witness
for a fraction of a second
the unbearable flash of the bomb

before they themselves were vaporized
These excursions niggle
in a small back room of his mind

As February gusts in
with another drenching rain
he sits working in the bus's cubicle
He thinks back upon the last months
It strikes him
that the wrenching desolation of *King Lear*
the memories of the Holocaust production
still tinge all he thinks   feels
Yet the scenario for the new event
has progressed
At first all the huge volume of his material
overwhelmed him
legends   myths   stories   histories
time
drifting back to antiquities
eons before Egypt was aware
For a time he drowned in such minutiae
Then Gillian dragged him to meals
but not to bed
for long discussions
to wrench insight
After they reached Vancouver
she had returned to her own acreage
the bus squatted by her house
She drove him to walk on the rain-drenched beaches
or to lookouts
to see the ranks of peaks
as they pierced the horizon
Slowly the incidents settled in his consciousness
as he began to sift through them
to find a shape   meaning
He had seen some time before
the many episodes of the little huts
onstage
with their parodies   ironies   satire

but that route he shuns
for the one vast event
with all its many colours

Now a basic structure
he begins to contemplate
three tectonic plates
First
land to which First Nations came
so many thousand years ago
rise of their tribes   nations
Inuit
Second
gradual invasion from Europe
taking of the land for settlement   wealth
evolution of the colonies
Third
construction of the Dominion
patchwork reservations
then a nation named
what occurred thereafter

But as this plan matures in his mind
he walks alone on solitary reaches
of the wintry beaches
the raucous quarrelling of seagulls
his sole company
At such times
the rain-soaked wind
tugging at his dripping slicker
above the sullen white-frothed waves
he feels a deeper chill
as if he treads on nothing substantial
All around is a misty void
in which he is implacably alone
no links to any human flesh
all memories devoid of life
or there to sever any further
touch or sight or sound or taste or smell

or warmth
His sixty years pace through him
no kin to reach for to refresh the past
no deep connection
with man or woman

Gillian is closest

Yet still he is absorbed in those he sees
his ear searching out what they mean
always
always
He has chosen this path
the drive to create
obliterating any human hindrance
Even now in this wintry desolation
his imagination stirs again
to shove the shadow
shivering
into some dark closet
until the latch is released again

Yet
Deirdre left me
before I was ready
to send her away

The memories of their later days
return to haunt him

But now the insight
into the source of his dark mood
releases him to forge ahead
flesh the mammoth skeleton
both in word   staging
With the now forming body
still warm in his mind
with Gillian he visits
his mask and puppet maker   designer

They find him in his workshop
in his old house
with his litter around him
of leathers of all colours   thicknesses
baskets full of scraps   pieces
of all imaginable substances
bales of cloth of many textures   colours   patterns
half-finished masks
some still in moulds
sketches pinned haphazardly
throughout the room
of costumes   masks   sets
Near the ceiling
circling the room
masks leer down
many sizes
many shapes
character masks   with fixed expressions   joyful or anxious
full masks   half masks
larval masks   large   abstracted mounds   hinting human or alien
animal masks   suggesting shape   or fang   fur coarse or fine
neutral masks   leather shaped   expression about to form   signifying
anything
all inscrutable
a chorus in his room
From the ceiling
like a forest upside down
hang
in suspended animation
puppets
marionettes   strings waiting to shape life   character
rod puppets   hanging among their dangling woods of rods
shadow puppets   gorgeous in colour   black in silhouette   twisting from
shape to thin line
glove puppets   large of head   absent of extremities   except in character
finger puppets   abstracted or defined
huge puppets
tiny puppets
In the corner beside a window

beyond which an old tree sweeps by
his drawing board
with its pencils inks T-square
paints glues papers

"George."

"Ray. Gillian."
George continues to work on a mask
seated on his stool
A short plump man
but with hands that seem far too big
far too thick   strong
yet he works delicately   surely
his supple fingers working at the surface
He wears a smock
but around his waist
as if a second flesh
is his utility belt
brimming formidably with
tools pencils pens measuring tapes
He does not look up as they talk
but finishes carefully the task in hand

"The scenario's now ready."
Archer produces a binder
bristling with sections

"How much time?"
The sausage fingers keep working delicately

"Two months before we use the basics."

A quick glance at the thick binder
as the hands continue their journey
"I'll need help."

Gillian intercedes
"You will have it when you need it."

A grunt
whether to affirm what Gillian had said
or because he had finished for the moment
Archer and Gillian could not tell

George rises   takes the binder from Archer
then crosses to his drawing board
sits on his high stool
The others perch on either side
Archer knows better than to speak
as George swiftly reads the outline of the piece

Silence for some time
save for the rustle of the pages
turned by a thick forefinger
At last another grunt
then one hand paws out a new sheet
while the other reaches for a pen

The two suppliants know
that he is interested

"Now you can tell me about it."

Archer spells out the concept of the staging

"A tent won't work.
Even a circus tent has too little space
for what you have in mind."

Archer frowns
"A field is too open;
no way to control it."

During all this time
the agile fingers restlessly sketch
doodle
High poles appear
great sails of cloth
shaped   reshaped
platforms emerge
travel to many locations
great puppets jump from the white surface
rays of light pick out
tall figures in the cross-hatched dark
above massed heads of a standing audience
Faintly can be seen
a perimeter to enclose the turmoil

Fascinated by shifting lines   shadings
Gillian suddenly exclaims
"A stadium!
It's got the space, the control,
no ceiling for echoes."

Archer laughs happily
as a stadium arises
around the previous sketch

George quickly strokes a driving rain
that pelts down upon its hapless victims
reflected in some enthusiastic lightning
"Will you play there in bad weather?"

Gillian looks at Archer
He nods
She sighs
"We'll take our chances."

The fingers move quickly again
The huge sail-like cloths
become canopies over the crowd
At the side of the sheet
a detailed drawing emerges
of metal carriers staked into the ground
"These can be used to anchor the cloths throughout."

Gillian exclaims
"But what if we play in stadiums with artificial turf?"

The restless fingers fly again
Now the carriers are attached
sometimes to moveable platforms
sometimes to stationary heavy objects
that form part of the setting
then another sheet
There grow with these heavy objects
high poles upon which the lights are found
that streak the space with light
are located just below where the canopies
can be anchored

In one structure
perched above the level of the setting
a platform for the lighting operator
evolves
"We will have to waterproof things.
This is going to be expensive."

Gillian grins
"I've taken care of that."

George glances at her but says nothing
"Tell me about the characters."

As Archer talks about the mythical creatures
the fingers work again
creating huge puppet or stilt figures
already roughing out shapes
from the different Indigenous traditions
As he moves on to historical events
masks
some half masks
some full
litter the white sheets
As Archer turns to stories
of individuals
faces appear
along with costumes
from each period
As Archer finishes
the table is piled high with sketches   drawings
George looks up   permits himself a smile
"I think I have enough to start with."

The others grin at him
Archer stands up
"I'll be back to pick up some things
sometime in March—
and I'll have another draft for you then."

George nods
then turns again
to work on the interrupted mask

Archer and Gillian look at each other
smile
"Goodbye, George."

Without looking up
George nods and continues working
The two quietly let themselves out

Filled with ideas
from the design meeting
Archer works through the draft
revising
cutting away
reinvigorating the stories
adding new elements
Slowly the script takes firmer shape
Gillian spends more time with him now
getting him to meals
walking with him
in the rain forest
on the beaches
only speaking when she sees
he is ready to talk
to construct with her
the growing vision of the work
Other times she is busy
working out details of the tour
the new situation of the stadium
as well as foraging for more grants
more funds
more angels
for the increased cost
Archer has estimated
sixteen for the company
with others for support
Gillian now budgets
over many late nights
for at least twenty for the whole troupe
But there are times

when each is aware of their intimacy
There are nights together again
murmured   alive

During this time
Archer finds the stage manager
he needs   wants
Amy he has worked with before
trusts her completely
They meet
He finds she is as she always was
solid   bluff   strong
unflappable
always calm
with sharp-eyed honesty
As he tells her about his plans
she listens closely
then asks him perceptive questions
states she will need five more at the least
He accepts her conclusion
She remains with him for the rest of the planning

One day Archer asks Gillian
to contact a composer   musician
who has worked with him before
They meet in a small bistro
quiet   comfortable
The musician is much older than Archer
but he has worked in jazz
played in burlesque houses
knows every style of music
intimately
He is as tall as Archer
his back now slightly bent
but he is lean
sports a small grey moustache
wears glasses only to read

"Ray, good to see you again,"
he says as they meet

shaking his hand
"And the beautiful Gillian."
As he gives her a warm hug
she kisses him on the cheek

"Kent."

Gillian has previously given him
a copy of the draft
After some catch-up conversation
over the main course
they get down to work
Kent speaks pleasantly
even-toned
with the occasional chuckle
a gentle man
He has made notations in the script
but before he goes into detail
he suggests an approach
"From what I can see
you want to give the flavour of each time,
but it appears to me that there needs
some way to tie everything together.
Let's start with some of the specific music."
He goes through the many possibilities
Indigenous dances   drums
martial drums   fifes   trumpets
music of the fiddle   the violin
music from the European centuries
music drifting into the present
"I'm not sure yet about the links.
And it is not a musical.
What ideas do you have?"

Archer confesses that at present
he has none
"Work on what you have for now,
and we will meet
when the final draft is done."

Then they look more specifically
at the possibilities he mentions

determine that the music would be played
by actor-musicians
"I can promise you no more than five."

Kent smiles
"I'll use what I can get."
They break up
after the several hours they had talked

Late in April
Archer holds a week of workshops
to choose the cast
A number of those who try out
had worked with Archer before
but others had seen the *Lear*
have travelled to Vancouver
to work with him

The workshops are rigorous
To begin
many physical exercises
the hymn to the sun
movement exploration
centres
effort qualities
firm/fine touch   direct/flexible   sudden/sustained   bound/free flow
the body as mask
the inevitable introduction to Tai Chi

After the first day
several candidates drop out
This pattern repeats
as the week wears on
Next
more improvisations
that explore moving
knowing the space
where others are
without sight
rhythm explorations
dance exploration

ensemble exploration
Then
work with poles
transformations
the great puppets
poles with huge cloths
the rhythm of their movement
their shapes together
Vocal exercises
vocal exploration
use of vocal rhythms
choral exploration
sounds of all kinds
songs of all kinds
with those who play instruments
exploring with the others
with Kent observing intently
exercises in focus
As well
shapes in space
individual   in groups
sound prompting movement
movement prompting sound
Finally
all kinds of mask exploration

Even those from before
find the variety   rigour
of the exercises
new to them
They have to work hard
to stay with the work
particularly the older ones
Ursula   Jack   James from *Lear*
others as well

By the end of the week
a few more than needed are left
Archer has meetings
with each of them

Finally
a cast is chosen
including those who play instruments
the first meeting scheduled
for the beginning of May

Gillian has found
an old mission hall
large enough for their work
with a wooden floor
that Archer with some volunteers
has refinished
It is here that the cast assembles
on an early May rainy day
Archer and Gillian greet each one
as they enter
Ursula and Jack come together
both showing that they have kept
as fit as they had been during the tour
James   Gary   Michael   Patrick
come early as well
along with Yumiko   Ann
They all greet each other
with the easy familiarity
of actors who have worked much together
Then the new ones gradually arrive
all well before the appointed time
Jean
Québécois
lean   medium height   hair curly black
in his late twenties
carrying his fiddle
Nora
Nova Scotian
Irish descent
auburn-haired
in her mid-twenties
bringing her flute
Bob

from Victoria
hefty big sandy-haired
in his mid-thirties
a trumpet case in his great paw
Ron
Winnipegger
Métis
stocky saturnine
in his late thirties
Peter
Albertan
Ukrainian descent
middle height build
steady dark eyes
in his forties
Ingrid
Saskatchewan
Scandinavian descent
blond striking
early twenties
Mahira
Vancouver
Punjabi descent
small agile
gorgeous
just turned twenty

All had seen each other
in the workshops
but there had been little time
to socialize
Those who had worked together before
are clustered together
but Gillian quietly goes over
to speak to them
They disperse to talk
to the newcomers

Finally Archer calls them together
"Welcome to this project,

which we will for the time being call
"This Northern Land."'
As he speaks
Gillian distributes copies of the script
to everyone
Archer then speaks of the intention of the work
which is to explore the history
the nature of the country
how he sees the piece being performed
in a stadium

All the cast gasp at this

Then he introduces George
who moves the group
around the designs
that he has placed on the walls
pointing to each item
which he then tersely discusses
as all gawk at the profundity
of setting elements
costumes
puppets
masks
with occasional interjections from Archer
When he finishes
Archer thanks him

He then brings forward Kent
who has been sitting quietly
in a corner
watching listening intently
Kent tells them briefly
about what music he intends to use
At the end
Archer thanks him
then introduces to him
the cast members who are musicians
Kent smiles asks them
to show their instruments

Jean has taken out his violin
Kent asks him to play
a classical piece
A sweet quiet melody
from Barber he strokes into the willing air
then without pause
he launches into a fiddler's reel
whose rhythms dance through
the space   bodies
Kent   the others laugh delightedly
Then Kent asks Nora to play her flute
As she begins a Handel sonata
Bob's quiet trumpet joins her
They soar through the sonorous convolutions
to which Jean adds his contrapuntal violin
When the delicious mixture drifts away
all applaud enthusiastically
When all are silent again
"I think we have good possibilities here."
Kent motions Ann to come forward
produces a deerskin-covered drum
which he has had warming by a light
"I would like you to play
this West Coast drum."
He taps the now taut surface
a note reverberates quietly
Ann takes to the drum well
showing her own innate sense of rhythm
Now Kent turns to Yumiko
whose drums were set up in a corner previously
"Let me hear you play."
Yumiko carries them all through a rhythmic journey
from quiet notes up through a scale
to the thunderous roar of her great drums
"Now let us explore a bit."
He has Ann start a rhythm on her drum
Then Yumiko joins in
to create a complex conversation
among the skinned instruments

Then Kent brings forward a snare drum
rat-a-tats
showing Yumiko how to use the sticks
She works tentatively at first
but it is clear that she will soon master
this new form of drum
He then gives the musicians scores
"Take these away and learn them
as a beginning to what we will do."

By now it is the lunch break
The company go off together
chatting animatedly about the morning

At lunch several blocks away
the group breaks up at smaller tables
Amy leading the technicians
to a table away from the others
Archer and Gillian sit with George and Kent
to discuss their future plans
At another table
the actor-musicians sit
Bob looks at the others with interest
"Where are you from, Ann?"

"Haida Gwaii originally.
And you?"

"Oh, I'm another island man—Victoria.
What about you, Yumiko?"

"Vancouver."

"You, Nora?"

"I'm from Dartmouth and proud of it."

Chuckles and smiles
"And you, Jean?"

"I'm from Montreal,
but I've lived in villages in Quebec as well."

Bob nods   then goes on
turning to Ann   Yumiko

"You've worked with him before, presumably?"

Yumiko nods but Ann says
"Yes. But what about you?"

"No, I've never worked with him before,
although I know his reputation.
I've done some acting and some puppetry,
that's all."

With the ice broken
the conversation grows more animate
Nora volunteering that she too
is a puppeteer
had seen *Lear* in Toronto
"It was magnificent!
I wanted to work with him,
and I came all the way out here
to take my chances."

Jean nods vigorously
"The same with me!"
To Ann and Yumiko
"I saw you in Montreal
and came here
as soon as I heard of the tryouts."

The three eagerly question
Yumiko and Ann
who answer as best they can

At another table
Ursula Jack Patrick
sit with Peter
As usual the two men banter
keep the other two laughing
but finally Patrick turns to Peter
"So, Peter, tell us about yourself.
Where do you come from?"

"Vegreville—Ukrainian, of course.
I trained in Edmonton

and have toured a lot,
but this is the first time
that I've worked with Ray."

"Well, you're in for a treat!"
The two men tell stories about him
some of which Ursula knows
from being there
but others that she is afraid
they have made up

At a final table
sit Gary   Michael
with Ron   Ingrid   Mahira
The men cannot help
showing interest in the two attractive women
The conversation begins with them
while Ron sits watching with
a slight sardonic smile
Gary addresses Ingrid first
"So, Ingrid, I'm from Halifax.
What about you?"

Ingrid smiles
an inner nervousness
hidden behind composure
"I'm just a prairie girl
from a small town—
nothing much."

Gary decides to leave the question
for the moment
lets Michael ask Mahira
the same question

"Vancouver."
With this terse reply
she remains silent
to the slight surprise of the men
but Michael decides to continue
"What have you done?"

"I trained in Canada,
but I've also worked in commedia
with companies in Italy."

The others
except Ron
look suitably impressed

"What about you, Ingrid?"

"I trained in Edmonton
and have done some workshops,
but this is my first real touring company."

Ron speaks for the first time
"What about you, Michael?"

"I'm from Vancouver.
And yourself, Ron?"

"Winnipeg."

"Have you worked with Ray before?"

Ron smiles
"Oh, yes.
He and I go back some time."

The three men start to share stories
of their experiences with Archer
the two girls listening attentively

But then Ron asks
"Who is he with now?"

Gary   Michael look at each other
Gary replies
"On the *Lear* tour he was close to
the girl who played Cordelia and the Fool—
Deirdre was her name—
but she decided not to try out for this show,
and so far as we know left him."

Ron's brow shoots up
"*She* left *him*?

That must be a first.
Usually he lets them go."

The two men look at him
slightly uncomfortable

Mahira asks
"What do you mean,
'let's them go?'"

"I mean that when he thinks
they have learned all they can from him,
he sends them off."

"Were they living with him?"

"Oh, yes, usually during the time of a production."

Michael hastily intervenes
"The relationship between Deirdre and Archer
was very positive.
She is a fine actress, and he treated her well."

"But he did not treat her any differently
from anyone else in the troupe,"
Gary quickly adds

Ron nods
but says nothing more

Mahira's eyes narrow
"Do you think he will try that
in this company?"

Gary
earnestly
"He does not pick up actresses
or come on to them.
In terms of Deirdre
it was a mutual attraction
that took some time to mature."

"That is always the way it seems to work."
Ron adds

"He is a very attractive man,
even at his mature age."

Mahira says nothing more
but they can see that
she is thinking hard about what they have said

In the afternoon
the work begins
Tai Chi
patient training for each slow precise
cutting of the air
but first
twisting repetitions
shifting push
like an articulated puppet
each segment adjusting
to the diverse demands of other segments
quiet work on strength
on basic function
pattern
then the start
meticulous
on each form
each with its exotic name
each with the purpose
to strike or press or slash
but now a slow abstracted form
in which each part's travel
is minutely examined
corrected
as all follow the master
One hundred eight forms
comprise the sequence
Today
four are worked carefully
in three hours

A break
then work on stance   breathing

the unforced making of sounds
the capacity to make all kinds   lengths of sounds
when on the floor
standing
travelling through space
passing sounds to each other
focusing sound to one person
while keeping it from others
filling the space comfortably
so that all can hear
Rhythms
clapped
made by the mouth
tapped or stamped on the floor
rhythms improvised among each other
rhythms organized in complex patterns
rhythms that provoke movement
dance
With a last wild rhythmic group gyration
the first day finishes

For several weeks
the training   exploration go on
the Tai Chi sequence begins to form
Poles of various sizes
some relatively small
others so tall that several actors hold them
they move   manipulate in many ways
Forests appear
great masts   sails
on the poles cloths soar overhead
like clouds or snow-topped mountains
or strange ghostly creature-like shapes
huts or teepees
carts
barricades
ranks of rifles
Voices
develop range   versatility

The space
becomes something to be filled by all
or in small pockets of intimacy
The sense of ensemble
is begun
Then puppets
finger   hand puppets
full-size puppets
each with several operators
giant puppets
towering above
as a head   fist
Finally the masks
neutral masks
larval masks
character full masks
mask   contra-mask
character half masks
character cheek   nose masks
mask eyes
mask body parts

While the troupe trains in the hall
outside the previous spring rains
have given place to the richness of May
With the gradually lengthening days
when the long arduous hours are over
many go to walk along the beach in English Bay
watch the sunsets tint the mountains
the sea   the sky

During this time Ingrid   Mahira
watch Archer closely to see if he would
choose a woman
especially one of them
but he treats everyone with courtesy
They see that those
who had worked with him before
trust   respect him
As the days progress

the troupe begins to become closer
with each other
Patrick   Jack discover
that Ron has a wicked wit as well
But friendly as he is
he still keeps more to himself
So does Mahira
who works hard at all she does
but still finds the ensemble difficult
One day Archer asks her to lunch
Ingrid   she exchange a look
but she agrees

Archer takes her to a quiet
booth in a café not far away
After some general talk
about her experiences in Italy
the connections with
some he knows there
he comes to the reason
for their meeting
"You seem right for this work.
And you work harder than
most of the others."

She looks down
"Thank you."

"The only area where you seem uncomfortable
is the ensemble exploration.
Do you know why?"

She continues to look down
"I don't know, really."

"Do you have any problems in the company?
Difficulties in working with anyone?"

"No, I like all of them.
They are wonderful to work with."

"Difficulties with me?
Anything I've said or done?"

314

For a moment she is silent
Then she raises her dark eyes to his
"I don't know whether I can trust you.
All the others do, I can see.
But I've heard stories about you
and women in your companies."

Archer laughs heartily
"I don't know what you've heard,
but I've never been on the lookout
for new conquests."

Mahira's eyes grow darker
"I'm not sure I believe you."

He looks closely at her
now serious
"I have never begun a relationship
that my partner did not help
to initiate.
Have I done or said anything
in this present company
to suggest that I might
come on to you or any other actress?"

"No.
But I have heard that you are the one
who breaks off your relationships."

He smiles wryly
"Most of those who have lived with me
loved me for what I could give them.
And when I saw that they had learned
all that they could for now
and needed to move on,
I broke off the relationship.
In all cases they are still my friends.
And my last relationship,
she broke off.
She knew, I think, that she had learned
all she could from me

either professionally or personally.
And she may work with me again."

Mahira's mouth twists
"Relationships are all a game!
I've never been in a relationship with a man
that wasn't full of tricks and deceit.
Why should I think you're different?"
She becomes silent   still
but continues to breathe heavily

Archer looks at her searchingly
"You are a beautiful woman.
Did your men see more than that?"

"None."
she says bitterly

"Let's be clear.
I can see that you're beautiful
and attractive.
But I am interested in you
solely as an actress
in this company.
What you do in your own time
is your own affair,
so long as it does not interfere
with the work.
I chose you because you have the talent,
not because of your looks—
in fact, despite your looks,
because you are so distinctive—
and I don't mean your ethnicity, either."

She looks away
still unconvinced

He tries again
"All right, then, let's make a pact:
If I do anything that reflects what you say,
then call me on it.
But you must let yourself

become part of the ensemble.
Trust here is between performers,
not between possible mates
or seducers,
and you must see it that way.
Agreed?"

For a long time she studies him
her eyes locked with his
Then
"Agreed."

But he sees that she still is skeptical

She's like one who has been hit
too many times to believe
that the arm will not be raised again

They return to the rehearsal space
but Archer is still sensitive
to the eddies   flows of her unquiet sensibility
marks the need to keep his lookout

Now exploration blends into rehearsal
as they begin to explore the script
what could be involved
Kent comes in with music
or suggestions for what sounds could be used
Over the next few weeks
scenes begin to form
the vast shape of the piece
uncoils

Ursula finds herself
working harder than she ever has before
dealing with the poles   platforms
the masks of different kinds
almost daily brought in by George
the small scenarios   scenes
with such diverse characters
the sounds   music
After the *Lear* tour

she let Jack see her on occasion
but still remained guarded
with too many memories
of quick attachments made
in runs of shows and tours
But as those months ebbed away
she found herself anticipating
such occasions
She noted that Jack himself
seemed less his normal clown
more vulnerable   concerned
Now that they are both engulfed
in the new project
it seems only natural to her
that they should meet daily
at lunch or dinner
One day after the rehearsal
dinner
a walk on the dusk-tinted beach
he walks her home
Apparently without a thought
they kiss
It is the first time she has truly kissed
since that last catastrophe
For a moment the desperate feelings
evoked then come raging back
but she lets Jack's kiss
continue
The past is dissolved
in the new feelings of kissing
a man whom she has come to trust
No further moments now
as they stand fused together
then without a word
she leads him in
For the first time
the two shed clothes   experience
create lovemaking anew
letting acquired skills build afresh

They lie together through
the night that they build themselves
Rehearsals now progress
through their new eyes
reanimated feelings

Now moments in the work
begin to gel
some of the story-theatre scenes
become sharper   clearer
stilt figures more articulate
great puppets begin to stir
cloths transform with relative ease
music too fuses with each event
musicians sense their connection
Finally the sections of the event
are brought together
The first run-throughs
show where the gaps   creases are
these are filled   smoothed out
At last the lights are brought to play
The whole piece
as a giant liner slipping newborn into the water
arises in its majesty

Canto 14

VANCOUVER: REALIZATION

Now begin the previews
to test the effect on audiences
High schools are bussed in
older audiences are found
Gillian has made sure
that the publicity has made the show intriguing
After adjustments are made
from the first audiences' responses
she sells tickets for several preview nights
which are well attended

At last opening night itself arrives
By this time news of the unique nature of the event
has passed around by word of mouth
There is a sense of excitement
among the spectators in the milling crowd
all two thousand of them
who have nowhere to sit
but find themselves in the middle of a stadium
among platforms   poles   paraphernalia
A fine July night
no moon flashlighting the space
Around them they can see
the bulk of the stadium beyond
the lights that define the space
in which they stand
Only after a time
do they realize that these lights
are almost imperceptibly dimming
until at last each winks out
They stand in darkness
the glow of the city
shielded from them by the stadium itself

Then
almost as indiscernible as the lights had been
a low deep rumbling is heard
that slowly begins to mount
even as new lights creep slowly up
to silhouette great shapes
forming around them
Tall peaks
slope to a horizon like a plain
then to smaller peaks   ridges
until they are surrounded by these huge forms
as the rumbling increases
with other sounds barely grating through
the mounting reverberation

Suddenly the roar stops
an Indigenous drum pierces the silence
joined by high-pitched songs
from all sides
as new light picks out
on the perimeters
the still   immense   figures
of the Creators
Raven
elongated sharp beak
cruel   quizzical
sly sharp eyes
brilliant wings now wrapped to the body
feathers patterned with the shape
of the bones of the West Coast bone game
his existence always caught on the toss
Old Man
tall   lofty   in his robes
his white hair simply braided
his face grave   chiselled
his ancient hands grasping
his plain staff
Earth Mother
a leather band

holding back her braids
her deerskin jacket
bright with beads
heavy with fringe
shoulder   arm
her soft trousers
edged with complex decoration
as are her supple moccasins
her graceful hands
ready to touch   embrace
Great Manitou
stern-faced
his vast headdress
with its bright feathers   beads
cascading over his broad shoulders
his braided hair
falling on the bones
of his armoured chest
the necklace of bones about his neck
where also dangles his precious globe
cradled in his long gloved hands
his sacred rod
With them
the Thunderbird
massive beak
wings
body
elaborately decorated
fierce-eyed

Then
with one motion
the huge figures
begin to move
through the crowd
that hastily parts before them
With them come
platforms at shoulder height
on which are found

Indigenous figures
from all parts of the country
who enact through story movement
the tales of their beginnings
their lives
to each of the now segregated audiences

The drum now silent

Haida Kwakiutl Salish
the many other coastal interior peoples
prairie Bloods Blackfoot Cree Peigans
arctic Inuit
northern Ojibwe
Algonquin
eastern Haudenosaunee
Huron other tribes through
this country of lakes rivers
Mi'kmaq in the Maritimes
Beothuk in that far-off eastern isle

As their stories conclude
the platforms the figures
drift toward each side
When they reach there
the drum begins again
this time throbbing a war chant
joined in by strident voices
On the sheets shaping the country
shadows appear of warriors
battles massacres
augmented by stories cried out
on each of the four sides
of the raids wars catastrophes
as the nations brush against each other
with stockades of poles
shadowed against the cloth
Then for a moment peace descends
Each group turns quietly
to its domestic life

in mountains
on plains
among the forests
lakes
tundra
on the islands

Gradually light dims to blackness
the audience finds itself
dazed and blinking
at intermission
Much chatter as they find
refreshments at the side
where those who
need them
find chairs in which to rest
Then lights signal return
they move back

Suddenly a trumpet note
clear   high
all changes
The large figures move back
to the edge of light
at each end
the sheets transform
into the sails of European ships
their masts extending tall
Attention shifts
to first encounters
at one end
then at the other
finally in the middle
Then as scenes of exploration
play out through the space
at the "eastern" end accumulate
gigantic figures of European royalty
in their rich costumes of these early centuries
before them the strange figures
of the two corporations

Hudson's Bay Company
North West Company
The sheets transform again
to allow for shadow puppets
platforms for masks puppets characters
to enact the horrors of
the Indian Wars
as the Creators begin to withdraw

The British king moves to the opposite end
with allies
to face the French king   his companions
as the trumpet   fife   drums
snarl   beat
for the war over the coveted land
Puppet regiments of red   blue uniforms
appear on the platforms
now massed at each end
to fire volleys at each other
on the Plains of Abraham
Din and smoke
the agonized cries of the wounded
attack the space
The fife   drum signal retreat
gradually fade
as the regiments disappear

Stories are again enacted
on the platforms
of those who had to live
through the expulsion of the Acadians
the fall of Quebec
the disintegration of the tribal nations
Exploration for new routes
is enacted
The platforms
now carts   wagons
again move through the area
as settlers west   east
invade the country
their stories told

For a brief moment
the early American flag
is seen upon the canopies
as revolution trumpets
in the colonies to the south
its echoes reverberating north
Colossal puppets fade away
the stories performed of the United Empire Loyalists
the New York Mohawks
led by Joseph Brant
who all must settle in the Canadian colonies
the shrinking of the tribes
now decimated by disease   war
by government policy
removed to reservations
nudged from their ancestral lands

Now the deep drums throb
as forests of poles arise
filling the space
the audience caught
in the dense multitude
Then they begin to topple
people scurrying away
as the tall sticks are levelled
to reveal on the sheets
now risen one each side
the silhouettes of growing towns
then cities
the rhythmic sounds of industry

A brief skirmish at one end
signals the War of 1812
its stories
the 1837 rebellions
their stories
the huge Irish migration
through the potato famine
the Métis in the west
the Red River migration

Large puppets appear
dressed in their beaver hats
Victorian formal dress
Fathers of Confederation
to argue   debate
negotiate
make deals
to bring forth the Dominion
during which each one
attempts to persuade members of the audience
of his colony's need   stance
The assassination of Thomas D'Arcy McGee
The building of
the Canadian Pacific Railway
with platforms   poled rails
connected rhythmically through the space
a giant William Cornelius Van Horne
roaring out orders
The Ballad of Batoche
Riel   Dumont prominent
played out with its aftermath
throughout the whole space
The last spike of the CPR
at Craigellachie
Change throughout the country
the many stories of the individuals involved
Chinese
First Nations   the residential schools
Métis
more Irish
more Scots

As the stories finish
the figures stand
in their numbers
on the platforms
as the lights
slowly dim on them

After a moment
of darkness
intermission lights rise

The babble of the audience
again arises
But this time
it is not the effects
discussed
but those elements
in Canada's past
that some knew
and others had little knowledge of

Then signalled back
an expectant
darkness
Greying of the light
more trumpets   drums
the violin
heard before in the old reels
now with familiar melodies
as the Great War breaks out
Soldiers march in parade through the space
Then large newspaper pages
cover the screens
with news of war   casualties
Through the audience
come nurses helping bandaged soldiers
limping or in wheelchairs
who tell their tales to those nearest them
nurses with bloodied uniforms
those at home
giving their stories throughout
The strains with Quebec
At last peace
with streamers throughout the crowd
characters laughing   kissing
throughout the audience
But the Spanish flu

interrupts
victims masked   dying
into darkness
Then a march of workmen
ending in the Winnipeg General Strike

Now the mirror balls
music of the jazz age
dancing among the audience
the arrival of a great wave
of immigrants
Norwegian
Swedish Danish Finnish
Russian   Ukrainian
German
Eastern European
small numbers from Asia
Jews Mennonites Mormons Amish
all Christian sects
Buddhists Muslims Hindus Sikhs
all religions
their stories

A great cloud of tickertape
over the audience
The Depression begins
large puppets of Prime Minister
Company Owners
at one end
at the other
Workers   Farmers
between
the prairies
from sod huts
to the farms
wheat to dust bowl
their stories
freights
the work camps
On to Ottawa Trek
ending in the Regina Riot

Sudden blackout
then at one end
as the trumpet   drums go mad
Second World War begins
the marching off of Canadian soldiers
all the busy machination
of industry   destruction
The stories are told
Again the streamers
as peace comes
More immigrants
the cities grow

Oil is found
The space is ringed
with the red of gas flares
The throb of growth
is heard everywhere
with the distant sounds
sights of
the Cold War
the Korean War

The celebration
one hundred years
repatriation of the BNA Act
the Charter of Rights and Freedoms
Changes in Quebec
the referenda for separation
Free Trade Agreement

Then
after all the enactments
puppets
masks
silhouettes
all the paraphernalia
of the production
a maze of rough fences
is woven through the audience

Characters speak intimately to those
beyond or behind the fence with them
about their present lives   concerns
global warming
housing   jobs
drugs   crime
the decaying infrastructure of cities
loss of farm land
family   relationships
Then they   the maze
slip away

On platforms at one end
the cast comes forward   bows
The audience realizes that the show is done
they applaud
General lights from before the show
rise

The audience exits
a few remaining
to speak to Archer
Their comments
like a wind that shifts restlessly
its direction no sooner sensed
than it seems to come from elsewhere
are admiring   puzzled
not certain of where
to place judgment
Archer
busy with his own notes
has little time to recognize
those who have spoken to him
but Gillian listens more carefully
takes note of their remarks

After all has been stored away
the company goes to a restaurant
to hear Archer
to unwind

"Only a few things to refine.
We'll come in about two tomorrow
and take a meal break.
Oh, and by the way…"

Archer smiles

"…you did well."

Then the party begins
as Archer sits with Gillian
George   Kent
Amy
whose technicians
sit at a table by themselves
"It looked very good."
George says
He quickly gives
some terse notes   sketches
Kent agrees
also gives several suggestions
for the music   the sounds

Gillian smiles
but says nothing
"I'll talk to you tomorrow.
Let's relax tonight."

While they talk
Jean   Bob   Nora
start to jam
The others
like a flock of birds
that suddenly soar up
following their leaders
begin to dance
Ursula   Jack
sweep around the room
to one of Jean's reels
Patrick carries off Ingrid giggling
to join them

as does Michael with an intrigued Mahira
Gary with a surprised Yumiko
Ann confronts a reluctant Ron
pulls him onto the floor
where he proves adept
to her own wonder
James   Peter watch amused
from a table at the side
drink companionable beers
The trio plays old reels   waltzes
the dancers continue
with enthusiasm

During a break when the three
drink   laugh together
the various couples chatter
Ann over these weeks
has been interested in finding out
more about Ron
but this is the first opportunity
she has had to speak informally to him
for though he has worked well
in the company context
he keeps to himself
with the occasional sardonic comment
"So you work out of Vancouver?"

They exchange stories
of the events   their rehearsals
the tours
during which Ann finds him
more relaxed   with
a wonderful sense of humour
but still enigmatic

At another table
sit Patrick   Ingrid
Michael   Mahira
Patrick as usual
is outrageous

the table is awash with laughter
but Michael
who feels strongly Mahira's attraction
notices that although she now
is more relaxed than when rehearsals started
still keeps up her guard
however subtle it may be
He also notices
that she glances covertly at Archer
several times

Soon the trio take up their instruments again
this time play
slow foxtrots
As the dancers rise
Mahira quickly excuses herself from Michael
crosses over to Archer at his table
"May I have this dance?"

He glances at her
then smiles   rises
They start off
Mahira keeps close to him
is agreeably surprised
to find that he dances well
For a time they glide around the room
saying nothing
their bodies attuned to each other
Then
his lips beside her ear
"Have I kept my side of the bargain?"
For a moment they continue
to dance in silence

"Have I?"

He chuckles
"Yes. Now answer my question."

She says nothing
but continues to dance close to him

a union in the dance
"You find me attractive?

"Extremely so. Very desirable."

"And you want me?"

"Any man would."

"And you can dance with me like this?"

"Of course. You are an excellent dancer.
And we dance like this
because this is what dancing should be,
and we can enjoy it to the full.
But as I told you before,
none of this means that I will
start an affair with you.
I will dance with you
and, if you wish, be a friend,
but not your lover."
They continue to dance in silence
still close together
Then he chuckles
"Have I passed the test?"

She looks at him
slightly in shock
from the conversation
but still dancing gracefully with him
He laughs   twirls her
Despite herself
she laughs too
They finish the dance
with great enjoyment
return to their respective tables

The merriment continues
with dancers exchanging partners
animated chatter
Finally the musicians
sit with the others

Sometime later
the evening comes to its pleasant end

The next day Gillian reads the reviews
which are striking in their differences
Some are wildly enthusiastic
praising the originality   breadth
of the production
others wildly antagonistic
finding it a spectacle
but not a play
No middle ground
She smiles
Controversy is good publicity

At lunch with Archer
she summarizes the response
He chuckles
"We knew it would have this effect,
didn't we?"
They both laugh heartily
then get down to complete
the plans for the run in Vancouver
for the tour of the country

In the afternoon
final adjustments are made
The company breaks early
for dinner
A two-hour warm-up
then the second show
full
with an audience much younger
who respond enthusiastically
at the end cheer the exhausted actors

As the two weeks of the run continue
the audience becomes more diverse
The actors begin to notice
that some older people

the restraint of a theatre seat gone
become deeply involved

"My name is Thomas D'Arcy McGee,
Irish and Catholic!"
a character roars
Half the audience cheers
half boo

The episodes concerning Quebec
produce similar responses
as does the building of the CPR
the battle of Batoche
the Indian Wars
at times many other episodes
The atmosphere of the performance space
begins to resemble in part
that of a midway
only the power of the actors
keeping the audience in check
Newspapers begin to report the incidents
as news rather than criticism
By the time the run has finished
the production has become notorious
across the country

Canto 15

CROSS-CANADA TOUR

Now the tour begins in earnest
the bus packed with actors   technicians
equipment
a trailer attached behind
Victoria for three days
Kelowna for one
Calgary   Edmonton a week each
Saskatoon   Regina
Winnipeg the same
Brandon a day
one at Thunder Bay
then off toward Southern Ontario

Skirting the rims of the lakes
the bus drones on
with Archer spelling off Gillian
at intervals
Gillian sits with Mahira
A conversation
that she has had many times before
takes place
about Archer
about herself
She answers
in her customary open way
for a time does not question Mahira
but instead
talks as well to Ingrid and Peter
The four of them discuss the tour
share anecdotes about it
then Gillian turns more directly
to the two behind her
"So you both are from the prairies?"

They nod

Peter takes up the question further
"Yes, I'm from a farm not far from Vegreville,
east of Edmonton."

Ingrid looks at him with surprise
"I knew you were from Alberta,
but I didn't know you came from a farm.
So did I, farther south and east of you."

For a few minutes
they talk about their farms
where they were located
Peter then changes slightly
"I was lucky in some ways,
I guess.
My family came from the Ukraine
after the Second World War
and had to start from nothing.
But we had been sponsored
by the Ukrainian community,
and although my parents were poor
they worked hard
and finally bought a farm,
which involved mixed farming—grain,
cattle, and the milk and eggs
my mother sold.
I was a late addition to the family,
in the sixties,
and so got some of the benefits,
although I still had to work hard.
Because the Ukrainians were so strong in the district
the discrimination I heard about
from those who had been there
for several generations before us
wasn't apparent anymore."

Ingrid interrupts excitedly
"That's what happened to us too,
although my family history here

goes back much farther,
to the 1920s.
I remember my grandmother
telling me about her parents,
who had come from Norway with little
and worked hard
with the help of a generous Norwegian
in the community there
and finally had their farm.
The fact is, my great-grandfather
had never been a farmer in the old country.
He was a carpenter by trade there,
and by chance found himself out on the prairies.
But, of course, by my time the farm was large,
and his sons went their different ways.
It was my father who finally got the land,
and I was brought up to do chores
and work with my mother in the kitchen."

For a moment the two of them
share recollections of the work each did
on the farm
Then Ingrid grows serious
"But my grandmother told me
that when she was a young girl
her mother could not speak English
but learned from her
when she came home from school,
gave her fresh-baked buns to eat
and listened as she did her homework.
And my grandmother always remembered
how when she walked into town
that mile or so,
the town children, most of whom were English,
looked down on her,
for before she had gone to school
she had spoken only Norwegian
and had to learn English the hardest way
as she struggled in the school and playground.

Of course, all that seems to have gone now—
I never had those problems in school."
She smiles bitterly
"Of course, money always helps,
as it did with us.
Then, I wanted to act,
and that was a different matter for my family.
My mother couldn't understand
why I would want to do such a thing,
but my father made a bargain with me:
Go to university; take a first year;
then audition—for we had looked at the calendar—
and if I get in, then he would finance the rest.
If I did not get in, then finish a degree,
one that let me have a profession
like teaching or nursing,
and return home to use it
and to get married."
She sighs
"I was lucky.
I got into the acting program."

Yumiko
her eyes bright with the memory
of her own story   so similar
embraces Ingrid

Peter laughs
"Just what happened to me!
And the situation was even tougher for me,
for there was no theatre where I lived,
and my family thought it scandalous
that I would consider such a career.
I had to finance it myself.
I took several jobs each summer
and also worked secretly during the school year,
for I also made it into the program.
And when I got out, the theatre
was expanding in the city
and I managed to get work,

both there and in touring companies."
They look at each other
a new sense of connection between them

Mahira suddenly twists in her seat
bursts out
"It may have been tough on the farm,
but you at least have a family
you can return to!"

The others look at her
startled and shocked

"I was born in Canada
but my parents came from the Punjab,
and when I was young
my father left us.
Oh, we had enough money,
but I was brought up by a mother
who was more concerned with herself
and her male companions
than with me.
And I still had to work for what I've done—
as a waitress, a picker,
anything that would earn me money
while I was at school.
I fought my way into Theatre School,
I fought my way through the course,
I fought to get to Italy,
and I fought to get here.
I fought my mother's men,
and I fought those men
who wanted me,
once I learned to play the game.
And I didn't take jobs
that involved the director's couch."

"It's all right, Mahira,"
Gillian says gently
"We may regret
what has happened in your past.

But the point is that you are here
and a valued member of this company."
She puts her arm out to her
but Mahira refuses it
sitting back in her seat
facing straight ahead
Nothing is said among the four
for the remainder of that afternoon's drive

The next day
as the bus begins to leave
the uppermost shore
Ann
who yesterday sat
while Ron read
oblivious to her
or anyone
finally attempts to start
a conversation
"I never saw you in Vancouver."

He glances at her
Then
sardonically
"You probably didn't see the right shows.
I used to do improvs when
I toured as a comedian."

She refuses to take the slight
"No, I was never interested
in that kind of theatre."

A shrug
From this terse beginning
they gradually begin to talk
He learns about her life
as a Haida
She learns about his Métis life
on the verge of the prairies
that he had been married
the marriage was disastrous

he became an actor later
had worked with Archer
toured with him before
As they talk
she realizes how well read he is
how informed
how his tongue
can be sharper than her knife
that women are now
to him
a race apart   dangerous

The bus drones on
Yumiko   Michael
enter more deeply
into a discussion
of their separate
East Asian
backgrounds
the vision that infuses each
how they have altered
with the work in the company
Each takes pleasure
in the talk together
without interference of attraction

Gary   Bob
enter into a friendship
with the technicians
who have adapted
to the way of working
now through Amy
beginning to relax
with the company
with whom they play cards
tell jokes
reminisce
while Amy smiles quietly
Bob plays his trumpet
to the amusement of the rest of the bus

Jack   Ursula
just like to sit together
occasionally talking
joking
but essentially
just being together

Two days later
in London
the university stadium
with its flanking bleachers
more open at the ends
woods seen
cajoled for them
by the Artistic Director
for two performances
despite the outcry
from the now fully birthed
football team
in a glorious September week
In the maelstrom
of the university's new year
curious students somehow
find time to come
urged by faculty in history
other subjects
that turn an eye
on the nation
or on the arts
or both
As before
actors   others come
from Stratford
Londoners
who had attended the production last year
Natives
for whom the grapevine
had sent reports
from the shows
around the lakes

The first show
five hundred in the space
as the sunset still glimmers
then the episodes
in which the East twists through
its many strands of struggle
begin to affect all
particularly Natives
older men   women
The finish
the applause
but the actors cannot
drift away
as people cluster about them
to tell their own stories
their anecdotes
their own memories
flooding into speech
Archer and Gillian
stand by
fascinated
The A.D. joins them
"I never really knew
what you had in mind
but you have done it again.
And look at what is happening—
I've never seen an audience
involved this way before."

Archer grins
"Neither have we.
But we must find a way
to let them have their chance."
The three stand there
for some time
while the noise swirls
around the surprised actors
those from Stratford
who had never seen the like before
as well

Finally Archer leaps onto one of the platforms
roars
"Thank you, ladies and gentlemen,
for your kind response
to our event
and for your own contributions.
Those who are interested
should speak to Gillian…"

He gestures toward her

"…and she will give you our email
if you wish to send us your own thoughts.
We will try to let everyone
have access to a site to see them.
Now we must ask those of you
who do not wish to see her
to leave
so that the actors can change."
Then he gets down
The startled Gillian
is swamped by those
who take up his offer

The A.D. goes up to Archer quickly
"Archer, we have a small reception
in the stadium facilities
for the company.
Would you mind
if some of the actors from Stratford
join us?"
He smiles   agrees
After the company
has cleaned up the space
themselves
Ann and Ron
have finished their conversations
with the Indigenous people who had met them
they all traipse up to the room
filled like a well-used palette of oils

with different groups
local sponsors
the theatre board
actors   directors
from the city   Stratford
university people
The A.D. greets them
introduces them
to general applause
then
drinks   food in hand
they circulate
Some they had met at Stratford
the previous year
These discuss
with much animation
the show   what they have done
The locals are more mixed
bemused by what they have experienced

The new members of the company
are fascinated by the potpourri
of people   the conversation
that scatters like shattered glass
in all directions
The reception goes on
for some time
until gradually people
sweep or drift away
Archer explains to the Stratfordians
that the company this year
will have no time to visit them
Goodbyes   final praises done
the exhausted company
makes its way home
to collapse in dreamless sleep

The next day
as before
a coffee session

with the A.D.
Gillian and Archer

She shakes her head
in mock bewilderment
"Well, Archer,
another wonderful surprise.
But it is a dangerous approach,
isn't it?"

He looks at her
appreciatively
"You're right, of course.
It's too easy to get lost
in the spectacle
and lose the experience.
Can you see the places
where this happens?"

She shrugs
"A few."
The three of them
work through her notes
discussing each deeply
thoroughly
as Archer sketches
ideas
from what they wrestle with
When they finish
he gives her a warm embrace
the three part
happily

For the next day
Archer thinks through
the changes
as they finish the short run
in London
drive to Hamilton
where they set up   perform
the same day

The next day
he calls the company together
in the afternoon
works carefully
on one episode only
making sure that any change
is thoroughly rehearsed
incorporated
so that no confusion will exist
in the night's performance
Again the next day
he works in a similar way
Then
the run finished after three days
they travel to Toronto
where in the first   second weeks
of their three-week run
he carefully completes the changes
The company becomes aware
that the show has become sharper
that each movement they express
each scene portrayed
each mask   cloth   element
now seems invested with more significance
that the great waves
of the country's history
roll on with purpose
punctuated by the individual stories
like a powerful madrigal

Toronto
for Gillian has proved
a problem
with two major stadiums
tied up with professional
university games
but she finally has found
a solution
a place

As usual
the audience
on the first night
is mixed
with those who know his work
those who are curious
for newspaper reports
have proved intriguing
many actors   directors
some Natives   the critics
For a short time
the audience resists
the space
the unique style
but then
as they become involved
in the history
that they know
or at least have heard of
they begin to coalesce
As in other places
their responses are specific
to their well-worn attitudes
Where on the prairies
the episodes dealing with
the CPR
provoked the farmers
into angry mutterings
here the struggles
of the East become
a strong focus
for different responses

Orangemen
Irish Catholics
the threat from the States
the boys off to fight at Batoche
the World Wars
At the end

the audience
exhilarated
roars its approval
The actors stay
to talk
Gillian gathers more
stories
volunteers

The next day
Gillian collects the reviews
which are mixed
Many highlight
the spectacular staging
some see the sweep   breadth
others see it more like a circus
or like a pageant
with no criteria
by which to judge it
keep only with the surface of the work
She summarizes the results
for Archer
"You'll have to speak to the cast, of course."

"Of course."

That afternoon the cast assembles
curious to hear what Archer would say
Those who had not worked with him before
are confused   concerned
by what they had read
but the others
who now know
how Archer thinks
wait to see what he will say

"As you know—
or at least as many of you know—
I don't read reviews.
I respond to what I see
the show means to an audience

and what I think it should be.
But Gillian has described to me
the confused response
that reviewers had.
Some apparently understood
what we intended.
Others were lost in effect
and had no critical footing
on which to stand.
And that is appropriate
for what we have done, I think.
Some people will be confused.
Some will look only for the spectacle.
But for us, the true sense of the event
comes when, after we have finished,
people come up to share their own stories
and histories,
for they have been provoked
by what they have seen
and felt
and responded to
and feel the need
to add to the whole mosaic
that we have presented.
And you know as you play
how the audience is with you,
whether in confronting what they see
or agreeing with it.
If we can let them experience
the great sweep
and the long struggle
of this land,
then we have done our work."
He gives them a few minutes
to ask
discuss
argue
then begins the work again

The media are intrigued
by the odd nature of the show
television networks
want to film parts of it
but Archer refuses
all requests
"Only with a live audience
can this be seen—
it is designed for them
and not for something picturesque
with the camera watching them
watching the stage
with the television viewer
wondering what all the spectacle is about."
Again he has interviews
in which he patiently explains
that the work
is not a pageant
not a circus with words
that it is not superficial
but tries to deal with the country
in its complex history
in a way that can be comprehended
experienced

So the three weeks wear on
the crowds gather
the night air becomes crisper
Then they leave for Ottawa

The week in Ottawa
their last of this tour
a new audience again
Those who saw them
at the National Arts Centre
now return to see this new event
bemused by its format
As word gets around
many from the embassies come
so that the audience fractures

between those who are caught up
in their own past
those who watch a strange
alien country
as it stirs into its many lives
Those from the NAC congratulate them
The cast finds itself
continually adjusting
to unexpected responses

Finally the last night comes
the audience applauds
the actors disappear
to begin the strike
When finished
they all go to a party
again in a private room
this time in the Chateau Laurier
a wry gesture from Gillian
It is a different kind
of occasion
like a farewell
tentative
temporary
for someone
who will return
again
but the parting
still stirs the blood
This time no Québécois
burst into the room
instead the company eats
drinks
chats
After a time
Archer calls for their attention
"Well, we have finished this year's tour,
and I think finished it well."

Cheers and applause

"As you know,
we have done only half the country,
and next year we will tour the rest."

Happy acquiescence

"But I have more news…"

They become more attentive

"…which I will let Gillian tell you."

Gillian joins him
eyes glowing
"I have just received an invitation
from the Irish embassy
for us to perform in Ireland
at the end of the tour next year."

Stunned silence
then an uproar
of cheers   laughter   applause

"However…"

They become silent

"…it depends on finances.
If I can wangle some money
from Foreign Affairs,
the Irish government will put up the rest."

 Quiet muttering among the group

Archer takes over
"Knowing Gillian,
I'm sure she'll find the money."

Relieved laughter

"And so tomorrow,
please tell me if you are willing
to continue on the tour.
Next year
we will start in April

and probably make revisions
as you know is my habit."

Rueful laughter

"The rehearsals will be
in Toronto.
But if any of you
wish to bus back
with Gillian and me,
you are welcome.
The money that would go
for your airfares
can be used partly
for motels,
but you still may be able
to save some money.
Please tell me tomorrow
about that as well.
And now,
enjoy yourselves.
You deserve it!"

A babble arises
as various groups
discuss the situation

After a time it grows quieter
Then the musicians of the troupe
gather together
The evening
goes on for hours
with the jam session
the dancing
until
exhausted   content
all return home
to end the tour
with a little sleep

Canto 16

THE RETURN

The bus growls through the scarlet hills
Gillian at the wheel
Production in Toronto slumbering
on racks shelves in boxes in ranks
in hibernation until the spring
Jean off to Quebec Nora to Nova Scotia
Patrick James in Toronto
the rest choosing the bus for the long journey to the western coast
Before they left Ottawa
Gillian had excavated the mines of the government
used the influence of the Irish ambassador
the influence of her artistic bureaucratic friends
carried with her assurances
of the riches that awaited them
for the leap across the water
Now the Shield envelopes them
as the bus winds its familiar trail
to Georgian Bay and north

Behind Gillian sits Archer
Mahira beside him
Ingrid behind Mahira
Peter alongside her
across the aisle
Ann Ron
Yumiko Michael
then scattered around
Gary Bob together
behind all
Jack Ursula
Amy
several technicians
the others staying in Toronto
The atmosphere in the bus

much different from before
As a brisk wind sweeps all before it
people lean into it
or feel it pushing them
its vigorous air
fondling their flesh
ruffling their clothes
its sound
a symphony of gusts   heavy whisperings
a hoarse conversation
always with them
then dies down
the air is still
but yet the memory
of the rush   sound
tarries for a time
so in the bus
the anticipation of performance
lingers like a faint perfume
but the sense of when
is lost
All sit in limbo
letting the scenery drift by
lulled by the sensation
of the vibration of the tires
the vagaries of motion
the muted roar
of engine   rush of air

For an unfolding time
all is silent
with vacant stares
at the speeding landscape
or dozing
too lethargic to read or talk
Then Mahira stirs
touches Archer on the arm
He opens his eyes
retrieved from his reverie

to look at her
Since that dance
when the performances began
he has noticed that she has changed
working just as hard
but reaching out more to the others
leading in the building of the ensemble
taking time to know
the technicians as well
that with him
she has been far more open
her eyes direct without guard
taking in all he says   does
He has noted
her terrible drive
to find each character
to explore their limits
release them to the audience
in her need to perform
all else set aside
She has asked him questions
during the tour
but always specific
about her characters
or movement
or relationships
Now she has come to sit with him
which she has not done before
He is intrigued
"Yes, Mahira?"

She moves slightly closer
so they can talk
without the effort
of distance in the bus
"I worked with an Italian company
on commedia and masks
and physical theatre,
and I can see similarities

360

in your work with us—
is all that you do
based on Lecoq?"

He smiles
"He has certainly been an influence
on me, as on many others.
But his main mission,
apart from the specific trainings,
and through them,
was to let each of us find our own way
and find the means to examine
continually what we do.
So I have used what he gave me
and what I learned from others
and what I learn from myself
to fashion my particular art."

She nestles closer
her shoulder against his
so that she can hear more comfortably
"Tell me what he was like
and what kinds of things he did."

He smiles
pleasantly surprised
to see that she can be at ease with him
in this way
then
memories rush back

les vingts mouvements

the work on mime
the former student
who demonstrated at command
the walks   runs   gallops
of animals   insects
with a slight movement
of the head
the wind against a cheek
the strange paths of the neutral mask
the character masks

le traitement

the work of the master
with architects
having them design rooms
in which one could not help but smile
always the probing eye
to force one to find the truth
of the act
even in its impossibility

All these memories
more
he tells to Mahira
who listens   entranced
Then he looks at her
takes her hand
"But all this happened when I was there.
Later students learned other things
as he kept exploring many trails.
That is perhaps the deepest thing he taught me—
to keep stretching
to let what sparks you
grow to a conflagration
as you search for the way
to best bring it to life."

She looks at him
her eyes burning
at what she has heard

"And so I have learned
from others as well
and other ways of working,
the darker realms of the mask,
my own techniques,
and use these insights
when and where I can."
He stops

She presses his hand
in thanks

362

Behind them
Ingrid suddenly speaks
her eyes wide with what she has heard
"I had no idea of what you tell Mahira.
What you have done with us
has opened up a new world."

Peter beside her nods
For a time an animated conversation
like a brief burst of sun
passes among them
Then Archer turns back
to rest
his head back   eyes closed
but Mahira still holds his hand

The bus drones on
passing through
the thousand lakes
Mahira
continues to sit
with Archer
or Gillian
at times with Ingrid
When she sits with Archer
Mahira becomes absorbed with his words
is comfortable
with his physical presence
which she now feels poses
no danger to her
He tells her of other approaches
of the work of Laban
Alexander   Feldenkrais
the different physical disciplines
the nature of style
the need to find the vision
of a play
or an event
the nature of performance   an audience

One night
now in Winnipeg
Gillian sits with him
in a bar
"You know what's happening to Mahira?"

"Yes. She is learning much from me."

"You're becoming her surrogate father, you know."

"I suppose. But she needs to go through that
before she can deal with men again."

"I hope you're right."

"We'll find out soon enough.
By the way,
I'd like us to stop a day or two
in Edmonton."

Surprised
"Edmonton? I thought we were going
the southern route."

He says thoughtfully
"I need to spend a little time there.
For myself.
The others might as well meet
directors there."

She shrugs   nods
They turn to other topics
before they return
to the motel   the bus

As the bus crawls across
the undulating prairies
under the vast skies
Archer gently excuses himself
from talking further
sits   eyes closed
letting his mind drift

Too much have I seen
too quickly
Too many persons
all so unique
now blending into a crowd
These vast themes
movements
like seeing a grand panorama
that strikes the eye at first
for its immensity
then bewilders
with its detail   diversity
Now
all these in the bus with me
who know me
only for what I teach them
direct them to do
nothing more

The cold wind of isolation
arises
its first chill breath
barely felt against his mind
then its frigid gusts
enveloping his feelings   his thoughts
He thinks back
to the women he has known

All needs   desires on their part
on mine
I knew when the time with each
was finished
except for Deirdre

Gillian
mutual respect in the business
a pleasure in bed
closest to a friend
but nothing deeper
if anything can be deeper

My parents dead
when I was just eighteen
no relatives living

He tries to remember
his parents
now wraiths in his memory
his mother who doted on him
slight   pretty
who loved to read poetry aloud
loved to act
loved to play the piano
his father who took him
on treks to the Rockies
or in a canoe
along prairie creeks
but although somewhat affectionate
always seemed to be at a slight distance

Is that why my mother
lavished her attention on me

Though they had many friends
held parties
no relatives did he know
nor did they talk of any
no grandparents uncles aunts cousins
But there was one person
whom he still remembers
who he now realizes
was slightly younger than his mother
a girl who helped her
became close to him
when he was a young child
but whom he has not seen
for many years

She must be very old now
if alive at all
I must see her in Edmonton

In his depths
he feels a need growing
to see her
see old acquaintances
from that forgotten youth
He continues to sit
eyes closed
lets the whir of the tires
carry him through the void
exposed in his mind

The actors
cavorting with the technicians
find no trace of the fences
the technicians built
at the beginning of the tour
when they became their own coterie
maintaining it assiduously
while showing themselves
proficient at what they do
With this year's tour ended
all are relaxed
no work now to distance them
Amy
thirty   stage manager
tall   solidly built   reliable
laughs heartedly at their pranks
joins in lustily
joking as only a Newfie can
her laughter matched by Josh
just nineteen
her ASM
from Saskatchewan
big   arms   legs like oaks   agile
who works out each day
beyond the warm-ups
now talks amiably
with the little group

while Ryan
twenty-five   from northern Alberta
the master of the lights
tall   thin
sits quietly smiling
when he is not absorbed
in his laptop
his PC games
None had worked with Archer before
at first were disconcerted
by the whole nature of the event
but soon became enthusiastic
found ways
of making things work more smoothly
Now
relaxed
returning to the vagaries
of the theatre in Vancouver
they let their world shrink
to the bus
its shifting portals on the world
match anecdote with anecdote
with the actors
As the bus sails
across the ocean of the prairies
the groups begin to break up
merge in different ways
as different mixtures blend
while still keeping their identity
in colour   texture   stained pattern

In Edmonton
like drops of mercury
that skitter across a surface
so the troupe disperses
some to friends
some to check out the theatres
some to relax
walk the trails   ravines

Archer avoids for the moment
those he knows in the theatre
heads for an older area
on the south side
finds the house he looks for
still there
huddled on a renovated street
that he barely knows
Up to the door he goes
past the tiny yard
with its neat grass
old concrete walkway
up to the small porch
rings the bell

A pause
Then he hears a shuffle
the door slowly opens
there she is
now stooped
She looks at him for a moment
puzzled
then with surprised delight
"Ray?"
He answers her with the old nickname
he had used since a child
They embrace
"Come in, come in!"

She leads him into another age
the living room exactly as he remembers it
but even smaller than before
"I'll get some coffee."
She canes off to the kitchen
as he sits on the old worn couch
looks about him
the room furnished with her rocking chair
an armchair
fastened on one wall
a long curved pipe

ornately carved
with a hinged embossed cap
on the large bowl
below which
on a handmade bookcase
her now dead husband a carpenter built
knickknacks from the old country
Denmark he remembers
and an intricate Chinese puzzle
carefully carved by her husband
on the mantelpiece
surrounded by framed photographs
that include himself as a child
the ancient mantle clock
He senses again
the still silence of the room
accentuated by the steady tick
of the clock which many times
was the only conversation in the room

He sits there
lost in memories
until she calls to him
"It's ready.
Please carry it in for me."
He goes into the neat kitchen
brings back the tray
laden with its treasures
the old serving pot
the worn cups saucers
the dish with its sugared delicacies
Together
they retreat into a past world
For some time
they talk about his childhood
his parents
punctuated by lengthy pauses
When the old woman

drifts into reverie
he gently brings her back

Finally
both of them comfortably immersed
in this rich sea
"Can you tell me about when I was born?
My mother never talked about it."

For a moment she looks startled
shakes her head   looks away
only sound the clock's slow insistent tick

Archer can wait no longer
"At least tell me what you know."

She glances at him anxiously
her expression strained   conflicted
then looks far off
only the tick of the clock

He takes her hand
holding it
as they had done so many years before
"Please, Nan,
tell me."

She looks at him again
a brief smile at the old word used by him
then an odd expression flits across her face
She sighs with resignation
"Ya, it seems long enough ago.
I was, as you know, a young girl then,
my family just come from the old country,
and I came to live with your parents,
for we were poor and I did not know English yet,
and help your mother out
with the washing and the cleaning
and later, when you came, with you.
You know that you had no other relatives?"

He nods

"Well, your mother and your father
kept to themselves
and did not talk about their families,
I don't know why,
and no one came to visit them
except their friends here.
Ya."
She shakes her head
sighs again
falls into a lengthy reverie
through which he waits patiently
while the mantle clock
ticks inexorably on

Finally she rouses herself
her face determined
"But after I had been with them a while
I learned English as well as I could,
and one day I came into their bedroom
to clean
and found your mother there
with a white face
and the sheets below her
stained with blood
just as her husband rushed up the stairs
and quickly took her to the hospital.
After I had cleaned up
and he returned,
he told me that she had had a miscarriage
and that she could no longer have children."

Archer   startled
listens closely

Again she shakes her head
sighs
pauses while the clock ticks on and on
"A very little time after that
they returned one night with you,
a tiny baby, almost newborn,

and told me to tell anyone who asked
that you were their child
and that you should be told that too
as soon as you were old enough to ask.
I never knew where you came from
or who was your real mother and father,
but you know that your mother here
loved you, as did I."

The world lurches about him
his breath caught in that instant
as he realizes
in his very bones
on the electric surface of his skin
in the beating of his heart
sounding over the insistent clock
the import of what she has exposed

Then he feels her hand squeeze his
sees the love in her face
Images race through his mind
how the old woman had cared for him
when his parents weren't there
how he had nestled in her arms
as she rocked him
in the very rocking chair
in which now she sits
He realizes that neither woman
had had children
but had lavished their love on him
Then he remembers
when he was in his late teens
the terrible accident
when both his parents were killed
in a collision
that at the funeral
there were a few of their friends
his nanny   her husband
but still no family
that with the money

he inherited
money that was a mystery
he went away to train
left Edmonton
the old woman here
All these things
rush into his awareness
from her touch on his arm

For a moment there is silence
as he lets his breath return
as they look at each other
He returns her press on his hand
"Thank you for telling me this, Nan."

She smiles   hearing the old word again
he had always used
"I can't tell you any more, I'm afraid."

He pats her hand
"It's all right.
You've told me what I need to know."

They drink their coffee
eat the sweets
talk some more
their words punctuated still
by the omnipotent clock
Then he embraces her
they say goodbye
at the door
He leaves
knowing that he will
never see her again

In a daze
he walks
walks
until he reaches
the riverbank

that overlooks the great valley
He walks on
until he finds
a place he used to go
when young
that looks out west
over the far bend of the river
secret in the protecting bushes
He sits as he always did
looks at the winding river
the valley
flooded by the brilliant sun's light
hears the whines   buzzes
of mosquitoes   flies around him
all that are left on this crisp fall day
the trees yellow-leafed or bare
stark against the evergreens
the fading grass
He feels utterly alone

There is no point now   none
to thrash thicket   brush
to hack out discovery
of those who begot me
no point   no point at all
to pull back the dark veil
shading my adopters
their story so secret
fragmented   private
like chatter of the thrush

For a stark moment
fury like a banshee
screams through his booming skull
goading his thought to flail

A cipher my whole life
no stream   a rivulet
in shadows abandoned
left defenceless to wail

Or was I ripped from them
by violence beset?
Brief liaison's result
unfortunate love child?
What did I inherit
from that defiled union?
What genes prompt my actions
my impulses assail
inclination create
unknown drives abet?
Insidious the thought
my life unreconciled
ignorant history
hapless oblivion
Beyond the pale facade
upbringing beguiled
no touch of filial blood
only false assumption

All these decades   so many years   past my childhood   perpetually watching
old   young   all kinds   studying all I met   to understand their character
what I could use in my portrayals   the slant of the neck   shift of the
shoulder   curve of the arm   bend of the spine   the casual sudden gesture
the strides and hesitations   set of mouth   flare of nostril   line of brow
shade of the cheek   eyes darkened   wide   abstracted   glazed   innocent
vicious   whoever I met or lived with   searching within   sensuous presence
sensual touch   guarded apprehension   withdrawn fear   unfettered laugh
strain of anger   release of affection   source of humour   depth of anguish
all the scales   ornaments of emotion   the food for the actor

As a director   the journeys clarified from the ricochets of life   meaning
suffused into haphazard acts   always the spectator   even when making
gestures at demonstrations   protests   helping at accidents   fighting when
needed   all for my art   none for my life

His mind rebels
forces him
to create
find order
some meaning
within this maelstrom

of his thoughts
He responds
still within
the gales
of his mind

Song of the Actor

In the evening with its glare
On the footing with its abyss
Toward the darkened cavern dare
To make the metamorphosis

Expose the written figure's pain
Trace the tortured path he takes
Let your body show the strain
That his inner struggle makes

Find his voice and cry his word
Let them stroke or strike at those
In the harsh arena heard
And reveal the acts he chose

Lead throughout the unseen eyes
Force the throats to catch their breath
Help compassion's tears arise
From his misadventured death

Receive with grace and studied bow
The struck palms and throaty roar
But with the accolade know how
When to exit, keep from wanting more

So each night passes on the stage
So each repeats the tragic tale
So each word rises from the page
So each performance must prevail

Among the bushes
on the edge of the great bank
he sits in a maelstrom of terror

vulnerability
caught in the pitiless bright sun
Only after an eternity of minutes
has passed
can he breathe properly again
reassert his customary discipline
Only then can he arise
leave the old nest on the bank
walk the long distance
back to the bus

When he returns
he sees Gillian
"We should leave tomorrow."

She looks at him
surprised both by what he says
the tone in which he speaks
"I thought you wanted to stay several days."

He looks at her distantly
"I've changed my mind."

Disturbed by his manner
"Is everything all right?"

Brusquely
"Just do it."

Hurt by his abruptness
she nods   goes off
to tell the others
but she is worried
for she has never seen him
in this light before

That evening he cannot eat
Lies in the cubicle
His sense of his age
suddenly focuses
crystal clear
his six decades
a blur of action much of the time

with fragments of memory
that thrust out with jagged abruptness
He begins to sense
the first foreknowledge
of what it means to be old
to have lived long enough
to see perspectives
to have sketched his map
now to study
although his body
is still firm   strong
disciplined
the steady onset of the degeneration
Again the shredding in his mind
forced again
to clarify
by composition

Song of Despair

Always the inquisitive eye
gathers in the questioned landscape
contours of hills and people

Surges and sings the sea   the blood   dark brothers
in our blind propulsive youth
Those dawning early days when I stood tall and slim
restless from the blossoming muscle
a panther on the prowl   ready to devour
flesh and fact   enticement and allure of knowledge
carnal and prosaic   discovered and sublime
eager to learn all   but foremost   the mystery
of martial arts   the travelled symmetry
of rhythmic pattern   balanced mayhem

Always the inquisitive eye
probes the quintessential move
flashes new arrangements to the mind

Adrift in the waves   searching for the shore
we swim against the troughs and peaks
I learned the catechism of myself
from those who grew around and with me
the glances of those with whom I trained
admiring   some envious
witnessing my height   my uncoiling body
with ripostes physical and vocal
of the newly minted women
who in their covert notice of my presence
flushed   not with embarrassment
as I gradually discovered
catching the colour on the grocery clerk
the girl passing in the hall

Always the inquisitive eye
surprises the unexpected glance
the natural betrayal of response

To fight the rolling waters   find the way
our own navigation we create
even in the twilight exploration
of willing flesh and hopeful adoration
in the sustained and choric motion
of the martial class   of fellow exercise
Alone   apart   always on my own
discovering and possessing my particular thoughts
in the many routes I travelled
delving in exhilaration through the libraries
afforded by my young questing life
avoiding the normal minutiae of existence
testing the extravaganzas of my body's limits

Always the inquisitive eye
receives the flood sensation pours
without let and little hindrance

Or let the current lead us on in tide and wind
billowing our wayward-taken course
in the fascination of stretching
my range of portrayal   characters   personages
exploring the expressiveness of incorporation

pressing the limits of my voice's flexibility
riding the crest of rehearsals   performance
the pleasant distractions of a tour
plunged into the agony and mirth of plots
removed from those found in the streets
of towns and cities   of the pew and legislature
in all those places through which I sped

Always the inquisitive eye
looks inside only for the mirror
to shape the ricocheting exposed world

But in the lull   no trough nor wave
on all sides the illimitable ocean
Besotted in performance in all things
the demonstrations where I gesticulated
the stage   the meal   the night's entrancement
all a meal to masticate   to digest
looking for the limits of self
the boundaries of wonder
the full palate of emotion
always moving on
all a journey with no destination
other than the travel

Always the inquisitive eye
finds its station   place to focus
from which it sees in its refracted light

Where is the shore from which we came?
Where is the shore to which we labour?
My only anchor   my roots themselves
my parents   my only family
those who remain in feeling   in touch
the granite of my existence
as much the fiction of a drama
as any play that passes on the stage
I come from nowhere
with nothing as a hook   a starting point
cut loose   freedom that is no freedom
a void

Canto 17

LACUNA

The next morning
they leave on the final trek
to Vancouver

In the long winter
of Edmonton
sometimes
perhaps once or twice
perhaps not that winter
there is a terrible sky
of a bright metallic grey
a psychotic sky
that leaves those who see it
in a state of utter depression
that drags at them for hours
until night can give blessed relief
In the bus
as it speeds from the city
west toward the unseen Rockies
Archer brings the feeling of that sky
At breakfast he eats alone
he acknowledges no one
he enters the bus first
strides to his cubicle
leaving the troupe
disconcerted
discomfited
uneasy
Gillian tries to cheer them up
as she checks them out
their luggage
tries to hide her own concern
but when she takes the wheel

the bus trundles onto the highway
no one speaks
everyone sits gazing out the windows
lost in their own thoughts

When Gillian wheels into Jasper
she stops for their lunch break
While the troupe scatters off
to look at the town
decide where to eat
she goes back to the cubicle
discovers Archer lying on the bed
his eyes open
but seemingly vacant
not even brooding
"Ray, what is the matter?"

He says nothing
still staring at the ceiling of the bus

"Ray, please talk to me."
She sits on the edge of the bed
"Please tell me what is happening to you."
She takes his hand
unresponsive
Now more concerned by his
strange behaviour
she becomes softer
more intimate
"Ray, you mean a lot to me—
to the company as well.
If you can't tell me,
at least try to respond to me.
The atmosphere in the bus
is unbearable. Everyone is disturbed
by your behaviour.
None of us have ever seen you like this before.
Can you try to get up?
Come to lunch with me.
We don't need to see the others yet."
She tugs at his hand

He finally turns to her

She is shocked by his eyes
that look at her
with such a sense of desolation
that her breath catches in her throat
"Ray!"

She covers his chest with her body
holding him
stroking his hair gently
until finally she feels his breath
change
slightly

Then he stirs

She sits up again
still holding his hand

He sits up slowly
says nothing
but nods to her

They get up
leave the bus
her arm tightly around his waist
She finds a coffee shop
where she buys them sandwiches
coffee
She leads him to a small park
where they sit   silently eat
"You don't have to say anything,
but please sit with the rest of us
this afternoon?"

A long   indecipherable pause
then he nods

She gives him a hug
until he responds slightly
Then they return to the bus
her arm about him still

She seats him just behind her
so that he is close as she drives
then waits outside
to greet the others
as they straggle back
To each she says quietly
"Ray is not feeling well—
I would leave him alone
this afternoon
if you don't mind."

Concerned
each nods agreement
All smile at him
as they go to their seats
but none speak to him

Little is said that afternoon
but they let themselves
be lost in the sights
of the great gaunt mountains
rearing about them
Gillian stops a moment
at Mount Robson
to let them stare up
at the immense rock
in a rare moment
revealed without its normal
shrouds of clouds
She leads Archer out as well
but she notes that although
he looks upward
his attitude seems to
make it for him
an alien jagged menacing shaft
Shaken
she takes him back to the bus
They rumble off
through the final province
stopping again for a break

just outside Blue River
at a comfortable wooden
restaurant run by old-country Germans
where they have coffee
Archer with her at a separate table
drinking mechanically
looking as if with new eyes
at the scene around him

Back into the bus
the final run of the day
into Kamloops
Settled into the inevitable motel
the company goes off in small groups
for the evening
Gillian leads Archer
to have dinner in a restaurant
that looks out over the city
its valleys
its mountains
They sit there
as the city shines its own stars
into the firmament
As they eat
she chatters on
about arrangements for next year
about what they will do
when they reach Vancouver
Archer says nothing
but sits
empty-eyed
eating mechanically
As in the spring
the torrents from the melting peaks
rush down to swell the river
which as it now swirls downstream
rises to threaten its resisting banks
so Gillian's concern
distends to desperation

With dinner done
she wheels the bus
into its nocturnal home
then leads Archer
silent   unresisting
to his cubicle

Like a mother with a sleepy child
who helps her passive son
out of clothes   into bed
so Gillian with Archer
For a long moment
she watches him lie
passive
eyes staring at the ceiling
then she sits on the bed's edge
takes his unresponsive hand
in the shadowed space
talks quietly to him
of the present tour
the members of the company
of Vancouver
of the months past
when he lived in the bus
next to her own house
Finally
as she jerks upright
realizes that she has begun to doze
she sees that his eyes
have shut
Wearily
still uneasy over his condition
she returns to her motel room
to collapse exhausted
into a restless sleep

The next day
Archer appears for breakfast
no longer abrupt

or silent
but still distant
In the bus
he sits alone
staring at the waves of peaks
as the bus soars over the Coquihalla
then down   across the Delta
over the innumerable ridges
into the busy ant hill
of Vancouver
Gillian lets off the company
at different locations
then eases the bus
into its familiar slot
As the day declines
she walks around her house
chatting continually with him
but still finds no response
even when at sunset
they walk among the trees

That night
not letting him return to the bus
she leads him to her bedroom
undresses him   herself
then lies against his still body
flesh against flesh
whispers close to his ear
all that they have done together
As she relives her life with him
holding him close
now exhausted from the stress
of caring both for the company
for him
her own feelings well up
uncontrollably
As tears trickle
from her cheeks
to his

she whispers
in involuntary gasps
how deeply she still loves him
then
nothing left to give
lapses into silence
A long   heartrending   silence

Then
with a cry
Archer turns to her
to her surprise
then swift surrender
fiercely makes love
At last
both soaked
Gillian lies in his arms
as he tells her
what he has learned
his sense of being in a void
no links to any past
any meaning
his fear
of never making real contact
with anyone
that all of what he is doing
has done
has lost its meaning
along with his own
that over this time
as she has struggled with him
finally this night
she has pulled him back
her confession
the true breaking of his spell
She smiles at him
presses close to him
in relieved exhaustion
falls asleep

For a time
he watches her
in the soft glow
of the moon
through the shaded window
sees
her face softened   innocent
as she had been
those twenty years before

halos of light   slight heat on face   touch of flesh   on my side   my chest   the cradle of my arm   shoulder   the soft light through the blinds   late morning not the bus   her bedroom   her hair across her face nestled against my neck across me as well   that face   so relaxed   at peace   contentment not seen before   those well-known lips   slightly parted in their serene curve   her white arm relaxed across my chest   her fingers slipped from my cheek to neck   her body   familiar terrain   now fresh discovered territory   her leg warm over my hip   all new   everything given in the night   not taken

As he wonders
searching through the desolation
of these recent dark days
like the slow inexorable pull
of a sluggish tide
against the swiftly moving current
of the emptying river
he feels again
the vacant past
the shroud of substitute affection
his descent to an infinity
of absence
fought by her
with all she had
to spark new feeling in him
She stirs
her eyes open   wide
as she realizes him beside her
She glances at him
unguardedly
her body tenses

He smiles   gently kisses her eyelids
She sighs
snuggles closer
lies there in complete relaxation

As an old house revisited
after a long age's passage
seems somehow familiar
its dust still invested
with inconsequential memories
yet is now seen fresh again
corners   ledges seen
as if for the first time
angles of light through elderly glass
shining on floors from which are removed
the carpeted remembrances of days past
all seen through the lenses
of wavering time
so in the next few days
these two old friends   lovers
find themselves
as if in the first new continuing hours
apart from bed   brushing by each other
in the unexpected surprises of domestic intimacy
old habits pried apart
new customs haphazardly erected
Archer had always felt compassion
for his women
for all of them he had made
small deposits of affection
enjoyed their company   their bodies
but never had he entered this strange wilderness
where vulnerability brushed against vulnerability
reaching out   reaching in   were matched
Days alternate between a haze of strange emotions
the sharp clarity of the new discovered movements
Actions   tones   expressions
of the other
intensify as they spend much of the time

on her property
or walking on the beaches
except when dealing with
the unexamined prospects of shopping
the minutiae of a daily maintenance

Over the days
when fog drifts in
with its hoarse bellows
or the laden clouds
dark   grey
give up their torrents
so that all glistens green or slick
the euphoria of those first new-found days
begins to drift away
like the mists on the still water
Dreams begin to jostle in his mind
with the sense of betrayed loss
Then he turns inwards once again
broods
until Gillian
works gently   persistently
to bring him back to her
each time reaches   never lets him go
But still the dreams creep back
within his sleeping   unprotected   mind

*out in the bushes   the trees   fall days   leaves not yet ready to drop   sound
of the two pairs of boots   cracking twig   rustle of dry vegetation underfoot
air crisp   chill   cheeks reddening above the windbreaker   the rifle long
heavy barrel cold with metal grey   cradled carefully   checked for no 22s
lurking in the chamber   all their little leaden noses   neat metal bottoms
snug in their cardboard bed   looking ahead   pushing the raking branches
from before the face   a space opens up guarded by the barbed-wire fence
old tin   rusted past its days   smells   carefully balanced on the post   father
leaning over me   showing me how to load the side chamber   slip each little
missile past the yielding gate   then kneeling so that the four arms work
together   butt against shoulder   left arm on the distant stock   cheek
against the cold metal   one eye closed   the other sighting the tiny slab to
intersect the far-off   vee   farther off the can   keep from wavering   assisted*

by larger hands   hold still   gently pull the expectant trigger   the sudden sharp noise   slight kick into the shoulder   can off the post   father laughing happily   his look   his look   no chill nor cold now   he likes what I have done   he likes me

At times
as she struggles tenderly
to wrench him from the abyss
he seems to shift in his body
like a badly synchronized rotogravure
sense himself
sense her deep released love
sense his own response
as he writhes back to her

so young   light from the sun   slowly flickering out   as my mother   father dress to go out   mother in a silk slip drifting over her slender form at the dresser mirror brushing her hair   its sheen caught in the dresser lamp father adjusting studs in his tuxedo shirt   fragments of their conversation floating past   not understood   "deal   work on him   I'll take the wife prospects look good   we'll arrange it"   I don't know them with these words quietly spoken between them   oh   shut out   oh   left out   oh   oh   leaving me   mustn't go   cry   father looks at me in irritation   cry harder   mother sighs   puts down her brush   picks me up   holds me against the softness of her breast   want to stay enclosed by that warm scented softness   mother calls   Nan comes   passed over to another warm softness   but the wrong smell   cry   but held   walked until the smell no longer matters   just the breathing softness   until I   sleep

Long slow walks again
along the beach
vague   indistinguishable
in the fog
or on other grey days
in clear curves against the leaden sea
but different from those previous walks
awareness of two walking now
together
as one
subtly linked

discovering how the other walks   moves
sees
conversation
wrapped in this awareness

One morning
light dim through the blinded windows
Gillian awakes first
turns to look
at the man
so relaxed in sleep
beside her
She lies there
absorbed in him
looking more clearly at him
than she had for a long
long time
She sees his hair
still luxurious
losing the battle
with its grey invader
sees the face
drowned in sleep
now has the lines
of his experience
etched sharply
on brow   forehead
mouth and jaw
as she remembers
twenty years before
when they had lain like this
how then his hair was still dark
innocent of age
how the lines had just begun
how firm his profile
his chin
the chiselled lips
which now are slightly
very slightly

thinner
She remembers
how she
so young
had been lost in him
his maturity
vigour
Now
as she studies him
she sees his age
beginning
almost imperceptibly
to make inroads
She realizes
herself now at the age
he had been then
how the erosion of the years
wears gently
on them both
Her love for him
grows more
in the flickering insight
She lets herself
lie close and still
beside him

Then Archer has another dream

*coming up the porch   step into the hall   doors closed to the living room
but the sound of mother's voice   can't make out the words   but the tone
desperate   look through the glass panels of the doors   do not be seen   she's
talking on the phone   vehemently gesturing   but the look on her face never
seen before   anguished   up to my room   hear her leave hurriedly   last
time I see her   that day the accident   but the look   the look*

The haunting of this dream
stays with him several days
but still he keeps from himself
the circumstances of their death
remembering only

the sense of loss
the tidy report made by police
With the new sense of loss
he feels no compunction
to open that door again
tries to lock it shut
but finds the lock broken   unusable

At Christmas
Gillian decides to hold a party
for those members of the company
still in the city
Almost all come
except for Ann
now at home with her family
Archer has been reluctant
for he has always been
a solitary man
who shuns most parties
not dealing with his companies
but she persuades him
that his last moments with them
had been unsettling for them all
what better way to test
his new-found attitude
than at such a gathering
As it turns out
he even helps her decorate
the tree   house
finds
much to his surprise
he takes pleasure
in the work together
Gradually the house fills
with people   warmth
As they arrive
each person is curious
apprehensive
of how Archer will be

but all are pleasantly surprised
at his open friendly manner
in greeting them   talking
different from that last brusque departure
even from his slightly distant manner
in the past
As food is consumed   drink flows
the happy babble in the crowded rooms
grows to a good party's din
Then Archer and Gillian
herd them together
He addresses them
"Gillian and I..."

All note both their names mentioned

"...are very happy that you all have come."

Chuckles   enthusiastic response

"But before all else..."

A hush

"...I want to apologize
for my behaviour those last days
as we returned."

Greater stillness

"In Edmonton I had a shock,
received a great personal shock,
which I should never have let interfere
with us."

No dissent
but still attentive silence

Then
turning to her at his side
"But Gillian has worked hard
to help me in my distress.
I give her my deepest thanks

and gratitude.
I owe her more now than I can tell."
He takes her hand
smiles at her
In the glowing expression
on her face
all can see now openly
the deep feelings stirred between them
The rush of good humour
stays through the party
for the two
into Christmas itself
which they celebrate on their own
exchanging gifts
a carved Haida bracelet for her
that Archer had requested Ann find him
for him a tiny mask carved from argillite
in the old Haida style

Now in the dank   wet
deep in Vancouver's winter
even as Archer works on the inevitable revisions
to the Canadian epic
still with the smart of unknown parents
unsettling him
he begins to look in the past
turns to what he finds
he has become

For over forty years
no home
so many countries   places
on the road
even by Gillian's house
living in the bus
searching   responding
looking with clear eyes
at people   at our lives
exploring
always
a wanderer

He glances at the books
on Gillian's shelf

Odysseus—
strange   my eyes drawn to him—
a wanderer too
an exile
fighting to get home
I have no home
My life a search
to explore what we live
what it means
and the way to present it

As he thinks more
about the intricate past
he finds his sense of his own ordeal
is deepened
and the first hints of a new work
begin to infiltrate his mind
But he pushes them away
to lurk in dark recesses

The green months
in Vancouver
with the rains   showers
let the buds burst gloriously
everywhere
But the company has no time
for this vernal episode
as all converge in the east
in a Toronto awaiting its first blush
of spring in April

On the first day
the space buzzes
as those from Vancouver
tell the others of the strange episode
with Archer
his new relationship
with Gillian

The buzz ceases as they enter
all eyes anticipating what they expect to see
but the two are utterly professional
as Archer tells of the new revisions
Gillian gives the details of the eastern tour
Then the work begins as before
but Ingrid   Mahira watch avidly
for any sign that might betray
the new relationship
but none appears

So the month wears on
as the troupe gets back in condition
learns the adjustments Archer wants
the crew refurbishes the equipment
the costumes   masks   elements
learns new cues

May opens with a sunny day
with the show in Toronto
for its first week
As usual
Gillian has made good use
of the past run
Critics come to see
what changes have been made
if there is improvement
The audience includes
some who saw the previous version
some Natives
more younger people
curious to see an unusual show
Now that the epic is better known
those who have driven in
from historic towns in the region
respond with great animation
to episodes that reflect their past
The tides of those
who believed in one side or the other
roll to and fro

as do those sections that depict the First Peoples
All the currents
highly charged
bring new dimensions to the work
as the grand sweep of the country's struggles
becomes more vivid in the political colourings
that blaze out in the excited audience
the shape of the whole
shifting according to the regions affected
At the end
enthusiastic applause shouts
then in clusters
the audience streams away
still deep in argument
the occasional quarrel
Reviews the next day
centre on this new dimension
almost to the neglect of the work itself
but the result is that
a new sea of people come to see it
during that short run in Toronto

In Ottawa the next week
the atmosphere is almost the same
except that many embassies are present
to observe this Canadian phenomenon
find themselves jostled
by the different factions that rise up
in response to their storied places
Then off to Montreal
where in the Olympic Stadium
the splits show most among the first three great inhabitants
First Peoples French English
as the struggles roil throughout the centuries
Then the Maritimes
fraught with their own embroilments
Acadians Loyalists
the ever-present First Nations
Finally to Newfoundland

with its own struggles to survive
shame of the Beothuk extermination
turbulent union with another country
Then   finally   the country covered
the tour ended
all prepare for Ireland

ACT THREE
2007

Canto 18

IRELAND

After the time-shifted night drones by
the eastern sun lingers on the tops of clouds
wisping below
the glinting ocean
that floods horizons every which way
before it shifts to illuminate
first a thin edge of land
then the land itself in all its mottled glory
that now comes closer in the long descent
until hills rush by   then lush fields
winding ribbons crawling with ants
that now clarify into roads   then streets
then houses   then the landing strip
rushing up   the jolt   squeal of tires
straining under the huge weight
then the settling down in the long taxi
the quiet stop at Dublin airport
The usual interminable wait as aisles pack
with those reaching for bags   all other things
associated with long trips
before released into the articulated passageway
the journey to Customs
declarations of living elsewhere
the stamping of passports done importantly
by bored courteous officials
then the exeunt to the main hall
where a sign held by an attractive red-haired woman
as if from every Irish movie made
wearing a summer print dress
greets Archer   Gillian   all the rest
of the sleep-shorn troupe

"Mr. Archer, I presume?" she says
as they move near her

He nods introduces Gillian beside him

"Ah, you're the one for me to really know
with all you've sent me and our words together.
Well, I'm Maura, as you may have guessed—
and no jokes about my Irish name and hair!"

The whole group
now a tight bundle round her
chuckle are disarmed
"If you're an example of what we can expect,
we must have landed in Paradise!"
exclaims Patrick
never one to miss an opportunity

"Ah, get on with you! You must have Irish blood
to talk so—what's your name?"
When she hears she gives a light clear laugh
"There! What did I tell you?"
Then abruptly businesslike
she explains in her soft voice accent
how she represents the Council
giving its Gaelic name so strange alien
to their ears
"But this is not the place to have a conference.
Let's get you to your lodgings first."

Outside in the teeming access
a minibus large van drivers
Troupe piles in one
luggage piles in the other
Maura leads the caravan
into the maw of Dublin
down narrow streets
some still cobbled
to a small hotel
modest but neat clean
briskly deals with reserved rooms

sends off the troupe
still slightly dazed
to their respective quarters
then leads Archer and Gillian
to a tea room
"No time yet for the pub, I think."

There they hold a council of war
"Well, I must say we have received high news of you,
both from our embassy and yours—
you'll have a lot to live up to."

Taken aback
Archer and Gillian look at her sharply
see she may have spoken with some wit
but what she says she means

Archer smiles   looks straight in her eyes
"Embassies always have high hopes
for what they sponsor.
We'll just try to live up to those expectations."

Their eyes lock for a brief moment more
then she smiles   lowers her gaze
Gillian sees that she is now
more impressed with them

"Now, about your schedule.
I see you require stadiums,
and we have worked hard to get them,
what with the leagues gearing up as well."

Both Gillian and Archer understand
what she must have gone through

"I thought, since you play at festivals,
it would be grand to travel down the coast road
to see some of these venues
before you start off in Cork."

They nod   happy to see in advance
where in some places they will play
Then she gets down to details

the minibus   van   drivers
that will be at their call throughout
the schedules of festivals   their playing dates
accommodation
the need for their technicians to check the electrics
Then   smiling
"A few quiet words of advice, if you don't mind,
that may help you in the long run.
We Irish are a relaxed people,
and our sense of time has the same flavour."
Another clear laugh
"You have no idea what I went through
to get to you on time.
As it went, the delay in your coming through from Customs
saved my life!"

Appropriate chuckle from the others

"And another thing.
We tend not to like authority—
too much of it in the past, if you get my meaning."

A nod of understanding

"As a result, don't deal in an officious manner
with those assigned to you at each festival
or with your drivers.
Things will go much better if your dealings
are amiable."

A grin from them
"We will try to be congenial—
but if you are any example,
how could we not?"

"Ah, get along with you!
I expect you'll do all right,
given you've learned the blarney already."

Universal chuckle

"Now, I'll tag along with you
while you drive down the coast

to help you with your contacts along the way,
and see your first performance in Cork,
at which there will be lots of high mucky-mucks,
let me tell you!"
Then as she pays the bill
"Oh, and another charming Irish custom is
that since I paid for this round
it's only proper that you buy the next—
and I expect a round from each of you!"
Then she leads them back to their hotel
sweeps off down the cobbled street
leaving them bemused
at this first encounter with Irish culture

A day of rest   casual exploration
knowing that they will have more time
in Dublin at the tour's end
Then the real business begins
finding the container now arrived
transferring the exotic contents
to the large van whose driver watches
with undisguised fascination
They stay in Dublin that night
with the troupe taking their drivers
to a pub of the two Irishmen's choice
Next morning   or part of it
the troupe straggles together
some showing the effects of Irish conviviality
All check out   stow their luggage
Maura arrives in her small car
to lead the procession off on its voyage
followed by Paddy driving the minibus
Kevin driving the van
accompanied by Amy
with whom he has already struck up
a warm   garrulous relationship
Down the M50 they proceed
where in the bus Paddy reels off the names
of the small places

which are clearly signed
then into Wicklow itself

"Wicklow."
Paddy intones
"Cill Mhantáin, the Church of the Toothless One."
Laughing he brings the bus
to a stop behind their leader's car
the van close behind

They are on a street before which
a great expanse of beach curves round
a hospitable bay
When they look the other way
they see the inevitable pub
to which their leader with the flaming hair
wearing yet another immaculate print dress
leads them now
Inside   like a cabin in an old sailing vessel
the place is of dark wood   smells of ale
with light fighting its way through front windows
leaded   latticed
Rising at a table to greet them is a threesome
an older woman   imposing in skirt   light wool sweater
her face composed in a mixture of greeting and authority
two younger persons   in their late twenties
one a woman with thick curly black hair
pert face
dressed aggressively in T-shirt
GREYSTONE ARTS FESTIVAL!
blazing from her bosom
tight inexpensive jeans
the other a man with thinning sandy hair
sharp-featured
also in a FESTIVAL! T-shirt   jeans

The older woman   in a constrained majestic voice
"Good morning to you, Maura..."

Although it was just past noon
her tone implied that they had been expected
a little earlier

"...it's good to see you again."

"And you, Mrs. FitzGerald.
Please let me introduce our Canadian troupe."

She introduces each of the troupe
with what Archer suspects is a sly twinkle in her eye

"And this is Mrs. FitzGerald,
who leads the Festival Council,
and two of its members, Nora and Sean."

All nod to each other
the Noras smiling at each other

"Now, please join us for lunch."
Mrs. FitzGerald's look   tone
make it clear that only Archer   Gillian
Maura are intended by the invitation
to sit with them
Amy catches Gillian's eye
leads the others to tables
tactfully away from the vicinity
of this special table
which it is evident has been held
and used
by the Council members
well before the troupe has arrived

They sit down as Mrs. FitzGerald intends
Archer on one side   Maura on the other
Gillian between the other two
Conversation is first punctuated
by her suggestions as to what Irish dishes they should choose
to which good-naturedly they accede
then she expounds on the scenic virtues of Wicklow
which she is pleased to hear they do not know
not having stepped before on Ireland's sacred turf
Everyone is now warm with food   ale
but Gillian notices that the other two keep silent
Mrs. FitzGerald herself
seems worried about something

yet reticent
given the circumstances how could they do otherwise
to speak of it

At last the meal finished
a drink in hand
she turns to the subject of the festival
extolling its virtues   uniqueness
A slight hesitation
then
"But there is a small problem
about what you require.
Sean can fill you in."

All eyes turn to look at him
He swallows   then says
"Your show sounds fantastic…"

"Yes!" seconds Nora enthusiastically

"…but apparently you require a stadium,
which we do not have."

Archer   Gillian look sharply at him

He bravely presses forward
"The closest one is Aughrim Park,
about twenty kilometres away,
which is nothin' in your huge country,
but would keep it far
from the festival proper here.
We're wonderin', then,
what to do."

A long silence
even against the garrulous bedlam of the pub
while Archer and Gillian look at each other
Maura closely watches both
Then Archer smiles
ignoring Mrs. FitzGerald
speaks to the two nervous ones
"I'm sure you can come up with something.

We need a stadium for four reasons:
to shield us from noise outdoors;
to provide some way of limited access
for our audience;
to give us a source of power for our equipment;
and to provide a well-groomed
level ground on which our objects can move smoothly.
Now, the last is the most important,
along with the need for power.
Can you think of what you might have
in this line? A soccer pitch,
or playing fields with lights,
or even the playing grounds of a school?"

The faces before him lose their strain
Soon both are babbling enthusiastically
about possibilities
"Those pitches beside the town?"

"I don't know if they have lights."

"The school would have the power."

Archer interrupts amiably
"Why don't we go have a look right now?
Thanks for the lunch, Mrs. FitzGerald.
I'm sure you don't want to be involved
in these technicalities.
We look forward to seeing you
when we come to perform."

He gives her a disarming smile
before she can reply
ushers the group out
making sure Gillian tells Amy
to bring the technicians with them
send the troupe off to the beach
away from pubs
of which for the moment some of them
have had their fill
then organize themselves

In the minibus Archer   Sean sit at the front
Amy   Gillian on the other side from them
Maura   Nora behind Archer
the technicians behind Amy
They cruise the city for appropriate venues
checking for mains   facilities
noise separation without their own disturbance
for a neighbourhood
finally fix on the playing fields
with Amy   technicians
in deep consultation
with the dazed happy festival reps

When in the late afternoon they return
to the other vehicles
Maura turns to Archer
gives him a mock bow of respect
"Well, you've won your spurs today!
I had no idea how you would solve this one,
over which we have all been scratching our heads,
let me tell you!"

Archer smiles
"We can solve anything if the possibility exists.
But it would be nice to know ahead of time
what the problem is."
With a look that Gillian knows well
he stares at Maura
"Do you have any other surprises for us?"

Startled
slightly shaken
her smile now slipped away
she answers seriously
"No, thank God! And I here apologize
on behalf of all of us
for putting you in this position.
Forgive me, Mr. Archer."

Her sincerity
as well as the quaintness of her formal address

makes him smile again
"All is forgiven, believe me.
But now what happens?
It's getting late to be on the road again."

"I'm surprised you solved the problem
so easily. I anticipated you would probably take much longer
and so have booked you into a hotel here."

Archer laughs
"Gillian, you and Amy round up everyone
and we'll check in.
And warn them not to dawdle in their rooms—
we'll do a session on the beach in an hour."

They look at him in amazement

"We're not here on a holiday.
We've been apart two weeks
and must get in shape again."

Off they go
Maura shakes her head
"A taskmaster, that's what you are.
But you're right, you know."

In the late   golden   afternoon
the sun still proud in the sky
the inhabitants of Wicklow could see on the beach
among the late splashers   sunbathers
a group flowing through
the stately beautiful motions
of Tai Chi

Soon after
dinner at another pub
that Maura knew
where all sit together
"There is a nice little band here
that you might like to hear."

Ears perk up for the troupe's musicians
who look at each other   grin

During the meal Maura sits again
beside Archer   Gillian
with Patrick close by
The conversation ranges both ways
with Maura fielding questions
about the festivals in Ireland generally
those in which they would play specifically
the troupe
particularly Archer
responding about their work
the theatre in Canada
In a while a small band drifts in
tunes up   starts to play
The atmosphere is warm
the playing sweet
but then Nora whispers to Paddy
who   startled   nods   rises
leaves with several of the others

Maura is concerned
"Do they not like what they hear?"

Gillian grins
"You'll know soon enough."
Sure enough
in a few minutes they return
with the instruments

"Can we join you?"
With a dazzling smile
Nora asks in a way they cannot deny
Room is made for them
instruments are tuned
then fiddle answers fiddle
flutes correspond with the drum   the *bodhrán*
the trumpet darts among them all
More of the pub regulars arrive
Soon pleasure overflows
including that from the bartender's spigots
Tunes vary from the sprightly
to that unique plain of Irish melancholy

Maura is entranced by it all
"You seem to have no end of surprises!"

"You haven't seen our show yet,"
chuckles Gillian

Maura looks at her with speculative eyes
"I'm looking forward to that."

Archer rises quickly
"I'm going for a walk on the beach."
Gillian sees that he needs to be alone
nods goodbye
he silently disappears from the pub

"What an interesting man your director is."
her eyes following him out

"More than you will ever know,"
Gillian wryly replies
"but he is unique in Canada too."

"Well, you've had your work cut out for you!"

A laugh   part proud   part wry again
"It has had its problems—
but the excitement of the quality
not knowing what to expect next
makes it all worthwhile."
For a moment she looks where he has gone

"Ah," says Maura
"Are you two in a relationship?"

"You could say so—among the many relationships we've had
over the past twenty years."
Maura sees Gillian does not want to pursue the subject
lets it drop
turning to a discussion of what it is like
to be a woman in the arts
in Ireland   Canada
They talk until hoarse
through the happy bedlam of the pub

until Patrick attempts to get involved
without success

Archer leaves the pub   its sounds
far behind him
as he walks along the great sweeping beach
Clear unbeclouded night
a moon still waiting for her fullness
lighting the calm rolling sea
with the oily sheen its gift
the restless   restless murmur of the sea
as it caresses the passive sand
He surveys the comfortable harbour
with its south punctuated by Brides Head's rocky headland
that of Wicklow Head

The most eastern point of the Republic's mainland

In the west the rolling Wicklow Hills
rising stark in the clear night sky
Archer
who as always has done his homework
turns back again to the harbour

He chuckles
then loses himself in the beauty of the night

Morning sidles in
on the backside of a drizzle
matching the mood of a subdued troupe
many recovering from nights of conviviality
Gillian trundles them into their respective vehicles
after a low-keyed breakfast with Maura   Archer
With a wave to the lead car
off they drive again
Archer is very quiet
subduing somewhat Paddy's narrative
Gillian can see he has been brooding
but she knows he will talk to her
when he is ready

On this rush through dreamland
Archer
who has been gazing across Gillian
at the passing scenery
finally speaks
"This will be more dangerous than I had thought."

Gillian looks at him quizzically

"All this conviviality and beauty."

Reproachfully
"Oh, Archer, we haven't even begun the tour proper!
Surely we can enjoy ourselves for these few days at least,
get rid of jet lag, and get to know the country."

A sigh
"Of course. It's good to have this break
after a long tour—and you're right,
we do need to know the country.
But we also will be performing within a week
and will have to be back in shape
physically and mentally
to work under such conditions as we just saw."

Gillian grimaces   shrugs
"I understand that.
So what do you suggest we do?"
He leans closer to her
to describe his plan

Farther along
Waterford approaches
Archer again peering out

Even as he ponders
the procession winds into the town
passing through the Georgian Mall
parking near the town square
with its bricked road
streets veering from it
with its dark stone-slabbed benches

its three lines of trees
pleasantly shading the thoroughfare

Again a pub for lunch
again a small delegation
but this time no problems
After lunch   pleasant conversation
with representatives who are young   bright
knowledgeable
all go off to see the stadium
Walsh Park turns out to be a fine location
The technicians quickly make note
of all necessary for the show
while Gillian checks the business details
By mid-afternoon they have finished
Archer leads them in a full physical routine
Then all return with a satisfied Maura
to the town
Again she has booked them for the night
anticipating any problem that might rear up
They take the time to stroll about
That night they scatter
to eat   enjoy the pubs
the musicians taking their instruments with them

The next dry-eyed morning
they leave at ten for Cork
Then to their lodgings in this early afternoon
then to lunch
While the others stay there
Maura takes Archer and Gillian
to the office of the Manager of the Festival
a maelstrom of activity
from which streams before them
dispersing like a spray
musicians   clowns   actors   others in strange dress
all colours   languages

Out from her office to greet them
comes the Manager

young dark-haired harried sunny
who gives them a bright smile
shakes their hands vigorously
"Well, I must say we're all looking forward
to seeing your show.
And you've certainly brought in the big guns politically—
ambassadors and ministers and God knows who else.
I suppose the members of your Council are sitting up there
waiting to see what happens here and how they should act
when it plays up there?"

Maura makes a good-natured face at her

"Now, you're on for the second week,
and that first show should be something
with all those Important People attending.
To soften them up, Cork is sponsoring a luncheon
for you with the guests coming down from Dublin
the day before you open."

Until this point no one else can say a word
but now Archer speaks in a voice that permits no interruption
"Thank you for all that you are doing for us.
Maura has shown us how much you help us."

Maura herself is uncertain how to take this

"I will leave Gillian to deal with the business side,
but we need to know when we can have the facility
and for how long each day,
both for our rehearsals and performances."

The Manager grins
"Ah, sure, that's no problem.
We've got the teams to give up the turf
these two whole weeks."

All three of her guests smile with relief
"Then I should ask if you can have someone
take us to the stadium
so that we can check it out
and begin unloading."

She looks at him   surprised
"You mean now?"

"I can't think of a better time."

For a moment she is still
thinking furiously
then she pulls out her cell phone
gets someone on the other end
to find   bring to her office
the appropriate production manager
"I can see that you don't waste any time."

"With this show we can't afford to.
And I'm glad to see you don't waste time either."

"With this festival I can't afford to."

They grin at each other

"Now, Gillian, let's get the rest of the details sorted out,
then you can go off and do your showy things."

She drags Gillian into her office
even as a sweat-stained young man
hurries up to them
"You must be Ray Archer, am I right?"

Archer nods

"Then let's go get done what must get done."

"Do you want to come with us?"

"I wouldn't miss this for the world,"
replies Maura
her eyes shining
"I haven't had this much fun for years!
Working on a council is not the best way
to have adventures, you know,
and I'll take them when I can get them."

"I won't guarantee that this will be fun,
but you're welcome to come."

Off they go in her car
to collect the van   the technicians
drive to the southeast of the city
to Páirc Uí Rinn Stadium proclaiming Christy Ring
"Famed Cork and Glen Rovers hurler,"
the host technician explains
"You've no doubt heard of him?"
All   except Maura   acknowledged their ignorance
Sighing at the Canadian lack of education
he leads them in
All looks well
The task of setting up begins

In the afternoon the whole troupe assembles
by the now-completed set-up
Maura continues to attend

"Well, here it is, thanks to our technicians
and our hosts…"

Appreciative responses from the actors

"…and now it's up to us all to be ready."

Appropriate serious hush

"Three days from now we open,
and Maura…"

Enthusiastic cheers from some of the troupe

"…Maura has informed us that
there will be many dignitaries attending,
so it will probably be the most important
of our performances."

An even more serious hush

"We have not performed for over two weeks,
and given the demands of the show,
we need to get back into condition.
And so, here is the schedule.
This afternoon, a full warm-up,

then break for dinner,
then back for exploration,
and finally a tech run
to make sure of everything.
Tomorrow and the next day
warm-ups, explorations, tightening of scenes
in the afternoon;
in the evening, the usual routine and performance.
On opening night, the usual routine again,
with a warm-up late in the afternoon."
He pauses briefly
then seems to grow taller before them all
"Until after the first performance
you must stay away from the pubs,
from any distractions from the festival itself,
and think through your characters and what you do.
We are rusty, and we need to learn to concentrate again.
In ten minutes we will start."

The troupe   now purposeful
moves away to prepare
while Maura looks at him   shakes her head
"Well, you're the Puritan now, aren't you?
The whole thing sounds like an army camp."

He smiles at her
"Wait till the day is finished.
Then tell me what you think."

She looks at him dubiously
then is directed to sit in the stands
For the next two hours
she watches the extensive regime
of exercise   exploration
that by this time the company
can enter into fully
to gain back what is lost from
two inactive weeks

After dinner
the sun still fighting off the night

she watches fascinated
as the masks   puppets are revealed
the exploration becomes more complex
Finally twilight   the tech begins
She begins to realize the size   scope
of the production through its sheer visual impact
as well as the music   the sounds
The tech progresses slowly and patiently
By the evening's end
the old habits   the timing begin to assert themselves
As everything is carefully stowed
the actors return to their own clothes
she approaches Archer again
"I think I'm beginning to understand.
Can we talk about it over a drink?"

A look
"I'm just like them,
barred from socializing
these next few nights.
If you like, we can talk at lunch,
but I have to think through adjustments
that may need to be done.
I'll see you then."
He leaves her to join the others
in the minibus
as she   still shaking her head at what she's seen
drives off alone

Over the pre-show days
each member finds a place to work alone
each rehearsal deepens
as old impulses are newborn
Maura sees the huge production
slowly emerge as from a chrysalis
each night with new wonders unfolding

All this time Gillian has been busy
working the media
checking the business details

Interviews with Archer   others
occupy the mornings

Finally the day arrives of the luncheon
with various dignitaries
Maura   her boss from the Republic's Council
the Manager   her group
Canada's ambassador is there
along with several representatives
from Foreign Affairs
Although it is evident
that he has never really heard of the group before
he has been briefed
gives a bland welcome from the Government
as does the Irish representative
with much more charm
the Mayor who says how grand it is
that this show would come all the way from Canada
at which the Manager raises her eyebrows
given that many of the events have been international
for years
All say
with varying degrees of sincerity
how much they look forward to seeing the production
Archer responds with gentle humour
but lets his own formidable authority show briefly
to impress the crowd
All leave satisfied in mind   stomach

Opening night
Special buses bring some audience from downtown
cars begin to fill the stadium parking lot
limousines drop off the important guests
who   bemused   find themselves without seats
standing with everyone else
The production is scheduled for nine-thirty
while the sky is still tinted with the sunset

In the gloom the show begins
as it always has

The audience of seven hundred or so
are first absorbed by the physical nature of the event
its sounds
particularly the drums of Ann   Yumiko
but gradually the strains of the story
begin to form for them
they are caught up in the action
At intermission the babble is good-natured
the bar   carefully designed for the event
is well attended
Then with the second half
the Irish elements begin to sound
the audience becomes more attentive
as time goes on
the immigrations
before the potato famine
during
after
Fenian raids
Orangemen
Donnellys
great construction stories
the Irish influence
Many in the audience lose themselves
in such old events
shouting encouragement or attacking
figures such as D'Arcy McGee
or John A. Macdonald
The atmosphere in the space
becomes electric
even more so
as the two World Wars
with the Depression between
barrage them with their tragedies
igniting memories of Easter 1916
Civil War
the ripping apart of the island
with the creation of the new Republic
the entrenchment of the six provinces

The story of Canada is almost lost
for the audience
as they remember   revive their own legends
Only the strength of the playing
the power of the production
finally bring them together
When it finishes
the weary cast stumbles forward on the platforms
the audience give way to cheers   tears
The dazed actors cannot leave the area
because of those who crowd around them
eager to tell their own stories
Archer is surrounded by the dignitaries
who congratulate him
particularly those of the Canadian delegation
their Irish counterparts
relieved yet apprehensive after the
electric moments they have witnessed

When they are finished
Maura rushes up
gives Archer a huge kiss and hug
"Ah, I've been wanting to do that for a long time now!"
she says breathlessly
"And here are my compatriots
and the Manager and hers.
What wonderful work! What wonderful,
wonderful work! And I'm so happy
I could watch it come to life here! Thank you!"
She gives him another long passionate kiss
Then the others crowd around excitedly
to give their congratulations too

"Now, surely you can release your poor benighted people
to enjoy themselves this one glorious night!
We'll not hear no! Come on, all of you!"

Archer smiles   then says firmly
"They'll follow as soon as all is cleared up."
Maura stays until this is done

Then off they traipse to a pub
where they are cheered   treated royally

After her third pint
Maura turns to Gillian beside her
"I don't suppose you could lend me him for a night?"
An amused look
"Ah, I thought not. But you must adore a man
who can do the things he has.
I'm sorry that I have to leave you here in Cork,
but you'll see me when you get to Dublin, no fear!"
She gives Gillian a tearful embrace

Archer is in deep discussion with the Manager
who tells him how thrilled she was with what she saw
"I had no idea how involved the Irish were
in your country. Of course, we knew about
the immigrations at the time of the potato famine,
but the rest never really sank in."

Archer is silent for a moment
thoughtful
Then he leans forward
"Everything we do is true, if dramatized.
The Irish events were a true seam in our story.
But I had no idea of the impact
they have had here.
And in some ways it worries me.
What if some of the audience gets out of hand?
Some almost did tonight."

The Manager thinks for a time
then says reluctantly
"I suppose we can make sure
there are constabulary in the stands—
unobtrusive, of course—
to deal with such disturbances.
But this would be the first time
we will have encountered such a thing
during the festival."

429

Archer is silent for a long time
finally says
"Let's have a compromise.
Invite some to come in plain clothes
to attend the show and let me meet them.
If anything does begin, I'll take care of it.
Let them clean it up."

The Manager looks at him dubiously
uncertain what he means by
taking care of it
but she agrees
particularly as it will give a bonus to the police
whom she wishes to keep on her side
She prays fervently that they will have no work here

The evening finishes off in high form
with the troupe's musicians joining with others
for a long jam together
even some room made on the floor
for those who wish to dance
Ingrid   Mahira are both centres of attention
dance gaily through the evening
with a variety of smitten men
watched over with good nature
but carefully
by the men of the troupe
Amy has another group around her
convulsed with laughter
as she trades Newfie stories with the Irish
Nora
who has joined the group on a break
joins her in good-natured banter
among the entranced Irish

Next morning
Archer is up as usual
thinking through any adjustments
that need to be made
the arrangement made with the Manager

Gillian is left to fend off the reporters
Those from the media
who either saw or now have heard
of the power of the production
are eager to discuss
the Irish Question
as it is seen in the show
She promises them that the next day
Archer will hold a press conference
The reviews are positive
but much is made of the Irish incidents
less of Canada itself
At lunch she tells Archer of this
"After last night I suspected that would be the case.
There's not much we can do about it, I guess,
but play it as it is and let them pick up
what they want.
Still, I'll address it in the press conference."

Afternoon spent
in warm-ups   adjustments
then the second performance

Before the show
Archer meets with the police in plain clothes
jokes with them
tells them to enjoy the show
that if anything untoward occurs
to watch what he does
Word has reached out
not only through the media
but through word of mouth
a thousand attend
Again a response similar to the previous night's
but no incidents take place
again the audience is rapturous
at the end
the actors   forced again
to listen to the many tales
brought bubbling to the surface

They all go to a pub afterwards
but this time they stay for a shorter time
exhausted   return to their lodgings

At the press conference
the next morning
Archer fields the questions
that barrage him from the crowded group
"Did you insert the sections about the Irish
for the tour here? What are your views
about the Irish as seen in your production?"

He waits for the bedlam to cease
"What you see here is what we played in Canada.
We have made no changes.
You can see from our portrayal that your countrymen
have played a strong role in our country's development.
As for what they did for good or ill,
we have tried to show each event as honestly as we can,
without making judgments,
as we have with every people and element
of our society."

Again a bedlam of questions
from which he chooses one
"What is our response to how we have been received here?
We are pleased and grateful, naturally,
for the reception you and your audiences have given us,
and now understand what a truly hospitable people you are."

Pleased murmurs   scribbling of notes

"But what has hit us forcibly
is how deeply you feel about the events that we portray
so that even today they live with you.
We are impressed by this passion and involvement
and thank you for it."

Again furious scratchings
After this general questions about how they like Ireland

"Very much, all of us. We're delighted to be here."

The festival

"We haven't seen much of it, but hope to do so
when we finish playing."

Their itinerary

"Gillian can supply you with the whole schedule,
but we're off to Clonmel next."

The cast   crew

"You're welcome to talk to any of them
any morning, but we work in the afternoons
and evenings."

Some general   ill-informed questions
about Canadian theatre
which he answers as tactfully as possible

The conference begins to trail off
The Manager
who has conducted the meeting gracefully but firmly
thanks all those who came
reminds them that any requests for interviews
should be made through her office
All traipse off
Archer   Gillian   the Manager
go off to lunch in her usual pub

After they have sat down   ordered
"Well, I think that was a grand session!
You certainly know how to deal with the press."

Gillian and Archer smile at each other
before he says
with a straight face
"We have had some experience in this line."

Conversation turns toward the festival
which the Manager is only too happy to discuss
Then she praises their work again
says how happy she is with the growth in the audience
They finish in a convivial atmosphere
Gillian being careful to pay for the Manager's lunch

Canto 19

THE MAN IN BLACK

That night the audience is even larger
From the beginning the power of the show affects them
but Archer is disconcerted by a strange occurrence
Every once in a while as he watches
from the corner of his eye he seems to detect shapes
human   golden
but when he looks he sees nothing
Throughout the performance the feeling persists
in an unnerving way
but the audience is unaware   enthusiastic
At one point after intermission
it appears that an argument might turn into a brawl
among some young well-lubricated youths
but as he begins to move toward the spot
he seems to catch glimpses again
of golden figures
surrounding the men
who   dazed   disperse into the crowd

After the performance   the usual crowding around the cast
Archer is approached by an older man
thin   with a pinched face   eyes that pierce
from beneath his scowl
dressed in black
"You don't know me yet,
but I'll meet you again at Clonmel,
where you must come to my place to talk."
He disappears back into the crowd leaving the stadium
Archer is as nonplussed by this as by
what he experienced throughout the play
but he keeps it to himself

The very next morning
he has an irresistible urge
to visit the stronghold of Kilcolman
Edmund Spenser's ruined home
He phones the Manager
to ask for someone to drive him there
and to Youghal   Raleigh's home
Startled by his request
she finds what he asks for
but he is aware that she is not happy
with where he is going
nor is the driver
yet another young woman
slim as an Irish sapling
wearing the uniform
jeans   T-shirt

The sky roils with clouds
as up the N20 they speed
toward Mallow
passing the verdant fields
between rolling hills
then past Mallow
up to New Twopothouse Village
then out on the R581
a very secondary road
through Old Twopothouse
to Doneraile
not far from there
the bird sanctuary on the grounds
into which they are permitted

After a walk through the grassy fields
they come upon the ruins
broken stone stark against the sky
with the small river   lake on one side
the rolling plains   trees
drifting off to the horizon
the Ballyhoura Mountains slouching behind
Archer   his driver walk up to the mouldering rock

435

untouched for centuries
except for signs of archaeologists' spikes
He walks through the remnants of the bawn
up to the crumbled tower itself
in the sound of thunder from the threatening clouds
seems to hear the ghosts of battle sounds
from that fatal time
For a few moments he loses himself in it
then motions to his driver
who has stayed a distance back
They move off   back to the car
As they go she turns to spit on the ground
before the ruin

Astonished
"What did you do that for?"

She glowers at him
"What did you want, coming up here in the first place?
We don't like this place, never did,
Bird sanctuary or not."

He looks at her in wonderment
"Why?"

Scornfully
"Why? Why? Why not, indeed?
One of those who stole our land from us?
One of those who fought against us?
One who wrote that we should be starved to extinction?
Well, bad cess to him I say!"
She spits again   strides off
Archer following

As she starts off
he says impulsively
not knowing why
"At Doneraile, please take us down to Fermoy
by the straightest route
if not the quickest."

She looks at him   puzzled
but shrugs   nods   agrees
As they reach the car the heavens split open
a fierce downpour floods upon them
Fighting for control of the car in the vicious gusts
she takes a narrow road down to Castletownroche
then across on the smoother route
through Ballyhooly to Fermoy
At Fermoy as they cross the sullen Blackwater
swelling in the torrents that rage down
he has another shiver of insight
Following his direction
even as the skies abruptly clear
she drives from Fermoy to Tallowbridge
up to Lismore   then down the spectacular drive
to Youghal
where they walk through Raleigh's house
luxuriating in the new sunshine

"I don't know why you see his place too—
he stole more than Spenser did.
But at least he had his head cut off!"
she says with savage satisfaction
"And even he is not as bad
as the one who bought him out—
Boyle, who made his own kingdom here
and industry.
Do you know why there are so few
of the famous Youghal yews?
Because he cut down forests of them
for his ironworks, bad cess to him!"

Lunch in Youghal
For a few minutes nothing is said
then Archer
looking directly at her
"In Newfoundland an Indigenous tribe
was exterminated by the new settlers,
who made it a sport to hunt them down.
I do not condone what they did,

but I had to see for myself where it happened,
the kind of country,
imagine how it could happen.
You see the results in our production."

"I don't see at all what it has to do with us here,"
she snaps
avoiding his look
"Why do you make this pilgrimage
if not to honour those two?
After all, aren't they the grand poets,
two of the glories of the English back then?"

"I know little about them,"
Archer admits
"In school we studied some of their poetry.
I have always kept Raleigh's ironic poem
about life in my memory,
but they were mostly a postscript
in our education.
I've never read *The Faerie Queene*
nor much else by Spenser.
Until you told me, I knew nothing
about his life."

She looks at him   puzzled
"Then why this great fuss?
And why did you have me drive the route you did?"

A look of confusion on his face
"I don't... I don't know.
All I know is that I had to see these places."

She looks at him
skeptical amused
but with a trace of fear as well
"Don't tell me you're touched!"

He looks at her uncomprehendingly

She sighs
"Ah well, you'll probably find out soon enough.

In the meantime I apologize
if I have been hard on you.
You can see why, I hope."

"Yes, I think I do..."
he replies with more confidence
"...and thank you for your assistance
despite how you felt."

They raise glasses to each other
The lunch   the drive back to Cork
are far more pleasant than the outward journey

Each night more come
After each show company members
begin to meet with other performers
who are in the festival
For Mahira it is particularly satisfying
because she can talk to the circus performers
others who do physical theatre
It takes her back to her training in Italy
There is much good-natured give   take
among them all
perhaps more so for the musicians
who are now continually jamming with their colleagues

On one occasion
Nora brings along some things
she has quietly brought with her
from Canada
After they finish a jam
to rest among the happy performers
who have been listening to them
she produces two pieces of cloth
two tennis balls with a hole in each
"I thought you might like to see
what else I can do."
She smiles affectionately
at the objects in her hands
Then she places a ball
on each forefinger

439

drops each cloth
around a hand
Two figures appear
a woman in a dress
a man in a cape
who bow   curtsey
to each other
Those around her watch fascinated
as the little scene
goes on before them
Some children passing by
stop   fascinated
Then Nora lets the two cloths drop
yet still the balls seem alive
Nora smiles
at the fascinated faces before her
then pulls off the balls
puts all carefully away
Both performers   children
ask her wondering questions
but she puts her finger to her lips
to silence them
picks up her flute
to start the jam again

When they have finished
are walking back
James says
"I have never seen that before."

She grins   replies
"You don't need much
to bring something alive."

From then on
the others view her with more respect

For most it is a pleasant time
in which they keep the discipline of the production
still enjoy the companionship of peers
After a flurry of interviews the media leave them alone

to talk to others
to explore the city   its surroundings
Only Archer
as Gillian notes worriedly
seems less happy   more...
she searches for a word
...haunted
but she can find out nothing from him

Each night he seems to see
from the corner of his eye
more of the strange golden shadows
at the performance
When asleep or awake
he feels a strange undefined urge
grow stronger
so that he grows more restless
as the run finishes

Last night
triumphant finish
a final farewell party
Then the next day
loading up   on the way to Clonmel
Again Archer finds himself
travelling up among the plains   rolling hills
that lead to Fermoy
His strange feeling clings to him
as the weather shifts above their heads
Then farther north
they find its streets hung
with hundreds of flags made by children
giving the town a slightly giddy look

First stop to see the Festival Director
a man with a long craggy face   little hair
who greets them with some enthusiasm
"Word has gotten out of your show—
you should do well here."
He sends them off to their venue

not a stadium but another playing field
only with lights
now with a new improvised
brightly coloured fence
for crowd control
two vans to act as concessions
They set up
but the rest of the day is off

Amy introduces Archer   Gillian
to a burly man who salutes them
"I've been assigned, sir,
to make sure nothing of yours is stolen—
and have no fear, nothing will be taken.
We're on shifts through the night as well."
Archer congratulates him on his vigilance
The troupe goes off to find their lodgings

A day of rehearsal
looking over the festival
at which some of the events from Cork
have come as well
Then another opening night
another large audience
During the performance
Archer glimpses uncertainly
more of the golden shadows than before
He finds himself in a strange state of mind
somewhere between awake   dreaming
At the end the man in black comes up to him
after most of the crowd has dispersed
"Now you'll come home with me."
Gillian sees him go off
but is too busy to check with him

The two walk together through the town
past all the excitement of the streets
to cross over the dark Suir
climb into the hills

where a small stone cottage sits
Inside the man offers Archer a chair
beside the stone hearth
then brings him a drink
"Now we can talk."

Archer looks about him
sees a place that seems to have been lived in
for centuries
with not much changed
for they sit in candlelight
their faces shifting in the flickering flames
shadows dancing about the room
Archer would like to speak
but holds his tongue to hear what the other will say

"An interesting play, yours,
catching a country's whole life
in a few little hours,
caught up in all its struggles
and its uncertain understanding of itself."

Archer says nothing yet

"Ah, I wonder what would happen
here in Ireland if we tried the same thing."

Archer notices that though the man
speaks precisely   somewhat dryly
when his emotions are aroused
a nervous click in his throat is heard
before he speaks
"What do you think would happen?"
Archer asks quietly

A click

"Ah, to be sure,
what would happen indeed.
We are a poor fractured nation,
our top lopped off
and everyone every which way
even if prosperity has come.

The church doesn't know what to do with us
except to shake its finger
as we merrily go on our way
with only a modicum of guilt.
And all the parts are different,
have been through the ages,
Munster from Connacht,
Connacht from Leinster,
and Ulster from all three."

"Can't you portray those differences?"

"We can. But consider.
Although we can be hospitable,
as you well know…"

Archer nods

"…our lives are layered with resentments
from the past,
for we have been for millennia
an invaded country.
Now our bile still rises over
our subjugation by the English,
subjugation by the Normans,
by the Vikings,
each other,
or by one family against another.
Look at Kilkenny up the way.
We won't go back into mists of old history…"

He smiles   the candles waver slightly

"…back into the first century after Christ.
Let's start with the Osraigh,
or the Ossory to you.
The next thousand years and more
the county was fought over,
this kingdom of the Ossory,
with battles and massacres and treacherous slayings,
until finally the house of Butler prevailed
as the Normans overrode all other minor kingdoms.

And for the next thousand years,
the Normans and the English kept the power,
until here we are with the power ourselves
and not sure what to do with it
or who now to trouble about,
except for those of us in the north
where the blood has spilled for decades
and where breath is now held
that enemies for centuries
can keep the peace
and the thugs can be brought from fake myth
to the welfare of the country."

"But where else has it been different?
You see in my country
the invasions and the struggles
and the blood that has been shed.
Memories are still strong there,
even as mottos: *Je me souviens*
is the mantra of the Québécois
with which the rest of us must deal.
And Indigenous memories are longer still."

Another click

"Ah, but you have such a big country,
a huge country,
where such things can be swallowed up,
and I don't see the blood still fresh on your hands.
You may have such as the French
who nurse their bitterness at losing,
and their fear of disappearing as a people,
but here the memories are kept fresh
throughout a country much smaller than yours
and ingrained in our children
and in each region.
As for disappearance—what of our native language?
What is the major language here?
What language have our greatest poets used?
English!

Our old language must be tended
like a delicate and sickly plant,
to survive with forced feedings of regulations."

A short pause as the candles flick shadows about
Click
Click again
"I write in the old way myself."

Archer is immediately interested
"You're a bard?"

Click
"I suppose you could call me so,
though today such have dwindled
almost to nothing."

He begins to speak in the old language
with its soft gutturals   alien vowels
The music of his words
none of which Archer knows
fills the room with their intricate lines
intonations
as even the candles' flames steady
in the warm embrace of that poetry
He recites for some time
if time exists during that spellbound utterance
Then he finishes
The room returns to its flickering reality
A silence

"That was beautiful. Thank you."
whispers Archer
who cannot think of words
to describe what he has heard

"It is beautiful."
agrees his host
without a trace of arrogance
"The bards of the ancient days
could have been Druids, you know.
They trained for decades and were said

to have powers of divination,
among other things.
And they go back even farther,
it is said,
to a time now shrouded in myth and antiquity,
when the first peoples came to our isle,
wresting it from each other."

A click
Again a click
The candles seem to grow brighter

"And it is said that the bards were trained
by one of those first peoples
who hated war and strife
and moved into the bowels of the hills and mountains
after their own defeat
to escape the continual roils of those who followed them.
So the bards have sung praises,
but always with an eye to truth and to best conduct,
and have sung with scorn against all that is false and vicious.
And so still today—except that few can understand their songs."

His last words are bitter
He lapses into a long silence
the candles dimming as he does so

It is Archer who breaks the quiet moment

"A wonder it must be to follow in their line,
to trace your ancestry back millennia.
I cannot do so. I have no line at all.
No knowledge of my true parents,
no knowledge of their calling,
or their parents' calling and so back through time.
I am the first and probably the last
of my abbreviated line."

He has not intended to speak
but the months of aching loss
now break out with a bitterness
he cannot control

surprising himself that he speaks of it
that he feels so deeply

In the flickering light
Archer thinks he sees
the trace of a smile on the thin lips

"Your line may become longer than you think.
You know how Ireland reeks
of the stories of fairies and little people
and all the supernatural stirrings
that attend them?
How do you think these came to be?"

As he speaks the light in the room grows brighter
Archer   bemused
now sees that the light is golden
does not emanate from the small flames
but fills the space from its perimeter
When he looks around
he sees standing in the corners
along the walls
what he has before glimpsed as golden shadows
sees them now in all their glory
as men in ancient riding dress
tall   with long golden hair   pale   faces
who stare at him with curious intensity

They move to surround him
Partly in trance he moves with them
outside the cottage
where more wait for them
mounted on huge black stallions
dark as the night
but whose sleek mighty muscles
are outlined in the sheen of the glow
snorting   prancing
their eyes blazing red
He   the ones around him   mount
Immediately the steeds gallop off
with vast bounds

The night is now obscured
with roiling clouds
from which lightning forks incessantly
with never-ceasing thunder
from which great torrents of rain
are flung down upon the battered trees
that bow almost to the ground
from the turbulent gusts
As they gallop on
Archer feels the wind rushing at his face
but no drop does he feel
despite the deluge surrounding them
His horse needs no guidance
nor do the others so far as he can tell
but all rush on purposefully
with little of the country seen
except for that ground streaming
beneath the blur of hooves

As they fly on Archer notes those about him
sees that their long hair now streaming behind them
is not all golden
but that there are different colours
all subdued in the sheen of the unnatural glow
On they go
and on
while time seems submerged
against the swift rhythm of the hooves

Finally the deluge subsides
the night sky begins to clear
He begins to make out
the bases of hills rushing by
until the group begins to climb along the side
with strange outcrops of basalt
hexagonal pillars
thrust from the ground

Suddenly before a looming hill
the horses rear up   stop

For a moment all is still
Then a rider raises a horn to his lips
sends a long clear note soaring forth
Another stillness
Then Archer hears
a rumbling deep within the hill
immense and powerful
Before them
the sides of the hill grind open
like a gigantic gate
Golden light
blinding against the night sky
blazes forth

Into this golden incandescence
the riders trot
When Archer's eyes adjust
to the new light
he sees that they are beginning to descend
along a broad highway
of intricate stones
secured to its sides
an immense pit
the other side of which
can be seen in the distance
As he looks below he sees
the graceful turrets of
a palace of unutterable beauty
its towers soaring
that what they traverse
is not a pit but a cone
which is expanding as they descend
to reveal a town attractively laid out
surrounding the central structure
its streets broad
with fair parks
rivers streams ponds
creating a pleasing asymmetry
How the road winds down

he cannot understand
but wind it does

As they reach the base
he sees a broad thoroughfare before him
lined with stately trees
paved with shining stones
in a complex but harmonious design
that leads to the gates of the palace itself

The stallions' hooves
he suddenly realizes
make little sound as they trot along
As he listens
he realizes that the sounds of the town
are unlike those he has lived with
where both day   night a hum is heard
in the mechanic cities
Here there are live sounds
of women's voices chatting
laughter from a distant window
singing from blocks away
the distant rhythmic beats of a smithy
the rustle of leaves in a slight wind
all clear   distinct
The smell of the place is different too
with the earthy smells
of leaf   blossom
grass   bush
scenting the air
against the harsh scent
of the horses' sweat

Now they reach the gates of the palace
dismount
Attendants take away the jet-black stallions
He sees the walls are made of whitest marble
without a sign of joins
almost unbearable to look at
in their alabaster purity

The gates themselves
high   of shining bronze
upon which figures intertwined
rise up to the limit of each gate's height
Again a single clear note from the horn
From inside a note returns
higher   sweeter
The gates swing open
slowly   quietly

Inside is a courtyard
in the centre of which
a fountain shaped with figures
of strange fish
plashes gently
Around it a marble square
inlaid with brilliant designs
then small lawns with trees   flowers   borders
around which a loggia extends
with slender pillars
An official greets them
leads them to the far side
through golden doors
again embossed   this time with strange figures
into a large airy hall
along which stained-glass windows
portray warriors in ferocious battle
against grotesque creatures
on sea   on land

At the far end is a high raised dais
upon which sits a throne
elaborately carved in marble
before which stands a queen
tall   in ancient regal dress
at each side groups of ladies-in-waiting
equally in splendid costume
all the women
but particularly the queen
of a luminous unearthly beauty

The group comes before her   bows
as does Archer   seeing it the custom

> "Welcome, Ray Archer.
> We have been expecting you."

greets the queen in a rich melodious voice
She smiles

> "I'm sure you would like to know
> more of us and why you are here."

Her voice now changes
charged with authority
He sees her eyes fixed on his
In them he sees golden flickers swarm
as her gaze grips him
her voice now powerful
intense with deep passions
that she fiercely keeps from bursting forth

> "But first, understand that we have watched you
> and deemed you worthy to be brought here,
> seeing the power of your vision,
> the beauty of your words and songs
> revealing the true nature of your land."

For a moment she subsides
He sees all the women before him
with the same intense stare
wildness he had seen
among the riders
Then she relaxes
returning to the majestic voice
with which she had first greeted him

> "Now, one of my ladies will minister to you
> and tell you what you wish to know."

She says a name in a language
Archer does not understand

but sounds with its soft consonants   vowels
like music itself

From one group a young woman steps forward
tall   lissome
her lovely pale oval face
framed by her rich black hair

The young woman smiles
at the dazzled Archer
takes his hand
leads him away
up a winding staircase
to a room   airy   bright
where she invites him to sit
with her at a low table
laden with bowls of fruit
a pitcher   goblets
She pours him a fragrant drink
another for herself
then salutes him   they sip
a taste tangy   invigorating

"We are honoured to have you with us."

A voice also musical   rich
tinted with a slight accent
that makes what she says
delicious to hear

"Have you questions you would like me to answer?"

Archer
who has not spoken since the cottage
finds his own voice rough
"Where am I?"

She smiles

"Within what the people here
call Nicker Hill,
close to their Pailis Ghréine."

Her answer confuses him the more
"Why within?
Who are you?"

Her laugh rings lightly through the room

    "If I answer your second question,
    it may help with the first."

Then she speaks gravely
but he can feel beneath the words
powerful feelings stirring deep within
He sees in her eyes
the golden flickers
he had seen in the eyes of her queen
that now glow with her intense feeling

    "We are an ancient people
    who came here so long ago
    that we know our origins
    only from our legends sung
    down through the ages."

Her deep-lashed eyes close
For a moment she stops
to take a sip from her goblet
To encourage her he does the same
Again her eyes open
but now look far away

    "Long,
    so long ago,
    we lived elsewhere,
    far away on the eastern sea
    on our own island
    to which we had earlier escaped
    from the huge, brutish sons
    of our God,
    the father of us all.

    "As a sea people
    we lived peaceful, happy lives,
    our black ships sailing everywhere

and often rescuing those in shipwreck.
But our Father-God was displeased
that we saved these mariners
whom he had ruined
with his wild gales and tempests,
and a hero whom he wished to punish."

Her breathing quickens
her golden eyes flash brighter

"For this great transgression,
we were forced to leave the isle we loved
and watched it sink forever
under his shattering earthquake and vicious gales.
We had to travel in our black, far-sighted ships
to a harsher land,
transported up a dark river
to a deep valley,
thick forested,
frigid in winter,
where we waited and endured."

She pauses again   breathing quickly
Then looks at him
This time a longer draft for each

"And after a prophecy had been fulfilled,
our black ships sped back down the river
to carry us across the seas,
transported us to this isle,
doomed to exile here forever."

Each sips again

"All we have left to remind us of that time
are our sacred black horses
who take us where we wish
without direction.
Sometime before we landed here
we started to explore our new powers,
some of which you have seen—

our gift to make ourselves
unseen by others;
the power of our red-eyed horses,
so swift and tireless;
our mastery of light."

As they sip again
suddenly she bursts out bitterly
He sees her as he saw the golden men
wild   passionate
her hair swirling around her shoulders

"We are not a warlike people,
but your kind forced us
to learn to fight.
When we first arrived we struggled to defeat
a monstrous race, and were successful.
But invaders came whom we fought to a draw.
We could see then that conflict would succeed conflict,
battles further battles,
until this green and then wooded land
would be stained red beneath these barbarisms."

She shudders
More sips

"And so we signed a treaty
and retreated to the hills,
where through our developing powers
we disappeared into the interiors of mountains
as you can see.
Here we have stayed for millennia,
watching the lands soaked in blood by some
and scarred, wasted by others,
and the pattern has continued up to this day."

Sips

"But we made sure not to be discovered.
In the early days,

to disguise our origins
we insinuated among the peoples
myths that we had swept down from northern seas,
descending from the air
with fabulous objects
such as the four treasures:
the Coire Ansic, a cauldron bottomless;
the invincible spear Lúin;
the Lia Fáil, the king's stone of right and rejuvenation;
and the Claiomh Solais, the irresistible Sword of Light."

They drain their goblets

"And then as centuries passed
and new invaders came,
more worldly,
we carefully changed our image,
starting among the peasantry
with tales of the little folk,
the fairies and the leprechauns,
and using a few simple magic tricks
to give some credence to the stories."

She has become more relaxed
although her eyes still glow
and Archer himself feels pleasantly the same

"But we still keep in contact with your world.
First the Druids, and from them the bards,
we have fostered, and they have learned from us
the arts of song and poetry to add to their own
skills and talents."

She pauses   seems reluctant to go on
her pale cheeks now delicately tinged red
her lips fuller   more red as well
her breath more uneven

Archer himself now feels his blood coursing
his body becoming younger
feeling as it did when he was in his twenties

He asks her   his own breathing now affected
"And what is the second way that you keep contact?"

She answers unsteadily
gazing at him
her golden eyes flashing

> "It is sung by our priest
> that when in our exile we were forced to flee,
> our black ships swiftly sweeping us
> to another country and its dark river,
> brooding mountains,
> there came to us, in a way wondrous,
> a hero whom we had succoured some time before,
> a brilliant man, fierce warrior,
> great teacher of the ways of war,
> a noble king himself, who mated with a princess,
> the daughter of our first exiled king.
> Since then men are chosen who can help keep us rich in blood,
> and we have spread across the land
> with both kings and queens through the mountain ranges.
> Here reigned Grian of the Bright Cheeks,
> renowned for her beauty and her erotic power over men,
> and here her descendant continues to reign,
> and we continue to find those who help us
> to perpetuate our race."

She stands   raises him to face her

> "I have heard the reports of you
> and myself watched you and your wondrous art..."

She looks at him with dignity and pride

> "...and I have made the choice of thee as my mate.
> Nor will I forget thee for thyself once I bear thy child,
> but thou wilt live in my heart in every beat until it stops."

She looks straight into his eyes
He sees the truth of what she says
in the power of her eyes

459

the hunger for him
His body surges with the needs   desires
that it knew forty years before
She takes his hand
in the electric touch of hers
leads him to a room close by
in which a bed rests behind
layers of filmy material
She releases his hand
tormented by her touch
Motioning him with a wild grace to stay there
she moves through the light materials
At the bed she slowly removes her clothing
until she stands naked behind the many layers between them

Never has he seen so lovely a sight
her beauty enhanced through the transparent barriers
her eyes glowing fiercely
He quickly sheds his own clothes
For a moment they stand there
devouring each other with their eyes
until he bursts through the flimsy cloths
embraces her
their two young bodies fused
Then he gently lays her on the bed
All his years of experience
come to play against the passion of his younger body
as he makes love to her
until she can stand it no longer
with a cry opens to let him in
Many times they make love
and the night passes in their writhing ecstasy
Then all becomes a blur
dressed again   galloping upon the ebony stallion
wind and country rushing by him in the last gasps of the night
the first tiny glow of dawn as they arrive at his lodging
Then he knows no more

460

Canto 20
THE GOLDEN ONES

Light   fresh light   new light   warm on eyelids   arm over eyes
"Ray?"
Gillian's eyes shaded with concern
He finds himself in his room   on his bed   still clothed
"What happened? Where have you been?"
He looks at her   still bewildered   in a quicksand of exhaustion
Body aches   more insight of what age means

"Ray?"

"I… don't know."

Suddenly   as a wrenched image   distorted   unclear
snaps into bright focus
so the memory of the night pierces his mind
the room before him lurches for an instant
He is about to tell Gillian
the wonder of the golden men   the ebony horses with fire-rimmed eyes
the city beneath the hill   the lovely girl
when the ordinary daylight of the room
jerks him back to this world
Gillian   anxious   beside him
He feels he cannot tell her
the experience he has been through
if it was real
"I'm sorry… can't tell you for now."

Perplexed   she looks at him
about to say something
then decides against it
"It's almost noon. Lunch?"

Surprised
Then a raging hunger devours him
"Yes. Let me get ready."

After a shower   other preparations
he is ready
off they go
but he cannot place his universe
the day   bright   warm
the Irish town   the café
the murmur of the cadenced voices around them
Gillian's talk of the show
of whom he needs to meet
all somehow crisp   distinct   different
as when asleep a life unfolds
in persuasive clarity
then interrupted by awakening
only to be immersed in the folds of another dream
He tries to talk to her
but she herself he sees
sharply   distinctly
a familiar stranger
That afternoon
he leads the troupe in Tai Chi
as if he sees himself
his body working on its own
dissociated from his own sense of himself
He lets the others explore
with his tongue making comments
apart from his mind
The show he watches
in the same detached   observant way

But the golden figures glide through the audience
At the end
he murmurs something unintelligible to Gillian
leaves the grounds
finds them waiting there
mounts the fierce black horse
the same whistling ride
with distance leaping by
the hill opens
the heart of the city opens
and he finds himself again with the girl

Sight obliterates the moment
as we each gaze
with our remembering eyes

Erect   proud she stands
thin fine cloth
caressing   enhancing
each enticing curve of her graceful body
But her eyes   her eyes
shining with their golden flickers
her stare filled with the memories
of my body as it met with hers
in that entangled night before
devouring it even now
her look so open
frank in her desire for me
her lips part slightly
awaking my need to blend them with mine
"Welcome, Ray Archer!" she says
her voice melodious
as she restrains her feelings
then speaks what are words foreign to me
but said with each sound caressed

She sees my puzzlement   incomprehension
laughs
sounds lightly tossed
petals in a still air
"I've just said in our language,
'I love you, my own man.'"

Must go to her   embrace her
but she gestures to me to sit
In that moment
even as I do her bidding
I sense a power in her
not experienced by me before
as she herself now sits opposite
I realize that she is now frank
fully open to me
no suppression of what she really is

She raises her full goblet to me
I do the same to her
We both take our first sip
This time I feel its strange power
already beginning to work on me
as my senses start their new activation
my body starts its first minute shift
Now I hear her beguiling voice
as she tells me stories of old times
undergone by her race
punctuated by mutual sips
the shifting of body   age   perception
for even as the wonder of my youth proceeds
I become aware of the currents of her emotions
powerfully throbbing in accompaniment to mine

Then   goblets empty   we arise
go to her room
each watching as the other strips
then meet passionately

O the ecstasy of bodies   emotions
so combined   so powerful
All was lost in these ultimate couplings
each submerged in the other's ecstasy

In the quiet following such union
she murmurs into my ear
before the next surge together
"In our past
we women were considered weak,
suitable only for domestic matters,
but in our exile,
after the great battles
that reduced our numbers,
even as our powers grew
that let us create
what you see now,
as this took place
our women changed as well.

464

It is not by chance
that we now have queens
that we guard our future
as I do now with you
whom now I love with all my being
in the shrunken time we have."

Fiercely she presses tightly to me
her eyes shining fully into mine
Powerful our attraction grows
as we couple again

Then all is obliterated from my mind
with only lost glimpses   touch of lips
the blurred ride home
a return to present matters

The week drifts on in the same way
and each day he becomes more fey
Gillian is at her wit's end
Each night he disappears
each night she waits for him
but falls asleep
to awaken with him there
Each morning he sleeps late
wakes exhausted
The troupe as well begins to note
his condition
Gillian has to reassure them
that he is all right
although it is clear to all
that she is haggard with worry

Finally the last day of the Clonmel run
Gillian holds on to him
as they strike   arrive at the party
The Golden Ones see that she keeps him
they mount   ride away
without him
Gillian makes sure that he is surrounded
with either guests or cast

465

throughout the party
She nudges him into attention
to speak to them
She has made sure that there are questions
that he must answer
or statements to intrigue his mind
Though
like someone who speaks to others
while an argument rages in his head
or some event fills his mind
Archer replies
yet this attention infiltrates his consciousness
By the time she takes him
back to their room
he is less bewildered than before
but beyond measure
his bones ache with exhaustion
She must help him to bed
where he plunges deep into a sleep
a tiny death

Off the next day
to the small town of Tipperary
All this time
dimly conscious of place
Archer sits in front with Gillian
what he has learned of the country
through which they now pass
asleep in the back of his mind
Paddy's voice a drone in the distance
But as they drive toward Tipperary
Archer is suddenly caught
by a new tone in Paddy's voice
a rougher edge
a deeper note soaked
in angry memory
"Would ye look now,
and see before yis the town of Tipperary
rapidly approaching us.

It was once a stronghold of yer King John
in the old days
and has been a market town since then.
D'ye know what the name means, now?
It means 'the well of Arra,'
for there was a well in the townland of Glenbane
in the parish of Lattin and Cullen near
where the river rises.
But ye might know it better
because of the song,
and ye'll soon see the signs sayin'
'You've come a long way.'
Now, they're meant to be a joke, sure,
but that's not how we here in Ireland
see them—for us they're a terrible catmalojin joke
made by a luddar.
And there's a grand reason we think that way.
Ye see, this town became famous for us
when it was the place for the first engagement
in the Irish War of Independence on the nineteen days—
the nineteenth of January, nineteen hundred and nineteen, sure.
It was that glorious day when,
near Solloghead Beg quarry,
Dan Breen and Seán Treacy
led their immortal band of volunteers
to attack the Royal Irish Constabulary,
who were in the process of transportin' gelignite.
It was a devil of a bang heard across the country.
But then, ye see, the poor town was where
a great British barracks and military hospital
was located, and it was from there
the fecking Black and Tans, bad cess to them,
roamed about the town and district,
with their guns and terror—and it was they,
they, who made the Tipperary song
their own marchin' song.
And so for us it leaves bad memories in our ears
and a stink in our nostrils
when we hear it.
And here is the grand town itself!"

He wheels them through the streets to Main Street
from which wide avenues radiate out
shows them statues commemorating heroes
in their war
then comes to a memorial arch
in the midst of beautiful landscaping
"Ah, here in 2005 our president,
Mary McAleese, Máire Mhic Giolla Íosa,
thought fit to make this arch a memorial
to those bad days and for recognition
of our heroes in the future.
She thought it would reconcile us all
to what had happened in the past—
but ye'll find no one here that sees it that way, sure."

Then he stops the procession
at a nice place for a morning tea
At the tables the troupe chat amiably
but all watch covertly how Archer acts
When he shows more life   attention
than they have seen for a week
they visibly relax
particularly Ingrid   Mahira
who have been disturbed by his manner
so different from the director
they have grown used to
Gillian continues unobtrusively
to keep him interested
in what is said around him
Gradually he begins to emerge
from the strange cocoon
in which he has been wrapped

A brief stop
then across the rolling farmlands
sumptuous in their green vestments
to Limerick
Paddy's catechism of the city
to which Archer listens
Lunch now in the city

at a pub of Paddy's choosing
where Gillian quietly makes sure
that others of the troupe sit with Archer
that he joins in the conversation
Though they find him more like himself
his eyes still retain in their depths
a haunted air they cannot define
that sends a tiny   almost unnoticed   shiver
down their spines

Then the trek to Galway starts again
along the N18
glimpsing the broadness of the Shannon
at Bunratty
then through the tree-tinged
wilder waves of fields
on up through Crusheen
the view bleaker
Gort An Gort   Ardrahan   Kilcolgan
Clarinbridge
then into Galway
the great bay

Their hotel is in Salthill
not far from Pearse Stadium
where they will play
but the day is too advanced
for contact   inspection
Dispersal to rooms
dinners
exploration
The festival has begun that day
parade now only debris in the street
but events are beginning
performers are roaming
The troupe spends a merry evening

Archer and Gillian walk along the streets
taking in the gaiety of the spectators
the excitement   the banners

the street performers
Then they walk to where they can see
the bay   the shadows of the hills
in the still glimmering twilight
Nothing said in this saunter
but as an insect moves carefully along
its antennae delicately probing
to sense in its own inimitable way
what unknown path to take
so Gillian feels beside her
her man watching all about them
but his thoughts still recessed deep
his eyes searching always
for something not there
Now   looking across the water
that shifts unobtrusively
in the dimming light
she still cannot find the vital moment
to prompt his answer
to the mystery
of the last few days
nights

Suddenly
as the last rays flicker out
the sky explodes above them
with huge brief rosettes of colours
soaring arcs of incandescence
bursts   showers of sparks
that drift slow tracks
as they fade   die
Faces uptilted they watch
even as the water below
echoes the bombardment above
with brief distortions
evanescent colour

Abruptly
"Let's go back."

470

They walk silently through the noisy celebrations
the trek to their hotel
As they pass along more silent streets
"Even that seems dull now."

She looks at him wonderingly
but he says nothing more
She can see
the haunt returned to his eyes
Again she chooses not to speak but her resolve deepens

They reach their room
There
as if for the first time
she entices him to make love to her
As they explore each other's bodies
he remembers the nights he has just lived through
his youthful primacy
but now his fingers trace an older
familiar body
her hands touch his older body
he feels in all his muscles bone skin
his veins heart breathing
to his deepest core
the inexorable descent of forty years
For a moment he plunges deep
into this insight of age
but then
as he looks into Gillian's face
which he has seen so many times
now sees anew
as she responds to him
with her open look
willing body
he is pierced by deep emotion
their link reforged
with mature bonds

The day freshens with Archer once more alert
After their late breakfasts

the troupe gradually drifts to the hotel lobby
Archer and Gillian have gone to see the Artistic Director
a genial harried woman
who greets them warmly
"Grand to see you have arrived.
You have brought fame with you, it seems."
They smile at her wry comment
then the three briskly get down to business
publicity   program   other minutiae
their technician summoned
a goodbye   amiable warning
that she   yet more officials
will be at their first performance

With the technician in tow
Archer and Gillian return to the hotel
where they pick up the troupe
All travel the brief distance
to Pearse Stadium
with its large pitch
ample stands
With well-practised efficiency
the crew unloads   sets up
Amy working closely with the festival staff

During the flurry of activity
Archer leads the cast in Tai Chi
All realize
that he has returned
to his customary alertness   absorption
Their mood lifts perceptibly
At the finish
Yumiko   Mahira grin at him
he smiles back
He speaks quietly to Amy
who calls them all together
"All right, everyone,
the rest of the day's schedule:
technicians to finish after lunch;
cast call for warm-up at six,

then a short tech and full rehearsal."
They all return to the hotel
Then at a pub for lunch
Archer   Gillian meet with Amy   the festival rep
to work out any unfinished business

That afternoon
the usual interviews   appearances
That night the rehearsal goes smoothly
all return for a drink
then retire
in preparation for the next night's opening

"Let's go for a walk."
Archer and Gillian walk the few blocks
to stand again looking out over the bay
The night is dark
save for the city's lights
that cast a dim glow
on beach   water
but Archer's face is shadowed
Gillian cannot see his expression
"I'm sorry that I have worried you so."

She shakes her head   is about to speak
but he stops her
"It is difficult for me to tell you
what has happened.
First, I have not been in our room each night
until the early morning, is that right?"

She nods   heart beating

"Do you remember an old man
who spoke to me
the night before I disappeared?"

She thinks back
a thin black figure briefly flashes into view
A nod

Hesitation
Then as he becomes lost in his memories
he tells of the meeting at the old man's house
of the golden figures with their fierce black horses
the bewildering   land-swallowing ride
the hill fissured   the golden city within it
the queen   the young lady
the drink   the metamorphosis
the vague return
his second visit
Throughout all this
Gillian listens in wonder
caught between disbelief at such fantasy
the chilling detail of his telling
When he finishes
dark-faced he looks out over the night bay
silent   brooding

She takes his hand in hers
"If I did not know you had been away
on those nights
that you have always told me the truth
whatever it may be…"

She grimaces for a moment

"…I would think you made up all of this.
And I still find it almost impossible
to believe. A fairy tale?"

His figure still   dark   face to the bay

"And you have been so strange
these last days.
The whole company has noticed it."

Still silent

"But now you are back with us,
and at least able to talk to me about it.
But Ray…"

Pressing his hand

"...please, please tell me if more
starts happening."

A pause
A nod
Silence for a moment
Then
"Let's go back."

She knows he could not talk more of it
for the present
Without a word
they return to their room
their own intimacy

The next evening
their run begins
As the Artistic Director had foretold
many officials
trying to look dignified
but unsure what they will see
a large audience
including performers
whose shows are not on at this time
people from the city
others from regions round about
It is evident that the show's reputation
has preceded it
also the stories of its Irish strains
The Artistic Director has heard
from the previous festivals
that there could be trouble
She has provided some quiet
off-duty forces with passes

The night brilliant with its summer trappings
the sun still reluctant to lie down
as the reverberant start to the huge pageant
focuses all attention
except that of Archer
for with a quickened pulse

he sees scattered throughout the throng
the golden wraiths
among them the girl

Gillian sees his white face
quickly moves close to him
"Ray, what is it?"

"They're back.
Can you see them?"

She looks about
but can see nothing
not even their glimmer
"No. Where?"

He points

"I don't see anything."
Fearful
she stays close to him
as the play rumbles on

As before
when some in the audience
begin to respond to the Irish events
in a belligerent way
the golden forms step in
to quiet them
but always Archer cannot keep his eyes
away from the golden girl
who watches the show   absorbed
in all it conveys
Gillian sees where his gaze is fixed
but   desperate   sees nothing
At the end of the first act
she tries to speak to him
but sees to her horror
that he again looks fey
his gaze distant   fixed
But she sticks to him
even as people crowd around them
already teeming with praise

With the second act
the sun has called it quits
the lights of the play
enhance the action still more
but for Archer
the golden hazes are still brighter
the girl still enslaves his eyes

At the end an ovation
the crowds about the actors
as always
The Artistic Director
then guides them to a reception
Gillian keeps always with Archer
not letting him away from her
but he himself is aware
too clearly
that the girl is there as well
watching him
smiling
proud of what he has done

Ignoring those who wish to talk to him
including the Artistic Director
to whom Gillian gives a helpless shrug
an apologetic look
he crosses straight to the fair shimmerer
Gillian close to him
"You've come. Why?"

Her soft voice with its alien accent

> "To see again what I have seen before,
> to hear again what thou hast told."

Gillian is aware of something
like the sigh of a breeze
against the babble around them
She shivers

> "And is this thy woman, then,
> my..."

She smiles proudly

"... Archer?"

His heart strained
"Yes, this is my woman.
Can't you show yourself to her?"

A wan smile

"Not here. I have but power
to show myself to one only
when in such a crowd.
When thou finish here,
come to the bay,
where no one will be about."

She glides from him
her gown gracefully drifting about her
Archer watches her go
his face drawn

Gillian   desperate to know
"Ray, what is going on?"

He turns to her   haunted again
"She wants us at the bay
when we finish here."

Both now endure the reception
Gillian making sure that Archer
apologizes to the Artistic Director
engages her in conversation

An eternity later
after talking to relieved   impressed officials
to members of the energized company
they leave
make their way to the bay
where several of the golden men
sit on the black steeds
But the girl stands on the sands
before them

Gillian gasps
astonished
for she can now see them

> "I do this for thee, my Archer.
> But both must promise
> never to tell of us in any way.
> Will ye do so?"

She speaks with such authority
the golden warriors
look so stern upon their fiercer steeds
that both vow immediately

> "Thou toldst her about us?"

He inclines his head
"Yes."

A laugh
light as a breeze

> "It must have been grand
> for you to hear, then."

Gillian gasps out
"Yes."

A smile

> "No doubt you did not believe him?"

A wry smile in return
"I must say I found it difficult."

The girl smiles again   sadly

> "Ah well, that would be natural,
> would it not?"

Then she turns to Archer

> "But I must tell thee, my fair man,
> that I am proud of what thou hast done,
> and that I will never regret the choice I made."

For a moment their eyes blaze at each other
Gillian is chilled by the look

> "We will come to each of thy performances,
> and I invite thee both to return with us
> to our home this next night."

Seeing Archer's face she laughs merrily

> "Nay, there will be no drink as before,
> so thou can'st rest thy mind at ease."

More seriously

> "But I wish to know more about thy life,
> the life of the two of you,
> as thou may'st wish to know more of us.
> Will you do so?"

Archer and Gillian look at each other
"Yes."

> "Then tomorrow night so be it."

With that   her steed is brought to her
she leaps upon it gracefully
Before the two can respond
.the group gallops away
without a sound

Gillian stands frozen with Archer
spell-struck by the encounter
her world wrenched awry

A smile no longer distant
"You believe me now?"

Like an animal huddling against another
to be enveloped in its warmth   heartbeat
so she slips her arm under his
to nestle close
They walk slowly back
as he tells her more of the golden city
that they will visit that next night

This night they lie quietly together
each ranging in a solitary mind
through the wonder of what they have seen
Sleep comes to them
only in the early glimmering
of an Irish summer dawn

For Gillian the new day
becomes a haze of activities
in which she finds herself
dissociated from herself
her body   her mind   busy
with all the multitudinous business
of the company
the warm-up
meals
but her true consciousness
absorbed in this new life
thrust upon her
and the questions that are born
rush through her

How can these strange figures be?
What other powers do they have?
The girl
so beautiful   alien
with her "my Archer"
I called his "woman"
his woman
Those stallions
so powerful   weird
with their fiery eyes
The speed with which
they galloped off
so knowing
so effortless

Finally the time of the performance comes
As it progresses
she can see the wraiths

like gold dust
scattered among the audience
making sure that nothing takes place
that would affect the progress of the play
She sees the girl
alone
again absorbed
watching
the ungainly history unfold
At intermission they remain
dispersed about the space
make no contact
nor do they
when at the end some of the audience
crowd about the actors   Archer
to tell their own tales
But when most have dispersed
the opportunity has emerged
the girl comes for them
They make their excuses to the others
follow them out
to where the midnight steeds
snort impatiently

They mount
the men surrounding the three of them
each woman beside Archer
Off they blaze
in the crystal night
Gillian had learned horsemanship
at a young age
knew what it was to gallop
but never has she felt the power
that surges under her
nor the implacable purpose of these creatures
as they move at an unearthly speed
to rush across the terrain
without effort

Once she has grown accustomed
to the pace at which they travel
that the wind which should attack her face
seems only like a brisk breeze
she turns her attention to the riders
In the shock of their first appearance
the day before
she had taken little note of them
but now she sees that what they wear
is of ancient origin
not of any age she knew in Ireland
but they are dressed as if for battle
eons back in ancient Greece
with tunics   capes that flow freely
as those must have done in that lost past
with their hair flowing behind them
When she studies the girl
she sees again a tunic   a cape
that seems borrowed from the men
her hair caught in a golden diadem
that lets the long strands stream behind her
But it is their faces that shock her the most
for all without exception have an unearthly beauty
their features perfect   unmarred
the girl unbearably lovely
yet all are set in an ecstasy of concentration
their eyes flash
as wild as those of their mounts
Around them sounds the thrum
of the hooves as they briefly strike the ground
with a hypnotic rhythm
which she fights but cannot conquer
Time starts to fade from her consciousness
as the stars wheel round them in the heavens
All incoherently passes in the sounding rush

Finally the pulse slows
the horses rear to a halt

before the black shape of a mountain
thrusting against the starlit sky
One of the men takes a horn
its sheen seen even in the starlight
blows a long single note
eerie   alien
When it finishes
the deep rumble begins
the side of the huge bulk
is riven apart
the brilliant light streaking through the wound
The procession canters in
winds down the strange trail
of the inverse pit
to the dazzling town below
Gillian can scarcely breathe at the sight
watches
past surprise
as they canter silently
down the broad thoroughfare
with the sounds of the town
heard clearly from the surrounding streets
They reach the palace walls and gates
that shine immaculate
All dismount

A second soaring note on the horn
A note soars back
The ornately figured gates swing open
Even Archer
who has experienced the entry before
continues to marvel at the sight
of the great plaza before them
but Gillian notices that when the gates swing shut
the sounds from the town fall silent
Only the plashing of fountains
the quiet melodies of birds
the quieter rustling of leaves and vegetation
can be heard

484

Even the scents in the air seem changed
from those outside the walls
which mingle the smell of flowers   trees
with the faint odours that emanate from the houses
merged with the fresher scents
the aromas of exotic perfumes

This time the square is empty
no queen greets them
Instead the men leave them
The girl leads them upstairs
to a room with a large balcony
that overlooks the town
There they sit
in comfortable chairs
of ancient design
with fruit   golden goblets
upon a low table before them

The girl speaks with a charming smile
as she pours from a pitcher ornately carved
with images of sleek black vessels
upon a boundless sea

   "Do not fear. This drink is harmless."

Beyond their height
they can see the town stretched out below
to the limits of the immense inverted bowl
in which it is situated
the streets laid out in spokes leading to the palace
each fringed with trees of different kinds
many bearing fruit
all rich in their various leafy colours
The streets are not paved
but inset with tiles
that from their vantage point
show pleasing designs throughout the town
Occasionally a small square is seen among the spokes
where what seem like shops congregate
At the verges of the town can be seen

smithies   other industries
but no smoke nor dust appears
to disturb the clarity of the air
either from these or from the houses
in the town itself
From here as well
they can again hear the town's sounds
Music drifts up from different sites
to create a pleasing disharmony

When they turn back
Gillian notices the girl's eyes glance away
She realizes
that the girl had been studying her
The girl toasts them
They toast her back
drinking a liquid unrecognizable
but with a tang   flavour
that leaves them refreshed
exhilarated
After they have quaffed that first draft

"I assume, my Archer..."

Always "my Archer" Gillian notes

"...that thou hast told Gillian
about us and where here we must live."

Gillian is aware how her name is pronounced
with a harsh beginning   lighter later consonants
also the slight attitude
that marks her as a rival
in Archer's affections
Her look is intercepted
a sad smile
in which resignation
frustration
vie for dominance

"Ah, I see what you are thinking,
Gillian.
You have nothing to fear from me.

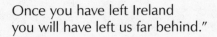

Once you have left Ireland
you will have left us far behind."

Gillian gasps as the girl's eyes
suddenly blaze golden
as she turns to Archer

"But, my Archer, I will miss thee,
more than thou knowest,
and with a reminder to me
of what thou wast like
and what thou art."

Both of them hear
the naked regret
sense of loss
that tinges her voice
Gillian can see
that Archer is moved
by what the girl says
that they share an intimacy
far different from that
between Archer   herself
She finds herself caught
between a sharp pang of jealousy
for something she cannot share
yet pity for the situation of the girl

A decision
"Why have you let me see you,
and why have you brought me here?"

Again a smile
but one more generous
as her golden eyes
look deep into Gillian's eyes

"We have seen how my Archer has been
affected by us
in the sight of others,
and though you have strained
to believe him,

it has not been enough.
Now that you have come here,
you will know what he has experienced
and help to smooth his way."

Gillian nods at the sense of this
although she can already guess
what the cost to both of them will be

"But now…"

continues the girl
sitting slightly back to observe both

"…let me hear your stories.
Your play has told me much
about your country,
but I want to know more
about your lives."

As she says this
she looks at Archer
in such a way
that Gillian sees
her hunger to know
all of him she can
to keep locked fresh in her memory
over the long   distant years

For a moment he cannot speak
Gillian finds her senses sharpened
more than she has ever felt before
Her breath catches
as she suddenly thinks
of those young actresses in other years
Then as Archer begins the story
of his life
she becomes aware
that he feels as she does
They sense the same
in the girl intently listening
As he speaks of

his childhood in Edmonton
his education
training in Europe
work over the decades
with a kaleidoscope
of other artists
actors   directors   choreographers
designers   technicians   managers
he becomes acutely aware
of what he has done
feels with unutterable clarity
his own physical presence now
bone   muscle
flesh   hissing blood

Is this what self-knowledge is?

Gillian is caught up
as he is
but now senses herself
in contrast to him
her hair still dark   long
her face with its sculpted cheek bones
mouth generous   full
her body trim   figured
legs long
tall
but only up to Archer's cheek

Then Archer finishes
She finds herself
compelled
by those searching eyes
to tell her own story
as self-aware
as he was
a happy childhood
in Vancouver
single child
of prosperous parents

used to social occasions
accustomed to knowing
notable people
her university days
Archer
working intensely
finding her forte
in management
her long artistic relationship
with him

During both their stories
the girl asks questions
about the small details
of their daily life
what their homes are like
their houses   apartments
cubicles
their sense of
streets   parks   mountains   animals
As they respond
she shows wonder at the difference
between their lives   hers
They each think

How I forget
all those whom I brush against
family   friends   associates
lovers   strangers

The two see
the crowds of those
they remember
extending beyond
their horizon

When Gillian has finished
a silence while they sip
Then Gillian stirs
"How beautiful your town is."

The girl smiles   nods acknowledgment
but with a strange look
that reminds Gillian
of the more extreme expression
during the ride

> "Much love and art have gone into
> its building and its maintenance
> over these centuries."

Archer
has been listening
noting the girl
carefully
has also looked over the town
studying its design
observing the few people
who venture into its streets
"It is a magnificent place,
including all that I saw before…"

A look between the two
that Gillian cannot bear to see

"…and I understand to some extent
why you keep yourselves apart.
But could you not have more freedom
above ground?
Wouldn't your powers help you
to keep back anyone
who wishes to harm you?"

A look of sheer horror

> "Why would we want such a thing?
> In our first days here we endured
> the battles that wounded us
> and only in this way
> have we found peace.
> You know that we still travel
> above.
> You know how we inspire

the island's bards
and how we keep ourselves healthy
as a people."

For a moment she pauses
looks away
Then, her eyes blazing

"You know we watch carefully all that happens
in your world.
But to enter into such struggle again
for us, who so abhor such combat,
would return us to depths
to which we wish not to descend
and would be our destruction."

A shudder through her slight frame
For a moment she broods
looking across the town
then softly
eyes now with only flickers

"We live here in peace and beauty,
our voices used for music or for poetry,
our hands to make lovely things,
our eyes to show us what to paint and sculpt,
our ears to let us hear our tales.
What can you offer us
that would be better than this?"

Silence

Then Archer
"A chance to see the world beyond this island.
A chance to know the vast array
of peoples, landscapes, seas, and animals.
A chance to understand more deeply
the science of this world and others,
to understand the nature of all things
in our need to know ourselves."

A deep profound sigh
Archer and Gillian

see in the girl's face
the haunted expression
that they had seen before

> "We can only watch you
> discover these things.
> We cannot leave this island
> ever.
> Such is our fate."

A look at Archer
naked with longing   despair

> "Dost thou think I wish to stay in my home
> when I have lost my heart to thee
> and will bear thy child
> when thou hast long gone from here?"

Racking sobs in her grief

Both Archer   Gillian freeze for a moment
then Gillian moves to embrace
the pain-ridden girl
The two women huddle together
for time interminable

Gradually sobs subside
All remain silent
the sounds of the subterranean town
on the fringe of their consciousness

Composure regained
the girl presses Gillian's hand
She returns to her chair

> "Forgive me for my outburst,
> I prithee."

Archer reaches forward
takes her hand gently
"In all this time
we have not learned your name...
And what would you call our child?"

Her look to them
strikes them to the heart
as she says quietly

> "I cannot tell thee either.
> We must not be named
> in the outer world
> to keep our secret close."

Still holding her hand
"I may not know your name
but I will not forget you.
And I'll think of what our child
will be and imagine each day
how it grows older."

A wan smile
Then

> "This shall be the last time
> that we will speak together.
> But you will see me at the performances
> of your strange play
> with its struggles so different
> and yet the same as here.
> And I will wave to you,
> and my people will watch over you
> while you be on the island.
> But always remember your vow
> and do not betray us."

A mask of composure
She rises
They realize that
the conversation is at an end

> "We will see thee back safely—
> and I thank thee, Gillian,
> for thy understanding."

The two women embrace
Then   eyes rich with golden tears

"And thee, my Archer,
for what thou hast given me."

A long embrace   kiss
while Gillian looks away
then back through the spacious ways
of the palace
across the square
past the imposing alabaster gates
where they find the men and horses
waiting for them
They mount
canter up the long spiral
out the cleft side
leave the rumble of its closing
as the horses surge
into the power of their gallop

This time Archer
senses all around him
feels the girl at his side
her hair blowing in the wind
as they stream back
to where the hotel is
Gillian   Archer dismount
Archer takes the girl's hand
for the last time
Then the horses wheel around
vanish quickly in the distance

Gillian and Archer in a daze
find their room
without speech
fall asleep

Canto 21

---•---

IN THE WAKE

When Gillian and Archer
wake after they have returned
it takes them some time
to speak while they prepare for the day
Gillian is first to break the silence
"How are we going to keep the day going?
Remember what you were like,
and how long before you came back to us?
Everything here now seems different,
as if this is the dream
and not what we just went through."

A bleak smile
"We will have to rely on each other
to keep focused on what we are doing."

What others see
is that both are closer than they were seen before
that each is closely attentive
to what the other does
at every moment
Archer accompanies Gillian
as she busies herself with all
necessary for publicity
for the festivals
swiftly approaching
She stays with him through the warm-ups
the performances
at meals
after the shows
The company relaxes more
as they see Archer focused on the work
but they also see
that both cannot conceal the strange look
seen before in Archer's eyes

After each show
when they are close in bed
they are driven to discuss
the golden town
This particular night
sated   with opened thoughts from their lovemaking
Gillian unlocks the subject
"A lovely woman."

"Yes."

"Do you love her, Ray?"

"In a way, I suppose.
Yes."

"Would you like to stay with her?"

"I have thought of that.
Sometimes the desire to be with her
is so strong I cannot bear it.
But then..."

"But then?"

"But then I look at her life,
and the lives of those about her,
and what they have become
over the centuries..."

"What would you find wrong with that?
They are artistic,
they watch our world
and comment through their arts on it.
Don't you do the same thing?"

"Yes..."

"Then what stops you?"

"Well, you for one."

She snuggles closer to him
pleased

"But did you see anyone there
like us?"

A question she has not thought of
She thinks a moment
"No."

"Nor did I.
And I've been thinking about that.
There must be some like myself
who have been taken there—
why didn't they stay?"

"I don't know."

"I have thought of two reasons.
First, they have not been allowed to stay.
You notice that we were not given that option?"

She thinks a moment
then   doubtfully
"Yes..."

"I know the girl is in agony
for me to stay with her,
but it wasn't put that way:
she could not—would not—
come to stay out here with us."

"That's true..."

"So those not of their kind may have to leave,
even if they were so intimate with them..."

Gillian stiffens slightly
He senses her unease
strokes her gently

"But I have found a deeper reason,
I think."

"Yes?"

"Their life is based on an enclosed escape—
but look at the cost to them.

Look at their eyes,
so haunted,
and with expressions that chill us to the bone.
They have strange powers
and those strange horses,
but what have those powers done to them?
Have they not ended up in a gilded prison,
forever shut off from full relationships with others?"

For some reason
Gillian is moved to argue for them
"But look what they have managed to avoid—
all the bloodshed and poverty and injustice
that swirls around us right up to today.
Look at our play and how bloodstained
our own past has been."

"True..."

"And what you do with your projects,
digging into our human condition,
which I struggle to see accomplished,
they do as a central part of their life.
Would that not be a wonderful way of living?"

"In a sense, yes..."

"Then what is truly wrong
with a people who wish peace
finding a way to live their lives
and surviving for centuries
by doing so,
creating a second Eden?"

"Nothing should be wrong
except...
they have themselves changed
beyond us in ways we do not know.
Do you know how I see them,
in a way?"

"No..."

"Like Milton's fallen angels,
beautiful to begin with,
but then changed utterly
in their fall
for their transgression against their God.
I don't mean that these people are evil—
but somehow they have grown
into something other than human."

"Is that so bad?
Are we so ideal ourselves?
Perhaps the changes would be for the good."

"Perhaps...
But the changes do not appear
to be altogether for their good.
There seems to be peace within
the confines of their mountain,
but outside they must use stratagems
to keep others from them.
And watch their faces.
The men show their disturbance,
a look of the lost,
of what they have been driven from.

"I have seen no old people among them,
although some mature and still beautiful.
Would you like to grow old there
among such?"

A reluctant shake of the head

He takes her hand in his
"Strangers in a strange land
is more than a cliché for us."

She squeezes the hand he holds
A sigh
A wry smile
"Well, in our present situation
we are not much different,
given the way we live."

"Yes...
But at least we observe our own world
and make events for those around us."

"Yes..."

The night now late
the discussion peters out
Gillian falls asleep
snuggled close to Archer
but he remains awake
listening to   feeling
the softness of her breathing
his sense of himself
sharpened by his growing sensitivity

I should know as strongly as they
what it is to be cut off
for them   the world
for me   my roots
Yet they have found ways
to continue to live
despite the cost
watching what turbulence
occurs beyond them
reaching warily to those
apart from them
to engender the promise of sweet song
or the propagation of their race
What then of me?

For a moment
he cannot think
the old feeling snaking up
but then he feels
the faint breath against his neck
the woman's body
lying still   warm against his
The acuteness of his feelings
swamps his whole being
with his now full-formed love for her

Here is the only anchor
I now have
Here let it rest
if it may

Sleep takes him over
They both drown
in iridescent dreams
of the golden city

For the rest of the run
it is as the girl has said
Each performance the wraiths
are there to watch   aid
The girl watches
both the performance   them
At the end of the show
waves once more
before they all mount
the horses vanish from sight

The run finishes in the usual way
with final convivialities
the sharing of the pleasant time
with members of the festival staff
and festival performers
the number of whom have grown
that the troupe have come to know
By this time Archer and Gillian
have become accustomed
to seeing the wraiths intermingled
the lissome girl waving to them
Though their dreams continue
they have found a way to adjust
to cope with the busy life of the tour
They mingle well with all
on this final night
much to the relief of the troupe itself

Now Paddy drives them off
from Galway to Waterford
for their brief run there

502

then brings them triumphantly
to the Rock of Cashel
rearing up from the plains of Tipperary
"Now you're in the navel of our country,
and a grand place for it—
the seat of the ancient kings of Munster,
and then a great religious centre
until that devil of a man, Cromwell,
sent his army in and massacred
its inhabitants,
all three thousand of them,
God preserve their souls."

All get out   inspect the imposing ruins
suitably impressed   solemn
but as Gillian   Archer stand on the height
looking at the surrounding plains
they see shimmering not far away
a troop of the golden horsemen
who smile   wave at them
then wheel around   gallop away
fading as they do so
They conceal their response
from the others
but when back in the bus
some of the troupe
see that the fey look
has crept back

Then off again
to Waterford
The young representatives meet them
with enthusiasm
They go again to Walsh Park
to set up before the break for dinner

During the evening meal
the Director of the Festival
"The Spraoi Festival—

a grand name, don't you think?"
sits with them   tells them
how word has spread from other festivals
both from those who have seen it
from performers who were there
who now know them
of the unique quality of the show
"We had no idea how much of Ireland
would be in your work.
And it seems that it strikes many of us
to the heart to hear the stories
and the things that we have done
in your young country."

Archer murmurs his thanks for the praise
demurs that the reputation
is more than the show deserves
but Gillian sees that he is disturbed
When the company comes together
in the early evening for the tech   rehearsal
he speaks to them
"You have all done good work on this tour."

Smiles   a feeling of pride
but some of the veterans
knowing him
brace for what he has to say

"The result is that the play has achieved
a high reputation,
and one that is deserved,
to a point.
But it has also created a myth
about us,
one that makes the play seem far more
than it is,
and your performances impossibly good."

Faces fall or look confused

"There is nothing we can do to break this myth,
unless we perform badly,
which I expect you not to do."

504

Faces determined

"All we can do is play the best we can."

Nods

"Tonight we will do our usual rehearsal,
but tomorrow afternoon
we will do some more exploration
to see what new insights and life
we can bring to the show tomorrow night."

Looks pass among the actors
Little exploration has been done
over the tour
They have begun to expect
that they would continue as they have

But that next afternoon
explore they do
scenes   characters shifting
under Archer's influence
A new life sparks
It happens
that Maura drives down that afternoon
stops by to watch
along with those technicians   performers
not occupied at that time in the festival
which opens in a day or two
She is startled to see what he is doing
but soon becomes absorbed by the new life
being born before her
the old excitement of what she experienced before
rising again within her

During this time she has not spoken to Archer
or to Gillian
At the end of the rehearsal
she approaches to congratulate them
When they turn toward her   smile in recognition
she is shaken by their eyes
"Wonderful work, as usual..."

she manages to blurt out
"and would you like to join me for dinner?"

They agree
Off they go to a pub in the town
Drinks   inconsequential talk
as she babbles on about their reputation
among the festivals
what she saw done this afternoon
All the time she sees the look
still there
Finally she can stand it no longer
"Something, surely, has happened to you two."

They look at her
now guarded
Archer asks casually
"Oh? What makes you think that?"

She cannot help herself
"Ah, your look—that's not the way you are.
You have been touched, surely."

"What do you mean?"

"Something—or someone—not of us
has changed you in some way."

"Oh?" says Gillian
"And what way would that be?
And who could such be?"

"There now!
You're beginning to talk like one of us.
It's as if you have come across the Little People."

"Little people?"

Impatiently
"Oh, you know who I mean—the Little Folk
that you always hear about in Ireland."

A glance between the two
Then Archer

"I can tell you in all honesty
that we have not come across such little folk."

"Well, something has happened to you,
that's certain. You may not wish
to talk about it, but I must warn you—
things happen here that shouldn't,
and no fairy tales they are, either!"

They both smile at her

She sees with growing alarm
that they keep something from her
in concert
"Just be careful"
she pleads
"for it is dangerous to be so,
the way you are,
and I hope with all my heart
that you will lose
whatever affects you."

There she stops
They talk about Waterford
the future festivals
then go to the evening rehearsal
which   like the afternoon
is crowded with those working in the festival
The show glints with the result
of the afternoon's work
At the end they are mobbed enthusiastically
by those who watched
Gillian has to shoo them away
to let Archer give his notes
Maura listens
absorbed by what he says
at the end thanks the two of them
promises to come to the first performance

Two days later
they give the first of the two performances

for the festival
Maura attends
As before the Golden Ones
are flecked through the audience
Maura keeps one eye on the performance
but she watches closely
Archer   Gillian
A moment comes
when the girl meets Archer's gaze
they look at each other
her violet eyes intense in her mist-shrouded face
Maura sees the expression on his face
the fey look
now so intense
She looks to see where he gazes
but can see nothing there
Fear stirs sinuously deep within her
for she has heard of such things before
but never believed or experienced them
until now
When the play finishes
the usual crowd surrounds them
She quickly moves to them
stammers out her congratulations
then hurries away ·
to drive back to Dublin
shaken   disturbed

Now back to Wicklow
where they see again
Nora   Sean
the majestic Mrs. FitzGerald
where they set up
to play twice
to end the first week of September
Mrs. FitzGerald greets them as before
but does not go to the grounds
to see the set-up or rehearsal
The other two

who have now heard much
watch   engrossed with all they see
The first night is the usual triumph
with gold interspersed among the sweaters
the light jackets
At the end the three from the festival
descend upon Archer   Gillian
but when those two turn to them
all three are startled by their fey looks
no longer hidden or controlled
After stumbling through their praise
they leave as Maura did
deeply disturbed

Sean   Nora turn to the driver Paddy
ask him what has happened
"I don't know, and that's a fact.
It started some time ago in the west
is all I've seen.
But though I've not come to it before..."
he says darkly
slowing his words for impressiveness
"...I believe them to be touched
by the Good People."
He crosses himself vigorously
"But you are the first to notice it,
other than meself,
although I know the rest of them
are confused by how these two act.
What, then, do you think we should do?"

Nora quickly answers
"Nothing for the moment.
Let the tour continue as it is.
The performance works splendidly,
and nothing should be done to interfere with it."

Paddy nods in agreement

"But"
she adds
"tell no one else—

it will be our secret for the present,
will it not?"

Paddy agrees
but more reluctantly than before
caught between the glory of a secret
the desire to tell all
his story

During this time
Gillian finds herself
observing the actors
with peculiar acuteness
as if they now belonged
to a different race or species
from herself

Even as the rumbling undertone
hiss of a city
drifts through the open window
of a starlit bedroom
insinuates itself
into the foundation of our consciousness
so Gillian senses
as they sit in the minibus
absorbed in the moving green around them
occasionally Paddy's remarks
the tides of energy that radiate from each
feeling the strong sexual emanations
from Ingrid   Mahira
the younger women
the young men as well
that set up a current that flows among them
which she has not felt so strongly before
senses a different giving off from those more mature
driven slightly less by a sexual urge
but with more complex undercurrents
She can feel
almost like a scent
the emotions that drift about the hurtling space

But when she comes to Archer
she finds an energy blazing fiercely
but deep underground
deeply held
a turmoil complex   difficult
She feels her own energies
a sudden surge of intense attraction
to him that sweeps through her
out to him
for he senses it
looks at her
She knows he senses
just as she does
The wave of feeling
almost overpowers her
but he smiles
takes her hand
their currents settle
into a common river
that swirls them
through the emerald landscape

Before any can realize it
the tour takes off again
this time to Kilkenny
Archer forces himself
under Paddy's rhetoric
to review what he knows of its history
but even as he remembers
the image of the golden horsemen
stains his thoughts

What they watched here
through the centuries
the Celtic tribes battling one another
slaughter   pillage   betrayal
continually ravaging
the torn countryside
Ossory fighting to be a kingdom
within the kingdom of Leinster

the shifting of power among families   kings
They stood aside among the screams
of those raped   dying
still taught secretly the bards
as the bloody times went on
new alliances were made
King Cerball with the Vikings
ruling families overwhelmed
by other families in alliances
as his own   the "Mac Gill á Padraig"
by the MacMurroughs of south Leinster
then the triumph of the Butlers
in alliance with the Normans
Kilkenny itself
Gill Chainnigh   Church of Canice
then Strongbow's castle
laid waste by the King of Thomond
then Marshall's rebuilt castle
home two centuries later
to the Earls   Dukes of Ormond
the Butlers
They watched the town grow
around the castle   church   ancient buildings
its streets tightly packed
until I   they   see it now
with old two- and three-storey houses
cheek by jowl with the hulking shapes
of the industrial area
the river through it
the town sheltered by mountains on one side
plains on the other
the city of the Catholic revolt
crushed
Still all this time
they watch it
here far inland
At times
they gallop on their sleek black stallions
past the warding   shielding mountains

to stand on the cliffs
or on the curving beaches
look at the sweet bosom of the sea
As they look out
their hearts break again
their steeds snort   their eyes blaze
then they return
to the slow chaos
from which they close themselves
in the hollows of majestic hills
There they live
in the gilded way they have forged
cast their brooding
into the pits of their memories
with only the knowledge
that their way will go on
into an unimaginable future

By now they reach their destination
the ritual of the tour begins anew
Again Archer and Gillian force themselves
to concentrate on the business
But during the first performance
Archer finds himself absorbed
in the responses of the audience

How they enjoy the novelty
of our staging
sightseeing to begin with
then absorption in figures   events
the thrills of the ancient battles
the reversal of attitude
favouring the French
antagonistic to the English
just as in Quebec
so at intermission
exhilarated
but also expectant
from what they have heard
about the Irish in our country

Then how deeply they feel
about their episodes in the second half
the feeling of old animosities
breaking to the surface
their deep involvement
in what is happening
in their neighbours
their attitudes
The way my golden people
adroitly break up any quarrels
about to birth
I see my girl watching them
I see she senses them as I do
then she turns   sees me
oh   the look in her eyes
the look   oh
She turns away
I cannot bear to watch any more

The week in Kilkenny
is invigorating for the company
as one of the most prestigious festivals
in the country
They renew friendships
with performers they have known
in the previous festivals
see   admire new ones
As do those who come to the show
they take in the beauty of the ancient town
But all still feel a slight tickle of apprehension
about both Archer and Gillian
They begin to note that the two stick together
wherever they are
that they seem to go through the motions
for warm-up   response
but some of them catch Archer at the show
not watching them
but gazing far off
The fey look about them both

seems to increase as time goes on
Their drivers   Kevin   Paddy   talk quietly about it
both shake their heads
Those in charge of the festival
note the haunted features of the two
At night after the performance
they are seen standing together
beside the river
motionless

Patrick   Mahira
can stand the situation no longer
Both arrange to have lunch
with Archer and Gillian
They find a quiet nook in a pub
After ordering
the conversation wanders aimlessly
over the present festival
what the two performers have seen
but after a drink   the meal
Mahira looks at Patrick
He clears his throat
"I suppose it's no secret to you
that all of us are concerned about you."

Archer looks at him
but his expression is tinged with vacancy
"Really? Why?"

A snort
"Come on, Ray, you've never acted this way before,
pretending that nothing has happened
to the two of you.
You've always been honest with us—
don't stop now."

A look between Archer   Gillian
Then he speaks slowly   quietly
"There is nothing either of us can tell you.
Please put up with us as best you can,
and we'll keep our part."

Mahira bursts out
bewildered and frustrated
"That's not good enough!
Look at you both—
you seem to be somewhere else
far from us all."

Archer reaches across the table
to take her hand
He looks into her eyes
What she sees in his
what she sees
paralyzes her
frozen   she hears his voice
distant
"Please give us our own time.
I know you are all worried,
but we will be all right,
will we not, Gillian?"

"Yes,"
she says in the same tone
with the same expression
that Patrick now sees—
an icy knife thrusts down inside him—
"There is nothing we can tell you."

It is clear that nothing more will be said
The performers leave the luncheon
more shaken   disturbed
than when they began
"What can we do?"
Mahira cries as they walk along

"I don't know,
but we must keep the company
from being too worried
so that we can finish the tour.
We still have Dublin to get through."

Mahira nods
She yearns
to talk about the extraordinary looks
but finds herself scared to do so
sees that Patrick also is unwilling
to discuss what they have seen
so they walk back
silent
each brooding on the experience

Somehow the company gets through the week
with the show still burnished
Finally the journey begins
to the last destination
Dublin

Canto 22

FAREWELLS

All the trip
Gillian and Archer
gaze spellbound
at the landscape through which they speed
Like shapes barely seen
enveloped in their mist
or birches seen tinged with the last glow
of the dying light
the places where the race dwells
they see or sense
the hills   green to others
glimmering with what they contain within
Occasionally they see
riding along a tufted hillside
some of the golden horsemen
who turn their gaze toward them
The two feel the strange energy
of what they pass through
It mixes with the living energies
within the minibus
They lose themselves
in the rich undertow

Into Dublin
to their hotel
where Maura meets them
She pales slightly
when she sees how Archer   Gillian look
but she greets them all warmly
avoiding any contact with their eyes
"Well now, it's grand to see you again,
and after all the successes you've had!"

"And you as well."

murmurs Archer
"We'd like to thank you for all you've done,
and for letting us see so much of your country.
Don't you think so, Gillian?"

"Oh yes."
Gillian smiles
Then a look passes between her
Archer
so knowing
so secret
as if she peered
into a darkened shop window
dressed in shapes   objects
that she can sense
but not make out
leaving what exists in there
desirable but unknown

Maura so sees the two before her
She is chilled to the core
by their public isolation
"Well, it is too late today
to take you to the stadium.
I'll come back tomorrow morning
when you've had time to settle in here."

Both smile at her again
unnerving her
but at that moment
Patrick comes up to the three
"Ah, Maura the lovely.
Are you still keeping your distance
from the fine men of this company?"

For a moment she is about to agree
but suddenly finds a new road
"Well—Patrick, is it?"

He grimaces
knowing full well she knows his name

"Well then, I suppose I should not let you leave

this fair island with such a dark view
of the colleens here.
When you are settled,
let's go off to a pub
and you can treat me
to a dinner and a drink—
that is, if you don't mind?"
she says   turning to Archer

He smiles
"Not at all—so long as you
return him here
so that he can be ready for tomorrow."

They all chuckle
but Maura notes
that both Archer and Gillian
sense something about her
about Patrick as well
that they cannot fully make out
"Well then, Patrick,
I'll see you here in an hour."
She hurries out
again deeply disturbed
by the strangeness of the two

Promptly an hour later
Patrick finds Maura waiting
They go off to a pub
of her choosing
Maura notices that he
no longer chivvies her
He notes that she
is concerned   worried
After they have ordered
have a drink in their hands
Maura gazes into her glass
"How has the tour really gone, Patrick?"

A keen look
"Very well indeed.
We could not have asked

for a better reception—
wonderful audiences and hospitality,
a fine look at the country itself,
and I think that the show
has kept up its standard."

A nod
"Yes, I've heard grand things
about it through your tour,
and you should do well here.
And how have Ray and Gillian
fared throughout this?"

His look changes slightly
but he continues evenly
"In terms of the show
as well as could be expected.
Ray has kept us on our toes,
always with new challenges
that provoke us further,
and Gillian could not be better
as a manager."
A slight uncomfortable pause
"They have both worked
with huge energy.
I've never seen them
with such drive."

A longer moment
both looking into their glasses
Then Maura looks up
meets his eye
"But what else is going on?"

Patrick guardedly
"What do you mean?"

She shakes her head impatiently
her red hair swirling about her shoulders
"Ah Patrick, don't be coy with me.
You've seen how strangely they look.

What has happened?"

He looks back at her
his expression now darker
"I wish I knew."
He tells her of the meeting
that Mahira and he had with them
how frustrating it was

A long silence
while their meal is served
They eat
still silent
for a few more minutes
then
"Patrick,
in Ireland, as you may know,
we are a superstitious lot."

He nods but does not smile

"The country has changed much
these last few years,
but the stories of strange events
and the Good People
or the Little People
still can be heard in remote areas.
I put little store in them—
they are our fairy tales,
and, as you know,
we have a plentiful supply of them.
But one of their themes
is that when we mortals
come in contact with them
we are changed— 'touched'
is one way such change occurs—
and not always for the better."

A quizzical look

"Now, I'm not suggesting
any of these things are true—
but look at them!
They seem to see things differently,
and when I talked to them
but a little while ago
they were in their own world."

A sad nod
"Yes, we see the same thing
but don't know what it is
nor what to do about it.
I don't think they've gone crazy—
and how would both of them
turn that way at the same time?—
but the whole thing is worrisome
for us all.
And I have to tell you—
they seem to sense things about us
we cannot sense,
and things beyond us as well.
I have seen them during the show
looking at the audience
as if there were others in it
that we cannot see."

Maura looks at him
white-faced
Then with a strong will
she composes herself
speaks quietly to Patrick
"Has their strangeness
affected the show?"

"No. As I said,
Ray has kept us working well,
and the discipline of the show
keeps us together,
however worried we might be."

"Has anyone in the company
talked of this to anyone else?"

"Not that I've noticed.
And we all try not to talk about it.
Of course, I don't know
about Paddy and Kevin."

"I'll deal with them.
The important thing
is not to let this become public.
It might be fine for the papers,
but it would make the show
a curiosity."

He nods
The meal takes another turn
as each finds from the other
their backgrounds   history
A drink to finish
then Patrick looks at her
shakes his head
"Ah, Maura,
I have to say that I will miss you.
It's too bad
we could not have had a thing going
between us."

A softer look
"Patrick, you are a charming man,
attractive too.
It could have been fun,
but I'm not really into one-night stands,
and you will be off shortly,
back to Canada,
leaving me here
to regret your loss.
And I know you have no intention
of taking on a mate
in the near future."

A smile
an exaggerated sigh
"Ah, what am I to do with you women?

You're so practical,
what's a man to do?
I'm for passion when you can get it,
for it may not come again,
and it's a lonely life without it."

A wry wistful sigh
"That may be true—
but it's even a lonelier life
after it.
I've known too many of you performers,
and I know that your life
is wrapped up in your work,
with little room for someone else."

"Not always true—
look at Ray and Gillian."

"Yes.
But have they always been together?"

"Well, yes and no.
She has worked with him
for twenty years,
and they had a relationship
early on.
He has been with many women since,
but now, here they are,
together again
and—even in these last weeks—
happy together."

For a moment she looks at him
his attraction grows on her
Then
"Well, that may be true.
But they have worked together,
stayed in the same country together,
and she has known what he does
and what he is.
No, it's not good enough for me.

Let's go home."
She leads him back to the hotel
leaves him there

He watches her go
thinks with regret
what it would have been like
to be with her
in different circumstances

The next morning
Maura leads Archer   Gillian   Amy
off to their playing space
"Well, here it is—
Croke Park Stadium,
one of the finest in Ireland."

They cannot help but agree
as they look around
the huge stadium

"We were lucky to get it at this time,
just before the League
is in play again—
and with a little help
from the powers that be."
She introduces them
to the stadium technicians
watches briefly as they begin to discuss
the set-up
then quietly leaves

In the afternoon
Archer and Gillian leave Amy
to work with her own technicians
the others
They go off to a series of interviews
arranged for them
starting with the press
This time
Archer is much quieter

listens carefully to the questions
answers them mildly
As usual the questions deal
with the Irish materials in the show
how they have been seen
by the audiences

"Your people have been enthralled
by the stories of their own in Canada
and, I hope, see how the Irish
have been deeply involved
in our country's development...
No, we make no comment
on their political positions
but present their stories
as honestly as we can...
Yes, we have had a wonderful time here.
The tour has gone very well
and we are very happy,
both with the size and response
of the audiences
and with the great hospitality
we have been afforded...
No, we have no plans at present
to play in Northern Ireland,
although if the opportunity arose,
I'm sure we would be happy to."

Some other questions
about the style he had chosen
the work of the company
then Gillian ends the press conference
thanking them all on behalf of the company
offering to talk privately to them
if they wish more information

Then off the two go
for a major video interview
This time only Archer is questioned
Gillian watching from the side

The interviewer is different
from any they have had before
a woman in her early forties
attractive   as it turns out
highly intelligent
She begins by showing clips
of the show that her crew had taken
apologizing for the way in which
the audience is unaccountably
slightly blurred at times
blaming it on a fault in the camera
although privately the cameramen
have insisted that there is nothing wrong
with the camera
as evidenced by the shots
of the performance itself
However
she does not bring up their point
but asks Archer to describe
the scenes shown
uses his answers
to segue into the questions
also asked by the press
The interview goes on pleasantly
in this fashion
until suddenly she asks
"You've seen much of our country now.
If you were doing a show much like your own now,
what would you present of us?"

How would I show the history
nature
of this island
its soil   emerald verdancy
manured with so many bodies
so many generations
from the first peoples
viewed through the heavy mists
of time   attitude

the massacres   lootings
of the tribes themselves
then the conquering armies
the long occupation
while all around Dublin   the Pale
like firecrackers thrown aimlessly
battles broke out
the long trajectory of memory
nurturing its seeds of grief   hate
abstracted ideals
placed against the forested reality
the famines
even here
in this capital place
in its very centre
the rebellion   destruction
the slow prickly road
to independence
yet the island still riven
the old conflicts
still timing the trouble
with only now
the sifting of the ash of peace
over old embers
which might yet ignite again
in this earthquaked land
even as the ground below them stirs
Despite the former ages of poverty
during those ages
the word still sang
from bard   poet
dramatist   novelist
the word made action
by those who hoped for the light
those weary of perpetual strife
people finding a way to live
working out the pleasures
to be had or made
while still the rumblings
can be felt deep   far below

Archer becomes aware of silence
then sees the woman
looking at him strangely

Did I speak what I thought?

Finally
with some effort
"Thank you, Mr. Archer.
You certainly have a unique view
of our country."
She quickly ends the interview.
But she sits for a moment
then asks him
her voice barely heard
"What has happened to you here?"

He looks at her
"I don't know what you mean."

"I think you do.
I've not heard thoughts like that
said in such a way.
I have only heard of eyes like yours,
but never seen them till now.
They have been known
mostly by legend."
She is about to go on
when Gillian comes on to the set
to take Archer's arm
The woman gasps
when she sees Gillian's eyes
"Two of you!
Something must have happened
to have two of you!"

Gillian smiles
"All we have are tourists' eyes—
your country is so beautiful."
She leads Archer away
before the dumbfounded woman
can stop them

On the street
hand in hand
both are overwhelmed
by their acute sensitivity
to the people
the traffic
passing by
Like sunlight seen
through a light mist of droplets
colours refracted   glancing
confusing the senses
with its twirling kaleidoscope
so they are bombarded
by the energies
multitudinous feelings
that brush by them
so that they sense
the onrush of the city
as the heart beats blood
through the hissing arteries
They stumble along
through streets stately Georgian
or slickly modern
caught in the currents
swirling around them
Finally
after no time that they sense
they arrive back at the hotel
where a distraught Maura
awaits them

"For God's sake, you two,
what are you doing?
I just had a call from your interviewer
and had to calm her down
and also get her to edit the piece,
promising her that she could use the rest
after you return to Canada."

The spell bends
without breaking
Gillian speaks first
"Maura, we're sorry
if we have caused trouble.
We can't help it.
Please trust us,
and help us while we finish the tour."

Maura sees the strain
each is under
Though she wants fearfully to know
what has descended on them
she sees they need her help
"Well, at least you have to admit now
that something has happened,
even if you can't talk about it.
You open in two days,
and, as usual, opening night
will involve all the major dignitaries,
including the cabinet
and others in the government.
We even have guests coming from Ulster,
which should prove interesting.
I'll stick with you then
to make sure you don't give yourselves away."

Both smile gratefully

Maura is stricken to the heart
by their forlorn look
"I'm truly sorry that
this has happened to you
in Ireland,
but I fear that it could not happen elsewhere.
I hope to God
that you will return to your old selves
when you get back to Canada!"
She flees them
before they can reply

That night in bed
holding close to each other
they mutter quietly
about the dangers that accumulate
After a time they gradually fall silent
Archer sleeps
But not Gillian

So aware of him
his energy
his feelings
so strong
so enmeshed with mine
more intimate
than I could have dreamt
all our nerve endings
on our skin
feeling the winds   currents
of all that is around us
almost too much to bear
yet
the two of us now different
isolated from the rest
seeing what others cannot see
only the strange people
in common with us now
but also
sensing the fluctuations of age
Ray's so much older than mine
mine against the young one
in the golden city

She feels a pang of envy
at the ripe energies of youth
remembers now
her own drives   feelings
twenty years ago
In the confusion of these revelations
she falls asleep
still tight within his arms

As Maura had predicted
opening night is a glittering affair
with a reception held before the performance
in one of the large rooms of the stadium
As she had promised
Maura sticks with Archer   Gillian
introducing them to the various dignitaries
but making sure that they speak only briefly
to each
Finally
the show opens
As usual
the audience is streaked with golden shapes
As usual
the audience begins with the novelty of the production
then is caught up in the dramas
of its own flesh   blood
Afterwards another reception
to greet the performers
The run is under way

During the run
Archer manages to keep rein
on his new vision
keeps the performers
fresh   alive
for each performance
Gillian also plunges
into publicity   public relations
sometimes accompanied by
the ever-vigilant Maura

Then at last comes
the final performance
both in Ireland
anywhere
Maura joins them again
But as the show is about to begin
Archer and Gillian become aware
that the audience contains

large bands of golden wraiths
far more than they have seen before
They somehow sense that these have come
from across the island
for this final show
Even as they stand there
the lovely alien girl comes to them
As the show begins
she takes Archer's hand
together they watch
the show unfold
Gillian on Archer's other side
Maura uneasily aware
that something is happening among them
that she cannot understand

Archer finds himself
watching the responses
of the hidden people
He sees them absorbed
in the history splayed out before them
As he looks more closely
he sees in their haunted eyes
a sadness almost unbearable

What a drama their story would make
what meaning could come
from searching out their fate
their confinement
to this one island
How strange my art is
that feeds on tragedy   disaster
or on comedy   disaster
Those who watch
lose themselves in the experience
Those who perform
lose themselves in the acceptance
of those lost in it
What use is it all?

As the lights fade
at the end
leaving blocks of gold among the audience
a cheer erupts
the cast takes call after call

As they do
the girl presses Archer's hand
He looks at her
She smiles at him
her eyes now shining brighter than usual
He suddenly realizes
that she is with child
his child
He reaches to kiss her
but her hand stops his mouth
then strokes his cheek
She releases his hand
smiles goodbye
to Gillian
then to him
joins the golden horde
who now sweep from the stadium

Then the usual burble of stories unlocked
the audience drifts away
The technicians   the actors
pack up
They all go to the stadium club room
for the final party
With a huge effort of will
Archer   Gillian
move through the troupe
talking with each
the finality of the situation
hanging over all
Maura is there
banters affectionately with Patrick
then is thanked sincerely
by Archer   Gillian

536

But throughout
they sense the tendrils
of each person
release themselves
from them

Some speeches are made
tears are shed
they all dance   drink
chat among each other
The night creeps noisily along
then finally they return to their hotel
exhausted in many ways

Hurried tap-taps on door   sound of harried voice   female   Maura
"Ray!"   "Gillian!"   "Let me in!"   Eyelids open   Room in focus   Archer
to the door   opens it   Maura rushes in   followed by Amy   Waves of
excited anxiety rage over the two now fully awake   "You've got to get
dressed now!   Amy, help them pack!"   Confused   Archer   Gillian   find
clothes   as Maura close to panic speaks quickly   "It's everywhere—the
press, the media.   Paddy has told them, saying he has waited until the
tour had ended before warning everyone, as he said was his duty to
Ireland and the health of the nation, of you two afflicted, touched by the
Good People—the stupid plank!"   She spits out her words furiously
"You have to leave right away.   I've changed your flights to as soon as
possible today.   The press will be here any instant.   Amy..."   who had
been packing quickly as only she could do nods that she is listening
"...you've got your crew to get the others ready?"   Amy nods as she nears
the end of the packing   "We've got to get you out of here before they
actually see you—your eyes are worse than before!"   They are now ready
even as Amy snaps their suitcases shut   "We have a car at the back—I've
taken care of the hotel.   You've got your passports?"   They nod   still
stunned by the power of the emotions they sense in the others   Down
the hall   stairs they run swiftly out to a back street into the car idling
there   Maura slips into the driver's seat   "Now keep your heads down,
you two!"   The car edges quietly into the street near   then carefully
travels not to attract attention   "I'm sorry about this mess—it's all
happened so quickly, and I hope they don't find out we've gone
from the hotel."

As in the night for a young child a car's lights penetrate the void shadows   street lights   glancing by   always advancing   retreating so Archer   Gillian   huddling together in the cushioned back are overwhelmed by Maura's desperation   Amy's steel determination   the car's enclosure   its textures metal   fabric   glass   their odours   shapes building shadows streaming by   their own confusion   Time retreats before this onslaught of continually changing impressions   until the car stops   They get out   Amy quickly retrieves their bags   hers

Inside the terminal is worse   bedlam of noise   static of the currents of the crowds   dim awareness of the members of the company before them They are shepherded into the centre of the group to get their boarding passes   But as they stand in line   someone shouts "There they are!"   A pack of reporters with boom mikes   videographers   descend upon them but the company quickly surrounds the two   A melee starts   the actors physically resisting the reporters hurling questions as they try to reach the pair   photographers jostling for pictures as hands cover their lenses boom mikes shoved aside   "What do you say to those that say you're touched?"   "Do you see them now?"   "Have you infected anyone?" "Why did you denigrate our country?"   Maura finally gets the boarding passes with them   who at this moment are too confused to deal with anything   The confusion continues while the others get their passes Then the group behind Maura   Amy are led by security officers to the haven of the Customs area as the media follow them   passengers in the terminal watching   confused   Maura quickly says goodbye to them embraces Amy   then turns to confront the pack at their heels   but the couple sense her grief   her courage   as she becomes surrounded

In a daze they pass through Customs   Amy taking charge of everything for them   Then waiting exhausted   until they can board   When finally they are seated   strapped in   they fall into a deep sleep   know no more

Canto 23

RETURN TO CANADA

"Excuse me, sir.
Sir?
We're about to land now.
Please raise your seat to the upright position.
Sir?"
Archer opens one bleary eye
then the other
For a moment he is confused
bound to a chair
a figure hovering beside him
"Sir?
We're about to land?"

He realizes suddenly where he is
"Oh. Sorry."

He raises his seat to the upright position
turns to Gillian
who is just awakening as well
"Are we landing?"
she asks drowsily
as he helps her struggle with her seat
She glances out of the window
where wisps of clouds streak by
as the air crankily gives way to the intruder
and the plane smooths out below the sparse cloud
She sees the Ontario countryside
in its green coat spreading out to the horizon
then the clusters of houses   buildings
their roofs angling toward the sky
growing more numerous
until they swallow all but shreds of green
The plane falls toward them
they speed by

trees wave closely below them
then there is the runway
thump of the main tires
then the nose lowers for the front landing gear
they race down the long expanse
with flaps open   the engines roaring a retreat
Finally they slow
turn through various routes
until they gently glide up to the landing pad

All becomes bustle in the cabin
Archer struggles to get up
but Amy
who has the aisle seat opposite him
standing
puts her hand on his shoulder
looks down
to speak quietly in his ear
"Stay there.
They will bring a wheelchair for you."

He looks at her
startled

"We've worked it out.
After what happened back in Dublin
the press and media here
will want to intercept you.
Just let us do everything
including Customs
but keep your eyes closed,
look exhausted."

He nods
lets his body slump

When most of the passengers
except them
have disembarked
a wheelchair is brought to him
He struggles up

helped by Gillian   Amy
on each side
then collapses into it
Amy pushes it
Gillian holding his hand
as they walk the long way
to Customs
There they get their luggage
for inspection
as he continues to "doze"

In exiting Customs
into the passageway beyond
each of the company
has carefully chosen a passenger
made conversation with them
continued to chat
as they exit
making sure that they
are separated enough
not to be considered together

Just before he goes through the door
to exit Customs
Archer lets his body   face
sink into those
of an old man
with his chin
lowered to his chest

When the company gets their luggage
they continue to stick with their passengers
once they exit
into the main area
All see shoulder cameras
reporters with mikes
banded uneasily together
Each small group of passengers
looks curiously
at the media

who are searching
for the theatre company
mill about the passengers
with their bags
but do not recognize
the invalid   those
who wheel him out

Once in the street
they still find
news hounds
dashing around
looking left or right
their cell phones lit up
All take separate cabs
to confuse those
still hoping to intercept them
escape
dispersing to hotels or homes or friends

Gillian   Archer get the bus
from its guest place
find a friend   a friendly place to park it
clean up the dishevelled cubicle
fall into bed   deep dreamless sleep

Darkness
less darkness   hint of light
drifting up toward the light   closer   at the closed eyelid
Open
to an orange glow   irradiating the closed curtain
See
murky in the strange light   the familiar curve above   then wall   desk
all now
alien timed
Feel
body naked   against naked body   flesh to flesh   again   soft   warm   again
sheet   blanket   askew   her chest   moving   breathing on my   quiet   light
press   release   press   light release
Cannot yet look

Which woman?
Which woman?
Now
in orange light unfamiliar
soft hair stained   strands trailing over my face   shoulders
Now
familiar lines of face   relaxed in innocence
familiar shoulder   arm across to lie on mine
the known terrain of her back
the rest descending into the uncertain cave of the sheet
leg felt straddling mine
but all in this unworldly light
yet another world
yet another world
Eyelids close
Darkness

Sound far away
nearer
insinuating itself
in my mind
in my ear

"Ray."

Gillian
Whisper in my ear

"Ray"

Nuzzling my ear
Light again
Look
Sunlight
Gillian's face close to mine
her eyes glowing into mine
Lips touch my mouth
No more thought

Still strong
their heightened sensitivity
to themselves

to all about them
Toronto no longer familiar
a kaleidoscope of buildings   towers   coloured roofs
all up   down
the streets
nothing like Ireland
Like those in vans upon the veldt
seeing the wilderness about them
through the open windows
watching the herds   the life   the sudden leaping tearing death
smelling the odours through the window
but always removed from the earth   the air   the carcass
so Archer   Gillian
walk through the hustling streets
buildings sky-scraping on either side
watch the hordes of people hurrying on
hear the din of motors   horns   sirens   voices
as a cacophony   monstrous noise
When they find a quiet park   bench
read *The Globe and Mail   The Toronto Star*
the first time in weeks they have rustled such paper
they find the sores   wounds of the world
exposed to them in words   pictures
wars on most continents
corruption   economic craziness   poverty   famine   riots
crime   bigotry   vaingloriousness
side by side with NGOs   relief   food banks
heroic acts   generous deeds   recognition of good
the gorgeous panoply of the arts
The two find all this as if on another world
then find stories
about the mystery
of themselves
the strange disappearance
of the company
from the plane which they had taken
the search
to see if they had returned

to Canada
They stop reading
take long walks in quiet places
shelter in the bus

Three days pass in Toronto
Gillian looks up from her laptop
"An email from Maura."

"Oh?"

"She says that the woman who interviewed you
has been burrowing around
about us
has talked to Paddy and festival organizers
and herself.
The journalist has made a program about us with the interviews
and with excerpts from your interview
that she had not used.
The whole thing has blown up in the papers as well,
with stories of us being fey or touched
by the 'Good People'
and the whole apparatus of their fairy tales
landed upon us.
Maura warns us that the story is being picked up
in Canada as well."

They both grin
remembering what they went through
the stories they just read

"It's lucky we arranged to leave with the bus
tomorrow.
I'll call up the cast and ask that they make no comment."

"A good idea."

"And I'll set up a rendezvous
with those travelling back with us
and tell them not to reveal it to anyone."

"Good."

"Yes. I'll get to work."

Gillian spends the morning
on the phone
as Archer drives the bus
to a more secluded spot
Even as she phones
Gillian finds messages pouring in
from reporters that she knows
but she avoids returning any calls
except those from the cast
who now are phoning
upset
over reporters who have called them

She makes a decision
"Pack your things
and go to the place I suggested.
We'll pick you up there at four."
She calls again
those whom she has not told
Then she emails
those of the cast
who will remain in Toronto
or who have already returned home
to ask them to make no comment
Some she talks to directly
is relieved to hear that
they have not yet been contacted
They promise to speak only
of how successful the tour was

When they arrive to pick up their travellers
they find to their surprise
all but those who have gone home
Jean and Amy
Even the technicians who are staying on
are there
When Archer and Gillian
descend from the bus

Patrick   Mahira are in the forefront
representing the rest

Patrick moves forward
about to speak
when Archer
his eyes glowing
shakes his head
Patrick stops
frozen by the gaze

All look concerned but disturbed

Archer takes charge
"Gillian and I"
taking her arm
"are moved by your consideration for us
and we thank you.
But for our sakes,
if you are badgered by the media
please say you don't know anything."

Upset expostulations

"No, it is the only way
we can get through this.
Now, those who are coming with us,
into the bus.
And goodbye and all the best
to the rest of you."

He herds the dazed group
into the bus after they have made their goodbyes
to the others
The bus slowly wheels away
from the curb
down the street
finally out of sight

The drive to Vancouver
is done in stealth
The first night they find a small motel

at Port Severn
As they skirt Georgian Bay
they stop for lunch in another small town
end up that night in Port Lock
outside of Sault Ste. Marie

Gillian   Archer
frequently exchange places at the wheel
Looking out they sense
in ways they could not before
the size of the land
They find the trek
through the Canadian Shield
overwhelming in the starkness
of rock   tree

Inside the bus
they cannot shut out the emanations
from the troupe
still strong as before
as they fluctuate
Mahira still sits by Archer
keeping close to him
as if to protect him
although neither says much
does the same with Gillian
Both can feel her concern
her need to help them
but because they cannot filter
its strength
they find it heartbreaking
Both try to calm her
make her more peaceful
Gradually
over the days
she does subside
They sense at the same time
that Ingrid has become
more comfortable with Peter
sense that the two

have experimented as lovers
but that Ingrid has not yet
found herself fully involved
so that even as they sit
talk
their feelings
like the eddies in a stream
shift   change

At night
Archer   Gillian remain in the bus
but they say little
letting the experiences of the day
subside so that only
their own feelings can mingle

Around Lake Superior
next they drive
almost succumb to
the immensity
to stay at night
in a small town
outside Thunder Bay
That day they feel
Ann's perplexity
as she still tries to make contact
with Ron
but from him they feel
deep   swirling
a rage that he suppresses
through his wit
that cuts through them
with its lava intensity
so that night
they lie exhausted
with uneasy dreams

On again
through forests   lakes
lakes   forests

until they reach Keewatin
past Kenora
for the night
In this part of the journey
they can feel Yumiko   Michael
now as good friends
who appreciate each other's talents
who are comfortable
without sexual tension between them
They sleep well
without dreams

So into the vastness of the prairies
overarching skies
rolling plains   valleys
inside   the comfortable intimacy
of Jack with Ursula
the stops at small towns
as they travel along the southern route
the names involved
Moose Jaw   Swift Current   Medicine Hat
Lethbridge   Fort Macleod   Pincher Creek
the foothills   Rockies
Fernie   Cranbrook   Trail   Rossland
Grand Forks   Greenwood
Osoyoos   Okanagan Falls   Keremeos
Princeton   Hope   Chilliwack   Mission
home

Canto 24

FLIGHT

Gillian wheels the bus into a parking lot
where all can catch the SkyTrain
for their respective homes
They all embrace for their final goodbyes
but Archer   Gillian
sense that the others still view them
as different
even though they have remained friendly
loyal
Finally all are gone
Gillian drives on to their home
When they are still some distance away
yet can see down the hill toward it
they observe cars parked in the driveway
people lounging in front of the house
"Media."
Gillian mutters
Quickly she turns the bus around
They speed away
"I know a place where we can park the bus
without being seen."

"Do it.
We don't need to deal with them today."

She guides the bus
to a deserted area
beside a stream
where there is an old trail
but the trees and bushes are thick enough
to hide the bus
There they stay
For a while they sit together
saying nothing

letting the movement of the journey
seep from them

Archer sighs
"We'll have to stay low
for some time yet.
Do you know where we might go?"

Gillian thinks a moment
"I have a good friend
with a little acreage
just where the mountains
touch the delta.
She might let us stay there."

"Good.
See if she will let us come tonight.
I'm sure that the troupe will be contacted by now."

Gillian rings her friend
"Jane, it's Gillian."

Archer can hear the excited squawk
on the cellphone

"Yes, we're all right…
No, we haven't talked to the media yet…
No, we aren't crazy…
Listen, Jane,
may Ray and I stay with you
for a few days?
We can sleep in the bus."

More squawks

"Thanks.
We'll be there
in a couple of hours—
and Jane… please don't tell anyone, all right?
We really don't want to talk
to anyone right now…
Yes, we'll fill you in when we see you.
Bye."

She turns to Archer
"Everything's fine with her,
although we'll have to tell her something.
But for now we have to get there
without being noticed."

She gets out her map
searches for a route
that avoids main roads
Satisfied
she backs the bus out
Off they go
down side streets
then small paved roads
finally a dirt road
that meanders on for a mile or so
until they come to a barbed-wire gate
Archer gets out   opens it
The bus wheels through
he closes it carefully again
They drive slowly
along a driveway
more like a trail
until they come
to a log cabin
resting beside a small stream

The cabin is not old
but modern in design
like a chic antique
From inside a dog's bark is heard
deep in tone
The door opens
A woman in her early fifties
steps out
smiling when she sees them
In front of her bounds the dog
a gigantic Great Dane
who   when she sees Gillian
in several leaps ends up

with her paws on Gillian's shoulders
her stubby tail wagging furiously
her tongue ready to lick a face
which is already being guarded
by a hasty arm

"Grace, get down!"
calls out the woman   laughing
as is the encumbered Gillian
who takes the dog's paws
gently lowers them
The dog sits happily
while Gillian strokes her head
tousles her neck
"So you're the Ray Archer
she talks about so much!"

Archer looks at her closely
sees a woman
trim of body
slightly greying of hair
with a weathered open face
He feels the solidity
of her character

"Yes, he is indeed.
Ray, this is Jane."

They greet each other   shake hands

"Jane, do you have a place
where I could park the bus
so that it can't be seen
either from the air
or from the road?"

Quizzical
"I think so.
You really are hiding out?"

"Yup."

Shaking her head
"All right.
Just follow me."

Gillian in the bus follows Jane
who leads it around the back of the house
to a small area
over which trees arch
bushes congregate
on each side
Then they return
where Archer still stands
looking at the place
Grace has bounded after her mistress
now trotting back
with the two women
places more attention on Archer
who puts out his hand
for her to sniff
when she has accepted him
rubs behind her ears
"Come on in.
You must be ready to eat."
They walk through the porch
into a living room
Archer sees that the place
is larger than he had expected
that this room is furnished
with old solid chairs   sofas
the floor of golden planking
with rugs placed throughout
They don't stop there
but continue through a glass door
onto a large deck   overhung by roof
from which they can view
the stream   the mountains
on which is found
a planked wooden table
chairs   a barbecue

a comfortable sofa   armchairs
The table is laid
the barbecue smoking
but Jane goes through another glass door
into what Archer can now see
is a kitchen
returns with wine glasses
wines
They choose   wine is poured
a salute
they sit comfortably
in the sofa   chairs
"Now, tell me what this is all about."

"We can't tell you much."
says Gillian
"But look at our eyes."

Where they sit is shaded from the sun
still bright
When she leans forward
Jane sees the strange gleam
that lurks in those eyes
she gasps
"What happened to you?"

Gillian smiles sadly
"I'm afraid we can't tell you.
However, I can tell you
about the tour."
She gives a brief description
of where they'd gone
the reception they'd received
how near the end
both the troupe   others
had been disturbed
by what they had seen
"But the strangeness was much stronger
than it is now.
One reason that I asked you

if we could stay a few days
is that we hope the effect
will be reduced enough that we can
face the media without
betraying ourselves."

Gillian suddenly gasps
"But how did the media
know we were back?"

Jane
who has listened intently
saw the look
that passed between Archer   Gillian
when the change was described
senses that something secret
disturbing
has happened to them
nods her agreement
"Oh, they figured out
that you had actually been
on that plane.
They checked passenger lists
and descriptions from passengers.
I saw it on TV.
So it was decided
to stake out your place.
One of them caught a glimpse
of your bus
but was too far away
to intercept you.
They will be looking
everywhere for you.
You can stay as long as you like,
and I won't ask any more about it.
Now, let's eat!"
The meal becomes a time
when they can finally relax
feel freer than they have
for what seems too long a time

Afterwards
as the sun trails its light
over the mountains' slopes
the land
they stroll around Jane's property
as she tells them about it
warns them where neighbours
might see them
For a little time longer
they all chat in her comfortable
living room
but their exhaustion becomes
so apparent
that Jane shoos them off
to the secluded bus
They fall asleep
to the sounds of the stream
gurgling not far away

A week passes
in which they relax
talk   stroll
try not to think of the tour
their other life
but even as they do so
they still feel
that the landscape is filled
with energies   rhythms
of which they are not fully aware
as an insect in new territory
tries to accommodate
what its antennae provoke
They still sense in themselves
in Grace
the currents that emanate
in ways that they cannot name
so that this countryside   place
seem foreign in a way
they've never felt before

Jane senses their isolation
confusion
that they see   feel things
that she cannot
Loyal as she is
she finds at times
that she no longer knows Gillian
a chill invades her
as sometimes she sees their eyes
still shining as they stare

Finally they realize
that the spark will not diminish further
that they will have to return
to Gillian's place
face the media
As they prepare to leave
Jane says
"Why don't you wear dark glasses?
No one can force you to take off your shades."
They look at her
then laugh heartily

"Of course!
Why didn't we think of that sooner!"
Gillian gives Jane a big hug
"It's not as if we don't own any."
The bus yields up this small treasure
they don them   chuckle at the look
then a final heartfelt farewell
to Jane
The bus heads back to Vancouver

As the bus drives down the road
toward Gillian's driveway
like ants whose nest has been broken open
that seethe in all directions
so when the figures lounging
in the driveway
close to the house

see it coming toward them
they leap into action
photographers   cameramen
readying their equipment
reporters whipping out
their recorders
The bus drives past the cars
enters her driveway
stops beside the front door
crowding the drive on either side
as flashes explode
cameras are trained on it
photographers and cameramen
running ahead   to the side
to record the two inside
as they descend from the bus

Archer   Gillian are overwhelmed
not only by the bodies pressing at them
shouting questions
but by the waves of energy
feelings that assault them
rapacious
more than a pack of wolves would show
who attack merely for food
Because they cannot move farther than
the steps of the bus
they find themselves pinned down
by the press   the bedlam
until finally Archer rises
to his full commanding height
with a gesture
a voice that carries over all
silences them
"To what do we owe this honour?"

Again a bedlam of voices
with recorders thrust into their faces

Again he silences them
"We are quite happy to answer your questions,
but we don't know why you are here.
Please ask one at a time."

For a moment there is jostling for position
but Archer keeps silent
until only two or three
are shouting at the same time
"Where have you been?
What do you say about
the stories of you in Ireland?
Why did you take so long getting here?"

"Hold on. Let me speak."

Quieter
recorders thrust under his nose

"First, we went for a holiday,
and where we went is our own business.
We took our time,
and we have been away
from newspapers and TV and the net
and don't know what stories you're talking about."

More bedlam
Finally they quiet down again
One reporter speaks
"They say that you began to act strangely
over there,
as if you had been possessed by something."

"You mean by fairies and leprechauns?"
He chuckles
"The Irish have good stories,
but you do not have to believe them.
Do we look as if we are possessed?"

Some muttering
but the reporter holds her ground
"We've seen clips of the interview you did,

and you certainly seemed odd.
Also, the drivers and some of those
responsible for the festivals
commented on your strange behaviour."

Archer becomes more serious
"I was asked a serious question,
and I'm afraid I got carried away
answering it.
As for the others,
keep in mind that it was
an exhausting tour,
and we were showing the effects of it.
But let me say as well
that the tour was an enormous success,
as you may also have heard,
and we were treated wonderfully
everywhere we went."

The reporter is still not satisfied
"From what we have heard and seen,
it still seems more than you say.
Did you know there have been calls
to the government about it?"

"What do you mean?"

"Some people think that
what you said in that interview
is a blot on the relationship
between Canada and Ireland."

Archer snorts
"Oh, come on!
I answered a serious question
as seriously as I could.
I was asked my opinion
and gave it as honestly as I could."

"Yes, but the way you gave it
was peculiar, to say the least."

"Well, I'm sorry you think that.
If we offended people in Ireland,
I'm sorry, and I will apologize for it,
but my intentions were not to insult,
nor to act weirdly as you suggest.
Now we have nothing more to say."

He begins to move through them
but they try to get Gillian to speak as well
She shakes her head
"I feel the same way he does."

They fight their way to the house
gain the door
shut it behind them
For a few more minutes
the media swirl around
then
seeing that they will get no more
they pack up   leave
the place becomes silent

The two fall onto a sofa
exhausted by the energies
that have battered them
throughout the encounter
That night they must watch
to see what is made of their comments
What they see
themselves in their black glasses
like beetles among ants
Archer speaking calmly
but the reporters obviously skeptical
The commentary the same
using the clips from Ireland
which jolt Archer
who has not seen them before
asking what had really happened
Then interviews with some of the troupe
who are clearly uncomfortable

but loyal to them
in effect saying nothing
Then the Irish media
with interviews with Maura
who tries without success
to be non-committal
with the drivers
Paddy revelling in mystery
festival people
to give a general impression
that something truly strange
had happened to them
Worse
interviews with former members
Deirdre bewildered   defending them
Lance smug   attacking them
so that by the end of each segment
from each network
the situation is made even murkier
During all of this
both of them feel without defence
what emanates from each person
the commentators grave or excited
but with satisfaction at the story
surging underneath
the worry   concern of the troupe
Maura's suppressed fear
Paddy's pleasure also tinged with terror
Deirdre's terrible confusion
the hate that surged from Lance
When they finally switch off the set
neither can speak
They go wordlessly to bed

The next morning
the deluge begins
They cannot help but listen to the radio
hear solemn discussions
of paranormal phenomena

whether fairies exist
the strange psyche of Ireland
whether they suffered some form
of psychosis
or worse
More worrisome
are the phone calls
from grant-givers
government agencies
disturbed by the negative publicity
their bottom line
there will be no more grants
until their reputations are cleared
Despite her powers of persuasion
Gillian cannot change minds
finally gives up trying
They now automatically unpack
bring the house to order
then go out to look at the acreage
As they stroll they see
light glint off something
a distance away
"We're being photographed."
Archer says wearily
"I never thought that we would be
meat for the paparazzi."

"Just ignore them,"
Gillian says
holding his hand
"We're doing nothing wrong,
and we are still wearing our shades."
They continue their walk
then return to the house

The hardest time
turns out to be when they go shopping
The grocery stores   markets
that Gillian frequents
are full of clerks   people she knows

but although these acquaintances speak civilly to them
they maintain an uneasy distance
so that conversations sputter to a stop
Both of them see strangers
who recognize them
who watch them covertly
As well
photographers follow them
everywhere they go
become more emboldened
Finally a point is reached
when one blocks their way
starts snapping quickly
Archer with no seeming effort
takes the man by the arm
places him to the side
much to his astonishment
The episode turns out
to have been a mistake
The next day his photographs
appear with a caption
about Archer's mysterious strength
where its source might be
Now the tabloids spring into action
stories that they are possessed
that aliens have taken them over
photographs of them juxtaposed
with strange creatures
with their eyes enhanced
to blaze brilliantly
"All we can do is sit it out."
Gillian says disconsolately

They do
staying on her property
most of the time
except for shopping
keeping a low profile
The days   evenings spent

each reading
Archer exploring further
Gillian's extensive library
she curled up in her favourite chair

A month goes by
On the web
they discover that
the stories from Ireland have begun
to disappear
that little if any mention
is now made of them
They look at each other
"Our friends have been at work there."
Archer says wryly
They have also avoided making phone calls
are always careful what they say
if a friend does phone them
for they are concerned that
their phones may be tapped
They do the same on the computer

As the days shorten
the sky greys
the rains are released
they can no longer wear
their dark glasses all the time
They try to buy groceries
at the brightest times of day
but the unblinking fluorescents
show all pitilessly
They take to wearing
baseball caps
with the rim lowered close to the eyes
but always make sure
that clerks   others
do not catch a glimpse of their eyes
where a small flame still flickers
Now they begin to stock up
on non-perishables

so that they have to go out only
for groceries that have to be renewed
They hunker down
within the house   its surroundings

Never has Archer felt so isolated
He has never
at least until the Edmonton revelation
minded being alone
but now
so cut off from others
so cut off from anyone blood-tied
with his new awareness
he feels the world shrunk
almost to the doorstep
Only his relationship with Gillian
keeps him from brooding
more than he does
Both of them feel the weight
of their otherness
They begin to realize
what the golden race
has lived with so long
Gradually their reading diminishes
They find they cannot watch TV
or read the newspapers
They spend much time quietly
their conversations never lengthy
Music they do listen to
although Archer finds himself
turning from jazz   modern bands
to more classical pieces
Bach   Haydn   Mozart
now acquire a greater attraction
as does Shostakovich
with his string quartets

November sweeps its gales
through the property
with mayhem to leaf   flower

even breathes a thin coat of snow
They decide not to celebrate Christmas
or the holidays
have not contacted any friends
The emails in their box dwindle
as they neither read nor answer them

Canto 25
Winter

In December
winter truly trudges in
snow decides to stick around
with the hospitable cold
All around them
is twig   branch   evergreen
Still they keep
their cocooned routine
Archer finds himself numb
the winter wasteland
settling in his mind
No longer does he feel
the difference between
the Canadian   the Irish landscapes
his memory blanketed with its own drifts
Only Gillian exists for him
the familiar home   its surroundings
even she seems caught up
in the same dreamlike existence
so that they both keep things tidy
But silence creeps through the house
lingers long
They exercise automatically
their minds far away   void
enfeebled
caught between an outside world
hibernation
At night they lie nestled together
making no erotic movement
They may dream
but the knowledge of their strange happenings
disappears upon their awakening

A week before Christmas
seasonably unseasonable
for the area
sharp cold
the unexpected snow
invading the surprised land
with eastern drifts
unusual consistency
An early dark evening
They have not begun to prepare a meal
Suddenly
light sweeps through the room
sound of engines
crunch of tires
stamp of feet
in the driveway
a banging on the door
Archer gets up to go to the door
although he feels neither
surprise nor puzzlement
When he opens it
a roar is heard
"Merry Christmas!"
A horde streams into the house
laughing gaily
with parcels   objects
He realizes that they are
members of the troupe
who swirl around the two of them

"You don't think we would let you
hide here and not see you!"
Mahira cries to them
as the others start to put a tree
decorations through the room

Archer   Gillian are dazed
by the energies of the group
the vividness of the colours   lights
the noise of their chatter   cheerfulness

like those who   kept in darkened rooms   alone
suddenly are thrust into bright sunlight
or into a vast neon-lighted street
crowded with people
In their bewildered state
it takes them some moments
before they can recognize
who has come
Mahira   Ingrid   Peter
Jack   Ursula   Bob
Yumiko   Michael
even Ann   Ron
then
there before him
smiling
Deirdre

"Hello, Ray."
She looks straight into his eyes
sees the small flame
still flickering there
"You have changed."

He sees her still looking
curious at his state
but honest   unafraid
"Yes.
It's good to see you."
He senses her feelings
her energies
that she genuinely likes him
but no longer is infatuated

As he is considering this
Gillian
still slightly dazed by it all
comes over to them
"Deirdre?"

Deirdre gives her a hug
then looks at her as well
"So you've changed too."

"Yes."

"I knew that something
must have happened.
When the others called me
about coming here tonight,
I had to come."

"It's nice of you to do so.
We had no idea of this!"
Gillian says breathlessly

Deirdre laughs
they both find themselves smiling
"But we'll talk later."
She runs off to help
as Ingrid   Ursula
go into the kitchen
with pots   containers
they are laden with

Archer and Gillian
stand bemused
in the centre of the cheerful vortex
in wonder
as the room transforms
with ornamented tree blazing with lights
greenery   candles   other decorations
then everyone clusters around them
hugging   kissing them
in enthusiastic greeting
bottles are opened
wine poured
snacks placed out
everyone settles in
on couch or chair or floor
with Archer and Gillian
in the midst
Mahira close to him
Deirdre sitting opposite

"Well, you two certainly have had a time!"
Jack grins
but Archer can sense
the worry below the banter
"The publicity you've had!
How are you doing now,
hiding away here?"

"We've been having a long quiet rest,
which we needed badly."
The others nod   mutter their agreement
Mahira snuggles closer to him
Deirdre watches her thoughtfully

"Well, at least things seemed to have died down."
Ursula says
"But you certainly made the headlines."

"Yes.
And you may find your pictures
in the paper tomorrow.
I don't know if the paparazzi
have given up on us."

Everyone laughs
but uneasily

Then Ingrid sniffs
leaps up
"Everything's ready!"

Everyone rises
but she puts Archer   Gillian
down again
"You get served."
Off she goes with the others

The two sit there
the shock gradually fading
with the wine
a more comfortable feeling
insinuating itself

Ingrid   Mahira return
carrying plates heaped
with salad   chili
hot bun
place them in the two laps
handing them cutlery   napkins
see them started
then rush off to the kitchen again
The room fills up with laden people
delicious scents
everyone concentrates on the food
the conversation animated
between mouthfuls
Gillian and Archer realize
that the group has not come together
before now
They are all catching up
on what they have done
The two ask questions of the others
as well
As they talk
they are tuned in again
to the currents around them
Archer is surprised that Ron came
He watches him unobtrusively
realizes that though the anger still lies
like lava deep beneath the surface
a feeling of loyalty
even devotion
has brought him here tonight
This moves Archer
more than anything else
Mahira stays close to them
watching Archer
He looks at her   smiles
"You still are concerned, aren't you?"

She looks at the golden flicker
shivers slightly

but keeps her gaze
"Yes.
You won't say anything more?"

A sad smile
"No."

"What are you going to do?"

A shrug
"I don't know.
We've kept out of sight here
and just rested,
nothing much more."

"No plans for a new show?"

Another shrug
"There's no point at the moment.
What with our reputation,
we don't have the same sources
of funding."

She looks at him
more worried now
"But you've always been occupied
with another project,
at least in starting to think about it."

He looks past her into the distance
away from the merriment
surrounding them
"I'm not interested in anything right now."
Then he looks back at her
"But what about you?
What are you doing these days?"

She can see he does not want
to pursue the subject
She gives in and talks
about the theatre scene in Vancouver
for a few minutes
then goes off to get another glass of wine

Deirdre
who has come in with a laden plate
takes advantage of the moment
to sit with Archer   Gillian
They smile at each other
A moment of concentration on food
then
"I see you are still involved with
attractive young actresses?"

Both chuckle
"Yes, but I'm afraid he's become
a father figure now."
Gillian says
with a mischievous look at him

"Oh, is that how you see me!"

Gillian laughs
then gives him a passionate kiss
to which he responds
surprised
"You can decide that for yourself."
She turns to Deirdre
who is fascinated
by their easy familiarity
"Now, tell us about yourself."

"Oh, not much to tell.
I had a few things in Toronto,
and some work in TV and film.
But I wanted to come west
to Vancouver
and try my luck here.
Some of the actors here
are involved in causes
such as the homeless
and global warming,
and I've started to work with them."

Both sense her passionate feeling
need to work on such objectives
outside the theatre
but also that she still is driven to perform
Archer gently says
"I'm glad you are doing so well,
and I wish you luck in your other work."

She looks at him
with that openness he knows well
"Thank you.
But I'm more concerned with you two.
Something has happened—
you can't deny it."

They look at her gravely
She sees for a brief moment
how worn they are
also that the golden worms
still writhe   flicker in their eyes
She realizes that they can sense
more deeply than she could expect
her own feelings
It shakes her
but she continues to look at them
waiting for their reply

They are aware of her response
that she has seen their awareness
Both sigh

"Silly stories have been told about you."

"Most of what has been written or said
is fantasy, not true at all.
But we have to live with it."

"Is that why you have holed up here?"

Now Archer speaks
"Yes.
We needed a break,
and we are taking a good long one."

Deirdre looks at him sharply
"You say 'a break'—
does that mean you will do another show?"

A slight shrug
"No plans at present.
Right now I feel like
never doing another project again."

Deirdre shakes her head strongly
"I don't believe you won't do one.
It's like breathing to you."

"Perhaps I just want to stop breathing.
You don't know how things weigh on us."
Gillian and Archer take each other's hand
as if both knew the other would do so

Deirdre sees how close they have become
closer than she had ever experienced
shivers despite herself
both at what she senses
how they both seem defeated
in despair
She can't think of a reply
but is rescued by the sound of a trumpet
as Bob summons everyone into the room
with the clear notes of his instrument
Yumiko   Ann produce small drums
from out of nowhere
Soon everyone is singing carols
popular songs
while Gillian   Archer listen quietly
as the waves of sound   feeling
rush over them
They have been alone   in quiet
for so long
that they are overwhelmed
but soon find the joyous flood
too much to resist
are caught up in its current

They look at those around them
as if for the first time
seeing Mahira Ingrid Deirdre
faces aglow
Peter Gary James Michael
grinning singing as if it would open the heavens
Jack Ursula entwined with song themselves
Ann Yumiko drumming a conversation between them
Bob interjecting his comments brightly
Ron quiet but in a moment of uncommon peace
Because they can sense so deeply
their hearts go out to these beings
that they have known worked with
so hard so long
They feel the subtle threads
so slight so strong
that stitch them together
Within the two
so deep that even they cannot yet sense it
something asleep slightly stirs

Finally
exhausted happy
the choristers come to a last gasp
then go off to the kitchen
to find more drink for dry throats
Jack Ursula return
with glasses of wine for themselves
for Archer and Gillian
sit with them
as the others straggle in
to join them
Gillian smiles at them
still hand in hand with Archer
"So, you two, still together I see?"

The two chuckle
Jack says
"You're one to talk!
Look at the two of you,

like two adolescents
holding hands!"

Archer   Gillian laugh
but they keep one hand in the other's

Then Jack asks flippantly
though they can sense something below it
"So, how long are you going
to bury yourselves out here?
When are you going to start
on another project?"

The others suddenly become silent
waiting to see what Archer will say

"I've got nothing in mind.
I'm still too tired to be interested
in starting something."

"Besides..."
adds Gillian somberly
"...we have no means of funding.
Our usual contacts won't deal with us
because of what happened in Ireland."

No one moves
all focused on the two
who are quite aware of what they all feel

"And so we can't afford to pay anyone."

"There are ways around that.
We could form an Equity Co-op..."
James offers
"...but you have other reasons as well,
right?"

A disconsolate shrug
"Probably.
But the main reason
is that I'm not interested
at the moment—

in a project
or anything else."

No sound in the room
for a time
Then
quietly
"Whenever you are ready again,
whatever the conditions,
I will work with you."
Ann says
"And I."
from Yumiko
then from each one in the room
the same pledge
"And I, too."
says Deirdre firmly

Archer and Gillian sit there
stunned
both by the affirmations of loyalty
by the feeling that accompanies them
like a current deep in the ocean
strong   irresistible
Gillian's tears begin small streams down her cheeks
Archer says gruffly
"We are very moved by you all
and your loyalty and friendship.
I wish I could give you some hope
for something soon,
but I can't.
I can't."

All can see the strain in his face
the depth of his malaise
Again no one can speak
but each goes up to embrace
them without a word
Then Bob takes up his trumpet
plays quiet blues

while all listen
with the lights playing their small splashes of colour
over the absorbed faces
Then he plays a quiet carol
all sing it in the same quiet manner
After there is some subdued talk
while the kitchen is cleaned up
everything packed
except the tree   the decorations   the lights
Then Archer   Gillian stand
each embraces them again
as they make their goodbyes
the snow makes its crunching sounds
the cars start up
can be heard scritching down the driveway
in the house
all is still again

In bed that night
a full moon shining
on the glistening snow
they lie looking out
upward
sleepless

"They are good friends, you know."

"Yes."

"And they truly would like to work with you."

"I know."

"You have nothing in mind?"

"Not yet."

"I hope you find something.
For both of us."

"Yes."

Then they are silent
only the rays of the moon
searching the shadows of their faces
After a long   unperceived time
they fall asleep
each drifting from their solitary thoughts

Morning glimmers late
the next winter day
Silence wraps both quietly
as they clean up
the little remnants of the party
it lingers during the lunching noon
refuses to leave during their brief rest
Then Gillian
with a deep breath
shatters it

"We need to talk."

"Yes?"
A listless reply
even as each
senses the rising wave in one
the unfathomable pit in the other

"What have you thought about
since the party?"

"Very little."

"What have you felt?"

If there had been
a clock in the room
it would have been heard
ticking ticking ticking

Mouth open to speak
Then closed
Then

"Alone."

She does not move
senses his desolation

"Even with me...
here?"

"Yes."
The pit deeper

"Do you love me?"

No pause
"Yes."

"But you still feel alone?"

"We are all alone."

Tick   Tick   Tick

Quietly
"I love you.
I want you.
I sense you here,
can't help feeling your feeling."

"And I you."

Tick   Tick

"Then?"

"Always...
since I was a child...
I have watched people,
sensitive to their emotions...
their feelings toward me.
It has allowed me
to be an actor,
then a director,
then a creator.
And even with the women
who desired me,
who slept with me,
who lived with me,

I could feel their need—
sometimes for my body,
sometimes for what I could teach them,
sometimes for both—
and I responded to their urges and mine,
but still I felt apart,
distant from them and all others.
And when I discovered
that my parents were not my parents,
that my true parents nowhere existed for me,
you know what happened."

"Yes."

"And through you
I felt something new,
that we could be alive together,
not separately."

Tick

"And then what changed us
in Ireland."

"Yes?"

"Our senses now so penetrating,
even as we feel
between ourselves
now.
This multiplied
as at the party last night."

"Does that not mean
you are more connected,
more attached to everyone?"

"No!
I feel what they,
what you feel,
but those feelings
are their own,
your own,

which I sense—
but as an outsider
looking in
through a window always closed."

She says nothing
waits

"Alone,
how could I create
against both the static of so many,
and the sense
that I would examine
as a scientist some cells,
objectively,
with no passion,
not truly connecting
with an art skewed
from those with whom it should connect?"

He lapses into silence
The two sit silently
each aware of the currents
surging through the other

Then Gillian speaks
carefully
quietly
her eyes fixed to his

"We love each other.
We sense each other fully,
as you say.
And I want to be near you
as much
and as long
as I can.
But I am still myself,
a woman,
sitting in front of a man…"

She lets her face show
the fullness of her feeling

"...and glad of the difference.
Of course each of us
is an 'other' to the rest.
Look at all our friends
last night—
how various,
how different they all are.
But that does not mean
they don't connect with one other
or with us.
You sensed they came
because they wanted to,
rich in their feelings toward us,
in recognition of who you are,
what you mean to them,
eager to work with you again."

Silence
She refuses to break their gaze
together
even as she senses
the abyss of his despair

"I don't have
the depth of your artistic perception,
your power as an actor.
I see many people in the work I do for you,
the planning for what you intend,
the multitude of tasks to organize,
to publicize, to run the tour,
to shepherd everyone on the trip,
to meet all contingencies,
coping with any 'other'
I may have to do.
And I am fine doing it.
I'm good at it.
I feel fulfilled doing it,

both for myself
and for that 'other'—you."

She will not let him
turn away from her gaze

Silence again

Then
his face strained
"All you say is true.
I am deeply proud
of what you have done
for me,
for everyone.
But…
it's not that I don't recognize
what you say,
all of which I have experienced too.
The problem is not other people.
The problem is that I am an 'other' to myself.
You all exist for me
with pasts that are defined
from your beginnings.
Your histories involve your parents,
your relatives,
your ancestors,
an unbroken trail of becoming.
But my trail has no beginning,
parents, ancestry unknown.
Even those who brought me up
remain, along with their own pasts,
a mystery to me,
enigmas.
I have no places on a map
that I can refer to
as you can.
These new sensitivities
have forced me
to remember this,

not in a flash
but continually.
I have no referent now
by which to focus
on a new event,
or little reason to do so."

He looks at her
lost
lost
She wants desperately
to rush to him
hold him
but deep within
she constrains herself

"What you say is true…
up to a point.
You know I have parents,
that I am their only child,
that they are wealthy,
could give me anything I want.
My mother taught me her social skills,
which as you have seen have been useful…"

Her smile brings his smile involuntarily

"…and this house my father gave to me
as a graduation gift.
Of course, he thought that if I had it
I would follow the route he wanted.
But, as you know,
that's not the highway I took.
And look at these walls…"

She gestures at the bookshelves
covering each wall

"…where you can see the places my past
led me.
And still does!
Yes, I can see my past.

But I can also see now,
as an adult looking back,
my past is what I hoped it to be.
Nor would I wish to change it.
You may have had to start from scratch,
no ancestors to recognize,
but you have built your own past
through your own efforts,
and we can see the quality
of what you've done.
Your 'other' is yourself,
with all its contradictions,
all its great qualities
that make you what you are:
unique, extraordinary,
and the man whom I love
more than any 'other' that I know.
Yes, there are years between us
and someday you will probably die before me,
but you will remain with me always."

Tears in her eyes
that she makes no effort to stop
He looks at her
his face as open as hers

She rises
crosses to him on the sofa
sits
pulls his head
on to her breast
like a mother with a child

They remain there
as the winter light
fades out

That night
while Gillian lies in his arms
asleep
his own past

unreels in his thoughts
Again the memories
of his now-foster mother
when he was a child
the mysteries   intimacy
of his foster father
the hurly-burly of his school years
awakenings as a teenager
discovery of the theatre
mastery of his body for it
thrill of creation
struggle of accomplishment
unexpected intimate relationships
Gillian
He fades to sleep

In the morning
when she awakens
he keeps her there on his chest
As they lie quietly
letting their sensations spring
within their peace
Gillian now knows
he has begun to find peace
within himself

Like a flower's bud
too early in the spring
that rests poised upon its stalk
ready to bloom
but still closed tight against the cold
so they take small tentative steps
They visit stores
to shop for Christmas treats
celebrate the eve   then day
with appropriate food   drink
On New Year's Eve
again Gillian pursues the dream
of another project
Though he still feels reluctant

he does not dismiss the possibility
As well they now watch TV
read newspapers   magazines
their continual reading

As the next year
starts its uncertain birth
Archer begins a long awakening
From what he sees   reads
he broods about what he has learned

Tenebrae

I

In the flickering gashes screen bled and read
In comfortable anguish
The tiny figures in the clouding dust
Scatter against the objective noise
Their jigsawed surprise
With the sour symphony played by instrument and voice

And on the broken whiteness of each page
The silent murmurs surround
The pictures shrieking the horror
Sung in each glancing eye
Each mouth and cavity black with its crimson notes
To shrunken and hasty applause

In this wondered museum
The catastrophic treasures of the world are spilled
In murderous exactitude
The casual body browned or yellowed
Flung against the eastern green embrace
The hacked body in the twisted dust

Or in the blank face and reddened eye
The dead remembrance of the journey
For sticks or water

Interrupted by grinning violation
And finished with the shameful construction
Of shunning family and scowling neighbour

Or in the playground of the school or street
The memorized enactments
Of the bully or the gang
Or the tight circle of chosen friends
Casual in the torment of their victims
With shove of arm or word of text

Or the leaking and hushed print
Of the house-hoarded acts
Thud against a weaker flesh
Twisting of subservient limb
Creep of paddling hands
In innocent and forbidden places

In our careful storehouse of words
Crammed so many to describe
The wide-spectrumed acts of violence

II

Our reported eyes take in by season
The din of finding place
Through the indifferent vote
The calculated rush to tear reputation
The intricate mazes of solicited privacy
And the public blare of invested triumph

Under the childish shouts of adult parliament
Rich in their insult and formulated accusation
There prowl the vicious hounds of ambition
Scenting for a likely kill
Over which they may bound gleefully
For the site of greatest strength

In the classroom and the meeting place
Lurks the sometime need for power
Found in gloved control
Or in the poisoned word and deliberate hand

Clouding the right act's clarity
In the belching smoke of belligerent authority

On the exclamatory street
The instrument of law's delineation
May swerve toward law's declamation
Of a hapless presumed perpetrator
Without home or place but gutter
Harshly sited by those passing by

Or when confronted by mobbed organization
May find that power lies in instruments
That can bludgeon
That can gas or electrify
To swerve the shouted word
Into the battlefield of bone

And in the office the hierarchy
Plays out every day
And in the home the same pattern stamped
Who commands and who submits
Who is parent and who child
In the shifting sands of age

In these murky corridors
How ingenious the expressions
To clothe the naked need for power

III

Like our own diffident breath
Retiring quietly from our awareness
Or the obedient heart that beats ceaselessly
For the most part unobtrusively
So we forget the maw of appetite
That skulks with us without let

To devour us with its insatiable hunger
For all found in the buffet
Of edibles before us
So easily consumed beyond repletion
As some rich men kill themselves at their meal
Or gourmands sample courses all day long

Or those whose dreams of food
Dissipate in the hopeless bloat
Of famined bellies
In the long slope of fading desire
With each grain and drop slid away
As they slip into the lethargy of nothing

Or for the insatiable craving
For that outside our skin
The attraction of the outer surface
That clings or hangs loose
With all its sensual delights
Season shifted and remarked

And farther yet the grail
Of coin and paper
To supply accumulation's urge
In ways that skew the grasp
To shower some with too much
And laden others with too little

Eyes peer at living spaces
Envious of those of more luxurious size
Or seeing plans of larger yet
But cannot focus in swift passage
On the prone body in the dirty sleeping bag
In the littered and trashed alley

So many oscillations of the words
Yin-Yanging glut with starvation
Surfeit of wealth with abstinence of poverty

IV

O the wardrobe of the masks we wear
So painfully constructed for awareness
Bold-edged with the child's eye
The many discards of the shifting years
Those hacked out in the blazing time
Those flaking in the final consciousness

Most we see inside out
Sensed through the limits of the eye's cavity
Or in the forced perspective from our head
Only the sudden unexpected shock
Of accidental mirrored glance
Hints of the true delineation
Not the careful exploration of the silvered form

Or the masks we create with others
Seen in their defining looks
Heard in their vocal demarcations
Felt in their circumscribing touch
Sensed in their suggestive moods
Some which we desire and others fear

Sometimes we carefully construct the social mask
Crafted to affect for what we want
Sometimes we live within the mask
Unaware of its personal definition
Sometimes we yield to one forced on us
However solid or faulty it may be

And in our subterranean urges
We knead the image of the other sex
To prick us in assumed ways
With stamped copies male or female
To cloud the true intimate vision
And construct our separation and our void

And we let the delicate intricacy
Of the life-formed masks
Obliterate in the common forms
Of masks of race's colour   hair and eye
Language and nation
Class and station

So we define mask as disguise
Too innocent of its deeper place
As the one way in which we know ourselves

V

And as our masks define ourselves and each other
So we construct them for our world
As the figures hover about us
Mysterious and legendary
Never seen but said to intervene
The wraiths of belief and faith

And to cover the personal configurations
Set up the simple powerful masks
Leader/politician/soldier/sage/authority
And all the rest to recognize and follow
To sense an order in the confusing luxuriance
That can be followed for some comfort

And put great store in the masks of reason
As they peer at what we sense or think
The intricate convolutions of mathematics
The trickle of the scientific experiment
The acid permutations of philosophy
The gorgeous vision and the dure test

The masks make shift of our consciousness
At tripartite war
Or stare without comprehension
At suggested unknown dimensions
In the infinitesimally small
Or the infinite itself

Or the creator's masks
Thrown onto page or stage or screen
To scrabble in the determined vortex of action
Shaped and made recognizable to us
Against the thicket brushing against the book
The theatre and screen and house

Or those photographed or painted
Sculpted and shaped
Exploded in form

Or tickling spaces we traverse
Or incorporated in note and arrangement
To change our comprehension of what we sense

Around us all these trail
In their bedazzled extravagance
The decoration of what we are

Canto 26

SPRING

In January
winter makes a reluctant retreat
the snow trickling away
but then counterattacks
of gales   rain   defiant snow
before the weather settles down
to mists   rain   leaden skies
In all this elemental fracas
Archer takes long walks
climbs the slopes hedgehogged with trees
to find an open space where he may sit
look out around him
at the ponderous mountain ranges
disappearing off into the creased interior
or at the flattened or undulating landscape
escaping into the restless waters
invading harbours
or invested with intrusions of islands
or dotted with tankers   laden freighters
in slow traverse or anchored   dormant

Slowly both he   Gillian
try to accept their heightened sense
to know themselves more intimately
than ever they have experienced before
As they do
their intimacy becomes more profound
Much can be left unsaid
much is seen as one together
At night as he reads
watches the changeable screen
thinks of all the turbulence
found outside their comfortable citadel

the horrors   the perils that batter through the world
he feels impotent to alleviate the slightest blow

"I should do something!"
he exclaims one night as they sit together
their faces mottled from the screen's glare

"What kind of thing?"

"I don't know.
Creating my shows seems trivial
against what we see out there."

Gillian turns off the set
They sit by a quiet light
a fire burning in her hearth
"You don't think your work worthwhile?"

He hunches slightly
"I don't really know."

"Do you think your projects affect people?"

"Yes.
But what help will they offer for the wrongs we see here?"

"It may not help much.
But I don't think you create them
to get people to change their lives."

"No."

"What are you doing, then,
that other artists do?"

"I'm no longer sure.
Showing people themselves
in meaningful ways, I suppose."

"Is that all?"

"How I shape the work
can explore the vision that I have."

"Don't people feel intensely
about what you submerse them in?"

"I suppose they do.
Yes."

Gillian forces him to look at her
"Ray, why do you think I've stayed with you
all these years?
Not just for your body..."

He chuckles   gives her an intimate poke

"...but because you create works
that are beautiful and powerful,
and they affect me so profoundly
that I have spent my life
making sure you can create them.
And I will continue to work hard for you
as long as you will make them.
Whether you want to do something else
I think is highly doubtful.
Right now, what do you feel you must do,
not what do you want to do?"

A long reflective   pause
as they sit close together
both aware of the fire's erratic conversation
the shadows prancing on the walls
"I feel...
something   stirring inside...
...a need?
...a desire?
Not clear yet,
but it's pushing at me.
I have to find it."

She smiles   softly kisses him
"You'd better get to work, then."

He looks at her
In her senses
a feeling he had felt before
long ago
but cannot place

Watching him
she smiles
takes his hand
leads him to their bed
where she quietly undresses him
then herself
always looking in his eyes
her face open with a quiet love
brings him to bed
where she offers herself to him
without reserve

Through all this
he is lost in the power
of her complete love
in the height of their passion
fully absorbs the insight
of what a woman can give fully
in their union

When they have finished
exhausted   fulfilled
she pulls his head to her breast
as they lie   spent
Soon she falls asleep
but he lies there
still in wonder at what has happened
As he feels her peaceful breathing
the memory for which he had searched
springs into clarity
the same feeling he had had
on his foster mother's breast
when they dozed together
that she had given to him
all her love without reserve
What should have been clear
struck him abruptly
What he had given to others
in his work   relationships
was nothing compared

to the complete love
these women gave to him
his mother   Nan   Gillian
He had not been then
or now
alone
without connection

But Gillian has loved me
waited twenty years
for me to truly love her
all the while as she watched me
with the others
How this must have hurt her

In humility
in recognition
he sighs
falls quietly asleep on her breast

The birds awake them
that sunny morning
Gillian stirs   ready to rise
but Archer keeps her with him

She grins
"Again?"

He smiles gently
"Not just yet.
I want to talk to you."

"So early in the morning?"

They both grin
Then he says quietly
his face somber before hers
"I want to say,
from my very being,
something vital."

She can sense his powerful feeling
serious beyond anything she has felt before

looks at him
eyes wide   alert

"I…"

Overwhelmed
by the intensity
of his emotion for her

"I… love you…
deeper than I have ever felt before
and now must tell you
I am so sorry for these long years
that you have worked for me
and loved me without love returned.
You should not forgive me,
but deal with me as you wish."

He lowers his head   overcome

Gillian   herself overwhelmed
by his passion   contrition
for a moment is silent

Then she pulls him down to her
for the most passionate of kisses
But before he can go further
she pushes him off her
to lie beside her
Again   for a moment
silence
Then   holding him close
she speaks quietly in his ear
"Do you still think about the girl?"

"Oh yes."

She snuggles closer
"Do you think about your child-to-be?"

"Sometimes."

"And what about here?"

He looks at her quizzically
"Here?"

She grins
"What about a child here?"

As she sees the dawning
understanding in his face
she pulls him to her

A week passes
during which they learn to live
with their new-found understanding
of each other

Then one day
they stroll together
hand in hand
along the streets
of the hedge- and tree-filled neighbourhood
both silent
keeping the awareness
of hand   proximity
He mulls his need to create
against his sense of isolation
now recognized
no longer dark with desperation
then thinks abruptly

Why should I rail
against an unknown past
when those who struggle
in their stubborn art
who search for the right line
or ordered word
may find that they
leave all around them
choking in the dust aroused
that must streak their intimate lives
in rust
in regret

Does not company in creation
mark thresholds by which
loneliness still must lurk
the actor   stressed
in his own void tossed
To lose myself
in some new personage
is the cliché made
without further thought
that leaves apart
the basic recognition
of all those facets
hinted on the page
that still belong to me
us all   no threat
but the link that
sings of our condition

As he thinks about his own life
the mystery of his birth
his adoptive parents
his constant tours
his bus's cubicle
a life of journeys
until now
with his heartfelt relationship
with Gillian
he stops
turns to Gillian
who   still hand-held
has sensed the racing of his thoughts
now stands looking into his gleaming eyes

"Tomorrow will you drive us
to where we go in the mountains?"

She nods
accustomed to the task

"Will you walk with me there?"

Startled by his invitation
for he has always walked alone
she feels his grave question
smiles
"Yes, of course."

The next day
they both climb
to his accustomed spot
hand still in hand

As they walk
aware of the forest about them
Archer says
"I can imagine the Gaia that some say exists,
a sentient world."

Surprised
she looks at him
smiles

"But I know deep inside myself
that such is but another mask
extended beyond my limits to comprehend
what I can sense but not understand."

She looks away
considering the significance
of what he has said

"As I think of other disciplines
the mind has forged for itself
I imagine every process
as made of metaphor   image
that may connect to what is outside us
but can only strain to describe that world
that may exist beyond the senses."

She presses his hand
in understanding
smiles wryly

Then he takes her over
to sit with him
in the accustomed spot
where he puts his arm around her
She rests her head on his shoulder
as they sit
silent
sensitive to the forest
active around them

Then
"Thank you."

Surprised
head still on his shoulder
"For what?"

"For helping me discover
what love is."

She shifts her head slightly
but does not speak
waiting to hear what he will say
sensing his heart beating strongly

"I had never felt before
what this emotion is.
I knew desire,
that women desired me…"

She chuckles
but does not move

"…but only you awoke love in me
after you brought me back
from my abyss."

His arm tightens around her shoulders
he continues

"It may have something
to do with desire…"

She raises her head to look at him

Hastily
"...and you are certainly desirable."

A poke in his ribs

"But there is something extreme,
indescribable,
a profound connection..."

For a moment he is silent

As they sit
in that handed intimacy
feel around them
the slow pulsed life
of the forest
he begins to speak
quietly   intimately
by her ear

She feels in the strong currents of his body
his need to tell
of what unravelled
must be touched together
She keeps silent
absorbing what thoughts
could now be brought to word

"This is the first,
the only time
that I have tasted love.
What does it do to you and me?
It makes us join in golden chains,
not just in sexual desire
but in helpless attraction,
unfathomable devotion,
fused in body,
in our inner selves
so that we may remain
for endless years
so joined.

"It can support us in adversity,
has done so already,
and now I think,
yearn to believe,
that this profound emotion
is a tall tree
up which we climb
with other feelings,
with intent.
Kindness is a sprout on a branch,
a thicker branch holds courage,
another, self-sacrifice,
still more,
just laws,
need for community,
the thrust to help others.

"What frail creatures are we!
A chance to be born,
a certainty to die,
not to exist.
The tree bends to the fierce gales
of selfishness,
ambition,
the rage of war,
the acid need of ego,
and all the hideous births provoked.

"And here we sit
aware of our mortality,
our greed,
our resentment,
quarrelling,
yet still with
the inner peace
of our love
as we live on together.

"That's what art does—
shows us in all dimensions,

finds meaning in the order of our actions,
leads us into this revelation
in whatever form it takes.

"Look at what we just did:
celebrated the innumerable people
who have lived in this country,
both rich and poor,
rulers and rebels,
those wishing to keep what they had,
those wishing to create something bigger,
those who spent patiently their lives
in carving a living
for themselves, their wives, and children

"For although we die,
we also are impelled to reproduce
as do all living things
around us.

"Our world is cruel.
One animal eats vegetation,
another eats that animal,
we eat both.

"And yet…
And yet…
We do find ways
to live together,
whether in villages, towns, or cities,
through empires, governments, assemblies.

"We can have desire for power,
need for laws,
hunger for wealth,
grief for loss.

"All these…
more than these…
is what I search for
as actor, director, creator:
to discover as an actor

the character
in all its dimensions,
find the way,
both inside and out,
to share it with an audience;
to find as a director
the full dimensions of the event,
to help the actors find
what they must portray;
to search as a creator
the whole depth and dimension,
the trajectory of the event imagined.
Writers of fiction and poetry
can create through words their visions,
but on a stage the creator must use
the tools of bodies, lights, sound,
space and setting enclosed
within a limited parameter.

"Think of Shakespeare's *Lear*,
how in one play
he portrays so much
of our human condition—
ruptured families,
what hate can destroy,
what love can touch,
set against a kingdom
torn in its unrest,
an old king wishing to keep power
by division of his kingdom
among his daughters,
wrecked by his own ego and age,
ending in a country riven,
invasions,
death and a kingdom's wreckage,
few left to right the wrong—
all revealed in those three hours."

Gillian
finger to his lips

"I see all these
in what you create—
how you make us see
with new eyes,
new insights,
as you did with the masks
and the drum in *Lear*,
as you did in this
last big panorama.

"But now you and I see,
we feel things so much more profoundly.
One thing I know now—
why those Golden Ones moved
into the bowels of the hills.
Their feelings are so strong,
so sensitive,
that they could not bear
the sensing of our turbulent lives.
Their gifts were another twist
in their harsh sentence."

He looks at her
struck by her perception
that brought into focus
his own puzzling of that gifted people
in their ancient-founded doom

But she keeps still
her hand upon his mouth
as she continues to speak
"And we will have ourselves to endure
in this same chaotic world
with no haven as they have created."

Then she says quietly
"And it may be that our child..."

Startled
He looks at her

"Yes, our child.
I can already sense it."

She stops
face of love   fear
so vulnerable
takes away her hand
waits

He does not speak
but pulls her to him
their hearts beating
one close to the other

"We will have to protect our child,
watch whether it begins to undergo
what we will endure."

"Yes."
she breaths
"And that
even as you create
what you must create."

"What can I create?
What can we use?"

She smiles
still tight against him
"We'll see what we can find.
At the least, we can do a co-op project—
you have people faithful to you.
I'll try to pick up
some of the wreckage.
Just consider
what you need to do."

For a moment
they sit quietly
looking out at the forest surrounding them

In their new awareness
like that first moment in spring
when colour blooms fresh among the leaves
the buds of the flowers begin to stir

the air fills with the scents of awakening life
they are acutely sensitive to all about them
feel each other's full responses
Sometimes the mist strokes their faces
with minute droplets
each of which they feel
They are aware of
the conifers about them
rough-barked   darkly green
brooding upward into the indistinguishable sky
their needles   boughs heavy with ever-present moisture
slow-dripping to the soft floor below
mossed   ferned
with ancient   rotting trunks
other creeping growth
in all of which they sense the subtle currents of life
in insect   worm
the birds that sift through the forest
jays   smaller birds
crows   shadowy ravens
glimpsed above the tall trees
hawks   eagles
in their slow-wheeling hunts
They try not to fight the kaleidoscope
that assaults their new-burnished senses
but to accept them all
at times with sharp discrimination
at other times the whole orchestral roar
internal   felt
along with the sounds that envelop them
whether the birds with their chirped or whistled conversations
complex with rhythm   pitch   tone
the whirring of their wings
or even the wind brushing their wings high above
the sounds of water dripping   trickling
the faint sighing of the fern   brush
in the whispers of the secretive winds
As they look from this green cavern
out beyond to the open sky

they see in its grey face
the subtle shifting patterns
of its clouds in their overlays
of darker   lighter shades
as they glide   merge their soft edges
Both feel the might of the upreared stone
tops shrouded in mist
steep slopes white   black spotted
the fields below in their subdued patterns
the ocean married to the sky at its perimeter
They sense all together
Each feels an intercourse of vibrancy
of swirling currents of energy
manifest in form   touch   sound   taste   smell

As they sit there
within this quiet maelstrom
Gillian glances at him
"Have you anything
that has sparked your imagination?"

For a moment
he senses with a jolt
out of the gnawing at his bones
his mind go back
to earlier last winter
when
he was working on
revisions to the epic event
An idea had flared
in the dark recesses of his mind
tiny   bright   intense
but now the spark
has dimmed   lurks unrecognized

He shakes his head

Gillian sighs
"Think of yourself...
given what you create..."

He looks away from her

Silence

Then he speaks   slowly
tentatively
"I've never really had a home
since my parents died.
Lived in the bus,
travelled, toured—
except for your place.
I've been a wanderer
always seeking... something."

 Gillian looks thoughtful
"Like Odysseus?"

Archer looks at her
struck by what she has said
"Odysseus?"
Memory floods in
he sees himself   struggling
in that dank   wet   Vancouver winter
feels the new idea
sparking once more
Odysseus
that most famous wanderer
with his litany of unforeseen
tragic
consequences

"Yes, Odysseus.
A complex man.
His grandfather,
the notorious thief Autolycus,
named him, saying:
'Because odium has been what I have
seemed to create in my life,
let this child be called Odysseus,
Son of Pain.'
So Odysseus's name came to signify hate,

or, because of his prowess,
anger,
and finally, with far more nuance,
'he who inflicts and suffers pain'—
a far closer description, I think."

Archer looks at her
"How do you know so much
about Odysseus?"

She smiles
"I do read the books I have in the house,
you know.
I've loved to study
the ancient sagas,
epics of many countries.
And now that I think of it,
those ancient bards and rhapsodists
sang of the histories of their peoples
even as we have done."

Archer jumps up   paces

"Odysseus.
That is where I can start.
He lived in an uncertain world,
subject to the warring politics around him,
to the whims of erratic Gods,
thrown into unwanted adventures
with only his skill, ingenuity, strength
by which to survive,
forced to set up the conditions to stop civil war
that yet led later to the Trojan war,
which he then contrived to win."

Gillian smiles again   thoughtfully
"But didn't Odysseus,
returning,
butcher the suitors of his wife,
then take the female servants
who had betrayed her,

string them up
to slowly strangle?
And when he had won the civil war,
didn't he sail with his troops
to sack a coastal town
and take those inhabitants who still lived
as slaves?"

Archer intrigued
"That may be true,
but think what else Odysseus did.
Despite his decades-long wanderings
his centre was still his wife and home,
paying for it with his choice
of mortal rather than eternal life;
his ruthless purging when returned,
the compulsory second voyage
with its dubious gamble of success,
always danger, the uncertain,
always the will, striving to survive,
always the ominous outcomes
for his decisions, his acts
the great chasm of responsibility."

Gillian quietly answers.
"But think about the women
in that time—or for that matter,
even now in this world.
Helen was an object prized by men,
Penelope became Odysseus's wife
in a negotiation,
Trojan aristocratic women
became slaves as their own were.
How will you deal with this?"

A grimace
"I don't know yet.
But you're right,
I cannot let lie
what women had..."

She glances at him

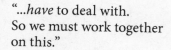

"...*have* to deal with.
So we must work together
on this."

Quietly again
"Yes."

She looks up into his eyes
her gaze more open   direct
than ever he had seen before

"It's strange how men portray us women.
Think of the powerful women
in the plays of the ancient Greeks—
Medea, Clytemnestra, Electra,
Antigone, others, who wreak revenge
or die for passionate principle.
And Shakespeare—
do you notice that Gloucester mentions mothers
only for what they have borne?
that Lear, only his daughters in his mind,
never his wife?
And closer to now, in *A Doll's House*,
Nora, who leaves her husband,
her children, to find herself,
and Ibsen, when asked, says she won't make it?
Enticers, breeders, other things were an afterthought
until now, and we're still searching for what
we should truly be in a world
that still lives more in its past."

She stops   still gazing at the forest
without seeing it

Then suddenly
she stares at him
and takes his hand in hers

"But for you to understand
what life was like for them,
how they made their choices,
you have to understand
what we women often face now.

"What I found irresistible in you,
to begin with,
was the power of your art,
how you could pierce through
to find meaning and truth
in the performances of your actors and actresses,
and I wanted to be part of such experience,
in my love for the theatre,
and learn all I could from you.

But in my innocence of relationships—
not sexual relationships,
because I had had a number of those—
and because I found you so intensely desirable,
more than I had experienced before,
I wanted you desperately
both for your artistry and your body,
and I gave myself to you.
You took me,
body and soul,
and it was a terrified bliss,
because, although I felt your passion
and your knowledge,
I never came to know you.
You gave me everything but that.
And when you judged
you had taught me all I needed,
you sent me off.
I was hurt,
profoundly hurt,
then intensely angry.
I felt I had been violated,
even though you had given me
as much or more than I could have wished.
And now, about twenty years later,
here we are."

As he listens
his eyes fixed on hers
he realizes

how open and vulnerable
she has become

*Have I truly been
both Son of Pain,
Inflictor of Pain?*

For a moment
she pauses
her eyes taking in his response
then continues

"And we must understand
what our relationship
which *will* be long,
now must be,
what it means
to have a child.
I know how your life has been engulfed
in your art,
but our lives will change
with these new responsibilities.
You will have to find the time
both for me
and for our child.
We must do this together.
Yes?"

Looking still into her eyes
he speaks from his deepest self
"Yes."

For a time they sit quietly
looking out again at the forest
surrounding them
Then they rise
start walking back
with no need to speak more
at present

Archer's mind awhirl
with what they have discussed

finds himself
with Odysseus in his mind
The more he thinks of the man
the more absorbed he becomes
in Odysseus's predicament
the more he becomes aware
that Odysseus   he
are indeed brothers
both driven to do
what they must
both wanderers
in this life
both in search
of what they can be
both blessed
with loyal   loving women
both sons of pain
inflictors of pain

Then Archer begins his new voyage
enriched with the love
he has discovered
with a woman of such depth
understanding   loyalty   love
and his heart wrenches with these thoughts

As he turns
with his new understanding
to what now engrosses him
gradually the new event
forms in his mind
the way it should unfold
starting with the dust of Ithaca

He glimpses the hulk
of a huge fallen tree
mouldering
as he had seen others
And he senses again
the slow growth

the disintegration
over millennia

And yet...
the story of Odysseus still lives
as do the tales of those who
created through their efforts
a country still restless
in its volatile evolving journey
We may die
but we continue to sing

Cynosure

"A wanderer is man from his birth
He was born on a ship
On the breast of the River of Time"
But where the ship sails
And what the wanderer undergoes
Is at the mercy of the currents of that river

Ejection from the warm thumping darkness
Is the shocking start
Hunger and digestion and budding senses the next
Then close hunched travel on the planks
And then the reach for railing
And the look past the ship itself

Wonder at the banks seen flowing by
All taken in without discrimination
The water with its currents
Its shades against the sun and moon
The vegetation at the water's edge
And all that rises past the bank's rim

And as the ship veers into quiet pools
Fascination with the upthrust
Of the vibrant blossoms
On the banks   the awe
Of inner currents with their urgent drive
For beauty   for procreation

Then the exhilaration and the terror
Of the currents rearing into rapid
The wrenching rear and roll
Spin and rise and dip
Lurch and shudder
And final exhaustion spent

Then with current swift and steady
New eye on what lies beyond the bank
Observation and segmentation
Naming the shifting landscape
Seeing high shapes in the distance
And restless what lies beyond

The final journey through the canyon
Huge and steep
Shutting out all except the sky high above
Showing only weathered stone on its face
The water thick and current torpid
Until its oily pulse sweeps into the inexorable cave

Thus our progress in this knick-knack world
Always in motion   on our way
Always change until oblivion
dust

Acknowledgments

ARCHER

For this volume, as I have done for the previous two, I made use of many books and articles found in the libraries of the Universities of Victoria and Alberta, as well as numerous sites on the internet. I have learned about Canada and Ireland from these many resources, including innumerable Indigenous and other sites, from all of which I have gained much and give thanks.

Among specific works, I am grateful to The Canadian Encyclopedia for essential facts; as an example of a good source, William Kilbourn's *The Firebrand* has given me William Lyon Mackenzie's actual words, which I used in this work. For sentimental reasons, I have referred to my father-in-law's old *Road Atlas* by The Western Producer (coupled with more modern maps). And for direct and valuable information on matters that they knew so well, I must thank Don Camp and Stefani Truant.

But what I must truly acknowledge for Canada is the immense beauty and diversity of the country itself, much of which I have seen first-hand through tours with theatre companies. I have been to Batoche; experienced the Winnipeg café and its Indigenous customers; worked in Montreal and the Saidye Bronfman Centre, where Muriel Gold, the artistic director, had Carolyn Zapf and myself create and produce *Voices from the Holocaust*, one of the most significant experiences of my life; and I retain the memory of performing in Wolfville, Nova Scotia, and driving black members of the cast to their homes late at night, as described in *Archer*.

I must also thank Shakespeare for the great play that he wrote. I have performed the role of King Lear and know deeply what that play and character entail; and I acknowledge here the great Russian film of the play. At a conference of Shakespeare experts in Vancouver, BC, the director brought the film cans with him for the first presentation outside of Russia. I have never forgotten the tragic scene, played on a dry lake bottom, between the mad Lear, the fool, and Edgar. Within a minute of the scene's start, five hundred hardened Shakespeareans, including myself, burst into tears; and at the end, as we staggered out, he met each of us at the exit, took our hands, and comforted us.

The idea of Archer's event I originated from two events: First was the extraordinary *Orlando Furioso* from the Spoleto Festival, which I saw at Les Halles in Paris as part of an audience of 5,000. To give you an idea of the nature of the event, imagine that you are in the audience and you are charged by ten armoured knights on horseback armed with long lances from which you must flee. And second was my own production of *Old Tomorrow*, created with Company One, which opened in the great ball-room of the Empress Hotel in Victoria, BC. In this production, the company used various types of masks and operated twelve-foot puppets of cloth, as well as a twenty-foot puppet of William Cornelius Van Horn, the man who oversaw the construction of the Canadian Pacific Railway. As in Archer's event, the stage was a set of wheeled platforms, and the audience literally followed them around in the space as they moved and changed the scenes.

It is, of course, Company One that I must acknowledge the most. An ensemble (company as one), they explored with me the many aspects of the mask work found in *Archer*, and we all grew together in the need to examine the art as deeply as possible, with Carolyn continually supplying materials to bring word to action, action to word. The company had artistic discipline—before every performance there were two hours of physical, vocal, and imaginative warm-ups. There is therefore full reason that I could visualize the performances in the book.

As well, I must again thank Douglas Campbell for his meticulous editing of my words in the mid-stage of the creation. But even more I must strongly acknowledge Carolyn Zapf as the principal editor. She began with me as the playwright and dramaturge for Company One Theatre, and we have intersected fruitfully many times since then.

ABOUT THE AUTHOR

Carl Hare in his long career has been a professor, actor, director, play-wright, and poet. *Odysseus* and *Spenser*, Books One and Two of his epic trilogy *On the River of Time*, were published in 2017 and 2018 respectively. Other recent work includes performances of his play *The Eagle and the Tiger* and his adaptation of Ibsen's *John Gabriel Borkman*; the setting of six of his children's poems to music by Canadian composer Malcolm Forsyth; a commissioned poem for Forsyth's *A Ballad of Canada*, performed by the National Arts Centre orchestra; and *A Weathering of Years*, a collection of poetry published in 2015.

For more details about the author, see Carl Hare's website at carlhare.ca

Revisit the adventure with the two earlier books in the epic trilogy
On the River of Time by Carl Hare

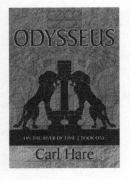

BOOK ONE: ODYSSEUS

Odysseus begins where Homer's *Odyssey* leaves off, and recounts the Greek hero's final quest to settle his debt with the god Poseidon. During his perilous journey he becomes involved in the intrigues swirling among the great Trojan War veterans and their heirs, and must also protect his own family and kingdom. Written in a poetic style reminiscent of the Homeric past, *Odysseus* is Book One of the epic trilogy *On the River of Time*. Published 2017. $26.95

BOOK TWO: SPENSER

Spenser portrays the last four turbulent months in the life of Elizabethan poet Edmund Spenser, author of *The Fairie Queene*, as he and his family are caught up in the 1598 Munster Revolt in Ireland. Critically wounded, Spenser is forced to examine the sweep of his life through memories and dreams, revealing to the reader the tragedy that happened in Ireland. Written in Spenserian stanza, *Spenser* is Book Two of the epic trilogy *On the River of Time*. Published 2018. $26.95

Visit the author's website: **carlhare.ca**

– ebooks also available; audio books coming soon –

Read excerpts from Books One and Two of *On the River of Time* by Carl Hare

Book Two: *Spenser*

[*The following passage describes an imaginary meeting between Edmund Spenser and an Irish bard.*]

63

That strange powers occupy this old room.
  Now, though large, much larger he doth seem to grow,
  His face entranced, and power him illume.
  Then, his arms raised toward me, eyes aglow,
  In ecstatic utterance, in this throe,
  He begins to chant verse in his native tongue
  Which should to me be something I can't know,
  When there grows in my mind the thoughts unsprung
Of what he says, and these ideas to me closely clung.

64

"Now your nature I can see in full scope.
  With your shining verse like the angels sing,
  But in your life you stray and cannot cope
  With all that must arise now as you bring
  The need for fame, the drive to find and wring
  As much from land and state as may be there;
  With stubbornness hold your faith and your sting
  To reap the conquest of a land stripped bare,
And scoff at art which you cannot ken, worth, or dare,

65

"Condemn the laws our country has lived by,
  Insert your own, and judge with foreign lie,
  Spawn viciousness from those who then must die,
  From the viciousness you yourself amplify.
  But heed this warning: those you crucify
  Will someday soon rise up against what you
  Have engendered; yourself will feel it nigh
  With loss of child, of home, and bid adieu
To what yourself has won, your verse, and your life too."

— from Canto 12: London, 12 January 1599

Book One: *Odysseus*

[*The following passage describes a feast given in honour of
Odysseus by Trojan war veteran Thoas, now ruler in Calydon.*]

Finally the time came for the banquet.
All assembled in the large hall; the bull was sacrificed
To Artemis and Apollo; they sat; and slaves
Brought in choice tidbits and served them drink,
Giving them goblets and pouring the wine from golden jugs.
Again Odysseus and his companions were startled
At the luxury surrounding them: all the dishes,
All the goblets were of gold, adorned with carvings
Of scenes of war and heroes. Odysseus, as he looked
At the sumptuous articles, began to recognize
Some of them—and realized, with a start, that he himself
Had drunk from the cup that he now held, had drunk
From it a libation for the Gods with Hector and Priam.
Many were from Troy, as he could tell from their decoration;
But others he saw came from many places,
And he realized that his host had been busy elsewhere
From Troy. As he waited for a female slave
To fill his cup, inadvertently he raised his eyes to hers;
Looking into large violet eyes that widened as he stared,
For he had seen those eyes before and marvelled at them—
She had been a Trojan gentlewoman renowned for her beauty,
Married to one of the great warriors of that ill-fated city;
Now she was reduced to a slave, and he could see how
The twelve years of slavery had left her drawn,
Although her beauty still showed despite her slave's demeanour.
She gasped slightly and almost spilled the wine she poured,
But quickly recovered, looking fearfully toward Thoas,
And again wore, if strained, the mask of submission.

— *from Canto 9: Calydon*